PENGUIN BOOKS

FLOWERS ON THE GRASS

Monica Dickens, great-granddaughter of Charles Dickens, has written over thirty novels, autobiographical books and children's books, and her works are beginning to be adapted for television and film. Her first book, *One Pair of Hands*, which arose out of her experience as a cook-general – the only work for which her upper-class education had fitted her – made her a best-seller at twenty-two, and is still in great demand.

Although her books arise out of the varied experiences of her life, she has not taken jobs in order to write about them: working in an aircraft factory and a hospital was her war work, not research. When she joined the Samaritans, it was the work of befriending distressed fellow human beings which she found compelling, although her novel *The Listeners* came from that experience.

She set up the first American branch of the Samaritans in Boston, Massachusetts, and lived nearby on Cape Cod for many years with her husband, Commander Roy Stratton, retired from the U.S. Navy, and her horses, dogs and cats. Monica Dickens now lives in England, in an old thatched cottage on the Berkshire Downs. She has two daughters. In 1981 she received the M.B.E.

Penguin have published her autobiography, *An Open Book*, as well as many of her other works.

FLOWERS
ON THE GRASS

Monica Dickens

PENGUIN BOOKS

Penguin Books Ltd, Harmondsworth, Middlesex, England
Viking Penguin Inc., 40 West 23rd Street, New York, New York 10010, U.S.A.
Penguin Books Australia Ltd, Ringwood, Victoria, Australia
Penguin Books Canada Ltd, 2801 John Street, Markham, Ontario, Canada L3R 1B4
Penguin Books (N.Z.) Ltd, 182–190 Wairau Road, Auckland 10, New Zealand

—

First published by Michael Joseph 1945
Published in Penguin Books 1962
Reprinted 1966, 1969, 1971, 1977, 1981, 1987

—

—

Made and printed in Great Britain by
Hazell Watson & Viney Limited,
Member of the BPCC Group,
Aylesbury, Bucks
Set in Linotype Juliana

To
Hal

Contents

CHAPTER ONE

Jane

THE cottage door stood open, as it did all summer, and most of the spring when the sun was warm. Jane had been up to the farm for milk, but no one ever locked their doors in this village. There had not been a burglary within living or hearsay memory, and what the policeman did with his time except grow carnations nobody knew.

The front door had been open the first time she saw the cottage.

She had stood by the gate as she did now, looking down the cobbled path between the disorderly flowers. When a woman in an apron came out of the door tidying her hair, Jane had known at once: I want to be that woman. This is it.

She wondered if Daniel ever stood at the gate like this to cherish the thought: I live here and it's mine. She had seen him pause here, but with an artist's objective eye, unbiased; the same that could paint Jane as she really was, not as his love saw her. Leaning on the white gate, he would study the way the apricot-coloured walls seemed to diffuse from themselves the soaked light of centuries instead of reflecting today's light from the sun, or how the thatch turned up at the corners like dogs' ears, and call to Jane to come immediately from whatever she was doing to see if she had ever noticed that one bedroom window was slightly higher than the other.

Visually he was far more observant than she, but in other ways he was more vague. Time meant little in his life, he was as careless of his clothes as a child and never put anything back in its place. Jane did not mind. She liked running about after Daniel. She had to do it discreetly, because she knew that it irked him if she fussed or was too solicitous. He would shy away from her with that fugitive, sidelong look, as if he were afraid of being trapped by too much cosiness.

Jane had prayed and prayed until she was nearly sick that her baby would be a boy. She knew that Daniel loved her, but it was

not only because she was a woman. Sometimes she thought that
it was in spite of her being a woman. He did not like excess
femininity. A bedroom full of scent and silk stockings in the bathroom were not for him, and if Jane wanted a mouse-trap baited
she had to do it for herself. He might not like a little girl who
wore frilly knickers and went to dancing class, which was the
kind of little girl Jane would like to have.

He was so happy now, taking so kindly to this first domesticity
of his life, that she was afraid of glutting him with females. So
it would have to be a boy. He – she thought of it resolutely as he,
as if that could change the perfectly formed being she carried –
bothered her now as the telephone rang and she hurried clumsily
down the cobbled path to answer it.

'Darling, look – something's happened.' Daniel invariably said
that and then paused, leaving you to panic through all kinds of
nightmare possibilities while he sought for words with the slight
hesitation that was not quite a stammer. It only assailed him on
the telephone, or when he was tired or nervous. Sometimes, when
he was hung up for a word, he would beat his arms about like an
exasperated child; but if you offered him the word you knew he
wanted, he would reject it, and have to think of another.

'Yes – what? Danny, what's happened?' A train, a car, a bus,
fire, pneumonia – Jane's pregnancy quickened her to morbid fears
for Daniel's safety. 'Where are you?'

'In London.'

'Oh, Danny, you've missed your train again.'

'Yes, because I'd forgotten about this staff meeting tonight. I'll
be a bit late. Listen, make me an enormous tea, will you, there's a
good girl. I'm starving. Didn't get any lunch. I met Bob Ricketts
in the King's Road and we went to the Stag.'

'Well, why didn't you think – ?' Jane was going to say: 'of
getting some sandwiches,' but that was the kind of thought he
never had. Other men made elaborate plans to ensure that they
got their lunch, believing that they would die without it. Daniel
lived in a pre-war illusion that he could get food at any hour of
the day or night, where and whenever he happened to be hungry.
He was always being surprised by midnight stations, crowded
restaurants, and shuttered snackbars. She could imagine him

today, drinking too many whiskeys with Bob Ricketts, realizing at five to two that he had a class at two, that he was starving hungry, and that all the sandwiches in the glass case on the bar had been bought and eaten long ago by more provident men.

When he had rung off, Jane went to the kitchen to make scones. She asked nothing better than to give Danny a big tea. That kind of thing fed her loving spirit as it fed his body.

She had wanted to look after Daniel for the last twenty years, ever since she was nine, when she had seen him at his mother's funeral. He was nearly fifteen, and his father had died when he was a baby. He was Jane's first cousin, but when he was suddenly an orphan she had been shy because of this that had happened to him and made him a stranger. She would never forget seeing him at the funeral. He was at Eton then, too small still for a morning coat and too large for his short jacket. His top hat and everything about him was spotted and scruffy. His face was spotty, too, and dead white, without any expression, not even one of sadness.

The undertaker's was in a mews, and it was there that Jane, getting into one of the funeral cars, had seen him, kicking his already scuffed shoes about in the gutter. Although he must have been the most important person at the funeral, no one had thought of telling him which car to go in, and he was not going to ask.

Jane, who had not been greatly upset by the news that Auntie Grace had gone to Jesus, cried then so much that her mother told her father: 'I knew she shouldn't have come. You'd make any excuse for a clan gathering,' and took her out of the car and into a taxi and home.

After that, Jane hardly saw Daniel. He was sent to live with some other relations, a childless couple who had priceless antique chairs in which a boy must not sit, and carpets on which a boy must not walk without changing his outdoor shoes, but who housed him in memory of poor Grace. He came to some of the family parties, but he had changed. It was not only because he was set apart by being an orphan that you did not know what to say to him. He did not want to be talked to. He leaned about round the walls, watching people disparagingly from under his eyelids, repulsing relatives who came at him with trifles and ice-cream, shunning the games, or spoiling the charades with some sly, irrelevant practical joke.

He became a problem child, a subject of family discussion. Jane wanted to defend him, but did not know how. After another term at Eton, something terrible happened. She did not know what it was, because people stopped talking about it when she came into the room.

He was expelled from Eton. For such a thing to happen to a Brett was unthinkable. It was hushed up, and Daniel packed off like the prodigal he had become to a great-aunt who had hitherto been outside the pale, but now proved her uses. She kept a majolica and basket-weaving shop in Anacapri village on the island of Capri. Daniel could go to the English school in Naples, and that settled him. He was still talked about occasionally, but in the past tense, as if he were dead.

'What a strange boy that was of Grace's, do you remember?'

'Of course, it was the worst age to lose his mother, and she'd always spoiled him so, but still ...'

'He would never have been any use in the firm.'

Jane thought about Daniel quite a lot. He had never before meant more to her than her other cousins, but now the idea of him haunted her like a legend. She bought a record of Gracie Fields singing 'On the Isle of Capri', but it sounded no different from any of those other places where people met or parted or sailed away to in songs. She could not imagine him there, or anywhere, going on with his life. He existed only in her mind, in static abeyance like far-off places which are not there without us, what-ever the map says. She saw him, not in Italy, but always in the rumpled top hat and tight black suit in the mews on that raw windy morning.

She did not see him again for twelve years. Her father saw him once. He went over to Capri when the great-aunt died and found that Daniel had not been living with her for a long time. He turned up from some room in a Naples alley where he was living (with a woman, Jane's father suspected). A bony Italian-looking boy with hair too thick and long, fisherman-brown skin, and clothes that – 'Well, the whole thing is not very satisfactory.

12

However, as he's studying art, I suppose he feels obliged to wear that costume.'

Jane's father, who had made the summer journey there and back in a dark city suit, starched collar, waistcoat, and watch-chain, could not believe that any Brett would wear a striped vest, washed-out cotton trousers, and sandals from choice.

But Jane went on thinking of Daniel in the top hat and black suit with that white, unapproachable face. It was a picture she could not get out of her mind.

When the war began, if Daniel was mentioned, it was: 'I don't suppose *that* young man will come back. Got himself snugly interned, no doubt.' But he arrived, surprisingly from America, and was in uniform before any of the cousins.

It was at a funeral again that Jane saw Daniel. There was the same raw wind that comes to winter buryings to make the mourners look more pinched and ugly than necessary; almost the same bleak black crowd, for it was another family funeral, and few of that long-lived stock had followed Daniel's mother.

The grandmother's death this November had brought the clan together as she so often had in life, for war had not yet dispersed them. A strange young man in badly fitting khaki was seen to be wandering about among the graves. People whispered, and swivelled their eyes round without raising their heads while the preacher spoke. When they had all thrown in their flowers and were straggling to the cemetery gates, Jane looked for Daniel, meaning to pluck up the courage to offer him a lift, but he had already disappeared. No one seemed to know what regiment he was in, and no one seemed to care. He was the only Brett without a commission.

Three years later, when Jane was an Army driver, she was sent one night to pick up a party of officers who had been testing defences on the cliff. She found the place where the road ran between a cleft almost to the beach, switched off her engine and waited, hunched in her greatcoat, half asleep, in the cold black silence. She waited for an hour and woke in a fright to a furious voice coming at her out of the night.

'God dammit, where have you been? We've been waiting an hour on the other road. Why the hell you women can't listen to instructions –' He came up to the car window and they saw each other's faces.

'Good Lord,' he said. 'I know you, don't I?'

'You ought to,' said Jane, calm with shock. 'I'm your cousin.'

It was a strange time, being there with him in that garrisoned seaside town where the stranded inhabitants went about quietly waiting for the war to be over and the soldiers and airmen to go away and give them back their hotels and beaches. Jane rid herself quickly of a mild liaison with a boy in the Air Force, for she now spent all her time off either with Daniel or within earshot of the telephone in the A.T.S. mess.

He did not always telephone when he said he would. He did not even always meet her when and where they had arranged. That might happen to anyone at this time and place; but, unlike other men, when she did see him, Daniel offered no excuses or apologies. He was spoiled, not from too much care, but from neglect; from having no one but himself to consider.

A lot of the girls were intrigued by him because he was a change from the three Service types of heavily married, wolfish, or cleanly pursuing. Like collectors who must trap and cage wild, exotic birds, it irked them that anything so attractive should be so free and independent. But he did not want any of them. He liked to be with Jane. He liked to talk to her. She thought he must need somebody to talk to, for except on the days when he was glum and stammering and bored with the idea of everything she suggested, he told her a lot of things.

She used to see other couples watching them sometimes, from benches on the sea front, or in the canteen, or the grill and bar of the White Hart. Couples with little to say to each other, without contact when they were not holding hands, wondering what on earth Jane and Daniel found to talk about all the time so eagerly.

When they talked about marriage, Daniel always swore that it was not for him. 'He travels fastest . . .,' he used to say, with a smugness that annoyed Jane quite a lot. After the war he was going back to Italy, if there was any of Italy left, to paint, or look at churches, or just sit about in the cafés at Amalfi and watch the coloured houses change in the taffeta light, and pretend that he could paint if he tried.

'But I could sit there with you,' argued Jane, who had admitted quite early in their time together – the first time he had kissed her – that she wanted him to marry her. The situation was not embarrassing. It was not even a joke between them, just an unavoidable circumstance. Jane wanted to marry him, but he did not want to marry anyone.

He catechized her, however, to make sure she had no other man up her sleeve. Daniel did not want to marry her, but nobody else might.

Jane's friend Edna, a proud, touchy girl, given to tossing her head and crying : 'What a cheek !' about Hitler, her senior officers both male and female, her reluctant batwoman, the mechanic who whistled at her from under cars, and her floating population of boy-friends, told Jane that she was a fool to let herself be Daniel's doormat. She said that Jane's technique was terrible, and tried to educate her with long nocturnal chats on Army cots. Jane surprised Edna by refusing, for once, to do what she was told. She was not worrying. These few doldrum weeks at the seaside when there was not much work and no danger were an island in time, sufficient in themselves, without ties of the past or plans for the future.

Looking back, she was surprised how shameless she had been in her attachment to Daniel. Foolish, too. Once, she had taken him home when they had a long week-end leave together and he had nowhere to go.

It had been a great mistake. Jane had known that he had known he was going to be bored even as they turned in at the gate between the dark and flowerless shrubs. She had lived in her home so long that she did not properly see it any more. Now she was nervous of his reactions to the glass porch and the ecclesiastical landing window, and hurried him indoors. He was not like one of the family any more. It was like bringing an outsider home.

Her mother and father were greatly relieved to find him so presentable. In uniform, of course, one could not look bizarre, although he seemed to have dodged the regimental haircut, and Jane's father was willing to forget the sandals and grubby sunburned toes. It was very satisfactory of him to have got his commission. Why, he was a credit to the family, not its black sheep !

In a heavy-handed way, they laid themselves out to welcome the prodigal home.

Daniel, however, would not cooperate. The minute he entered the house, he behaved as if he wanted to leave it. He made no attempt to settle down for the week-end, unpacked nothing but a hairbrush, sponge, and pyjamas, and when he sat in a room drummed his fingers and kept looking round as if to spy out the best way of escape. Jane's mother wanted to look through his socks, and kept harping back to the past with him, trying to draw him back into the family. Her father wanted to have long gruff talks with him about the war, but soon their enthusiasm for him waned. Jane felt a traitor to both camps, for whatever she did was wrong for one of them. Daniel did not like it when she went gossiping into the kitchen with her mother to wash up, or spent too long pasting cuttings into her father's war album. Her parents did not like it that he always wanted to take her out, for walks on the heath, or to the cinema, or for a drink before dinner, or just – out. Anywhere to get away from the house. The very furniture seemed to oppress him. At lunch, Jane caught him looking balefully at the crouching, sway-bellied sideboard. In his room, he slept the wrong way round in his bed, pretending that the light was in his eyes; but Jane thought it was because he did not want to see the tall scrolled wardrobe which looked as though it were going to topple forward – and once had, with a housemaid inside, in the days when there were housemaids.

She foolishly confided this to her mother, who said : 'You must remember he has the artistic temperament, darling, and forgive it.' As if Jane were trying to criticize Daniel !

On Monday, he made some vague excuse to go back to the coast much sooner than necessary, so Jane made an equally cursory pretence that she must go with him. The train was crowded. They sat on their suitcases in the corridor, hardly talking, and somewhere near Salisbury Jane apologized for the week-end, although it was really he who had spoiled it. Then, because she looked as if she were going to cry, he kissed her straight dusty-blonde hair and suddenly said for the first time that he loved her. He talked excitedly about this all the way to Yeovil, to the delight of a sentimental soldier who was jammed against the rocking wall behind them, listening to every word. Jane, resigned by now to the idea that she would always have to make the practical suggestions, mooted the question of marriage once more. Daniel, who had by now talked himself into a state of rapture, agreed as if it had been his own idea all along, and the sentimental soldier leaned forward and kissed Jane wetly, and insisted on giving her a clumsy lead signet ring he wore as an engagement present.

She kept it always. It had a horseshoe seal on it, and she looked at it sometimes and wondered whether the soldier had given away his luck with it and whether he were alive or dead. It was the only engagement ring she ever had. Before he could organize himself into buying her one, Daniel went abroad and was taken prisoner.

When he came home, nearly two years later, Jane had to start all over again with him. None of her letters had reached him, and he had not written to her because he had assumed, for some reason, that Jane would by now have attached herself to some steady chap with a safe job to return to after the war, who could give her the kind of home and family in which she had grown up.

'And God knows I can't do that,' said Daniel, who was gloomy now after his first proud joy at finding her still waiting for him. 'I never could have. We were kidding ourselves, you know, and I'm less marriageable now than I ever was.'

Jane patiently persuaded him towards marriage again. 'She got at me when I was weak,' he liked to tell people afterwards.

It was many months before his restless spirit could adjust itself to the freedom for which in the prison camp he had pined into sickness and nearly died. He could not settle down with her, even to the unsettled existence of furnished rooms and flats which at first was theirs.

In the self-contained university which grew up in the camp Daniel had discovered that he was a better teacher than he would ever be an artist. Long ago in Naples he had suspected that he would never paint or design well enough to make a living, or even to please himself. He admitted this now and found a job teaching architectural drawing and lecturing on Italian art at a technical college in Chelsea. He and Jane lived up and down the King's Road, hopping from room to horrid room, into a leaky flat and out again, like birds not knowing where to build their nest.

Daniel would not settle anywhere. Almost as soon as they moved into one place, he would weary of it and want to move on. He was sure they could find somewhere better. He could not suffer another day that colonic cistern, the engines racing at dawn in the mews, the smell of the landlandy's curry.

He had all the habits of the chronic homeless, Jane discovered. He did not want to eat at regular times, and when he was hungry would rather go out for a meal than wait for Jane to cook it. When they did sit down at a table together, he read the paper and ate too fast. He preferred to live in his boxes instead of putting his things into drawers. He accumulated dirty laundry in undiscovered places. He had no hobbies of any kind. He would not sit peacefully after supper, but walked about the room talking to Jane, or took her out to the pub or cinema or down to the river to watch the colours that followed sunset. He would just as soon make love to her on a sofa as in bed.

Jane accepted all these things, even the knowledge that he was not as happy as she was, because she knew that it would all be different once she got him into their own home. His mother had left him a little money, just enough to buy a house, but he would not begin to look for one. Jane wanted them to be in the country, somewhere with a garden, near enough for him to come up to London every day and back again to peace at night. He would not believe her when she told him how happy they would be.

'We don't want to clutter ourselves up with possessions,' he said. 'I don't want to have to poke in drains and mend broken fuses. What are you trying to do to me? I won't be made smug. I won't be made into a mild little man who travels back and forth like a tram with the morning paper one way and the evening paper the other and fools about all Sunday with a watering can. It's all right for you. You were brought up that way, but – well, I mean, honestly, darling, can you *see* me?'

Yes, she could. She did not tell him so, but went to agents on her own and saw one or two houses while he was at work. Then she came to the white gate and saw the cottage. There it sat, looking as if it had grown out of the earth instead of being built on to it. The thatch was so thick that you could sit on a bench outside in the rain and not get wet. The wood fires were laid on beds of never-cooling ash inside chimneys as wide as a little room. You could trace the traffic of four hundred years by the places where the red tiles were most worn, and the easiest way to go upstairs was on all fours.

Other people were after it. The owner wanted a quick decision, but Daniel would not make up his mind, so Jane had to tell him about the baby. She had not meant to tell him yet, because she did not want to use it as a weapon. He was staggered, almost as surprised as if he had been told he was going to give birth to a baby himself, but he bought the cottage for her.

They had not meant to have a baby yet. Daniel, who still had fits of class reserve in which he would hide all his thoughts from her, did not say much about it, but she caught him looking at her sometimes with a contemplative, conceited smile, and knew that he was pleased.

Jane was thankful now that they had not waited. She thought that the baby would be all that was needed to seduce him completely to this new home-life that was creeping over him with insidious content.

He liked it. He was happy here. He unpacked his clothes. He bought books instead of borrowing them, and knocked up shelves to hold them. He began to meddle with the garden, and then, when things grew for him, began to get possessive about it and bored visitors, just like any country husband.

People said that Jane had done wonders for Daniel, but she thought it was the cottage. Some of the family had been dubious at first about her marriage. They pretended that it was because they did not approve of cousins marrying, but she knew that it was because they did not approve of Daniel. They could not forgive him for having been a liability sixteen years ago. Jane laughed to herself now sometimes, wondering what they had expected to see at the wedding. Some of the aunts could not disguise their surprise at finding Daniel so normal – personable even, better than some of them had got for their own girls.

When the family got used to being able to stomach Daniel now that he was respectably married to Jane, they came down to visit them at the cottage. Daniel could stomach them, too, now that he was secure as host, with something of his own to show off, and could savour the pleasure of seeing them go and turning in again at his own door to a room empty of voices.

One Sunday he nearly killed a fat and foolish man from the college who made a joke about first cousins having idiot babies. Jane laughed, and the child moved within her as if he thought it funny, too; but Daniel went white and clenched his fists and stammered, and the man became nervous, fearing that he was going to be sent home before lunch.

When Daniel was angry, you could usually storm him out of it by making him laugh; but about this he had replaced humour with stubborn old-world propriety. He did not like the men even mentioning the baby, although Jane's slight frame was so monstrously distorted that she thought that it was only by mentioning it freely that she could avoid embarrassment.

That evening, after the people had gone, Daniel was in one of his moods when he hardly knew how to be loving enough to make up for the times when he was casual to her. When he felt like talking, he would talk all night to her if she could keep awake, and she would tell him of thoughts she scarcely knew she had until she wanted to put them into words for him. They would talk themselves into oneness until the birds stirred and tried a few notes and the sky crept into light and colour over the wide Cambridge fields.

That night, they talked about what Jane would do if Daniel died. He had found Robert Bridges's poem:

> If death to either should come,
> I pray it be first to me.
> Be happy as ever at home
> If so, as I wish, it be.
>
> Possess thy heart, mine own,
> And sing to the child at thy knee,
> Or read to thyself alone
> The songs that I made for thee.

'That's how I'd like it,' he said.

'That's a selfish outlook, Danny,' Jane said. ' "I pray it be first to me. . . ." It's all right for the one who dies first, but what about me here without you?'

'But I am selfish. You knew that, I thought.' Daniel was sitting on a stool, jabbing at the fire with the bellows. 'But what would you do, Janie?' he persisted. 'You'd give me a village funeral, I hope, with people saying, " 'E was a lovely gentleman," and children throwing posies of wilting wild flowers?'

He niggled on at the subject, morbidly attracted by the thought of himself lying dead in his grave. 'What would you do? Would you be brave and statuesque, and people would say you were "wonderful"? Or would you weep until they feared for your reason? How long would you weep for me?'

'How long? For ever. No, I wouldn't, because I'd die.'

'You're not an Indian wife. You don't have to die because I do,' said Danny, talking as if he were already moribund. ' "Possess thy heart," the poem says. You'd have to go on being yourself, the same as you did before we knew each other four years ago.'

'I knew you long before that. I've loved you since I was nine.'

'Oh shucks!' he said, pleased. 'Look, Janie, one day I'll write you a poem, then you can sing it to the child at your knee when I'm gone. Would you go on living here? "Be happy as ever at home. ..." Perhaps you could be. People would say: "She lives on there with her memories of him, like a shrine. His chair, his desk, his empty napkin ring. ..." '

He drooled happily on, but Jane wished afterwards that they had not talked like this. She dreamed of him without a head and woke screaming. He was quite cross then, although it had been his fault for harrowing her before she went to sleep.

He was inconsistent like that, and in other ways. Although he was growing more domesticated, he would still wander off at times into detachment. He would suddenly choose to sleep in the spare room, or to go out walking all Sunday when people were coming for lunch. He would stay late in town for no reason. Once or twice he didn't come home all night, but would arrive the next day with no excuses, quite serenely.

Jane tried not to worry. When she was not pregnant any more it would be easier. Today, for instance, she expected him home at half past seven after the meeting, but he might easily stop for a drink on the way to the train, miss it and not come home until nearly nine. For an hour she would have to pretend that she was not worrying. He would not ring up again. He never had enough small change to ring the country from a call-box. He only telephoned her from the college.

When he did come home he might want tea, and supper round about midnight, or he might want to have supper first, in which case they would probably have tea and scones in bed at midnight. There was no planning meals beforehand with Danny. He had cured Jane of any hidebound niceties she had inherited from her mother. She had to be prepared for anything, and was expert now at managing without fuss. He hated her to be in the kitchen all the time when he was at home.

She made the scones and put them to keep warm, cooked some potatoes, and put out eggs and a tin of beans. She prepared everything they would need for whatever meal he might want, then made up the fires, did her face and hair and fed her yellow collie, who went straight out again after eating to watch for Daniel. He had not transferred his devotion; he had simply picked up some of hers, growing like her in soul as Danny said he grew like her in face.

When it was nearly half past seven she went into the kitchen to put on the kettle. It gave a little 'phut!' and sparked as she switched it on. She was wary of electricity. Daniel terrified her by carrying lit lamps about and changing wall plugs without switching them off. Jane turned off the kettle and pushed the plug in more firmly before switching it on again.

She thought she heard the car, far away at the turning off the main road. Sound carried a long way over the broad flat fields. He had not stopped for a drink, so he would be dying for his tea. She listened again, but the kettle interrupted by beginning to hum. Vaguely, with her mind far away, she did what she was always telling Daniel not to do. She lifted the lid. Then it happened.

She could not lift the lid. Her hand was on it, but she could neither pull the lid free nor let go. She put her other hand on the kettle to push herself off, and that was held too in an iron grip that clutched vibrating right up her arm and through her body, and the roar of the kettle was inside her, splitting her head.

She opened her mouth and shouted, but could hear no noises.

She could hear nothing but the battering and hammering inside her head. Her baby kicked in his prison as if fighting to get out. She was shaking all over now, losing sight, sense, sound – the world, the world was going, spinning away above her as she dropped into the sucking blackness with the last very sad thought: 'Who will give Danny his tea?'

CHAPTER TWO

Ossie

IT was bad luck on any boy to be called Merlin. Especially a chubby, unmysterious boy with cheeks like rosy ping-pong balls, a mouth like a pink buttonhole for the button nose above it, and a cowlick of chocolate-coloured hair that would never do anything but stand up in a butcher-boy quiff. When he grew up looking like one of those dolls that won't knock over, no one but Mr and Mrs Meekes would have continued to call him Merlin; but having christened him that, they were capable of anything. Mr Meekes had been reading the *Idylls of the King* during his wife's confinement, and it was touch and go that the jolly round baby was not called Gawain.

At school, he was always called Wizard, and the name stuck to him through college and into the Army, until a girl in the Naafi canteen started to call him the Wizard of Oz. After that, he was Oz, or Ozzie, to everyone. Daniel called him Ossie, believing that his name was Oswald, so Merlin kept his real name dark, for Daniel and everyone else laughed at him enough already. He did not mind. He had been laughed at all his life, and it was better to be a buffoon than a nobody. He had discovered that at school, and exploited it. Although technically a mere dreg, a day boy, with no ability at anything, he had become a kind of court jester, acceptable to both masters and boys as a foil who could never be a rival.

When he was eighteen and disposed to *Weltschmerz*, he would have liked to be serious, at least for just a short wallow in the sumps of puberty, but boys from his school went with him to college, and so did his reputation. He had only to raise his voice in class for it to be drowned in a roar of laughter, even if he was going to be right. People did not like him when he was serious. He bored them and they walked away. Like a jolly mongrel, he liked all humanity and craved their approval, so he gave up being serious about anything, ever.

It had advantages. He loved his food, and could get away with untold excesses, because his greed was a stock joke. He never had to strive, because the more inept, the funnier and more popular he was. Before he could discover that it was not so funny to be unable to get a job, the war came and he fell happily into the position of regimental buffoon.

No one expected him to be able to drill or handle a rifle or look anything but ludicrous in battledress. He was Hitler's Secret Weapon. Before he was faced with the serious business of fighting, he developed varicose veins, which was a scream in itself, and was put to a desk job, where he could provide comic relief without danger of killing his own side.

He did not have to make many jokes. He had just to be Ozzie, uttering foolish exaggerations in that chirruping voice coming so inadequately out of the cushions of flesh wherein his mouth was bedded. Men in the mass will laugh at anything, and many was the wife who feared that the Army had deranged her husband's sense of humour when he tried to tell her of the absurdity of Ozzie.

'But what does he *do*, darling, that's so funny? Growing mustard and cress on flannel on the window-sill doesn't sound very witty to me.'

'Oh, but you don't know Ozzie. It's not what he does, it's the way he does it, you know. And that voice – and those double chins – if you could see him shaving !'

'Yes, well, look, darling, you've only got thirty-six hours, so don't let's talk about Ozzie any more. . . .'

How, after the war, he had ever chirped his way into a job at a college in Chelsea was the subject of a whole mythology of conjecture and fable. Some said that he was the illegitimate son of the Principal. Others said he was a spy from the Kremlin. There were those who maintained that he had wandered into the library one day to shelter from the rain and never found his way out. Anyway, there he was, in charge of the reference library and museum of specimens, and if he or anyone else suspected that he was quite efficient they kept it dark. One did not only go to the library for information. One went to have a laugh with Ozzie Meekes.

For two weeks now Daniel had not laughed either with or at Ossie. He came in and out of the library without seeming to notice that he was there. This was disturbing, since Ossie imagined that he was Daniel's friend, which was more than most people at the college could say. Ossie valued this. He himself was everybody's friend, of course, but the others were easy. Daniel had that tantalizing detachment of self-sufficiency that made you want to make him notice you, to need you, if only for the occasional laugh. He had asked Ossie down to his cottage one Sunday not long ago, when he had wanted light relief from his father-in-law. Ossie had earned his lunch. Daniel and his wife had been able to go off for a walk while Ossie entertained the father-in-law by telling him naughty stories into his little deaf-aid box, like a radio comedian going on the air.

Ossie, like the conscientious professional humorist he was, kept a notebook to fall back on when his own native drollery failed. In this book he copied out rude stories in the perky hand which was so like his voice and so unlike his figure. He also collected newspaper cuttings – advertisements from Continental papers, printers' errors, or naïvely-phrased remarks from public speeches. People saved them for him as if he were a small boy with a stamp album.

'Poor old Ossie doesn't have a sex life,' they said, 'so he has to get it this way.' But Ossie kept the notebook more for others' amusement than his own. He did not aspire to a sex life. It did not enter into his design for living. Pierrot has Pierrette, Harlequin has Columbine, but there is no girl-friend for Pantaloon.

When, after two weeks, even the sight of Ossie's bottom going up the ladder to the top shelf brought no response from Daniel, Ossie tried him with his prize new one from the notebook, a real collector's piece. Daniel listened gravely, grunted at him and went out. Ossie's smile drooped. The story had never flopped yet, except with Macintyre, who never saw the point of any joke until it was explained, and then saw it wrong.

'What's the matter with *him*?' Ossie asked Peter Clay, who was sketching a bone of the skeleton that hung from a gibbet in the corner. 'Looks like a corpse.' He rattled the skeleton's ribs merrily with a ruler, as if they were railings.

'Good God, you ass.' Peter looked up. 'Don't you know?'

'How should I? Nobody ever tells me anything.'

'Didn't you know his wife died?'

Ossie floundered and mumbled. He had no words for this sort of thing. 'But Peter – but I say – I knew her. It can't – chap's not wearing mourning –'

'I only found out by chance.' Peter bent over his sketch again. 'He never told anyone. Queer fish. Just like him not even to wear a black tie.'

Yes . . . yes, Ossie thought. Just like him. Didn't want to distress people. Ossie judged everybody's motives by his own.

Ossie lived in a little shoebox modern flat near Sloane Square. Once into the bathroom, he had to back out, because he could not turn round. He had many friends; but even though you go out every night, or have people round, friends must go home, or you must go home, and Ossie knew what loneliness was. He could not bear to think of Daniel alone at the cottage. When Ossie's parents had been killed in the Blitz he had needed to be with people all the time. When his room-mate went on leave, he had moved his Army cot in with the men next door.

It was bad to be alone. It made you think – futile, distorted, unbearable thoughts. Images of horror that seared into the brain like a branding iron. Memories in the cheating guise of nostalgia. Remorse where none was needed; false regrets . . .

A lifetime of having to keep to himself all the serious thoughts he could not express had taught him that you could think yourself into any emotion about anything, good, or bad, as Hamlet had discovered. He wanted to tell Daniel that this was why he should not be alone, but it was not in his role to say such things. He was not even supposed to know about Hamlet.

So he spun out his tea half-hour and waited in the canteen until Daniel wandered in. He nearly always went about with his hands in his pockets. Ossie thought this must be because he had lost his parents young, remembering how his own mother had been for ever slapping and pulling at his fat wrists. Daniel sat down at a table in the corner and opened a paper, but Ossie, like a missionary, tracked him down through the jungle of silly spidery tables, and sat down opposite him with a bump that slopped over

Daniel's tea and sent a plastic salt-cellar bouncing to the floor.

'Hullo sunshine,' said Daniel gloomily, pouring the tea back from the saucer to the cup.

'Greetings,' said Ossie. 'Mind if I sit here?'

'I don't. The furniture might,' said Daniel, as Ossie shifted uncomfortably on the metal chair that had been scientifically designed, but not for shapes like his. He laughed as if this were rare wit. At least Daniel had made a joke. That was something.

Daniel read the paper. Ossie lighted a cigarette. His mouth was so small that it looked as if he were smoking in the middle of it – puff, puff – like a daring novice. He had planned just what he wanted to say, but the Heavens only knew how he was going to get round to it. If they knew, perhaps they would come to his aid.

'How's – er, how's ye olde cottage?' he asked, removing his cigarette and affecting to examine its tip.

'The cottage?' Daniel glanced up. His face looked grey, but it was because he needed a shave. 'The cottage? It's O.K., I suppose. I don't know. Haven't been there for ages.'

'Haven't you? Where are you living then?' From the look of him, he might be sleeping on a park bench, or not sleeping at all.

'I've gone back to an old girl-friend of mine. Italian woman – keeps a lodging house in Battersea.'

'Oh, but look here, Brett, you can't – I mean –' This was too tragic. Ossie knew that place. He had been there once with a student whom Daniel had sent looking for a room. They had not penetrated further than the reeking hall and the one-eyed old Neapolitan trull who had come up at them from the basement with her blouse undone and her hair like a snake's nest.

'What do you mean, I can't?' Daniel was not annoyed. He looked at Ossie mildly, waiting for him to make a joke.

'Well, what I mean is this, my dear fellow. I mean, you can't live in that detestable place. That's no kind of a home.'

'Who said I wanted one?'

'But you must. Everyone does. Of course, I can understand you not wanting to stay on at the cottage, after – after –' Ossie floundered about among earnest words like a whale on the beach.

'For God's sake!' Daniel laughed at him without mirth. 'Don't be tactful. You of all people. Though I must say you're the first person who's ventured even to touch on the subject. I give you that. I seem to be an object of dread to most. Because Jane has died, I make them uneasy. I put a jinx on things – there, you see? You don't like me talking about her. But have no fear, Oswald dear, I shan't embarrass you again. Let's talk about the cottage.' He hitched his chair forward. 'Nice little place. First house I ever got half-way attached to. Don't imagine I'm staying away out of sentiment. What difference does it make? No, it just doesn't seem worth trekking out there and back now. And then, you know, I couldn't be bothered to buy things and cook and sweep, and whatever one does.'

The Heavens had given Ossie his chance. He pounced. The pepper-pot slid to join the salt-cellar. 'Let me come and stay there with you for a bit,' he blurbed. 'I'd run the house for us. I can do those things. I can cook –'

'Ossie, what is this? Are you proposing to me?'

'No, do listen, my dear fellow. It's a good idea.' Ossie's voice was rising so high, it was nearly through the canteen ceiling. 'I wouldn't make jokes at breakfast – honest. And I wouldn't get in your way when you wanted to work.'

'Work? Good God!' said Daniel in horror. 'I never do any.'

'That book about Italian churches. You could get on with it. I could work, too. I'm writing a book myself, as a matter of fact.' He lowered his lashes modestly on to his chubby red cheeks, then raised them, opening his eyes very round at Daniel in a goggling, golliwog way he had. 'It's a funny book about dogs. The sort of thing people buy at Christmas time. A man I know promised to introduce me to a publisher. He –'

But Daniel was not listening. He suddenly shrugged his shoulders. 'O.K.,' he said. 'We'll go, if you like. I wouldn't mind having a smack at the garden, anyway.' He picked up the paper, as if he weren't interested any more, and Ossie could make whatever arrangements he chose.

Ossie liked being at the cottage.

'Good of you, Oz,' someone at the college said. 'Lord knows it's no joke trying to see someone through the first hell of a thing like this.'

'Tripe,' giggled Ossie. 'I'm doing it for my own benefit. Free bed and board – jolly cushy billet.'

'Good old Oz,' they said. 'True to form. Never a dull moment.' And, 'God!' they said to each other behind his back. 'How on earth does Brett stand him – now of all times?'

Although Ossie saw himself as a man with a mission, Heaven-sent to keep Daniel from despair, he sometimes thought that his joke about cushy billets was almost true, and wondered if he had a right to be so happy there, when Daniel was not.

Not that he seemed actively unhappy, but he was restless. The cottage held a genial peace within its walls, as if generations had lived there without strife or spite. Most people felt this atmosphere as soon as they came in at the door, but Daniel might have been at a railway terminus for all it affected him. He seemed to be not properly there, more like a one-night lodger than a man at home in his own house. Sometimes he did not come home at night, and Ossie had learned, after the first time, not to ask him where he had been.

Daniel never spoke of his wife, and it was impossible to tell how much she had meant to him. He had been rather casual to her that Sunday when Ossie had seen them together, except just once, when Ossie had blundered into some quip about the babies of first cousins. Daniel, who had not even seemed to be listening, had nearly blasted Ossie out of his chair. It had been embarrassing for everyone, including Daniel's wife.

His silence about Jane was not deliberate and strained, but casual, as if her absence were no more unusual than her presence had been. It was almost as if she had only just gone upstairs to fix her hair, and although he had not spoken her name for weeks, if Daniel had suddenly called out to her to hurry up, it would sound quite natural. Her things still stood about the house in the most unnerving way. The bottom drawer in Ossie's room was full of her winter jerseys, and he knew that her dresses still hung in the cupboard in Daniel's room. The books she had been reading were still beside her bed. Her garden shoes were still in the kitchen. Her work basket was still on the table behind the sofa.

Daniel seemed not to notice these things, and Mrs Petter, who came from the village, simply dusted whatever there was and put it back in the same place.

Although Daniel did not talk to him a lot, except in spurts when he had had a few drinks, Ossie was not bored at the cottage. He had found a twopenny library where they had all of P. G. Wodehouse and was going through chronologically from *The Clicking of Cuthbert* onwards. Sometimes he wrote little bits of his own book. It was a slow job, because he had to keep thinking of puns. When he had made a good one, he would chuckle out loud, hoping that Daniel would ask what the joke was.

People dropped in occasionally, some because they liked Daniel, others because they knew he had some gin. He was an erratic host. Sometimes he could hardly bear to let them in over the doorstep. Sometimes he could not bear to let them go. If they stayed too late, Ossie went to bed. He felt ill if he did not get nine hours' sleep, and hoped the visitors would not make a noise and wake him when they left. He did not like being awake in the middle of the night with the earth so still. In Chelsea there had always been a car, or a sudden bawl of song, or quarrelsome voices echoing in the empty night like a clacking telephone, or the hollow tap of heels going home. Here, the sea of Cambridgeshire lay too lonely under the stars. The fields were too big. It gave Ossie agoraphobia if he looked at them too long from his bedroom window.

These were clear summer days with glowing evenings. As soon as they were out of the knockabout car which they left all day in the station yard, Daniel would mix a drink and go straight out to work in the garden, planting his glass in a handy place. Ossie did not drink. His parents had forbidden it before he was twenty-one, and afterwards he had never felt the need. He liked everybody anyway, so he did not need anything to make him sociable.

While Daniel struggled with the rampaging garden that had got the upper hand while he had been away, Ossie expanded his Humpty-Dumpty torso in a deck-chair in the last of the sun and thought about what he was going to cook for supper. He was no use in a garden. He could not tell flowers from weeds, and his feet crushed things that mattered. When he had tried to help by mowing the lawn, he had run over an old knuckle-bone and chipped the blades. He had pretended to Daniel that it was a stone, because he did not want to remind him of Jane's dog, which had run away the day she died and never been seen since.

Ossie tried very hard not to upset Daniel, although if he happened to say something tactless by mistake it did not seem to make much difference. He watched Daniel a lot, noticing his changes of mood, studying his brown, square, quick-smiling, swift-frowning face, trying to say the right thing when he seemed to be having what Ossie thought of as 'a bad time'.

These bad times usually came on him when he drank too much. Or was it that he drank too much because they were already on him? Ossie did not know.

If Daniel and Ossie finished work at different times, they would meet at King's Cross. If Daniel were not there, Ossie would wait for two trains and then go to the country by himself, although he hated driving the car, and did not like sleeping in the cottage alone, but he had nowhere else to go since he had lent the flat to his sister. If Daniel were going to stay away often like this, he thought he would get himself a little dog. A poodle. There was a white woolly one in the window of a dog shop, and Ossie always stopped on his way to lunch to tap and scratch on the glass and make kissing noises, although it could not hear.

One evening, when he had waited nearly an hour at the station, drinking tea in the sad buffet where the cruets were built into the table tops so that you could not steal them, Ossie got into the seven-o'clock train, feeling depressed. Something comic had happened in the library that morning and he had been saving it up all day to amuse Daniel. The carriage filled up. People began to arrive running instead of walking. Doors slammed. A liverish man in a stained grey hat wrenched open the door of Ossie's non-smoker and began to roll a cigarette as soon as he sat down. At the last minute, when the train was already moving, came Daniel, with his hair rumpled and his jacket flapping. He spotted Ossie, and hurled himself in, panting and giggling. There was a small space on the seat opposite Ossie, and the people on either side of it moved themselves away, cramping their thighs and tucking in their clothes, for Daniel was obviously a little drunk. After he had sat and laughed at Ossie for a few minutes, he fell asleep with his head on the shoulder of a woman in a hard velour hat, whose mouth looked as if it had just been sucking lemons.

'Is he your friend?' she asked Ossie, when she had pushed away Daniel's head and received it again on her bony shoulder for the fifth time.

'No, no,' protested Ossie, who was rehearsing the scene to tell Daniel later on. He liked to hear about things he had done when he was drunk, especially if they were impossibly exaggerated. It made him think that he had been more drunk than he was, which pleased him, because he was always complaining that these days he had to spend a fortune before he could feel any effects at all.

Daniel slept like a child, with a half-smile and lashes displayed on his cheek. Ossie caught the woman in the velour hat glancing down once at his hair, and for a moment her eyes were sad and her mouth looked as if it tasted wine, not lemons.

When they got to their station, Ossie hauled Daniel out, leaving the woman indignant, tricked: 'You said you didn't know him!' brushing the smell of Daniel off her collar as if he were scurf.

Daniel drank a lot more before and during supper. Ossie ate most of the supper, while Daniel talked. Afterwards, when they were sitting in their opposite armchairs, Ossie thought that Daniel had fallen asleep. But looking up from his book, he saw Daniel gazing at him with eyes half closed and unfocused, as if he were trying to blur the shape of him into another person sitting there.

Ossie felt uneasy. He hitched his slippered foot from its perch on the other fat thigh and got up.

'Get us a whiskey, now you're up, Oz,' said Daniel, without moving his gaze from the empty chair. For a long time afterwards he sat holding the tumbler on one arm of the chair while his fist slowly thumped the other. Ossie roved about doing little pottering jobs, not liking to sit in that chair again.

When the bronze bell outside the door clanged, he switched on the light under the thatch eave and opened the door, blocking the space so that no one could come in until he had vetted them.

'Hi there, Oswald!' It was a man from the next village, who called himself a gentleman farmer to let people know that he was supposed to be a gentleman. With him was his wife, who ran a kennels and smelt of dogs and stale beer and cigarettes smouldering in metal ashtrays, and a small man in a check suit, who looked as if at any minute he would say: 'A funny thing happened to me on my way to the theatre tonight . . .'

'Where's the boy-friend?' asked the gentleman farmer. 'We've come to cheer him up.'

'I'm so sorry,' Ossie said quietly. 'I'm afraid I can't ask you in. Daniel isn't very well – touch of flu, I think. He's just going to bed.'

'What the devil are you nattering out there for? Come on in and shut the door, whoever it is. Theo!' Daniel got up, spilling some of his drink on the floor. 'Thank God you've come. I've been screaming for company all evening.'

'Your nanny said you had flu,' said the gentleman farmer.

'Are you sure we don't intrude?' asked the man in the check suit.

'Flu my foot,' said Theo's wife, peeling off a leather Air Force jacket; 'he's half tight.' She laughed herself into a nicotiny cough. Everyone laughed, including Ossie, who never missed the chance of a cackle.

'Why, you're quite right,' said Daniel. 'I am. It's wonderful. Come on; what are you going to have? You've got a lot of catching up to do.' He went over to the drink cupboard, which was built into the thickness of the wall where the old backdoor had been when the cottage was two houses.

Ossie had some cider and sat with them for a while. He showed the man in the check suit his notebook and had quite a success with some of his stories, although Theo's wife maintained that she had heard them all before. The gentleman farmer began to tell a long and detailed story about how he and some other merry lads had assisted a cow's difficult accouchement by roping the feet of the calf to a lorry and driving away.

When Ossie went to bed they seemed to be settled in for the night, but when he woke later to a moonlit room and the dree of an owl the house was quiet. He could not get to sleep again. The moonlight made the room look cold, but he was too hot. He flung off the clothes and then was too cold. He would go down and get himself a biscuit. It was always a help to chew a biscuit in bed, or even two or three, if you could not get to sleep.

Going into the sitting-room, he nearly died of fright. Daniel's chair was empty, but there were feet on the hearthrug. Daniel was slumped asleep in the other armchair, the one that had been Jane's, his face green and puffy in the moonlight.

He cursed when Ossie woke him, and cursed all the time he was getting him upstairs and undressing him on his bed. Ossie found that he quite enjoyed doing all this, and could understand why women liked to be nurses. In bed himself, rolling over in a kindly glow, he fell asleep without remembering his biscuit.

Next morning, Daniel would not get up. When Ossie tried to rouse him, he said : 'For Christ's sake, don't nanny me !' and turned over, so Ossie got the car out and went to work alone.

He hurried back that night, driving much too fast from the station so that he went off the road going round a corner and had a sudden vision of what Daniel would say if he found him and the car in a ditch.

Daniel was mowing the lawn, looking surprisingly healthy in a terrible plaid shirt that Ossie did not allow him to wear.

'You're late,' he greeted him.

'I'm not. I'm early.'

'Well, it seems late. I've got company in there.' Daniel jerked his head at the house. 'Been there for hours. Jane's mother and her sister, collecting her things.'

'Oh,' said Ossie, 'how awful. You shouldn't be there.'

'Well, I'm not. I'm out here.' Daniel stuck in his pipe again and went on mowing.

Jane's mother – Daniel's Aunt Dilys – was a tall, swaying woman with a general lavender-coloured effect about her clothes, hair, lips, and skin. She had long narrow feet and legs whose thinness she tried to disguise with thick grey cotton stockings. Either sorrow or natural causes had made her droopy. Her back curved, shoulders sagged, her hair looped downwards and her hands when idle hung with fingers pointing to the ground, the edges of their long nails like drops of water about to fall. Her clothes looked too big for her and she trailed at arm's length a squashy bag into which she was sadly putting knick-knacks from the sitting-room.

Her daughter Lydia was still more colourless; not even lavender, but a fawnish no-colour which had spread from her personality to her clothes and hair. She was short and flat, and went about neatly, like a robot maid, doing the things that were necessary: folding clothes, sorting letters, packing books. When her mother, who was given to nervous repetition, asked her for the third time to do something she had already done, Lydia answered: 'Yes, Mummy,' with a natural patience that required no effort. Decorous and undemanding, they moved about the house like wraiths, and Daniel, coming in sweating from work, seemed by contrast excessively alive. It was clear why Jane, reared in the hushed and pallid atmosphere which swathed her mother and sister like a mist, had needed to marry someone like Daniel, nourished to full vitality on freedom and the sun.

His powers of recovery were astonishing. Looking at him, no one could have guessed that he had been dead drunk last night and incapable of speech or movement this morning.

'I must say, you look very *well*, Daniel,' his aunt said uncertainly.

'Me? I'm fine. I need a drink though. What are you going to have?'

'Well, you know I don't take anything usually, but I think today I would like a small glass of sherry, if you've got it, dear.'

'Good for you. Lydia doesn't, does she?'

'No, Lydia doesn't.'

When he brought her drink, Aunt Dilys half put out a hand as if to touch his sleeve. 'You're so – so very good and brave, Daniel,' she said wonderingly. Though relieved to find him so normal, for it made their sad task easier, it seemed that in a way she would almost have preferred him to look peaky and mopy, so that she could have mourned with him, and they could all have loosed together the tears with which her throat was dry and her breast aching. In her, gladness that he could master his suffering fought with an involuntary resentment that he was not showing more suffering for her daughter.

She got Ossie by himself in the bathroom. 'How *is* he?' she whispered, although Daniel was out in the garden again and could not possibly hear.

'He's not too bad. He has his bad times, of course,' said Ossie importantly.

'Oh dear. I do wish I could do something for him. But no one has ever been able to do anything for Daniel, even when he was a child. When his mother died we all tried to help him, but he was so – so obstructive and remote. Not like other children. Oh dear . . .' She had found Jane's sponge and stood looking helplessly at the hard, dry lump. Ossie went gently away.

It was time to cook the supper. 'Do we,' he asked Daniel, 'feed them before they start back?'

'If you like. If you've got anything to give them,' Daniel said, as if it was Ossie's house, not his.

Aunt Dilys offered to help with the supper, but Ossie wanted to show off his cooking. She stayed in the kitchen for a moment, looking round about the electric stove, as if seeking for something that was not there, and then went out to lay the table.

'Napkins. . . . Where are the napkins? Lydia, ask Daniel where the napkins are.'

'Daniel, where are the napkins?' relayed Lydia.

'What napkins? I've never seen any.'

'They haven't got any napkins, Mummy,' Lydia relayed back into the dining-room.

'Oh dear.' Aunt Dilys drifted round the table straightening cutlery and murmuring: 'It's all wrong, you know, these two men living here together in this way with no one to look after them. That village woman doesn't seem to do much. Look, Lydia, at this glass.' She breathed a sad little mist on to it and rubbed it on her sleeve. 'I do wish Daniel would –'

'Pom – tiddy-pom-pim-*pom*!' trumpeted Ossie. 'Soup's up!' He did not want Daniel to hear her fussing.

They had a quiet, polite meal. Aunt Dilys ate little, dabbing her mouth with a mauve handkerchief. Lydia ate whatever was put on her plate and would not help herself to anything, even salt, unless it was passed to her. When they had had coffee and the cases were in the car and it was time to go, and everyone was suddenly stimulated by relief that the awkward visit was safely over, there was a thud on the front door. It was not like someone knocking; it was like someone smaller than a person bumping against the door.

Ossie saw Daniel's face frozen into unbelief. He saw him look at the others, finding their gloves and being helped into coats by Ossie, but the sound meant nothing to them, until Daniel opened the door and Jane's collie dog slid in, gaunt and mangy, with one torn ear raggedly healed and half his tail gone.

Aunt Dilys gave a cry and burst into tears. Lydia clung to her and wept without noise, Daniel dropped on his knees and laid his cheek on the scarred yellow head. The dog, after greeting him no more effusively than if he had just returned from a day's hunting instead of two months' wandering, slipped away, down the step into the dining-room, over the cross-bar under the table and up the step into the kitchen, with the movements of old habit.

Nobody said anything. It was as if Jane's ghost, which had never troubled the house, had suddenly come back, with her dog.

'We must go ... must go.' Aunt Dilys groped to the door.

'Yes, Mummy.' Lydia straightened her hat. Her short figure steered her mother's tall one up the path in the dusk, while Daniel and Ossie followed.

The box-like family car jerked to a start and wavered away up the lane, for Lydia was still crying. Daniel stood by the gate with his hands in his pockets and watched them go, then turned back to the house to find something for the dog to eat.

Gradually Daniel was less and less at the cottage. Ossie did not mind so much sleeping there alone now that he had a dog. The collie became quite attached to him, which was gratifying, being the reverse of Ossie's usual relationships with people; but when his master came home, the dog forgot Ossie, who had fed and petted him while Daniel was away.

Ossie did not have so much time to worry about Daniel now, for shortly after the visit of Aunt Dilys and Lydia the most extraordinary thing happened. Ossie got himself a girl-friend. It was more that she acquired him than he her, for although they had chatted often in the library, for she was a student at the college, it would never have occurred to Ossie to make the first move that would lead to better things.

Even now, when she had made it quite clear that she liked him, Ossie could still hardly believe that he had a girl-friend. A regular girl-friend belonging to no one else. A girl who kept evenings free for him. A girl he could nuzzle in cinemas, and kiss in the dark doorway of her block of flats. A girl who let him say : 'I love you,' and did not laugh. He said it often, once he had overcome the first difficulty of getting it past his untutored lips. 'I love you, Doreen,' he said, and although she had not yet said 'I love *you*' in return, she appeared to like him saying it, and Ossie sat and dreamed about her in the late train going home, with a fatuous smile among his chins.

Sometimes in the mornings, when romance was null, Ossie would look at himself in the long mirror and realize dejectedly that she was kidding him, or he kidding himself. A man who looked like that – what could he mean to a red-haired Aphrodite like Doreen? But then there she was, popping into the library half-way through the morning to say : 'There's a new film at the Empire tonight. Shall we go?'

Sometimes in the late train, which wandered out of London stopping at every little station and picking no one up, Ossie dreamily wondered if one day he and Doreen would get married. It was an idea almost too revolutionary to be entertained, let alone voiced. It was an exhilarating thought, yet a disturbing one, too, because marriage had never entered into any of Ossie's plans for life. Not that he had many plans for life. He was young yet; he had always thought he would just drift on and see what turned up. He had never thought of marriage turning up. When he looked at his middle age, he saw himself as a jolly bachelor uncle taking someone's children – his sister's if she ever married – to the circus, the pantomime, the fair on Hampstead Heath.

Ossie did not tell Daniel about Doreen. He thought that it might hurt him. The idea of a man and a girl ... Once when he had been with Daniel at a theatre, they had been talking in the interval and Daniel had suddenly stopped in mid-sentence and stiffened like a pointer, staring at the back of a pale blonde head two rows in front. When the girl turned to her companion so that they saw her profile, Daniel had relaxed, let out his breath and gone on talking.

When Ossie stayed late in town he always told Daniel that he was going out with his sister or 'with the boys'.

'But where do you go?' Daniel asked. 'Where does one go "with the boys" if one doesn't go to pubs?'

'But I do.'

'God,' said Daniel, 'they're dreary enough if you drink. Must be hell if you don't.'

Sometimes Daniel came home by the late train, too. Sometimes he didn't come home at all. In September he had some kind of quarrel with Benita, the old Neapolitan woman in Battersea, and began to come home to the cottage again every night. Ossie felt bad then about going out so much with Doreen. If he was Daniel's friend, living with him for company, then he must do the thing properly, not leave him there to lonely darkening autumn evenings with no one to cook his supper.

He explained this to Doreen, but she did not understand. She was interested in Daniel and often asked Ossie things about him. Like most girls, she was attracted to him, yet peeved by the fact that girls did not seem to attract him. Not the ones at the college, anyway. He was polite with those he taught, or sarcastic if they were foolish, for all the world as if he were some sexless old professor who viewed them only as brains, not bodies. A girl might save herself the discomfort of an uplift brassière for all the effect it had on Daniel Brett.

One day Daniel was caustic to her about the perspective of her middle distances. It was that evening that she and Ossie had their first real quarrel.

'Gigli's at the Albert Hall next Wednesday,' Doreen said, in Lyons. 'I've got no late class. You could sneak out early and we'll queue like mad. We might get into the gallery.'

'Not a hope.'

'Why not? Don't be so defeatist. Someone's got to get in. Other people do.'

'Not us,' Ossie said.

'What's the matter? Don't you *want* to go? I thought you said you liked Italian music, or were you only pretending?'

'I – pretending? You know me, Doreen; George Washington's my middle name. It's me arches. I can't stand in queues.'

'You did for the Crazy Gang.'

'Ah ...' Ossie snatched gratefully at the joke, like a dog at a bone. 'That was "*underneath* the arches". This is on them.'

'Oh shut up,' she frowned. 'I'm serious.' That was one of the privileges Doreen had brought him, serious discussion for the first time in his life. 'I – want – to *go*,' she said, biting off her words like thread.

'Well, I'll see.' Ossie shifted his chair uneasily and a waitress knocked into him with a tray of tomato soups.

'I know.' Doreen leaned forward, her pale-lashed eyes narrowed. 'You don't want to abandon your beloved Daniel, that's it.'

'No – but well, in a way it does seem a bit mean. After all, we're going to the Palladium on Tuesday, and there's that film on Thursday. I don't feel I ought to go on the tiles every night. He's pulling down an old shed, and I have to help him.'

'I never heard anything like it in all my life,' said Doreen. 'All right, if you don't want to go to Gigli, I'll get someone else. Morris will take me, I know.'

'But Dor*een* –!' cried Ossie desperately, stretching a hand across the table.

'Daniel obviously means more to you than I do,' went on Doreen, with a noisy passion unsuitable to the crowded brasserie of Lyons Corner House. 'What are you two, anyway – a couple of pansies?'

'Doreen!' Ossie was shocked to the depths of his soul. If she could say a thing like that, he was not sure that he could go on loving her, but then he looked across the table and saw her fuzz of red hair, her thick creamy skin, her little sharp teeth, her shape under the green jersey....

She began to get up. 'Oh, don't let's go,' he begged. 'Sit down. Do. Have another Horlicks.'

'No *thank* you,' said Doreen, and went, leaving him to pick up his hat, pay the bill and flounder after her.

Ossie now went through a period of great mental distress. He could not be happy at the cottage; he could not be happy with Doreen. She would not let him kiss her now. He never kissed her without first asking: 'May I kiss you?' and now she said: 'No,' and went quickly up the stone stairs to her flat.

Was it to be a choice between Doreen and Daniel? He could not desert Daniel now, yet Daniel would not need him all his life, and by the time he had helped him over his bad times he might have lost Doreen. He, Ossie Meekes, whose only worry in life had been that nobody needed him – his worry now was being needed by two people at once. Was this he? He hardly knew himself. He studied himself in the mirror as if he were a stranger, and fancied that one of his double chins had disappeared. Doreen had gone to hear Gigli with Morris. She would not tell Ossie what it had been like. He suspected that they had queued in vain and never got in, but thrust this base glee from his mind.

'I suppose,' said Doreen, on a Friday, 'it's no use asking you what you're doing this Sunday? You're building sand castles with dear Daniel, no doubt.'

'Well, I don't know. . . . He talked of taking the car up to the Royston Downs and having a walk.'

'You walk!' Doreen laughed and ran her eye up and down him.

Oh, Doreen! cried Ossie's soul. Don't be like this. What has happened to you? You never used to mind my being fat.

A proud girl, she was. Before he could betray her further, she said huffily : 'Oh, don't mind me. I've got other plans for Sunday. I only wanted to tell you not to count on me since I have an invitation to go out.'

Ossie did not believe her. He knew her so well, had studied her face in so many moods across so many teashop tables. He knew that when she slid her nut-coloured eyes away like that she was lying. She never went out on Sundays. She usually washed and ironed her underclothes and wrote letters to her family in New South Wales.

When Ossie got home that night, Daniel told him that he was going away for the week-end. 'Aunt Dilys and Uncle Hugh have been at me for ages to go there,' he said. 'It's a hell of a bore, but I'll have to go sometime, so it had better be now before it gets cold, because they don't light fires till November the first.'

Ossie knew that Doreen would not come into the library on Saturday morning. If she was annoyed with him, she sent someone else for her books, or managed without. So he hung about in the corridor outside the ladies' cloakroom, where he could catch her before she went home at midday.

'What are you up to, Ozzie?' someone asked. 'Don't tell me

you're setting up as a D.O.M. That's a criminal offence, you know, loitering with intent at a place like this.'

Ossie laughed, and showed him a new joke on the same subject in his book, keeping an eye on the swing doors so as not to miss Doreen.

When she came out, he grabbed her arm, masterful because he was happy about having this week-end uncomplicated.

'Let go,' she said. 'You're pinching me. Great clumsy hand –'

Ossie took it away and looked at it. True, it was rather like a bunch of sausages, but she used not to complain of it. She had even begun to teach him how to use it in the days before they had quarrelled. It would be all right now, however. He put the hand back on her arm, more gently, and steered her down the steps as if she were Queen Elizabeth.

'Listen, dear,' he said. 'Daniel's going away for the week-end. You come down on Sunday, eh? I'd like you to see the cottage. It's really twee. I'll cook you lunch.' She did not object to that, because she could not do anything domesticated. If they ever married, Ossie had thought that he could do the cooking – well, what about French chefs? Doreen might even be the one who went to work while he stayed at home with an apron over his trousers. They could both be happy like that.

She said that she would come. Although she did not care much for the country, Ossie, as almost landed gentry, with a genuine old cottage almost as good as his own, had always appealed to her. Ossie wished he could have suggested her coming on Saturday and spending the night, but she might not understand that it was only so that she could have more time there. And perhaps – who knew – if he had her there on his own he might make a beast of himself. Doreen was not that sort of girl. Or was she? How did one tell? That was the trouble of never having had a girl-friend before. One was out of touch with modern social customs. Did people – or didn't they? He thought of what his parents had told him and remembered that no, no, of course they didn't.

But there had been those funny things Doreen had said once or twice when they were kissing. . . . But no, she was not that sort of girl.

She was the sort of girl for a sofa, though, all right, after lunch on Sunday. It was terrible of Daniel to laugh himself nearly sick when he came home unexpectedly and found them there. He laughed so much that he had to sit down on a chair and slap his thighs. Doreen was annoyed, and went away to tidy herself up.

Ossie passed a handkerchief across his face, looked at it furtively and jammed it in his breast pocket with the lipstick stains concealed. All he could think of to say was: 'Why are you back?'

'Couldn't stand it any longer. The old boy started showing me photographs of Jane as a kid. They'd planned a tea party for the locals to meet me today, to gaze on exhibit A – the bereaved husband. Mean of me, I suppose, when poor Lyddie had been making scones all morning like a mad thing, but I escaped. Don't let's talk about me, though. I want to talk about you. Why didn't you tell me this was going on?'

Ossie tried to explain, and Daniel, when he realized what he was hinting at, laughed more than ever. Even allowing for his upsetting week-end, with those old photographs and everything, it was unforgivably rude of him to say, with Doreen just coming back into the room: 'You thought I'd be reminded – oh God, how incongruous! Ossie, you must be even more naïve than I thought.'

Ossie would not let Doreen be offended. He took her aside and explained how sad it all was. She, infected, perhaps, with the kindliness of the cottage that toned down everyone's acerbity, played up creditably. She began to talk to Daniel in her intellectual voice about Italian architecture. She even asked him about his book, which was thoughtful of her. Ossie was proud of her, but Daniel got up and went out to the local pub.

There was no reason now why Doreen should not stay the night, with Daniel there as chaperon. Ossie made up her bed, bade her a chaste good night and lent her his dressing-gown. When he heard her going along to the bathroom, he sat on his bed and ground his teeth. He would not let himself go out and say good night to her again, because Heaven knew what might happen if he met her in his dressing-gown, without her corsets. It was not so much Doreen's honour as the thought that Daniel might come home and laugh at him.

Next morning Ossie got up early, left a cup of tea outside Doreen's bedroom door, and took a great deal of trouble prepar-

ing breakfast. Quite a family party they would be. But Doreen
only ate the yolk of her egg and left all the white, and Daniel
came down very late, gulped at a cup of coffee, said it was cold and
dashed out to the garage, shouting :

'Come on, you two – if you're coming !'

They all bought newspapers and read them all the way to
London.

When Ossie was washing up after supper that night, Daniel
called through to him, quite casually : 'I'm going to let the cottage.
I saw an agent about it today.'

'You're *what*?' Ossie came to the kitchen door with a plate in
one hand, a wet mop in the other, and his mouth like a goldfish.
'Let the cottage? But why? Where will you live?'

'No sense in coming right out here in winter. I'll get a room
somewhere.'

'Oh, Daniel !' Ossie's mission came over him like a hot flush.
'Please don't go back to that again. *Please*.' He stood pleading
earnestly to the empty dining-room, his face screwed up, per-
suasively, as if Daniel could see him. 'What's the good of having
a home if you don't live in it?'

'I don't want a home.'

'But you ought to. You know you've been better since we came
out here.'

'Have I?' asked Daniel's unseen voice. Ossie went through to
the sitting-room, still carrying the mop, to see from Daniel's face
whether he had said this sadly, or mockingly or gratefully. But
Daniel's face showed nothing. He was leaning back in the armchair with his eyes shut.

'I've told the agents I want to let it anyway,' he said. 'They're
sending people to see it at the week-end.'

'It's a pity,' Ossie said. 'Old boy, I think you're wrong.' Daniel
opened his eyes and grinned. 'You can't try and argue seriously
with me with that dish-wiper thing tied round your waist. How
on earth d'you get it to meet at the back? Turn round. Oh, I see.
Pins.' He seemed more interested in the tea-towel which was
wrapped round Ossie's waist like a flag round a lucky-dip barrel
than in talking about the cottage.

Saturday was a trying day. Three lots of people arrived to see

45

the cottage, each time when Ossie was just going to put food on the table. Daniel quite liked the first ones, and was affable to them. They said the right things about the cottage and were more interested in the garden than the plumbing. Because he did not like the others, he put the rent up ludicrously, and when they asked to be shown round, wandered away saying: 'Well, there you are. You can see for yourself what there is.'

On Sunday came two middle-aged spinsters, who made Ossie want to laugh, but Daniel, surprisingly enough, took to them at once and clinched the let without any ado. One spinster had long, untidy hair, a hand-knitted dress, pottery brooches, and a great many little bags and reticules. She went round the cottage with oohs and ahs of delight and sank on her knees to a clump of chrysanthemums. The other one had short neat hair which accentuated her square jaw and bull neck, and wore a suit made of some kind of sackcloth, shoes with sporrans, and plaid golf socks up to the knees over her stockings. She went round the house grunting at it, and fondled the dog in the way that he liked. Ossie was afraid they might be thinking of starting a teashop in the cottage, but no, they simply wanted to live there.

The hand-knitted one was Miss Adelaide Mallalieu, and the sackcloth one was Miss Freda. Daniel was enchanted with them and insisted that they must stay to tea. Ossie went into the kitchen to put the kettle on. While he was waiting for it to boil, he thought for the hundredth time how silly it was not to have an electric kettle like he had in the flat. He had always been meaning to buy one for Daniel. Now, of course, it was too late.

When he carried the tea things through, Miss Adelaide was saying: 'I'm afraid you'll miss this dear little place dreadfully, Mr Brett. How can you bear to leave it?' Ossie nearly dropped the tray when he heard Daniel say quite easily: 'Well, you see, my wife was killed here.'

Miss Adelaide's eyes filled with tears. She looked down at her hands, twisting them in her lap. Miss Freda leaned forward with the face of a trustful mastiff and said brusquely, but without embarrassment: 'I'm sorry. What happened?'

Ossie would never have dared to ask Daniel a thing like that. He had never heard anyone ask it, and he had never heard Daniel talk about the way his wife had died, but now he began to tell the Mallalieus as naturally as if he were used to talking about it every day. Adelaide sat looking at her lap, and Freda sat with her knees wide apart and her knickers showing, muddy feet planted on the rug, nodding and grunting while he told them about Jane and the electric kettle, and how he had to prise her dead hands off it when he found her.

'Go on, Ossie, pour the tea out, old boy, before it gets cold,' he said, for Ossie was sitting paralysed at the thought of how he might have come gaily home with an electric kettle.

Afterwards Daniel was rifling through his desk for some papers relating to the house. He found them among a jumble of unpaid bills, and Miss Adelaide took them over to the window, for the light was fading.

'Oh, excuse me.' She turned round. 'There's something personal got in among these.'

'What is it?' asked Daniel from his desk, where his attention had been caught by a forgotten file of notes for his book.

'It's a poem. By Robert Bridges.'

'Oh?' Daniel looked up, as if he were listening to something. Dusk was creeping out from the corners of the room, although it was still light outside, where the garden lay spellbound before the approach of night.

Miss Adelaide turned back to the window, her wispy head silhouetted. 'She copied this out.' She said rather than asked it.

'No.' Daniel stirred, and broke the stillness which lay on the room like water. 'I did. She didn't like it. She said that Bridges and I were selfish to want it that way. So you see –' He got up and switched on a light. 'Here's what you get for being selfish. I wonder if Bridges got it, too? Ossie will know. He runs a library.'

But Ossie did not know. He did not like this conversation. He had not liked any of this afternoon since tea-time and he wished these women would soon go away. He could not understand it. After all his weeks of tact and consideration, these imprudent women had got far closer to Daniel in a few hours.

When they had gone, and Daniel was looking through his

books to see which he must take away, Ossie thought he would try bluntness, if that was what Daniel wanted.

'I say, old boy,' he said bluffly. 'I've been feeling bad.'

'I told you kippers and leeks didn't mix,' said Daniel reading.

'No, but listen. I know you laughed at the time, but that day you suddenly decided to let the cottage – it was because of finding me and Doreen here, wasn't it? Made you think – made you think of you and Jane –'

'My God!' Daniel spun round. 'Don't make me sick. As if it could compare – How dare you even mention her name, you blundering fool? As if you and that toothy – that –' His stammer assailed him and he beat the air for words.

This was too much. Ossie was roused at last. 'I've had just about enough!' He hated the way his voice always went shrill when he got angry. He rushed squeakily on, before Daniel could become articulate: 'After all I've done for you – you talk to me like a dog. You insult Doreen. You let the cottage with no thought for me, when you know I promised my sister she could have the flat another month. I gave up my home for you! I –'

'I never asked you to!' shouted Daniel.

'Didn't you want me?'

'No!'

'Well, don't think I wanted to come!' They stood a yard apart and yelled at each other in the low room. Suddenly Daniel gave a shout of laughter and fell over the arm of the sofa on to his back with his legs in the air.

'Oh God, that was wonderful, wonderful. Done me a power of good. I like you a hell of a lot, Oswald. You're a great chap.'

Ossie felt wonderful, too, and next morning when he had packed up his things and left the cottage for good they parted better friends than ever before.

Ossie looked forward now to the future. They would go on being friends, and he would see Daniel a lot in London. They might even share a flat, and if Doreen did not like it, no matter. No matter either that she was still annoyed about what had happened at the cottage. If she wanted to be like that, and flaunt Morris at Ossie whenever he suggested an evening's entertainment, all right. He and Daniel could get on quite well without her.

A few days later in the library, when he asked Peter Clay to send Daniel along with some overdue books, he said: 'Don't you ever know anything, Ozzie? He's cleared out – chucked the job and cleared out. No one knows where he's gone.'

CHAPTER THREE

Doris

DORIS was getting No. 4 ready for a new guest. The floor did not trouble her much, but she spent quite a long time on the taps and the veneered top of the dressing-table. Dusting and polishing she liked – things that showed – but those bits of fluff and dried mud at the bottom of the wardrobe she just pushed back into a corner. There was no means of getting them out, anyway, with that ridge at the front. Furniture was always made as inconvenient as possible. Doris was used to that.

She stepped on to a chair and dipped her finger into the well on top of the wardrobe, looked at the finger and wiped it on her apron. No point doing anything about that. It would only make the dusters dirty. She banged all the drawers open and shut. She had not brought any drawer paper up with her, so the paper would do for one more guest. She threw a little knot of brown hair out of the window, likewise the hairpin and the razor-blade. A hairpin *and* a razor-blade in a single room? Yes, because Miss Riggs had been one to take trouble with her appearance, even though it was not the bathing season. No other explanation was possible. The Lothian Private was not that kind of hotel. There was a gentleman once who was asked to leave. No scandal. Mrs P had simply given him a more suitable address.

Doris threw the razor-blade and the hairpin without vigour, and they landed on the jutting lead roof below. Oh well. There were other bits of rubbish out there. This was not a window to look out of, giving only on to the roofs and side walls of the houses that climbed away from the sea.

Doris wiped round the basin and reminded herself to ask Mrs P to unlock the soap cupboard. She glanced under the bed and gave one scythe-like swish of the broom there. The bed itself she made carefully, tight and cold as a coffin. One thing she was good at was making beds. Her mother, who had been a nurse, had taught her. Since the age of ten Doris had had a passion for mitred corners and eighteen inches of turn-down.

When she had finished, she paused by the door for a quick look round. It was a nice enough room for the money. Whoever was coming had got the best eiderdown in the place, though some guests complained that it would not stay on the bed. The gentleman who was here last winter used to tie his dressing-gown cord right over, which was a great nuisance to undo when Doris came to make the bed.

Sometimes Mrs P chose to come up and inspect before a guest arrived, so – one thing more. Doris looked at the notice on the wall by the light switch to make sure that the last occupant had not written anything rude against the part where it said: 'TO FACILITATE THE ORGANIZATION OF THE HOTEL AND THE CONSEQUENT FELICITY OF THE STAFF, GUESTS ARE URGED TO ATTEND PUNCTUALLY AT MEALS.' It didn't mean a thing. Felicity was a girl's name. There had been a girl at Doris's school called that.

Not that Miss Riggs would have written a remark, but you never knew. Quite ordinary people did the queerest things. Doris never thought twice about it. She did not trouble herself much about who came and went in the rooms. It didn't do to think too much and fancy things. You could go nervy that way. You had your own life. The best thing was to forget the guests as much as possible and just do the job. Sometimes she forgot that she only had the job because of the guests. She was intolerant of people who wanted to miss breakfast and lie in late on a Sunday morning. It put her behind with beds, and after seven years of making their beds, cleaning after them, feeding them, Doris had come to think of cleaning, bedmaking, waiting at table as her business, not theirs. Mrs P had got like that, too. Once when an invasion scare had emptied the hotel, she had made Doris clean the rooms just the same every day. Doris had not objected. It gave you something to do.

Although she was what you'd call a mobile woman, they had not called Doris up, because her eyes were so shocking. They were better now, with these new glasses whose thick lenses made her eyes look like beads in the head of a teddy bear. She had read a piece in a magazine that said you must wear your hair soft and fluffy to distract from your glasses, so Doris had a perm every six months and washed her hair herself, without setting it, so that it stood out twice as thick. Jimmie always said that he liked her better when it was straight, needing a new perm, but men never knew.

'And another for No. 4,' the porter said, passing through the pantry where Doris was laying the early-morning tea-trays.

'He's never come yet,' Doris said.

'Oh, he hasn't?' said Ferdie. 'I suppose I didn't get out of bed at long gone twelve to let him in.' The door of the Lothian was locked at eleven-thirty, and anyone gadding later must take a key, which did not happen often with their type of guest.

'What's he like?' asked Doris without interest, spooning tea into the pots with a screwed-up mouth, for Mrs P would not unlock her cupboard to give her any more if she ran short at the end of the week.

'Nothing extra,' Ferdie said. 'Youngish for us.'

'Oh – traveller.'

'I daresay. I didn't see his looks much. A window got banging when I was opening the door, and while I was gone fixing it he was off upstairs. Smallish bag he had,' said Ferdie, with a Sherlock Holmes air. 'Short-term lodger – you'll see.'

Ferdie had not been at the Lothian as long as Doris. He had not yet learned not to take an interest. He had a married daughter in the other part of the town who was always on at him to tell her things. She wished he worked at the Queen's or the Imperial, so that he could tell her about famous people. No one famous ever came to the Lothian. Ferdie, however, always had it in the back of his mind that one day there would be a murder done there. That *would* be something. His picture in the London, as well as the local papers.

Doris slammed another plastic tray on to the pantry shelf. 'Just look at that!' She indicated the curling cigarette burn on the edge. Would they never learn that you couldn't treat modern improvements the same as the old stuff?

'I don't know what time he wants his tea,' Ferdie said. 'He'd gone up before I could ask.'

'Oh well,' said Doris. 'He'll get it now, while the kettles are boiling, and like it.'

When she went into No. 4, she screamed and had to lean against the door, collecting her heart together.

'What's the matter? Who's that?' No. 4 sat up in bed, looking round him as if he could not think where he was.

'Oh, he gave me a fright.' Doris drew great breaths. 'Rising up at me from under the bed like one coming out of the sea.'

'It's all right. He won't hurt you.'

'Ah, I can see that. Oh, you beauty.' Doris set down the tray and bent to rub the dog's head against yesterday's dirty apron which she wore for morning work. 'What have they done to your tail then? Fancy cutting your tail, poor fellow.'

'He got it in a trap.'

'Ah, they're bringing a law against that in Parliament.' Doris read the papers from end to end, after supper, with her shoes off. 'There's a good dog. They always like me,' she said. 'They know.'

'Know what?' asked the gentleman in the bed, but Doris went over to the window, where she rattled aside the curtains with the dramatic cry: 'It won't do!' She turned round, her humpy shoulders making a right angle with her squat square sides against the morning light. 'You can't keep him here,' she said. 'If Mrs P was to set eyes on him, she'd –' She did not know what Mrs P would do, for no one had ever tried to bring a dog into the Lothian Private, which had notices on its railings, in the hall, on the prospectus and on all the notepaper: NO DOGS.

The winter guests at the Lothian were mostly long-term, although this lot had the air of being there while they waited for something. Mrs Lewin was waiting with her twelve-year-old son Curtis for her Canadian husband to send for her. Miss Willys was waiting for a man. She had been waiting all her life. Old Mr and Mrs Parker were waiting for their daughter to ask them to go up north and live with her. Miss Rawlings was waiting for her mother to die in the nursing home round the corner. She went in every day and read the *Pilgrim's Progress* to her in Esperanto, but had not killed her yet. Mr Dangerfield, who was the MC at the Palace Ballroom, was waiting for the summer season, when he could stop giving private lessons and once more be Our Own Dudley Dangerfield in white gloves and tails to the ground, chanting into the microphone for the old-fashioned dances: 'Swing your partners and turn *around*. Knees to the middle and bow to the *ground*.'

Mr Finck had some job connected with building the new holiday camp outside the town. No one knew what he was waiting for. To pinch the spoons, Ferdie said.

Just now they were all waiting for their supper. Mrs P liked everyone to be there before she started serving – *to Facilitate the Smooth Organization, etc*. Five minutes after she had sounded the gong she looked through the hatch at the company docilely unrolling napkins in the cold shiny dining-room.

'Where is Mr Brett?' she asked Doris. 'Run upstairs and tell him.'

Doris never ran anywhere, but she went, at her own special gait, foot to foot, far apart, for her legs were set on square and wide.

'Supper now?' he said. 'It's only half past six.'

'Now or never. Didn't you see the notice?'

'No. Oh that. Tell me.' He was sitting on the edge of the bed, and he leaned forward and looked up at her with interest. 'If I do, will it give you felicity?'

'Mrs P is waiting to serve supper,' Doris said firmly and led the way downstairs. She hoped he wasn't going to be one of those who got larky. She'd had some of that. No thank you.

Mrs P was ladling out soups when they came down. She never let the cook serve out the portions. Doris showed Mr Brett to the table in the draught – the newcomer's table – and began to fetch soup plates from the hatch. There was a noise of spoons and of mulligatawny going through Mr Parker's moustache.

Mr Brett turned up his coat collar. 'What's the good of a gas fire if they don't light it?' he asked Doris, when she brought him his Cornish pasty.

'Mrs P lights it when necessary.'

'When is necessary?' But Mrs P was shoving not only vegetable dishes but her head through the hatch to see what Doris was up to.

After the semolina, jelly, or cheese and biscuits, Mr Finck stopped Mr Brett on the way out. He had a nose like a piece of Government cheese, with a blob on the end that quivered when he talked. 'Keep it up,' he said. 'We may get that ruddy thing lit yet.'

'Why don't you ask?'

'Oh, she'll do it if you *ask*. Most obliging. Do anything. But she has her subtle ways of getting back at you.'

How well Doris knew those small reprisals. The portion of stew all carrots and no meat. The outside slice of suet roll, from which the jam had retreated. The gravy poured back into the soup before the last plate had been wetted. 'For Mr Finck,' she would say. Or: 'For Mr Parker' (that day he had left the tap running in his basin and wet Miss Rawlings's clothes on a chair in the room below), pushing the sweets of revenge through and slamming down the hatch.

When Doris was going upstairs with an armful of hot-water bottles, Mr Brett came out of the first-floor lounge, passing a hand across his forehead, as if it had tired him talking in there. 'How am I going to get the dog in?' he asked.

'Gracious, you're never going to bring him back?'

'What did you think I was going to do?' Doris had not thought. 'I had the devil of a time getting him out this morning. People popping out of their rooms like jack-in-the-boxes. The care-taker in the art school has had him in his room all day, but he goes off at nine.'

'So do I,' said Doris, suspecting that she was about to be embroiled.

'Just wait while I fetch him, and watch out for me on the stairs.' He was gone from her and out of the front door. It made it difficult to say No to a person when they didn't wait for you to say it. Doris began to lay the breakfast-tables. Mr Brett gave her a start, looking round the door and saying: 'Psst!' She was always getting starts and turns, and wondered sometimes whether she had a funny heart.

'Where's Mrs P?' he asked.

'Having her supper.'

'Lucky woman. She gets it at a respectable hour,' he said although one of Mrs P's trials was that she couldn't sit down to a bite until turned nine.

Doris went up to stand guard outside the lounge door while Mr Brett ran up the stairs with the dog. She did not like doing this. She hated intrigues and secrecy, and liked nothing to happen in life that one could not speak about; but she hated upsets, too, so as he had already got the dog in the house, this was the only thing to do.

'It was awful,' she told him when she went in to turn down his bed. 'Someone started to turn the handle, so I locked the lounge door. Fancy! They were mad, in there. I pretended I'd been polishing the door-knob and turned the key by mistake. They must have thought me simple – at the Brasso this time of night. Oh dear.' She turned down the counterpane neat and taut. 'I wouldn't have done it but for being fond of dumb animals. Never again.'

'You won't have to.'

'That's good then. I'll be sorry to lose him though.'

'Who said he was going? Come here.' He was standing by the window. 'Look. Just the thing. On to this roof, down on to that shed roof, and into the alley.'

'Oh, but you can't,' Doris objected. 'I mean, you can't go in and out of the hotel by the window.'

'Why not?'

'Well, I don't know.' It was hard to explain, even to oneself, that however queer people could be, whatever things they might say to her or write on the walls, there were certain basic rules of hotel behaviour to which everyone conformed, and surely going in and out by the front door was one of them.

He seemed to have made up his mind to it, however, so Doris decided to put it out of her head. She was going out of the room when he called her back to the window. 'Who's that spying in the house opposite?' he asked.

'Spying? Whatever do you mean?' Mr Brett seemed determined to have things not normal. This was as bad as during the war when someone had heard Mrs P's electric refrigerator and reported her for having a radio transmitter.

'Look, that crack of light – ah, it's gone. See the curtain move? There she is again, peering round the corner.'

'Oh, her,' said Doris, turning away. 'She always does that. Been at it as long as I've been here. Oh, don't ask me what for. If she's got nothing better to do with her time, that's her funeral, not mine.'

Mr Brett put his fingers to his nose and waggled them at the house opposite, then drew the curtains across. 'I say, just do one more thing for me, will you?' he said, though it was after nine, and Doris had told him distinctly that she was off duty at that hour. 'Sneak me up something for the dog to eat.'

'Oh no,' she said, planting herself squarely. 'That I can't do.'

'He won't want much. He had something at the school. Just a few bits of meat –'

Doris had to laugh. 'Where d'you think I'd get meat from? That was the last of the joint went into the Cornish pasties – such as you could see for potato.'

'Well, bread or something, or biscuits. Do find something.'

He seemed to have no idea what he was asking. It meant getting past Mrs P's sitting-room into the kitchen, groping there in the dark for fear Ferdie should see the light, having her heart nearly let her down when a saucepan lid clattered to the floor as she reached down the big tin of stale cake and bread slices that was always on hand for trifles and charlottes and bread-and-butter pudding, creeping into the pantry to pour on as much as she dared from the milk left out for her early-morning teas. By the time she got back to No. 4, dodging into the bathroom once when she heard Mr Parker blowing his nose on the stairs, she felt as if she had been through something out of Dick Barton. She would have liked to convey to Mr Brett an idea of what she had accomplished, but although he thanked her politely – he had a nice voice, she'd say that for him – he seemed to find nothing exceptional in what she had done. Took it for granted. That was the way he asked you to do things. He didn't ask as a favour; just asked, and took it for granted you would do it. He could not have had much experience of private hotels.

Although it was long after her time, she had just to stay and watch the dog eat. He was such a dainty feeder. It always seemed so clever of dogs to teach themselves to eat with mouths that shape.

Mr Brett unwrapped a bottle of whiskey from brown paper and poured some into a tooth-glass. 'Oh dear,' sighed Doris, 'now that's two things you didn't ought to have up here. Mrs P won't have spirits in the house, except just for the Christmas pudding.'

'Oh — Mrs P,' said Mr Brett irritably, using a word that Doris did not like to hear said, even about Mrs P.

She lingered by the door, watching him drink the whiskey. 'Have some,' he said. 'Go and get yourself a glass.'

'Oh no, thank you.' Doris retreated a step. 'I've no objection to it, mind, for them who like it. I just can't fancy the taste of it myself.'

'Oh well, you miss a lot,' he said, pouring himself out some more and lying back on the bed with his feet on the quilt. 'I couldn't sleep a wink without this stuff.'

Was he going to turn out to be a drunkard, then? They had never had one of those. But the drunks Doris had seen in the streets were older, blobbier men, the kind you would draw away from instinctively, even without the danger that they might be sick on your shoes.

'I'll say good night then. And please, Mr Brett, hide that bottle for pity's sake.'

'I've got some more.' He grinned at her, but not blobbily.

'Hide them all then.' Doris went downstairs, took off her shoes and got herself interested in the papers.

There was one thing you could say for Mrs P. She did not try to catch you unawares. She told Doris: 'I'm going to do a round of inspection – everywhere,' and it would be everywhere, but it gave you fair warning.

Doris went up to No. 4 to get the dust out of the top of the wardrobe. Ah – he had hidden the bottles then, like she told him. She picked one up to get at the dust. It was empty. So were the others. Three empty bottles and he had only been there a week! No wonder he was so difficult to wake up in the mornings. Well, sooner him than her. If she had to drink one, let alone three bottles of whiskey in a week, Doris believed that she would be dead. She took the bottles away, and after dark dropped them over the low fence into the dustbin of the hotel next door. Mrs P was not above inspecting the Lothian dustbins when the mood was on her. There had been that trouble not long ago when she had found all that bread. That was why there was never any fresh bread at meals now. The old loaf had to be finished first, so by the time they got to the new one, that was old, and so it went on. Mr Dangerfield sometimes took a slice to his room to clean the stiff collar and cuffs he wore for giving dancing lessons. He said, with his smile, that stale bread was better for this. He was always one for finding the silver lining, and had Patience Strong verses stuck around his dressing-table mirror.

Mr Finck had tried to be funny one day by pretending to break a tooth on the bread. No one had laughed except Mr Brett, and they had both paid the price in jam sauce when the queen puddings came round.

Mr Brett continued to go in and out by the window, boosting the dog over the roofs. So far no one had noticed that he was never seen either going out to or coming in from work, and Doris herself had got quite used to it. It was as much a part of him as little Curtis Lewin's spinal jacket was of *him*, though it had given Doris a turn when she first saw it sitting on a chair when Curtis was in bed.

She had also got quite used to Mr Brett drinking so much. He was getting worse, and Ferdie did a lot of conjecturing as to where he got his whiskey, and why he drank so much all alone up there. 'He's drinking to forget,' Ferdie said. Doris did not speculate what, but Ferdie did. He had turned quite nasty one day when Doris asked him to get rid of some empty bottles for her, so she did not ask him any more. She smuggled them away in a suitcase when she went out, and dumped them in a corporation bin.

Sometimes Mr Brett did his drinking out. When he stayed out to supper, he never remembered to tell Mrs P beforehand, which put her out with her portions. One week-end he stayed out for every meal : dinner, tea, and supper. The other guests had talked about him in the dining-room, hoping that he was having a gay time and enjoying himself, wherever he was. They were becoming quite fond of him, especially Mrs Parker and Miss Willys and Miss Rawlings, with whom he would sometimes play whist in the lounge for a while before he went upstairs to his whiskey. Doris got quite a start when she went in to clear the coffee things to see him sitting there looking as out-of-place as a monkey at a funeral. Much too young, for even little Curtis had an old man's face, and looking as if he could suddenly jump up and run if he wanted to, whereas the others, even Mr Dangerfield, who was lazy after meals, thought twice about getting up to change the programme on the wireless.

They all took an interest in Mr Brett, for want of anything else in their lives, and when a young lady from the art school kept ringing up they teased him and wagged their fingers and said : 'Ah-ha.'

'A model, I daresay. Wish he'd bring her round here,' said Ferdie, who visualized models as more or less permanently in the nude.

That week-end, when he had not come in to any meals, nobody knew that he had not come home at all on Saturday night. Doris discovered this when she took his tea, but she could not tell Mrs P, so Mr Brett's Sunday egg was cooked in vain. Nobody else had it, for making distinctions in deprivations was one thing, but fair was fair and Mrs P did not think it right that one guest should have two eggs and the others only one. Doris privately thought it was because she did not like any of the guests enough to see them eating two eggs. The cook or Daphne would have liked it, but they could not eat it with Mrs P in the kitchen, and by the time she was gone the egg was congealed and nasty and even Ferdie could not fancy it.

That Sunday night, Doris had managed to secrete some chop bones from the plates after dinner. She forgot about them until she was undressed for bed, and then remembered that she had not taken up anything for the dog to eat. Her room, which she shared with the cistern, was on the top floor, so she had to creep all the way downstairs in her green wool dressing-gown and black slippers. Since Mr Brett had come with his outlandish demands, she had got used to skulking about doing things she ought not. It had become as much part of the job as making his bed or empty-ing his wastepaper basket.

Coming up with the plate of bones, she knocked on the door of No. 4 and called softly, meaning, since she was indecorously dressed, to leave the plate outside and go away. He did not answer. It was not like him to fall asleep so early, even when he had a lot to drink. She knocked again, but she could not stand knocking and calling there all night without doors opening on the stair-case, so she went into the room, clutching her dressing-gown tight in front of her as if its buttons were not modesty enough.

He was not back yet. The window was open a crack at the bottom, as she always left it when he was out, so that he could lift it from outside. She put down the plate and went to the window to look at the night and see if he were going to get caught in the rain. There he was, sitting on the lead roof below her, his back against the wall, cross-legged, with his dog sitting beside him as if they intended to stay there all night. Doris raised the window and he looked up and waved.

'Come along in, Mr Brett. Whatever are you doing?'

'Can't get in,' he said.

Oh dear, yes, he had had too much to drink. Doris had heard his voice like this so often before, and recognized it as dispassion-ately as if it had been hoarse from a cold.

'Funny thing,' he said, 'but tonight I can't make it. The dog can't make it, either. Funny thing.'

'No wonder,' said Doris crisply, 'since it's you that always has to lift him in. Come on, Mr Brett, give me your hands and I'll help you in.' He was heavy and he was foolish, thrashing his legs about and not trying properly. She got him and the dog in some-how, expecting every minute to hear windows go up because of the noise. He did not seem to notice that she was wearing a dressing-gown, so she thought no more of it and behaved as if she were in her black dress and apron.

He flung himself on to the bed, and she took off his shoes. She never liked to see shoes on that eiderdown. Before she had finished, he was nearly asleep.

'Come along, Mr Brett.' She shook his foot. His sock was full of holes. What did other men do, she wondered fleetingly, who had no one to darn their socks for them? Mr Dangerfield darned his own, she knew, but he was not like other men.

'Come along, wake up. You can't go to sleep with your clothes on.'

'Yes,' he muttered. His face looked crumpled.

'Now, if I go away, will you promise to undress?'

'Yes.' But she knew he wouldn't. However, she could not stay to prove it, so she left him. When she got to her own room, she could not feel easy, so she came down again and listened outside No. 4. There was no sound except the dog crunching the chop bones. She opened the door. Yes, there he was, just as she had left him, only more deeply asleep.

'Mr Brett,' she implored to his unconsciousness. 'You must, you simply must undress. It's my late morning tomorrow. Daphne will bring you your tea and she can't see you like this. It will be all round the hotel – after all the trouble I've taken to keep things dark. Mrs P –' But he obviously did not care about Daphne or Mrs P or anything but whatever he was dreaming about which was making him smile.

That was not the only night Doris had to help Mr Brett off with his clothes, although it was the only night she did it in her dressing-gown. He was getting worse, but the worse he became the more she got used to him, so the more she put up with. She did not mind what she said to him. He was not like one of the other guests. He was just Mr Brett in No. 4, and to be treated accordingly.

Sometimes he refused to get up and go to the art school. 'You'll lose that job,' Doris told him, dusting round the room. She would come back and make the bed later.

'I don't care,' he said. 'I'll get another.'

'Oh, will you?' said Doris, who liked to lecture him. 'And what about references, pray?'

'I write my own,' he said. 'That's how I got this job.'

'That's dishonest,' Doris said.

'Yes.'

'I wish you wouldn't smoke that pipe in bed.' She nagged at his reflection while she dusted the dressing-table. 'You'll set yourself on fire one of these days and burn to death; that's if you haven't already drunk yourself to death first.'

'When I do, they'll say of me in the lounge: "I can't understand it. He was always so charming," like they do when a murderer is taken away. It will give them something to talk about for weeks. That can cancel out my unpaid bills.'

'Mr Brett,' said Doris, turning round, 'do you owe Mrs P money?'

'Not yet,' he said, 'but I shall soon. I'm what is known as living beyond my means. I ought to find somewhere cheaper.'

That gave Doris a turn. It would be funny to have someone in No. 4 who went in and out by the front door. 'I've brought two pairs of socks back,' she said, putting them in the drawer. 'The others were like colanders, not worth wasting wool on.'

She did not tell Jimmie about darning Mr Brett's socks, nor, of course, about undressing him. She did not mention Mr Brett to him at all. This was not unusual, for she hardly ever talked to Jimmie about the guests. On her half days and evenings, when she went to see him, she liked to get right away from the Lothian. Sometimes they stayed at his home and had tea or supper with his mother and sister. Sometimes she and Jimmie went for a walk. At least, Doris walked, and pushed Jimmie, who had been crippled in his legs since birth.

She had known him all her life. They had been engaged now for five years and were going to be married when Doris had put by enough out of her wages at the Lothian. She would have to go on working after they were married, for Jimmie could only do part-time work at the electrical factory, but if they could ever find a flat or a prefab Mrs P had said that Doris could live out and go in by the day. She would not have liked leaving the Lothian after all these years. It would be funny not to be there any more, almost like leaving home.

Jimmie's mother said that she didn't think it right for a cripple to marry, but Doris thought she was jealous of losing him after looking after him all this time. She saw nothing wrong in marrying a cripple. Even if they could not have children, they could always get themselves a nice dog. Often, when his mother was out, she had to do things for Jimmie. That was why it was nothing for her to undress Mr Brett; but all the same, she did not tell Jimmie about him. Nor did she tell Mr Brett about Jimmie. He never asked about her private affairs, so why should she tell him?

Tea in the Lothian lounge on Sundays was quite an occasion. Everybody was there, and there was fruit cake as well as toasted Sally Lunns, and sometimes chocolate biscuits, to stop the guests questioning what became of their points. Mrs P did not want a repetition of the tiresome affair last summer when Miss Willys, who had been advised by her doctors to eat raw prunes, had demanded her ration book so that she could buy them herself. When it was explained to her that her points had been spent long ago on golden syrup and tinned salmon, Miss Willys had retorted that whoever saw tinned salmon in this hotel it certainly wasn't her, and that she, who took salt on her porridge, would henceforth regard her fellow-guests pouring treacle on theirs as, in effect, snatching the prunes from her very mouth.

It had blown over. They had all had salmon croquettes two Sundays running, and Miss Willys settled down again into the best armchair, ruffled but quiescent.

She was not quiescent today, however. While Doris and Daphne were setting out the tea-things on the side table, Miss Willys was having a carry-on in the monotonous, running tone with which she had before now driven guests out of the lounge with their heads humming.

'Feet!' she was saying. 'Feet over my head, last night, and then again this morning while I was washing before dinner. It's not the first time either, I may tell you. I've seemed to hear footsteps; and I tell you, when one suffers from migraine, that kind of thing doesn't help.'

They all murmured sympathetically, for they had learned by now that if they did not oblige at first Miss Willys would go on plugging her migraine until they did.

Mr Brett, who was sitting on a stool by the fire, hitched himself nearer to Miss Willys. 'Go on,' he said, looking up at her like 'The Boyhood of Raleigh', which hung on the wall of the lounge. 'This is thrilling.'

Doris looked hard at him through her thick spectacles, but he would not look at her.

'It may seem so to you, Mr Brett,' said Miss Willys, 'and I must admit that now you make me feel quite an adventuress, but I tell you frankly I was cold as marble with fear last night, literally as marble. I quite thought a man was trying to get into my room.'

'Thought or hoped?' muttered Daphne, who never realized what a carrying whisper she had. Doris hustled her out to fetch the tea and hot water. She was not sorry to get out of the room herself. It made her feel hot all over to see Mr Brett sitting there as cool as you please.

She did not think Miss Willys would mention it to Mrs P, for they had never been on much more than good-morning terms since the affair of the prunes, but one of the other guests might. Mr Finck was being very interested when Doris came back to pour the tea. The tip of his nose was waggling like a semaphore and he was even talking of setting up a patrol to watch the back roof at night. Mr Dangerfield had declined to join him, but Mr Brett was enthusiastic. There was a nerve for you. Doris would have to tell him off about it later.

Mr Brett, however, chose to stay out all night again. When Doris took in his morning tea, with a lecture prepared, there was his bed turned down just as she had left it, with his pyjamas and slippers laid out, and the food she had left for the dog congealing on the tiles before the gas fire. Doris put the plate into the bottom of the wardrobe, and tucked in the bed and pulled up the counterpane, to look as if Mr Brett was already up and out. When Mrs P inquired for him before she served the breakfast kedgeree, Doris surprised herself by saying that he was taking an early class at the school and would breakfast out. She was so little practised in telling lies, for she had seldom had anything to conceal before, that she was quite pleased to find how successfully she achieved this one.

Mrs P said no more. She had given up wishing that Mr Brett would tell her when he was going to be out for meals, and was considering a new wording of the notice about Felicity to cover this. If she did, Mr Brett would be the first guest to cause a whole new set of cards to be printed and tacked up. He could say that for himself, thought Doris.

He stayed away another night, and again Doris had to tell a lie at breakfast. Mr Parker, overhearing her doing it, remarked: 'What an energetic, industrious young man he seems to be.'

'He will go far,' said Miss Willys. 'You mark my words. He has the same phrenological traits as my brother had. I used to read heads, you know.'

Someone asked her if she had been bothered with any more footsteps, and when she said no, Doris was terrified that they might put two and two together. Although she was relieved when they did not, she felt a little scornful of them, too, for the dumb lot they were. It had never struck her before just how dumb, but now, seeing them sitting there like sheep, meekly swallowing their potato cakes, which were half cold again this morning, Doris was suddenly filled with despair at the thought that there was no reason why they should not stay on and on here for ever, until they or she died.

Never mind. Mr Brett would be back this evening. That would liven things up. She would tell him what they had said about him. That would make him laugh. Energetic! They ought to see him as she did, laid out on his bed half sozzled and half asleep.

He did not come back for supper that night, but after supper came a strange visitor for Mrs P. When Doris answered the doorbell and saw the woman in the black old-fashioned dress and crazy hat, she thought she had seen the white moon face before, although she could not think where.

'What name shall I say?' But the name was not familiar.

She showed her into Mrs P's sitting-room, and soon after, while Doris and Daphne and Ferdie were having their supper, Mrs P's bell rang with its own brisk buzz so different from the other bells, although they were all on the same circuit. Ferdie swore, although it was not he who would have to answer it. Daphne swore, too, which Doris did not like in a girl of her age. She liked it even less that Daphne was so lazy. She created so much about going up to answer the bell that it was simpler to go oneself.

'Put the coffee back on the stove,' she called over her shoulder. 'No doubt the visitor wants a cup.'

If the visitor wanted coffee, she was not getting any. She and Mrs P were sitting as far away from each other as the arrangement of the chairs in the small room allowed. Mrs P had on the cold face she reserved for guests who really did bad things like dropping shaving-cream jars into the basin and cracking the porcelain.

'Mrs Whistler wishes to go. Please show her out,' she said, and it sounded to Doris as if she meant: Throw her out.

'Ah-ha!' The visitor's little black eyes fastened on Doris. 'That's the person. There she is.' Doris stood stock still, frowning, mystified. 'That's the person I've seen looking out of the window, standing there as bold as brass.'

'Naturally,' said Mrs P, 'she might be seen at any window of this hotel, since she is head chambermaid here.'

Head chambermaid! thought Doris. That was a good one. What was Daphne then – the tail? You had to hand it to Mrs P. She did know how to lay it on when she got swanky.

Mrs Whistler, however, was unimpressed. 'Oh, don't tell me,' she cried. 'You try and make this out a respectable house, but I've had my eye on you for years. I haven't wasted my time.'

'I'm sure you haven't,' said Mrs P smoothly.

'You ask her.' Mrs Whistler pointed a glove with holes in the fingertips at Doris. 'You ask her if a man doesn't go in and out of one of your back bedrooms by the roof.'

Doris knew now what it meant when people in books wished the earth would open and swallow them up, although if the floor of Mrs P's sitting-room did that, it would land her on top of the knife machine in the boot hole. 'I don't understand,' she hedged. 'What is being talked about?'

'It's hardly worth repeating,' said Mrs P, 'and I certainly don't want it passed on outside these walls, but this Mrs Whistler' – her pronunciation of the 'h' made the name sound an insult – 'comes to me with some preposterous fol-de-rol about a man climbing in the window of that second-floor room at the back.'

'Oh – oh – you mean Miss Rawlings's room,' lied Doris wildly.

'No, no.' Mrs P tapped her foot and frowned. 'Hers looks to the front. You know that. No, this must be No. 4 she's talking about.

Why, that's Mr Brett's room! There you see –' She swept triumphantly round on Mrs Whistler, who stood her ground, nodding her great head grimly. 'You see – all your innuendoes, and that's a gentleman's room your precious apparition is supposed to be visiting.'

'Well,' said Mrs Whistler, hitching her voluminous dress up in front of her in a satisfied way, and chewing on her gums, 'that makes it even worse, doesn't it?'

Mrs P pretended not to know what she was talking about, but strode to the door, flung it open, and bade Mrs Whistler go before she called the police, which dramatic scene was deeply appreciated by Curtis Lewin, who was sitting on the bottom step of the stairs trying to think of something to do.

Although Mrs P was in a tremendous state of affront, she could not resist going up to see from which house Mrs Whistler had been spying.

'Is Mr Brett home yet?'

Doris made a mental review of the room – dog plate inside the wardrobe, whiskey bottles on top, tooth-glass washed – yes, Mrs P could safely go in.

They went into No. 4 together, just in time to see a dark bulk silhouetted half in and half out of the window, dragging after it a lesser bulk which let out a small yelp. Mrs P switched on the light with a click like a rifle shot, and Mr Brett gave a yelp himself and fell from the window-sill to the floor with the dog on top of him.

Doris had got to go. The guests knew that, although they did not know why. They only knew that all day she had gone about with a face like cheese, taking off her glasses if anyone said a kindly word, to scrub at her eyes.

When Mr Brett came home that evening, by the front door, with his hands in his pockets, moodily, without the dog, Doris was laying the tables for supper, the cruets swimming in the mist that had kept steaming up her glasses all day. When she saw him go past the door, she rattled a fork against a plate, and he turned, looked in and came to her.

'You look rough,' she said.

'I am. What is it about the seaside that's so depressing? You don't look so hot yourself.'

Doris turned her face away. 'I've got my notice.'

'Because of me? Because of the dog?' he asked incredulously.

Doris nodded, dumbly straightening Mr Dangerfield's pudding spoon and fork.

'Good God!' said Mr Brett. 'Where is the old —?' He used another word that Doris did not care to hear, but this time she did not mind.

'In her sitting-room – oh, but you can't go in now. She's having her quiet time.'

'I'll rowdy it up for her,' said Mr Brett, and left Doris palpitating.

What he said to Mrs P Doris never knew. He would not admit that he had said anything, and Mrs P would not admit that she had withdrawn Doris's notice for any other reason than the difficulty of getting new staff.

Doris had told Jimmie most of the story, because this now was too big a thing to keep inside oneself. It was Jimmie's idea that he should look after the dog for Mr Brett. They were out walking now, Doris pushing the chair with one hand, for Jimmie was very light, and leading the collie with the other. They went along the promenade, past the empty shelters and the empty bandstands and the closed pier gates with the torn notices of old concerts. There was nobody about but themselves and the wind coming off the sea.

Jimmie reached a hand back to touch the dog's nose as it trotted by the wheel of the chair. 'It is nice of you to have him,' Doris said. 'I hope he's not giving any trouble.'

'Oh, Mother will get used to it in her own time,' he said. 'It's made all the difference to me, having him. In any case, it was the least we could do for Mr Brett, wasn't it, after him getting your job back for you? He must think a lot of you.'

'I don't know, dear. It's only because there's nobody else there to take away his empty bottles and help him get to bed when he comes in the worse for drink. He drinks too much, poor gentleman.'

'Help him what?' Jimmie twisted round to look at her. 'You been putting him to bed? I don't like the sound of that. Why didn't you tell me?'

'I never thought to. It's all in the day's work.'

'No wonder he's nice to you. A darn sight too nice, I'd say,' grumbled Jimmie, making a show of male jealousy. 'You watch out, Doris. Maybe he's got his eye on you. You watch he doesn't get a bit too nice one day.' He spoke in fun, teasing her, for Jimmie had never been threatened with a rival yet.

Doris did not laugh. She walked on in silence, thinking about what Jimmie had said. She did not talk much at tea, even about the flat that a friend of Jimmie's sister had heard of, and she left early, kissing Jimmie on the cheek, which was the only way she ever kissed him.

Walking home, still thinking about what Jimmie had said about Mr Brett, she had a queer feeling in her nerves, not like her funny heart, but as if something exciting was going to happen. Although she was supposed to be off duty, she thought she would just go up to No. 4 in her new navy tailor-made, to see if he wanted anything. He had never seen her out of uniform, except that time in her dressing-gown, when he wasn't capable of noticing.

She approached Mr Brett's room with a new interest, a quickening of pleasure. When she went in, she saw that the drawers were open and empty, his clothes, his brushes, his sponges, his suitcases were all gone, only an empty whiskey bottle lay half in and half out of the overturned wastepaper basket. Automatically, Doris bent to pick it up. The bottle was broken and she cut her finger and stood sucking it, looking round the room with vacant eyes. When she found the five-pound note on the dressing-table, she took off her glasses and began to cry.

CHAPTER FOUR

Mumma

THE boys told Mumma that she was a mug to bother herself letting rooms, when money could be earned more easily in so many other ways. But Mumma had always had a lodger in that top back room, and intended to go on doing so. It gave her a bit of money of her own, without having to ask the boys or Pa, and it made one more in the house, which she liked. If the house had been bigger, she would have had more lodgers. She liked to live in a home with bulging walls, filled all day long with voices.

There were ten of them here now, since Esther and her husband and children had settled into the other top rooms. Mumma and Pa; Lew and Hymie; Esther, Morris and Joey, who was more trouble than six children, and the shiny, black-eyed baby Vernon; Rosie – no, one must remember to call her Rosetta – and this new lodger that Rosetta had brought home for her mother. Mrs Weissman had been a little nervous of having someone interested in Rosetta living under the same roof, although the male lodgers were usually interested in her before long. This one, however, seemed to be no more interested in her than she was in him. She had brought him home for her mother, not for herself, because the top back room was empty, and because he had nowhere to go that night she got talking to him at the Venus Club.

He had been drunk the night that Rosetta brought him home. He had been ill, too, and Mumma kept him in bed for a week, panting up three flights of stairs with trays for him of things he would not eat. Pa, who could not drink because of his ulcer and so had no sympathy with alcohol, prophesied trouble, but Mumma, sitting like a great collapsed jellyfish in the corner from which she could not get out when all the family were in the kitchen, said: 'No, Felix. He will not be drunken always. He is not the type.' She was right. He had been more or less sober after that first night.

'I'm off it,' he told her. 'I used to try and get paralytic every night to make me sleep, but after a bit it doesn't work. Gives you an hour or two of dreams that are worse than your thoughts, then the rest of the night lying awake with a head splitting with thoughts that are worse than the dreams.'

'It is terrible not to sleep,' Mumma said. She turned all her remarks into pronouncements. Trivialities from her were oracular, and people came from all round the Elephant and Castle seeking advice. This young man had not yet told her what was troubling him, but he would. Everybody did.

'You should not take those powders, however,' she told him. 'They will do you no good.'

'Mumma,' he said, 'but I *must* sleep.'

'They wouldn't hurt a child. Safest thing out,' Lew said in his quick, seller's lisp. 'Easy to get, too. I'll always see you right for them, Daniel boy. Don't you worry.'

'All the same, Lew, I do not like it,' his mother said.

'Ah, there are a lot of things you don't like, my dear,' Lew said, kissed her affectionately on the lips and went out with Daniel.

Sitting by the kitchen window, she watched their legs go past the area railings. It was true what Lew said. There were some things she did not like. Since the swelling of her legs had practically confined her to the house, she had given much time to thinking about the life she could not share, and what was wrong and what was right. She was old-fashioned, she knew, living in a bygone age, they told her, but one of the things she had never really liked was that Lew and Hymie were not in regular work.

'We are in regular work,' they told her. 'Regular profitable it is, too.' They brought home more money than their father made, but Mrs Weissman wished they would not clutter up the ground-floor back room with their buying and selling. It was always full of wireless and television sets, gramophones, cameras, typewriters, chocolate, rolls of silk, and boxes of nylons. They usually operated separately, rivalling each other in their deals; but when there was a big thing on, or one was in difficulties, then they became corporate as Siamese twins. Lew would trade in anything from a barrow-load of bananas to Cup Final tickets. Hymie, being younger and more flamboyant, went for things like furs and jewellery. He could not keep away from furs, young Hymie; and

Lew, scolding like a wife, sometimes had to extricate him from rash enterprises. Mumma flattered herself that she had brought them up to know right from wrong, so she did not ask herself why some of their business associates never came to the door in the daylight. She did not ask the boys either, for they would not have told her. If she did show too much interest in something that was causing them to talk to each other out of the sides of their mouths, they only kissed her and gave her a funny answer.

She did not mind about the petrol coupons, or the clothes ration books, which were brought to the door by little old women in black. There was nothing wrong in going one better than the Government, and coupons took up no space in the back room.

Since Pa had the ground-floor front room for his tailoring workshop, and the floors above that were full of large downy beds, that left only the basement kitchen for the family to eat, laugh, quarrel, drink, scheme, and entertain their friends in. As she sat there watching the legs going past on the pavement and finishing off hems and buttonholes for Pa, all her thinking always led Mumma round to the comfortable truth that she was a lucky woman to have her family closely round her. That was the most important thing.

She thought that she was lucky now to have Daniel in the house. She liked him better than any of her lodgers, even dear Mr Moss, who had died in her top back room. Daniel was different. Mumma knew that he was a gentleman, though she would not have breathed this to her family, whose vocabulary did not include the word. Either you made a success of life or you didn't. Birth was a thing no more important than the colour of your hair. They did not wonder, as Mumma did, what had brought Daniel here. They only knew that he had not made a success of his life, and treated him with tolerance and no respect, as if he were the family runt.

It was because he was not a success that Mumma was growing so fond of him. Like the ugly duckling, he appealed to her mother-hood. The others were so independent now. They did not need her as she felt that Daniel did. Lew, Hymie, and Rosie never asked for her advice. She often gave it, but they did not need or take it. Esther never wanted advice about the children. She would sooner

73

do things all wrong than draw on her mother's wise experience. True, Daniel did not want to be mothered. He turned his face to the wall and groaned if she fussed about in his room too long, but he was physically so low that he had to let himself be looked after, so Mumma took her opportunity. She would have kept him in bed much longer if she could, although the stairs were as tiring to her as a cross-country marathon.

When he was better, and mooching about the house in a pair of old slacks and a jersey, for he did not seem to have many clothes, Mumma liked to see him there at meals, laughing and squabbling as if he were really one of the family. Meals were her high spots. Everyone was together then, dependent on her for food, and she was the boss, serving out the things she had spent all day preparing, relishing their enjoyment of the food as keenly as she enjoyed what was on her own plate. One of the things that kept the family all at home and deterred the boys from marriage was Mumma's cooking. Rosie – Rosetta – would alternately bless and curse her mother; bless her before a meal, when she came in hungry from a dance rehearsal, and curse her afterwards when she thought what it had done to her figure. She would run round to the chemist to weigh herself and then get into a panic and hardly eat a thing for three days. Then she would get into another panic that she was starving herself ugly, and put on the pounds again in ten minutes by stuffing herself to indigestion with her mother's deep fat Krullers.

Mr Weissman was a little quiet man with an earth-coloured face and hair like grey lambswool. Ever since his family could remember he had been putting in nine hours a day at his sewing bench. He only went out to get materials, and once a week on the Sabbath, first to the Synagogue, then to the sooty gardens to watch the children playing. He did not need any exercise. He got enough treadling his machine and lifting the chunky irons from the gas-ring to the steaming cloth and back again. He emerged from the front room for dinner, when he would read the paper amid the noise and eat with a fork in his right hand, for he had worked in America for many years. At supper he would take off his spectacles and listen gravely to the events of everybody's day. Afterwards, if he did not go back to the workroom, he would sit neatly at the table and read a Victorian novel, which was his favourite, indeed his only form of literature. Now that they talked of ending clothes rationing, Pa had not been making so much money. The war had brought him a whole new clientele of people with more money than coupons, but if rationing was to end there was no point in coming all the way out to Walworth for a suit and waiting six months for it, for Mr Weissman was slow, and getting slower with each new rheumatic crystal that settled in his seventy-year-old knuckles.

One Friday Pa could not give Esther enough money when she went out to do the shopping. She went back into the kitchen, where she had left her baby Vernon playing round his grand-mother's feet.

'Mumma,' Esther said, 'Pa is either mean or poor. I must have some money.' She never said please or thank you. She was a blunt, noisy, determined girl who always got her own way through strength of limb if not of character. Although her mother admired her, she was disappointed that she had not turned out soft and slender like her younger sister. Esther's lips were thick and red, her nose high-bridged, her eyebrows densely black, and her hair so strong and wiry that it pushed her hats out of place. She had never got her figure back after her babies. She was going to be fat like her mother, but as yet everything that in her mother drooped and sagged and overflowed, in Esther was firm and taut, and solid as furniture if she knocked into you.

Mumma had hoped that marriage would gentle her down, but it had made her rougher, for she and Morrie were always fighting, with fists as well as words, and she manhandled her children as if they were rubber. It had made them rubbery. Seven-year-old Joey was a bouncing smart-Alec, whom no one could worst. The baby, who could not yet walk, hurtled about like a tennis ball with three diapers under his knickers as much for his own pro-tection as other people's.

He came at his mother under the kitchen table now with his rolling crawl and she dug him in the ribs with her foot, fairly gently. He bellowed with laughter and began to lick the polish off her shoe.

'Money, Mumma. Kopecks, shekels, pazzaza,' Esther said

impatiently. 'How do you expect me to do your shopping for you?'

'One moment, love. I'm looking.' Mrs Weissman was plunging about in the great swollen handbag that held everything – combs, hairpins, scissors, spectacles, letters, photographs, old newspapers, medicines. For years she had put things in and taken nothing out. The zip fastener had given up the struggle long ago and the whole bursting, overflowing pantechnicon was much the same shape as its mistress, who never moved a step without it.

The purse, when she found it, was full of newspaper cuttings. She took them out, looked for money, shut the purse, opened it and pretended to look again. It was an awkward moment, with Esther staring and hustling her. Lew and Hymie, coming in search of coffee and cinnamon *schnecken*, grasped the situation with the speed at which they registered anything financial.

'But you should have money today, Mumma.' Lew poured himself coffee and took a warm *schnecken* slice out of the oven, where they were always to be found in the middle of the morning. 'Daniel pays his rent on Fridays.'

'Or does he?' Hymie narrowed his eyes at his mother.

'Don't inquisition me, son. Sometimes I forget to ask him.'

'He's upstairs. I'll go and ask him for you.'

'No, Hymie, please. The rent is my affair.'

'How much is he paying you, anyway?' Lew asked, wiping his fingers on a silk handkerchief and taking a comb out of his breast pocket. 'I know what he ought to pay,' he went on, slicking his hair at the mirror, 'but does he pay it? Why do you never have any money?' He turned and pointed the comb at her, like a barrister intimidating a witness with tortoiseshell spectacles.

Mrs Weissman hedged. Daniel had not paid her anything for three weeks, and she had not dared to mention it in case he should leave. Lew and Hymie, who could smell out the truth of anything to do with money, were shocked and disappointed in her.

'It's not good business, Mumma,' Hymie said sadly, his big brown eyes sorrowing at her over his coffee cup.

'This is not business,' she said. 'This is a friendly arrangement.'

'It's the same thing,' Hymie said, twitching his upper lip, for he was growing a moustache, and it tickled.

'And while you stand arguing,' said Esther in a far more argumentative tone than anyone had yet used, 'I'm waiting to go to the shops. I do all the work in this house and get all the kicks. Ow! You devil, Hymie!' She kicked him back and they began to tussle, with the baby gurgling and crowing round their feet. Esther's hat came off. She bit Hymie and he released her and went out of the room whistling happily, flinging his head back in the stimulated way of one who has just taken refreshing exercise.

Mrs Weissman performed the large-scale operation of getting to her feet. 'Please go away, everybody,' she said, 'and leave me to cook the dinner. Lew, give your sister some money, and get off the table. I want to chop onions where you are sitting.'

Lew gave Esther some pound notes and she went out, pushing past Daniel who was coming in. He recovered from the impact and came into the kitchen heading for the coffee-pot, kissing Mrs Weissman good morning on the way. She insisted on being kissed by everyone. She loved to be kissed.

Daniel took his coffee and three cakes from the oven and sat on the table swinging his legs on the same place from which Mrs Weissman had removed Lew. Because she thought he looked tired, she took her onions and knife to another corner.

'A good thing you're not in a job, Daniel,' Lew said. 'You'd be late to work every morning.' He had on his shrewd face, soft grey eyes narrowed and bright as wet pebbles.

'Yes,' said Daniel, picking up the paper. 'I was always late when I was a teacher. Used to miss the first class. The students didn't care. They simply came late, too.'

'Well, I do care,' said Lew so nastily that Mrs Weissman said: 'No, no, Lew,' and waved the knife at him.

'About my sleeping late? It's your fault. You get me the dope.'

'On tick,' said Lew, even more nastily. 'I'm not getting you any more until you find some work to do.'

'For the good of my soul?' Daniel asked with his mouth full. 'Don't give me that, for God's sake. Why does everyone want to save me? I didn't think I'd get that in this house.'

'No,' said Lew, 'for the good of my mother's purse. How much longer are you going to live here on her charity?'

'Lew!' His mother banged the table with the handle of the knife. 'I will not let you talk like that to Daniel. Leave him alone.

My affairs are my affairs.' She sat down, the better to make this weighty pronouncement.

Daniel was not offended. He got up to get another cake from the oven. 'I'm terribly sorry, Mumma,' he said. 'Honestly, I'd no idea you wanted the money till the end of the month. I'll have to get hold of some. Trouble is, I'm not getting the rent for my house any more. The tenants left.'

'You have a house?' Mumma was astonished. 'Why don't you live in it?'

Daniel shrugged his shoulders.

'Why not get another tenant?' Lew asked.

'I can't be bothered to find anyone. The last two were all right. No trouble. But one of them went and died.'

'You must let it again or sell it,' Lew said. 'I can get you a good price for it.' He was interested now and had forgotten his grievance.

'What's the use,' said Daniel, staring at nothing, 'if people are always going to die in it?'

'Nonsense.' Mrs Weissman put her hands on her knees and pushed herself to her feet. 'If it's their time, people will die wherever they are. Not sooner, not later.'

'Let me fix a let for you,' said Lew, 'or a sale. Might be the right thing to auction it. There are some beautiful prices being paid for house property.'

'I can't be bothered,' Daniel said. 'All that fuss about inventories and sewers and repairs. Possessions are a curse. It's best to forget about them.'

'But it's such a crying waste.' Lew was really upset. He began to walk up and down in the narrow space between the table and the wall, planning what he would do with Daniel's house.

'Do leave it alone, Lew,' his mother said. 'Don't keep on at Daniel.'

'It's all very well, Mumma, but he's got to make money. Why should he be the only one who doesn't bring anything to the house?'

'Oh, all right, all right,' Daniel said sourly. 'I'll get a job. God knows what at.' He put his cup in the sink and went to the door.

'You can paint,' Lew said eagerly. 'I know a man who has a sweet little business copying antiques and old masters –'

Daniel went out, and they saw his feet going up the area steps and wandering away down the street.

Mumma took her pan of onions to the stove and stood there lifting saucepan lids and stirring. When she was at the stove she did not look so gross and unwieldy. She was a craftsman, appropriate to her environment. She even had a kind of ponderous grace as she reached to her spice shelf and shook nutmeg into a pan of dumpling soup, whose smell alone might have been enough to justify her whole existence.

'Not too much of that,' Lew said, watching her. 'I don't like too much.'

'Daniel does,' she said without thinking, and he flared up.

'So now he means more to you than your own son, is that it?' Lew's lisp was twice as thick when he became excited. 'We must all eat the way he likes. I suppose the next thing will be we mustn't have kosher meat because Daniel is a Christian.'

'Lew, you are unkind. Don't you see that it's because he is not my son that I must try and make up? It's no easy thing to be a lodger in someone else's house. Everything is all right, until something happens which draws the family together and then he is left out. Or something happens to him, but he cannot turn to anyone, because the family have their own affairs, and no one puts him first. That's why Daniel is like this and cannot work. He has kept some trouble inside himself and it has made him ill.'

'What trouble?' asked Lew suspiciously.

'I don't know.'

'Guilty conscience perhaps. I wonder what he's done.' Lew pursed his lips. Having no conscience himself, he could be quite smug about other people's. 'Perhaps his girl walked out on him. He seems to be off women.'

'We must find him another, then,' said Mumma, with homoeopathic optimism. 'I would have liked that he and Rosie –'

'Ro wouldn't look at him,' Lew said. 'She likes her men solvent.'

Nevertheless, it was through Rosie that Daniel found some work to do. She had a gentleman friend called Max, who had acquired a long low basement in Denman Street, which he was going to open as a club. Rosie was going to leave the Venus Club and exchange her sequinned trunks for the long dress of a hostess. Max, who was the jealous type and carried a knife which he had once used on a sailor in a brawl, would be happier to have Rosie under his eye and fully clad.

One evening after supper she announced in her clear, imperious voice: 'Max wants someone to paint the decorations round the walls of the new club. I said Daniel would do it.'

'I?' Daniel, who was playing chess with Mr Weissman, looked up in alarm. 'Good Lord, girl, you must be mad.'

'Why?' Rosie shrugged her shoulders elaborately. All her gestures were excessive. If she was only pointing to a smut on your nose, she flung out an arm like stout Cortez discovering the Pacific. Now, her thin shoulders worked like steam pistons under her silk blouse. 'No one in the family can paint, so you might as well be in on it.'

'Oh, fine,' Daniel said, 'except that I couldn't paint either now. I've taught, but I haven't put a brush on paper since – oh, for ages.'

'Your move, boy,' said Mr Weissman, who took half an hour over his own moves but only allowed his opponent half a minute.

'Of course you must do it,' Rosie said, flinging her body about at him resentfully. 'Don't annoy me. I've told Max you would. Anyway, Lew says you must do some work.'

'Not that kind,' Daniel tipped back his chair to look at Rosie. 'I wouldn't be much good.'

'That's all right,' Rosie said candidly. 'Max wouldn't pay you very much. You can paint women surely. Girls – you know the kind of thing.'

Hymie whistled through his teeth and made rounded gestures in the air. Daniel watched, shook his head and, letting down the legs of his chair, bent to the game again. 'No, Pa,' he said. 'You can't do that. A pawn can't go there.'

'So sorry, so sorry. It's my eyes.' Pa did not exactly cheat at chess, but he tried things on. His needle-pitted fingers hovered over the board, picking up pieces and putting them down again, not always in the same place. Daniel slapped his hand and moved a bishop back to where it had been.

'Oh, do stop playing *chess*!' Rosie almost screamed. 'Daniel, you are so lazy, you make me *ill.* You can paint. You said you could.'

'Not girls.'

But Rosie had promised Daniel to Max. 'Yes, girls. Any girl. You must have painted some girl or other some time. Goodness, I had a boy once who was an artist and we never had any fun because I was always sitting still while he drew me from a distance.'

Daniel looked up from the board, and seemed to speak to Mumma, not to Rosie. 'I used to paint a girl once,' he said. 'Yes. ... But oh no.' He gave himself a little shake. 'She wouldn't do.'

'A girl's a girl,' Morrie said and made a smacking noise with his lips. Esther reached a foot under the table and hacked him on the ankle.

'Let's see,' Lew said. 'Draw her now.'

'No. My move, Pa?' He moved a piece thoughtfully, then suddenly turned round and said : 'Yes, all right, I will. Anyone got a pencil?' Quickly he began to sketch the rough picture of a fair, wispy girl on the white scrubbed wood of the kitchen table. Everyone crowded round to look, criticizing. Pa got up to see and knocked most of the chess-men on the floor.

'There you are !' Daniel flung the pencil down and turned away from the picture.

'It's rotten. I do better than that in school,' said Joey, who should have been in bed hours ago, but kept coming down again in his pyjamas like a boomerang every time he was shut in his room.

'It's not,' Lew said, screwing up his lips as if he were judging it with a view to purchase. 'It's good, but –'

'She looks half starved,' Mumma said.

'She should have more –' Esther patted her own solid self proudly.

'Where's her sex?' Hymie said. 'You forget to put that in.'

'No,' Rosie said, 'she wouldn't do for Max's place. Do another. Who else can you do?'

'I could paint you,' Daniel said, running his eye up and down her.

'No, Max wouldn't like it. He wouldn't like to think you thought of me like that. Try another.'

'There was a girl in Italy –' Daniel picked up the pencil.

'Not on my table,' Mumma said. 'Someone get some paper.'

Hymie went upstairs and returned with a sample of 'export only' wallpaper. Daniel leaned his elbow over the picture of the girl on the table, and on the back of the wallpaper he drew a sultry-looking girl with a lock of black hair over one eye and an impertinent figure.

'Ah!' they all cried. 'That's more like it. Now you've got the idea.' They pushed at each other, leaning over the table to judge the masterpiece seriously.

'Max will go for that,' Rosie announced.

'You can do her all round the walls,' said Morrie, 'in different posi— sorry, Esther – ways. Now we must have a man looking at her. Like this.' He put on a look that made Esther kick him again.

'There was a wing-commander I used to sketch in the prison camp,' Daniel said. 'I could do him as he looked once when he found something in an American Red Cross parcel wrapped up in a page of *Esquire*.' He drew the wing-commander, with a lop-sided black moustache and eyes like prawns. Everyone was delighted, pleased for Daniel as if he were a child. He on his side humoured their enthusiasm without sharing it, as if they were children. He allowed himself to be dragged off by Rosie to the Venus Club to see Max, who was always there to watch her number, in case anyone else was watching her the wrong way.

'Don't you want to play any more chess?' Pa asked, rising from the floor where he had been picking up the pieces. Daniel had gone.

'I'll play, Gramp,' said Joey. 'Bet you I win. What odds will you give?'

'None,' said his grandfather, 'because you always do.' He would have preferred to read his book, but if Joey said he wanted to play chess he had to play.

Daniel bought paints and brushes and started to work on the walls of Max's basement. He seemed much happier now that he had something better to do than moon about the house wondering whether or not he felt ill. As the paintings progressed, he became more interested and developed quite a temperament about them, coming home to supper with the air of Michelangelo having just put in a hard day's work on the Sistine Chapel.

He could not take the sleeping powders any more, because Max, who was paying him by the day, was angry if he did not turn up on time. When Max was angry, he took it out on Rosie, who took it out on Daniel. Mumma knew that he was not sleeping well. Sometimes, worrying about him in the night, for she did not have to worry about her family, who could be heard snoring in different keys all over the house, she would get up and go half-way up the stairs to see the line of light under Daniel's door. Once she had heard him go downstairs, and following after, amorphous in her dressing-gown, had found him trying to wash the remains of his drawing off the kitchen table. Mumma thought he was sleep-walking. He looked at her in a bemused, hurt way, and she turned him gently round and propelled him upstairs again.

The whole family went to the opening night of the club. Daniel behaved as if it was opening solely to exhibit his pictures. At the last minute he refused to go. But they gave him some drinks and pushed him into a hired dinner-jacket and took him along. Mumma stayed at home to mind the children and to open the door to a man wanting to see Lew about a radiogram and another who had brought a fur to show Hymie, and to answer the telephone to Morrie's racing friends and a chilly-voiced woman who wanted Daniel.

She was sitting wrapped in an eiderdown by the kitchen fire, waiting for them with coffee when they got home with the sky already light.

'Hell,' said Daniel, when she told him about the telephone. 'How on earth –? I didn't think anyone knew I was here.'

'And why not?' shouted Esther, who was tired and not very sober and spoiling for a fight. But Daniel would not fight. He sat muttering about God-damn interfering families and how they couldn't keep their hands off a person, until Mumma began to think that perhaps Lew had been right and he had embezzled something. She could think of no other reason why anyone should not want to see their family. She got someone to push the eider-down in the small of her back to help her upstairs, and climbed into the vast double bed where Pa, from habit, lay neatly on the extreme edge, although he had lain there four hours without her.

Max got other jobs for Daniel, and he paid his rent. He called it prostituting his art, which Mumma interpreted as a reference to the kind of places in which he worked, and began to worry about Rosie. She was a good girl. She had been brought up right, but her very innocence might lead her into trouble. If only she would cast off this fat, cocksure Max who spoiled her with presents, and give up these clubs, and this dancing every night with goodness knows who, and settle down with someone that Mumma could love more as a son than a son-in-law. In August perhaps they could all go away for a holiday. Lew knew a man who had a hotel at Bournemouth. They could go away without Max, and Rosie and Daniel would walk on the beach under the moon, just as Mumma and Pa had walked at Southsea forty-five years ago.

Sitting in her kitchen, which in this heat-wave was getting more like an oven lit full speed for a *buffeten kuchen*, Mumma saw it all, down to the last blossom in Rosie's hair and the last whirl of icing on the cake that she would make.

In the evening when the sun was off the street, Mumma took a chair to the top of the area steps and sat there looking Italian, talking to friends, and greeting the family as each one came home: Joey from school, jostling another boy in and out of the gutter; Esther red-faced from shopping, with the baby submerged under parcels and tins in the pram; Rosie from the cinema. 'It's cooler inside,' said the posters and she had believed them until she paid her three-and-six and found that they lied. Daniel came sweltering from some work he had been doing on the new bar of Max's club.

'It's like Hades down there,' he sighed, draping himself over the railings while he talked to Mumma. 'Imagine – people go there for pleasure.'

'It's cooler at night, remember.'

'It's not. It's like an inferno down there with that mass of sweating, pawing bodies.'

'Oh dear,' Mumma did not like to think of Rosie down there among all that. Yet what other job could she do? She called this 'being an actress' and would contemplate nothing else.

'I'll have to get some thinner clothes,' Daniel said, trying to cool his cheek against the spear-shaped top of the railing and finding it burning hot. Pa was making him a summer suit, but it would be winter long before it was finished. 'I think I'll go to the cottage this evening and get some things.'

Mumma had quite forgotten about his house in the country. He never talked about it. She hoped that when he saw it he would not want to start living there again, for how anyone who had a house in the country could bear to live in Walworth in this weather baffled her. She never liked losing her lodgers. She hated break-ups of any kind, but when Daniel went it would be like one of the boys leaving home.

'I can't face that train,' he said. 'D'you think Hymie would mind if I took his car?' Hymie, who had begun to dabble a little in the car market, had brought home only last night an elegant blue Jaguar, which was now in a disused builder's yard at the back of the house.

'It's not for me to say.' Mumma did not think Hymie would like it. He was funny sometimes about his things. 'I'll ask Pa. Pa!' she called, but he had the window of the front room shut and could not hear. He smiled and nodded and waved to her.

'I'll risk it,' said Daniel. 'He won't mind. It's too hot to mind anything.'

When Hymie came home he did mind. He said that he had planned to drive out in the car to a roadhouse on the Brighton Road, although Mumma thought that had only occurred to him when he heard that Daniel had taken the Jaguar.

'After all,' he grumbled, 'it's not as if it was mine for good. It's a saleable article. In fact, it's going to be sold next week, with a satisfactory profit for little Hymie Weissman, thanks very much. But how do I know what Daniel will do to it? You shouldn't, Mumma.'

'I'm sorry, Hymie. I didn't tell him he could –'

'You didn't tell him he couldn't.'

Everyone was feeling sultry and cross in the kitchen, toying with their food, disinclined for rich, greasy cooking. Hymie would not let the subject drop. 'I mean,' he groused, 'it's just as bad as if Rosie took one of the minks up there and wore it to go out. She'd be sure to tear it.'

'I wouldn't.'

'You would.'

'Children, children!' But no one paid any heed to Pa, so he picked up his coffee-cup and his plate of cherry tart and went away to his workroom.

'I wouldn't,' said Rosie. 'I have often worn them, and you've never known – so there!'

This started a first-class dispute, in which everyone was involved. Whether Rosie ever had worn any of Hymie's fur coats, or had just said that to goad him, Mumma was not sure, but at least it took his mind off the car. They were still arguing, when there was a quick clatter of feet on the area steps and Max came in by the open back door. Rosie got up and went to meet him in the passage, but he pushed her aside and came straight into the kitchen. He looked at the family sitting in various attitudes of heat and fatigue round a tableful of dirty plates, laughed in a self-conscious way, and said casually: 'Any of you boys got a hot car?'

Hymie jumped to his feet, his face yellow, his skimpy moustache twitching. 'What are you talking about?' he croaked. 'I've got a car. Yes. But it's strictly on the level.'

The atmosphere was cold suddenly with fear, in spite of the airless heat. Mumma, at the sink, went on making the motions of washing up, not daring to look round.

'How d'you know?' asked Max in his clipped, nasal voice. 'Who did you get it from?'

'Hymie,' said Lew in a low voice. 'You fool. Who was it?'

'It was all right. You know Harry Speed –'

'Harry Speed! Oh, my God!' Lew covered his face with his hands and laid the whole lot on the table.

'Harry Speed!' said Max. 'This young boy wants a keeper. What in heaven made you think that Harry would come by any car that didn't either have something wrong with it or the price of a king's ransom on its head?'

'Max,' said Rosie, who was still standing in the doorway. 'What are you trying to say? Get on with it, for God's sake.'

'It's only –' he flashed his gold tooth at her, 'it's only that your beloved brother, whom the gods preserve, has come tonight within a split hair of the cooler. Saved' – he held up his hand for silence, as they all broke into a babble – 'saved, I blush to tell you, by the presence of mind of yours truly. I thank you one and all.' He bowed round the room as if receiving applause. 'Is that a chair? May I sit down? Is that a bottle of whiskey by any chance? May I? Ta very much.' He helped himself, and leaned back, enjoying the excitement he had caused.

'But Daniel,' Mumma kept saying, from the sink. 'What about Daniel?' But nobody heard her. They were too busy reviling Hymie. She came up to the table, drying her hands on her black flowered apron. 'Max,' she said. 'Tell me what has happened to Daniel. He was in the car.'

'You're telling me,' he said.

'Yes, and if he hadn't taken it, this would never have happened –' began Hymie heatedly; but his mother said: 'Hush, son, we don't know yet what has happened. Tell us, Max.'

Max finished his drink deliberately, and reached for the bottle again. 'O.K.,' he said. 'Here's your bedtime story.' Rosie came to stand by his chair. While he was talking, he put his hand on her arm and ran his fingers up and down it.

'So this Daniel friend of yours,' he said, 'comes round to the club, see about – what would it be? – about an hour and a half ago. Left his jacket at my place, with his wallet in it. Trusting kind of guy. I always thought he had an honest face. Who'd have thought he'd get mixed up in this kind of thing?'

'Max, please.' Mumma leaned forward, gripping the table. 'I beg of you, tell us what has happened. You talk as if you were enjoying yourself.'

'Well, it was a scream really, you know.' Max leaned back and played with Rosie's fingers. 'He comes into my office, see, and we were having a quick one. "One for the road," he says. "Oh," I says, "where are you going?" "Down to the country in Hymie's car," he says. "Hymie's car?" I says. "The boy's coming on in the world. Smashing job it is, too," he says. "Take a dekko." So I took one, but I can tell you, I pulled my head in from that window pretty damn quick. There was this car – dead right, too, Hymie, it is a smashing job. Was, rather, as far as you're concerned – well, there was this smashing wagon. Only snag about it was that there was coppers advancing on it from every corner of London, crawling round it like flies round a cow-pat.'

Hymie groaned. 'If I ever get my hands on that Harry Speed –'

Everyone shushed him, and Max, having collected his audience again, went on : 'Well, no offence, Hymie, seeing that I thought the car was yours, but naturally, being a man of the world, I put two and two together, and "Daniel, my boy," I says to him, "here's where you make-a da lightning exit, or make no exit at all, for –" Let's see, what is it for car stealing? About six months, isn't it? "Show me the door," he says, so I nips him away through my private escape route. Now don't get me wrong, but you have to have one these days, when they raid you just for the hell of it.'

'Yes, yes, and what happened to him then?' Mumma's voice was unsteady.

Max studied his nails. 'Last seen flitting down the mews in the gloaming. I wonder he's not home by now.'

'And the car?' Beads of sweat the size of hailstones stood on Hymie's forehead.

'Bottle stoppers took it, of course. Oh, they came in to see me, but I was O.K. Didn't know a thing.'

'Thank God.' Hymie slumped like a doll and mopped his face.

'Of course,' said Max cheerfully, 'I don't know whether anyone saw Daniel in the car. If they did, he's as hot as the car is, so watch out when the wandering boy comes home. With which pretty thought, I leave you.' He stood up. 'Ta for the whiskey. Coming, Rosetta?'

'No.' She looked at him sulkily. 'I've got to see you later, in working hours. That's bad enough.'

He chuckled. 'Happy at your work?' He raised her chin, gave her the kind of kiss one does not give a girl when her mother is in the room, laughed again when she struggled free and went whistling away up the area steps.

Rosie did not go to the club that night. She stayed with her mother waiting for Daniel. Lew came in and sat down on the edge of the bed, where his mother was propped against the pillows like a prehistoric mammal, and his father slept quietly, clicking in his nose a little at the other side. They had tried to tell Pa what Max had told them, but it was too involved, and with everyone talking at once he could not understand, so he had gone up to sleep, knowing that he could not do any good, whatever the trouble was. Someone would explain it all to him in the morning.

'Mumma,' Lew said. 'Daniel can't stay here any more. Too risky. We might all be on the spot. We're O.K. otherwise, because there was no record of the sale, and Harry won't be doing any talking.'

'We must stick by him.' Mumma tried to raise herself to a sitting position to emphasize her words, but gave it up and fell back on the squashed pillows. 'Wouldn't I have you or Hymie back if the police were on your trail – God forbid it should ever be.'

'But that's different.' Hymie appeared in the doorway, very tall and thin in a zebra dressing-gown. 'He's nothing to do with us. He's not the family.'

'Ah!' Mumma raised her hands, which emerged like pork cutlets from the frilled cuffs of her nightgown. 'That is what I always have said. Poor Daniel. He can be family with us when all goes well. When it goes bad for him, he has no one. Then he is only the lodger.'

'Not any more if I know it.'

'How can you say such things, Hymie, when it was your car? It's all your fault.'

'It isn't Mumma.' He whined as he used to when he was little. 'You let him take it.'

'Oh, very well,' Mumma spread her hands on the sheets. 'So it was all my fault. I got him into trouble. Well, I will make it up to him when he comes back. We shall all be happy as we were before.'

'He won't come back,' said Rosie, picking fluff out of a corner of the eiderdown. 'I have a feeling.'

' 'Sright,' said Lew, picking his teeth. 'He can get along without us.'

'But Lew – he has no one!' Mumma's voice rose, and in the room upstairs the baby gave a single aggrieved cry.

'Can the noise!' Esther yelled. 'Morrie and I want to sleep.'

Her voice woke Mr Weissman, although the voices in the same room had not roused him. He sat up, looked fuzzily round, rubbed his eyes and lay tidily down on his edge of the bed.

Although Mumma would not let his room to anyone else, and Pa finished his suit, Daniel did not come back. Even after he wrote from somewhere in Cornwall to say good-bye and ask her to send his things, Mumma still seemed to see him running down a shadowy mews, running home to her. And although there were so many others to fill her days and her heart – Pa, Lew, Hymie, Esther, Morrie, the children, Rosie, and now this Max – whenever Mumma baked cinnamon *schnecken,* she always thought that perhaps today he would stroll in with his hands in his pockets just in time to eat them as they came hot from the oven.

CHAPTER FIVE

Geoffrey

IF they told him, when he woke, that he had had a fit, Geoffrey would never believe it. Groping vainly in memory, muddled with sleep and headache, he thought it maddening of them to come and tell him these things, omniscient from their pinnacle of health. But when they had gone forgivingly away, and his temper was cooling into reason, he would begin to notice things.

Why was there no hot-water bottle in the bed? Why this extra blanket over the eiderdown? What, above all, was he doing in bed, with the sun at his window showing that it was afternoon? Wearily, he would get up and go to the mirror to see a fresh bruise or a cut added to the scars and scabs he always carried, the hall-marks of the epileptic.

Oh well, that would give him about three weeks of peace before the queer dreamlike warning came upon him again, that illusion of having experienced everything before. The '*déjà vu* phenomenon', he knew it was called. Geoffrey was deeply interested in his disease and liked to read about it, but he could not discuss it with anyone. Although his family coddled and sheltered and restricted him and found a hundred ways to emphasize his infirmity, they shrank from it verbally, as if it were slightly improper. Outsiders tried to change the subject if he broached it, watching him nervously, as if they feared he might talk himself into a fit. Geoffrey's companion-tutor Woodie believed that since he was taking Mr Marple's money, he must take his opinion as well, and Mr Marple's opinion was that if talking could not affect a situation, then why talk? What can't be cured must be endured, he thought, but he did not say that. He left it to his wife to make the fatuous remarks.

Now that Woodie was on holiday, therefore, his stand-in, this man Brett – Geoffrey at twenty-two looked on everyone of any age or sex as equals or inferiors – this man must be trained from the start to talk to Geoffrey about Geoffrey.

Geoffrey liked to talk, but although he needed an audience, he quickly became irritated by people and had to go away by himself. By himself! He could never be that for long. He was not allowed to do anything alone. He could not swim or fish or sail or bicycle to Marazion or lock the bathroom door. He had never been allowed to drive a car or have a gun. Although he never saw her, because the luminal he took gave him deep sleep, he suspected that his mother came into his room in the night to see if he were suffocating himself, in spite of these hard hair pillows on which they insisted. If he managed to elude Woodie, and sneaked off alone in the bus to Penzance, or took the out-board dinghy round the point to Praa Sands, his family would raise a hue and cry as if he were an escaped convict.

They were surprised that he himself had no sense of danger. They could not understand that he just knew he could do these things. A star watched over him. He could do anything. He could conquer the world if only they would let him. He had read in a book that this was 'morbid optimism', a sympton of his disease. All right, then he had morbid optimism. He was a good case, qualifying on all points like a champion show dog.

For two days of grilling weather since Woodie left, Geoffrey had not been able to swim. His father and mother could not go in after him in an emergency, for they had not swum out of their depths for years. Aunt Florence was away on the round of visits known as 'distributing my favours' to resigned friends and relations. The maids were not allowed to chaperon Geoffrey, especially after that incident with Ruby last year. His sister Eileen, a dull, faint-hearted girl who should have been born a hundred years earlier, was afraid of being alone in the sea with him.

'If anything happened, it would be *my* fault. I'd never get over it.' She had scarcely the hardihood to survive her trifling mistakes, let alone a monstrous one like a drowning epileptic.

As soon as the man Brett arrived, Geoffrey dragged him down to the sea. The house at Mara Rocks was built as if it were part of the rocks itself, dropping down with them sideways towards the sea, so that the ground floor at the road end was the first floor at the other. The front door opened among the bedrooms, and the stairs from it went not up but down to the living-room and down again to the old play-room and the door that led to the terraced garden, and below that to the sea. Above the thumbnail of beach, there was a little harbour, said to have been blasted out of the rocks by a smuggler called the Duke of Mara, although how he could have done it without bringing every coastguard for miles on the scene no one knew. It made a perfect natural swimming pool, and here Geoffrey and Daniel Brett, who had desired at lunch to be called Daniel, were sitting on the edge of the baking rocks with their feet in the clear green water.

Geoffrey was telling Daniel about his '*déjà vu* phenomenon'. 'One of the classic forms of aura. Napoleon was supposed to have it. That's why he lost the Battle of Waterloo. Toward the end, when things were going badly, he was going to give an order: "Fight on. *On ne se rend jamais!*" ' Geoffrey liked his French and aired it whenever possible. 'But he was working up for a fit, and when he opened his mouth to say that, he imagined he'd already said it, so he closed his mouth, had his fit, and when he came out of it it was too late to say: "*On ne se rend jamais!*" One had already more or less *rendu*.'

'I don't believe a word of it,' Daniel said.

'I'm not surprised. I made it up just now,' said Geoffrey cheerfully, liking Daniel for that. His family would have received the story with: 'Fancy, dear. How interesting,' not wishing to excite him by contradiction.

'Let's swim,' he said. 'I can't stand this sun much longer.'

'Bit soon after lunch, isn't it? Your mother said –'

Oh hell, thought Geoffrey. Was he going to turn out smug like Woodie? He looked at Daniel, sitting there in a pair of trunks, basking his tipped-up face, his body not burned golden with this summer's sun like Geoffrey's, but brown with the maturer tan that does not wear off in winter; the product of years of sun, or of natural colouring. He did not look the smug type, but you never knew with people who were no good for anything except to be tutors or companions. They were apt to be soapy.

'Don't fuss,' he said fretfully. 'You needn't worry about me. I probably shan't have an attack all the time you're here, if that's what you're scared of. I always know, anyway, I get this unearthly sort of disembodied feeling, this knowing that everything has happened –' Even as he spoke, he felt that he had said all this before to Daniel, sitting on the rocks with the sun exactly there and the same gull riding that very wave. He had seen him open his eyes to find out why Geoffrey had stopped speaking, had heard him say: 'What?' in that identical tone, like a gramophone.

Geoffrey got to his feet. His body began to float away from his mind. This was going to be a quick one. He had time to yell: 'Look out! Get me back on to the sand before I –' He just had a moment to hope to God that Daniel knew what to do, and then everything in the world was nothing.

He woke in his bed, in darkness. Strange. He did not usually wake in the middle of the night. He lay for a while trying to remember what time he had gone to bed, then switched on the light to see his watch. Darned thing had stopped. The glass was broken. He had not done that. His mother must have knocked it off the table when she tucked him in and picked it up without noticing. Why must she always go bumbling about without her glasses?

He was annoyed. Now he would not be able to go to sleep again. It had not mattered much about the time before, but now it began to be imperative for him to know it. His bed was a comfortable world, secure. His limbs felt heavy and his head was thick. He did not want to get up, but he must know the time. It was getting on his nerves. With a petulant exclamation, he flung off the bedclothes and got up into his dressing-gown and slippers.

The corridor light was on, which was not unusual, since his mother frequently forgot to turn it off. It was unusual, however, for the downstairs light to be on, for his father, who came last to bed, would as soon leave a light burning as forget to clean his teeth. As Geoffrey went down the stairs, he heard voices in the drawing-room : his father and the man Brett. What on earth were they doing up at this time of night when he had been in bed and asleep – long asleep, by the leaden feeling to which he had woken? Talking about him, no doubt; Daniel getting his orders. Orders ... ? Vaguely Geoffrey remembered a recent story about Napoleon giving orders. What was it? Who had told it him and where? He must try to remember, because there had been French in it, and he might want to tell it himself.

Yes, they were talking about him. He laid his head to the drawing-room door and listened.

'Poor boy,' his father was saying, and Geoffrey could imagine his diluted blue eyes winking and blinking as they did when he was venturing on a delicate subject. 'It's hard luck, hard luck indeed. All the things I'd planned for him.... Put him down for Rugby, of course, when he was born, but we had to take him away after a year there. And then no varsity – what chance has the boy got?'

Geoffrey could not hear Daniel's answer. He hoped he would have the sense not to say he had not been to Oxford or Cambridge himself.

He could hear his father's sigh, right through the closed door. 'Sad for him, and a great blow for us. Especially now that ...' A pause, Mr Marple cleared his throat and tried to speak briskly. 'My wife told you, eh?'

Daniel murmured something. There was the sound of Geoffrey's father getting up, shrilling the castors of his chair. The lid of the china tobacco jar clattered with a familiar clop. There was quite a long pause now while he filled his pipe, then he spoke jerkily, between the laboured puffs with which he bellowed it as if it were a sluggish fire.

'Oh well ... I suppose ... lessons to one ... start a family with too high hopes.' The castors of the chair cried out again as he sat down. The pipe was going now. 'Just bad luck. What? Oh yes, but three generations back, we never contemplated ... But these things don't die out, it seems.'

Geoffrey put his hand on the doorknob, but paused as he turned it, hearing his father say: 'Sorry about today, Brett. Distressing to have it happen your first day.'

So that was it! Geoffrey burst into the room. His father and Daniel were sitting in the bay of the window, with the whiskey decanter on a table between them, smug as you please, talking about him. Geoffrey was prepared to resent this now, although he had enjoyed listening to the talk.

'Here,' he said, as they turned surprised faces, and Daniel

pushed himself more upright to see round his chair, 'is that why I was in bed? What's the time? Don't tell me I've had a fit.'

His father hated that word. 'Well, yes, old boy. I'm afraid you did have a little attack.'

'Where?' snapped Geoffrey. It was exasperating not to be able to remember it.

'By the sea,' Daniel said.

'On the rocks?' Geoffrey put a hand up to his face. He should have looked in the mirror before he came down.

'No,' said Daniel, 'you got yourself on to the beach with the cunning of an old hand. Very proud of you, I was.'

Mr Marple began to blink, but Geoffrey liked this. No one had ever treated the things as a joke before.

'Two minutes later,' Daniel said, 'and you might have folded up while we were swimming. Then God help you, because I failed the life-saving test six times at Eton.'

Mr Marple blinked faster. That was no way to talk to Geoffrey. He should be reassured that he was safe with Daniel. That was what he was there for.

By casual, indirect questions, Geoffrey tried to make Daniel tell him what had happened. He liked to know, but he hated to admit that he could remember nothing, so when Daniel told him, he listened carefully, but said: 'Yes, yes, I know. I remember. You were telling me a story about Napoleon.'

'No,' said Daniel. 'You were.'

'No. I remember quite well.' Geoffrey became heated, and felt himself begin to sweat under his pyjamas. 'You were telling me –'

Daniel shook his head; then seeing Mr Marple frown a warning to him not to contradict, laughed and said: 'Oh, all right.'

'There, you see!' triumphed Geoffrey, who would never let a subject drop until he had been proved or faked right. It did not matter which, as long as he got his own way.

'What was the story – good one, old boy?' asked his father in the chummy voice he used with Geoffrey, as if trying to deceive himself that his son was anything but a dead loss as a chum.

'It was about Napoleon being epileptic. Did you know he was, Dad?' Geoffrey asked, to distract from the fact that he had forgotten the story.

'No. They didn't teach us that when I was at school.'

'Nearly all the great men were. Julius Caesar, Mohammed, St Paul, Marlborough, Duke of Wellington.... So you see, you shouldn't be ashamed of me. You should be proud,' he went on, ignoring his father's hurt protest. 'Epilepsy breeds greatness. It might be in me, you never know. Something to do with abnormal brain energy. Lom – what's his name? – Lombardo – Lombroso said that all genius was apilep – epileptoid.' He saw the way his father and Daniel were looking at him and realized that he was slurring his words. Damn. This often happened after a fit.

'You read too many books, Geoff,' his father said. 'How about going back to bed now?'

Geoffrey fought off the drowsiness that was clouding his thoughts and speech. 'I couldn't sleep now,' he protested.

'Have some whiskey,' suggested Daniel.

Mr Marple leaned forward and took the decanter from him. 'No. no. He's never allowed alcohol.'

'Never?' Daniel looked at Geoffrey with concern.

'Never in my life,' he said proudly. 'I don't even know what it tastes like.'

'Heavens,' said Daniel. 'You don't know what you miss. May I?' He picked up the decanter again and helped himself. Geoffrey did not know whether his father was frowning at that, or because Daniel had not reassured him that abstention was no hardship.

He sat down. 'I'll have some Ovaltine and sandwiches,' he said, as if he were ordering in a restaurant. 'I'm hungry.'

'The maids have gone to bed,' said his father, 'and Eileen and your mother have gone to the Women's Institute dress rehearsal. She didn't at all want to go and leave you, but I packed her off. It's good for her to get out and about a bit. Brett – I wonder if you'd get Geoff something to eat? He mustn't go wandering round the draughty kitchen in that outfit.'

'Ought he to eat last thing at night?' asked Daniel, who did not want to stir himself.

'Oh, yes,' said Geoffrey happily, settling back in his chair. 'I'm supposed to have snacks between meals, so as not to get too hungry.'

'O.K.' Daniel went off and Geoffrey laughed to himself because he could see that he did not like having to run about after a boy of twenty-two. He did not behave as if he had ever been a professional companion before.

Geoffrey drowsed a little and opened his eyes to see his father sitting watching him, his white hair like teased cotton wool, rabbit teeth showing under the colourless moustache that would never go properly grey.

'Dad,' he continued his drowsing thoughts. 'When Daniel answered your advertisement, did he send references from other people he'd been with?'

'Of course. Never take anyone in my house without a reference. Excellent ones they were, too. Why? You like him, don't you? Think he's going to be satisfactory?' He made a face, because the door was opening.

'Yes,' said Geoffrey, and: 'Oh *yes*,' he repeated as he saw the bursting sandwiches that Daniel had made for him with complete disregard for butter and cheese rationing.

Although he was not usually interested in the details of other people's lives, Geoffrey was intrigued by Daniel. He wondered why he had taken this job, since he seemed to know so little about teaching anything except drawing, and why he behaved like a recluse, never wanting to go outside the grounds of Mara Rocks. Once, when he had to go to Penzance to take Geoffrey to the dentist, he had worn dark glasses all the time, even in the dentist's waiting-room. Geoffrey, who had no respect for anyone's secrets, often asked Daniel what, if anything, he was hiding from, but Daniel only laughed and said: 'Blackmailers', or 'A Sicilian vendetta', or anything that came into his head.

One afternoon, when the bay was glass and the heat haze shimmered like oil vapour above the dusty flowerbeds, Geoffrey was pestering Daniel unsuccessfully to take him in the car to Penzance. He was lying under a tree on the lawn, with a rather effeminate straw hat on the back of his head, while Daniel, who could stand as much sun as a lizard, was perched on the wall above him, sketching the jutting corner of the house and the bay beyond.

It was a novel experience to be thwarted. Geoffrey did not mind as much as he had expected. It was refreshing to have someone who would argue with him instead of always giving in, although annoying if it interfered with what he wanted to do. At the moment he wanted to go into Penzance and eat cream cakes and ices at the Rosebud Café. He had a passion for rich, sweet food. He agreed with his medical books when they said that this was typical of his disease, but he disagreed when they said it should not be indulged. Like a pregnant woman, he ought to be allowed to satisfy a pathological craving.

Daniel went on sketching and saying: 'No,' while Geoffrey grumbled away on the grass. 'All right,' he said, 'if you won't take me, I'll drive the car myself.'

'You don't know how.'

'It's easy. I could do it. I'll take that old bit of mistletoe I picked last autumn at just the right phase of the moon.'

'What for?'

'Don't you know anything? The point is that as it's rooted on the tops of trees, it can't fall to the ground, so an epileptic who carries it can't either.'

'You're crazy.'

'Well, it's easier than going to that church in Wales where you have to take a cockerel with you and lie all night on the altar, and if the cock dies it's got your epilepsy and you're cured.'

He spoke as if he half believed this, and Daniel said: 'What a funny mixture of superstition and precociousness you are, Geoff.'

'Aren't I?' said Geoffrey with interest, but would not be side-tracked into talking about himself. He nagged on about Penzance.

'I thought you were supposed to stay quiet for at least a week after a fit,' Daniel said. What a relief it was to hear someone say that word here. When reference to it was unavoidable, it was usually 'a go' or 'one of your little attacks'.

Geoffrey's stomach, his gullet, his mouth were aching and wet for chocolate cake with a ball of ice-cream on top. He tried flattery. 'That sketch was pretty good yesterday. You'll only spoil it if you go on messing about.'

'Why don't you do some sketching yourself?' Daniel asked. 'It's one of the things I'm supposed to teach you. God knows there's nothing else I can tell you that you don't know more about than me.'

'I know all about sketching, too,' Geoffrey said, 'but that won't cure my hunger, or my colossal *ennui* with this dreary hot summer which just goes on and on and will only end with the even drearier return of Woodie. It always rains when he's about. His sponge-like personality attracts water. Daniel' – Geoffrey turned on his face and chewed grass because he did not want to sound intense – 'I wish you wouldn't go at the end of the month. I'll get Woodie pensioned off and you can stay.'

'Why?' asked Daniel, through a pencil held in his teeth while he rubbed something out.

'Oh – I don't know. I like you because you make me laugh. Everyone else here makes such heavy weather of life. You don't care a hang. Maybe it's because you've never had anything to care about. They have. Oh, I don't mean me. I'm a back number as far as tragedy goes. I mean, five years ago when the string that holds the sword of Damocles broke above Mara Rocks. No one has ever recovered from the crash. They never will. Sometimes I think they don't want to. You wait till Reggie's anniversary. This place is like the wailing wall. Don't put on that face, Daniel. I know I sound callous, but honestly, it gets on my nerves. I can't imagine Reggie likes it either.'

'*You* would,' Daniel said. 'You'd be furious if you thought people had forgotten you even for a minute.'

'True,' agreed Geoffrey, 'but that's different. I'm an epileptoid genius, don't forget.'

Presently, saying that he was going indoors to rest on his bed, he went through the house, out of the front door and up the lane to the main road where he caught the bus to Penzance.

When this was discovered, Daniel was very unpopular. Geoffrey's father was too much of a gentleman to say: 'What do you think I'm paying you for?' and his mother was too kind to say such things, or even think them, but Aunt Florence was not. She arrived back that evening from Cousin John's at Teignmouth, and almost before she was over the doorstep gathered the household reins into her large ugly hands again, summed up this Mr Blatt as she insisted on calling Daniel, and told him where he got off. Geoffrey, who found his Aunt Florence even more aggravating than most people, was glad to see that Daniel did not mind at all. He must be used to it.

Florence Marple had come to live with her brother after his eldest son was shot escaping from a German prison camp. Mrs Marple had disintegrated utterly and was quite incapable of running the house, and by the time she might have been capable again Florence was established in the best guest room with her sewing machine and the rackety old typewriter on which she typed noisy, newsy letters to friends and relations all over the world.

She had a firm hold on all the domestic strings, and no intention of letting go, so Mrs Marple, who used to enjoy running the house by inefficient methods which got her there in the end, was now relegated to small pottery jobs which she spun out as long as possible, to fill her day.

Her days were long, for she had no pleasure in them. After five years, her life was still dominated by sorrow. She had no unconnected interests, must be careful what she read in case something upset her, could not listen to war plays on the wireless, or hear 'Jerusalem' played without remembering speech day at Rugby in Reggie's last glorious year.

She and her husband, who thought her rather a fool, had nothing in common except their elder son's death. Sometimes Geoffrey wondered how they had ever got along at all before that. When he was a child, he could not remember them ever doing anything together, or any conversations between them, although there must have been some. In family photographs of Mr Marple in a Norfolk jacket and a cap like a cushion and Mrs Marple with a buckled waist, they were always standing well apart, not in deliberate pique, but as if they were unaware of each other's presence. How they had ever produced Reggie and Geoffrey and Eileen was a mystery as unfathomable as the night sky.

After Reggie was killed, there had been a period when they had come closer than ever in their lives, but soon Mrs Marple had driven her husband away again by talking too much about what had happened to them. However, it was still there between them to harmonize moments which before would have been discordant. When Mrs Marple said something particularly foolish, Geoffrey could sometimes see his father reminding himself, making allowances, and giving his wife one of the smiles to which she leaped like a beggar to a coin.

Aunt Florence had loved Reggie, too, but losing a nephew is not the same as losing a son, and although a doubtful advantage, this was the only one Mrs Marple had over her sister-in-law, who had pegged out for herself a prior claim to everything else in the house.

The only reason Geoffrey was glad to see Aunt Florence back was that the meals improved. She had a way of getting more out of the butcher and grocer and making more out of what she got. The cook hated her, although – or because – she had taught her many things. Nellie, the house-parlourmaid, hated her because she kept one forefinger permanently extended for running along shelves, and whatever breath she could spare from laying down the law for breathing on the spoons and rubbing them up in a pointed way at meals.

She would not rub them up today, however, for a guest was coming to lunch, so any censure of Nellie would take place by private appointment later.

Arthur Mew, who, by dint of saying that he wished to welcome Aunt Florence home, had got himself asked to a good lunch, came into the drawing-room in a blue alpaca jacket, oversized bow-tie, and narrow flannel trousers, which his sister had dyed from grey to an interesting shade of cinnamon. He was known in the district as 'our local archaeologist', because he dabbled a little in old churches and made humiliating remarks to people about their beams and plasterwork. He was much in demand to open fêtes and book weeks and village meetings that aimed gently at culture. Several years ago he had written a book on Cornish folk customs and had been trading on it ever since as his passport to the world of letters. He was the only visible author for miles around. There were a few real ones who typed doggedly away in cottages and kept their lights burning far into the night, but they were never seen at public gatherings so Mr Mew felt himself unchallenged as the 'Q' of Mara Bay.

He bent low over Mrs Marple's hand. 'Dear lady,' he breathed, as he always did, thus proving that it is not only people in books who say that. She was in the black which she would wear now for the rest of her life; and with the deference of a funeral mute, he led her towards the group by the window as if he were showing her to the first closed carriage. When he saw Mr Marple, he grasped his right hand and put his left on the other's shoulder. 'Splendid! Splendid!' he repeated in time to his pumping hand-shake, though Mr Marple had not yet said a word, favourable or otherwise.

He was as courtly to Eileen as if she were a raving beauty, in-stead of a plain, short girl with a big nose and flat hair, and he admired her dress, which had nothing to recommend it except a clean collar and cuffs. Geoffrey sometimes wondered if he would marry her in the end. She had broken off her engagement to the only man who had ever looked at her twice, to be a comfort to her parents after Reggie was killed. The archaeologist was her last chance, but she would not marry while her parents were alive, and old Mew would probably be dead long before them.

Geoffrey was sulking. He did not want to have lunch with Mr Mew. He had said that he would have a tray in his room, but his mother had begged him to come and be polite, and Aunt Florence, who had discovered that mice had invaded the house while she was away, was vetoing trays in rooms because of the crumbs.

'Geoff!' hooted Arthur Mew. 'Delightful!' Resignedly, Geoff-rey half rose from the window seat to shake his hand, sat down again at once and went on looking out of the window.

Mr Mew could turn anything, even rudeness, to conversational purpose. 'Those wonderful windows over the sea,' he said. 'I always say looking out of this room is like looking from the deck of a frigate.'

'Oh, do you?' said Mrs Marple as politely surprised as if he did not say that every time he came. 'I like windows,' she said. 'They make such a difference to a house.'

Mr Mew drank sherry with tittuping sips, to show he was a connoisseur of wine. No one could think of anything to say, but

Mr Mew said: 'Yes indeed,' and: 'Well, well,' which gave the illusion of conversation.

It was quite a relief when Aunt Florence came charging into the room from the kitchen where she had been putting the wind up cook, who was trying to dish up. She and Mr Mew exchanged noisy greetings, for she always talked at the top of her voice, and he had to exclaim: 'Home is the wanderer!' many times before he would let go her hand. She brought with her Daniel, whom she had roped in on the way to carry her mending, and introduced him as Mr Blatt. She had been calling him that for so many days now that no one felt equal to correcting her. It seemed a little late.

Aunt Florence, whose mind was still in the kitchen, said to her sister-in-law: 'What have you been doing while I've been away? I've just been round the cupboards checking the stores and we're low on nearly everything.'

Mrs Marple glanced at Mr Mew. This was not the time to say that she had been taking the opportunity of reducing the grocery bills while Florence was away. 'As it was so hot,' she said at random, 'I was afraid of things going off.'

'I've never heard of dried herbs going off, nor yet Oxo,' retorted Florence, appealing to Mr Mew, with a toss of her lichen-coloured head, to join her in a scornful laugh.

'Lunch is served,' remarked Nellie in an off-hand Cornish way from the door. She spoke to Mrs Marple, but Aunt Florence answered.

'Very well, Nellie, we will have lunch,' she said as if making a decision, although the soup was on the table and as far as Nellie was concerned they'd have it now or have it cold.

Lunch was wonderful. Roast chicken with crackling skin and white flesh that fell apart on your teeth almost before you could bite it. Cauliflower in a sauce like velvet, a purée of potatoes, of which Geoffrey, suspecting that Aunt Florence had palmed into it some of his extra eggs, took more than anyone else, as his due.

Aunt Florence, who was apt to speak to him as if he were a backward child, said: 'Piggy, piggy! There are others to come after you.'

Mr Mew held the table with an ornamental account of a meeting at a literary lunch with an author of whom no one had ever heard. At least, he held Aunt Florence, who was 'a great reader', and tore bits out of the book pages of the Sunday papers before other people had read them.

She told Mr Mew that she envied him his interesting life among the great and that she had always said that she would write a book herself if only she could find time. The others got on with their food, and Daniel, who had the gift of detaching himself, seemed to be somewhere miles away beyond the window.

When they were ready for the next course, Aunt Florence, putting out a foot to press the bell under the table, pressed Mr Mew's toe instead, and he let out a yell and swallowed a small splinter of chicken-bone that he had just succeeded in dislodging from behind his teeth. Debonair to the last, he managed to convey, even while he was coughing and spluttering out shreds of potato on to his chin, that it was worth it, indeed an honour to have his foot trodden on by so charming a lady. Aunt Florence looked at him quizzically over her bust while he said that he could, yes indeed he could be so naughty as to wish she had done it on purpose.

While all this was going on, Geoffrey took the opportunity of helping himself to both kinds of pudding when Nellie offered them for his choice.

His mother leaned across the table to whisper: 'Only one, dear. You know what Doctor Mount said about not too many sweet things.'

Geoffrey, who had been working up an increasing irritation and had been looking all through lunch for something to make a scene about, now pushed his plate away, spilling custard on the table, slumped in his chair and prepared to make life hideous for everyone in the room.

'Nellie,' said Aunt Florence, 'fetch a cloth. Mr Geoffrey has made a mess.' She sounded as if he were a child allowed in to dining-room lunch as a treat, but not to be trusted after all without his square of mackintosh. 'Take your plate back, dear, and get on with your pudding,' she said.

'I don't want it,' growled Geoffrey, although his mouth was watering for the whipped-cream trifle and blackcurrant fool.

Mr Mew, having finally settled the chicken-bone, was free now to make the best of this. 'I say, I say,' he said loudly, 'this won't do. Do you know what my nurse used to say to me when I refused my food?' No one asked, but he told them. ' "There's many little boys in slumland," she used to say, "who would be glad of that;" and do you know what I used to answer?' Still no one asked, but still he told them.

' "All right," I'd say, "they can have it!" I'm afraid I was always sharp to repartee.'

'Has there ever been any child, I wonder,' said Geoffrey, manufacturing a yawn, 'who wasn't supposed to have said that?'

'Well!' Mr Mew was nonplussed for a second, but quickly recovered as Nellie came at him with the trifle. 'My gracious,' he said, 'this looks ambrosial. I'm afraid I can't resist it, even if you can.'

Geoffrey gave him a sick look. 'I'm trying the starvation cure for epilepsy,' he said sourly.

His mother drew in her breath and shook her head at him. She did not like to have that word said before outsiders. Even Mr Mew, the ever-jolly, did not like it, especially in that tone of voice. He drew back his head like a tortoise and retired into himself, taking tiny bits of trifle on the end of a fork, sitting very narrow on his chair with cramped shoulders, like a passenger with a first-class ticket in a crowded third-class-only train.

Geoffrey pursued him with words. 'Remember the epileptic boy in the Bible – the one that had a devil brought out of him? The Lord said: "This kind can come forth by nothing but prayer and abstinence." Mine may come out any minute now. Look out you don't catch it.'

'Geoff, behave yourself,' said his father, and his mother looked distressed. It was nice that he knew his Bible, but not quite like this.

Mr Mew rallied. 'No, my dear boy! "By prayer and *fasting*." ' He looked round the table complacently. A misquotation was right up his street.

'Teach your grandmother,' said Geoffrey rudely. 'It's my devil, not yours. I ought to know what brings it out.'

'And I ought to know my Bible, dear boy. As a student of both the Authorized and the Revised version, not to mention the

Scofield edition, with its new system of connected topical references to all the greater themes of Scripture, with annotations, revised marginal renderings, summaries –'

'Geoffrey was only joking, Mr Mew,' put in Mrs Marple hastily,
seeing that her son was becoming excited. 'He always like to have
a bit of fun, don't you, dear ...' Her voice trailed away like a
run-down gramophone as Florence broke in crisply : 'Just ignore
it, Mr Mew. It's so boring. Do please go on telling us what Walter
Scholes said about the stream of consciousness.'

As Mr Mew opened his mouth to comply, Geoffrey cried out
and clutched at the air as if a dragonfly had flown past him.
'There it goes ! I told you it would come out. Look out !' He made
a swipe that knocked Mr Mew's spoon from his hand half-way
from the plate to mouth. 'Damn, it got away. Duck, everybody !'
Sometimes, when he had worked himself up to embarrass people
by pretending to be a little crazy, he could almost believe that he
was. His brain was hilarious now, his thoughts spinning about
in the top of his head. He did not care what he did.

It had been impressed on Geoffrey's family that he must never
be crossed. If he behaved like a tiresome child, they could not
treat him like one and haul him off to bed. A psychologist had
once told the Marples that violent opposition might bring on a
convulsion, and that in the dining-room would be worse than
anything he was doing now.

He was peering forward, studying Mr Mew's bow-tie, which
indeed was worthy of study, having been made by his sister from
an odd piece left over after making the loose covers.

'Keep still !' hissed Geoffrey, poising his hand, and paralysing
Mr Mew like a rabbit. 'I'll get it now. There it is – just under
your chin.'

'Ha, ha,' said Mr Mew with bleak bravery. 'Some family joke –?'

But the family were not laughing. Mr Marple's eyelids and
moustache were twitching. Aunt Florence was saying : 'Geoffr*ee* !'
and knocking on the table with one of the spoons she had so
often polished with her napkin. Mrs Marple had begun a quick
conversation about nothing at all to Eileen, who was too nervous
to listen. Nellie stood transfixed with a dish in each hand, drinking it all in to tell cook.

Daniel was scowling at Geoffrey across the table. He opened his mouth to say something, but his stammer blocked him and he gripped the edge of the table, his face intense with the effort of trying to get the words out.

Mr Mew, with his head back before Geoffrey's pin-point gaze, half rose from his chair. 'I'm afraid I ought to be running along,' he said in a cracked voice. 'So delightful, but I have several early appointments.'

'No you don't.' Geoffrey took him by his alpaca jacket and sat him down again with a bump. 'You've got my devil on you. You can't take that away – or do you want to have the falling sickness, too?'

Mr Mew gave a ghastly smile, raised a hand towards his neck and then jerked it away, as if Geoffrey's epilepsy really were sitting on his Picasso print bow-tie. He glanced sadly down at his plate of trifle, made an indecisive gesture towards his spoon, but lacked the *sang-froid* to eat.

What would happen? It was like a film when the projector breaks down. Geoffrey was quite prepared to go on sitting there all afternoon staring at Mr Mew's tie. He was becoming almost hypnotized himself by its whirligig patterns.

'Look!' Daniel suddenly jumped up and rushed to the window, knocking his chair over on to the nylons which Nellie kept to wear when there was company. 'Look, Geoff – your bike! I've just seen a man go out of the gate with it. Come on – we'll catch him with the car!' He ran out of the room without looking back to see if Geoffrey was following.

Geoffrey's bicycle was his fondest possession. It was the only machine he was allowed to have, his only means of swift escape when the urge came over him to fly from everybody and everything, pedalling like a madman down the hill as if he could flee from life itself.

The spell was broken. He dashed after Daniel, stumbled up the stairs and out of the front door into the blinding sunlight, skidded round the corner of the house to the garage and stopped short like a curbed horse. Daniel was sitting on the mounting block with his hands in his pockets, drawing circles in the gravel with his foot.

'My bike!' yelled Geoffrey. 'Quick, you fool, get the car out. My bike!'

Daniel jerked his head. 'In the garage.'

'What the devil –? But you said –'

'Oh, that was only to get you out of the dining-room,' said Daniel in a bored voice. 'What on earth were you playing at?'

Geoffrey was furious. The old grievance of trickery that always nagged within him came surging up and pounded in his head. He shouted obscene things at Daniel. He did not have to think what he said. His voice did it for him.

'Pipe down,' said Daniel, 'or you'll shout yourself into a fit.'

Geoffrey would like to. That would show them. Fits were his weapon. He would have a fit and show Daniel and all of them who was king of this place. But although he screamed and threw himself about, nothing happened. He had always been told that over-excitement might bring on a fit, but now here he was positively hysterical and it was producing nothing. Blast those doctors. They didn't know their job.

He rushed at Daniel and began to pummel him. Daniel fended him off without getting up, and Geoffrey stood breathing heavily on the gravel drive, waiting for the aura of warning that he was sure would come. It must come.

Daniel gave a yell of laughter. 'You can't imagine how funny you look,' he gasped, 'standing there solemnly trying to have a fit.'

Geoffrey went on waiting. It was a let down. It was like taking your temperature when you feel ill and finding you are normal. What could you do then?

'I'm going back to the house,' he grunted, 'to plague some more hell out of that man.'

'Over my dead body.' Daniel got up. 'Don't you know why I dragged you out, or were you doing it deliberately to spoil things? You're mean enough for that.'

'Spoil what?' asked Geoffrey blankly. 'I was only relieving my nerves. Why can't you leave me alone? You don't know what it's like –'

Daniel cut into his whine. 'Don't you know that your mother thinks there's a chance old Mew might be going to want to marry your aunt? She's pinning all her hopes on that. It's the only kind way she can think of to get the woman out of the house, that having been her dearest wish for seven years.'

'God!' said Geoffrey. 'I never knew that. How do you know all this?'

'Your mother told me.'

'Why not me? They treat me like a child. I mustn't know things. Why should they tell you things and not me? My mother likes you better than me because you were in a prison camp, too, like *him*. It isn't fair.'

'Where are you going?' Daniel asked, as he turned back towards the house.

'To take an overdose of luminal. I say –' he paused before he went round the corner. 'We shan't get such good meals, though, if old Flo goes.'

When Geoffrey went into the drawing-room, although he was looking quite normal, Mr Mew got up at once and took his leave. Mr Marple could not reproach his son then, for he had been praying for the last quarter of an hour that Mr Mew would go, because there was a Test Match being broadcast.

All afternoon the drawing-room was uninhabitable, because Mr Marple knew only two ways with the volume control – off and full strength, but the next day, although it was a three-day match, the wireless was silent.

It was the anniversary of Reggie's death. At breakfast, Mr Marple, who was wearing a black tie, opened *The Times*, cleared his throat, then lowered the paper and blinked across the table at his wife.

'It's in,' he said. 'Do you want to see it, dear?'

'Please, dear.' They called each other Dear all day on Reggie's anniversary.

He walked round the table with the paper and stood behind her chair while she looked at the front page.

'Let's see.' Geoffrey stretched out a hand for the paper. His mother gave it to him, then got up and went out of the room, weeping.

Reggie's *In Memoriam* notice covered twice as much space as anyone else's and included the last two lines of a poem that would

make you weep even if you had never known Reggie, or lost anyone in the war.

Mr Marple stood dangling his napkin, looking after his wife.
This was the one day in the year when he behaved like a husband.
'Should I go after her?'

'I'll go, Daddy,' said Eileen, who was wearing a black dress in
which she already looked hot although the sun was not yet high.
'You stay and finish your breakfast.'

Mr Marple did not want his breakfast. It was a waste to cook
eggs on Reggie's death day. It was a waste to cook for any meal,
for no one but Geoffrey felt like eating. Nobody spoke much,
and when they did it was in a cautious, considerate way, as if
they were strangers. Meals were quickly over. Nellie removed the
dishes less noisily, out of deference to the day, and the family
wandered out of the dining-room and went about the house as if
they were wearing carpet slippers.

Daniel stayed away for lunch, saying he wanted to finish a
sketch, so Geoffrey had no one to talk to. He wanted to swim,
but neither Eileen nor Aunt Florence would swim with him. No
one would do anything. It was as if Reggie had died yesterday
instead of five years ago.

All his photographs had flowers before them, or ivy twined
round the frames, and the framed telegram from the War Office,
announcing his death, was propped on the drawing-room mantel-
piece. When Geoffrey went into the study his father was taking
out of the desk drawer the German revolver that Reggie had
brought on his last visit home. For a moment Geoffrey thought he
was contemplating suicide, but it was just that he wanted to sit
and handle it with a faraway face. He wanted to talk to Geoffrey
about his brother, but Geoffrey would not stay. He had seen his
father cry once, and he did not want that embarrassment again.

In the afternoon he went down to the beach. Even the voice of
the sea seemed to be turned into sighs for Reggie, and above the
smuggler's pool where he had loved to swim water dripped from a
rock as if it wept for him. The gulls were not screaming round the
little island. They were settled on it, disconsolate as penguins,
hunched in the heat, piping thin echoes of their usual turbulent
cry.

The oars had been removed from the dinghy and the plug from its outboard motor. Geoffrey had read a book about an asylum where even quite rational patients were not allowed to have knives and forks or matches, and he knew how they felt, impotent and belittled. He sat down on the pearly sand with his feet drawn up and his arms round his knees, too depressed to make himself more comfortable.

'Where the hell have you been?' he asked, when Daniel came round the point, looking objectionably healthy and cheerful, with his hair wet and a rucksack on his back.

'In the cove. The boats are all in, and I think I've done quite a good one this time. Want to see?'

Geoffrey shook his head. 'I've had the hell of a day,' he said, without being asked.

'Sorry, old boy.' Daniel took off the rucksack and sat down by him. 'I knew it was a bad day for all of you. That's why I kept away.'

'Sensible chap,' gloomed Geoffrey. 'I wish I had. I told you how it would be, didn't I? They've been positively wallowing.' He un-wrapped his long body from its hunched position and lay face down on the sand, digging vehement little holes with his hands. 'It's always been like this,' he said. 'It was always Reggie, Reggie, Reggie, while he was alive, and it still is now he's dead. You know. I heard Aunt Flo telling you last night: Reggie was so brilliant, so handsome, so gay – oh yes, I've heard it often enough – so loving and popular, so everything, in fact, that I'm not. Do you believe all that, Daniel?'

Daniel did not answer. He sat looking down at Geoffrey, waiting to see what he was going to say.

'Because he wasn't.' Geoffrey began to speak rapidly, almost gabbling. 'He was mean. You've seen his photographs. Look at that head, how narrow it was, and his eyes were much closer together than mine. You know that I had to leave Rugby after a year because the boys jeered about my fits and made them worse? Well, Reggie was one of the ones who jeered. He did! No one be-lieves it, but he did, because he was afraid people would class him with his lunatic brother.'

'Rot,' Daniel said.

'It's true, I tell you. All my life, ever since I can remember, he made it harder for me by being better at everything. People compared us. I was the runt. I still am. The prize boy is taken and the runt is left – that's supposed to be always the way in war, isn't it? They wouldn't say it, of course, but I know what they think. They wish it had been me in the prison camp instead of him. But I wouldn't have got myself shot. I wouldn't have been ass enough to try and escape. Trust Reggie to do the spectacular thing.'

'There's nothing very spectacular about escaping from camp,' Daniel said. 'I had a shot at it once.'

Geoffrey shrugged this away as being irrelevant to the theme he was developing with increasing enthusiasm. He never had a chance to voice all these thoughts that rankled within him. No one let him talk like this. They hushed him or walked reproachfully away, but Daniel sat quiet, looking at the sea.

'Reggie had a car,' Geoffrey went on. 'He had a horse, a gun, a sailing dinghy of his own, everything he wanted. You should have seen this house when he was alive. People and parties all the time. I used to go away. I couldn't stand Reggie's gang. Then they used to talk about me, I know. Reggie was always laughing about me to his friends. He *was*, I tell you! Don't contradict me, Daniel. What do you know about it? You don't know what it was like when Reggie went to war and the maids left and we had to get rid of the car. I was in the way, a disgrace to the family because I couldn't go and die for my country, even when I was old enough.'

Geoffrey ruminated, remembering his father sticking pins into maps and listening to every reiterated news bulletin, his mother harrying him about the blackout, as if he were a German spy, and Eileen eternally knitting things for other people, never for him. He remembered the gang of soldiers who had passed him in a lorry, jeering as he pushed his bicycle up the hill, and the grocer's wife, who had said : 'Never mind, Mr Geoffrey. We can't all be heroes.'

'As if it were my fault!' he burst out, sitting up to gesticulate. 'I didn't ask to get this plague. That was Reggie's christening gift to me, his *chef-d'œuvre* you might say, of brotherly love. He never equalled that afterwards with anything he did.'

'Oh, come off it,' said Daniel. 'You can't blame him for what you inherited from your great-grandmother.'

'But I didn't! That's just the point. Listen, I'll tell you something.' Geoffrey lowered his voice and gabbled like an incanting witch. 'At my christening party Reggie picked me up and dropped me on my head. Oh, they say, of course, that there wasn't enough injury to make me epileptic, and they got the doctors to say so, too. They're all in league against me; but I know. I've read books. I've got more insight than they think.'

'You've got a more bizarre imagination, certainly.'

'But it's true! I don't imagine things. My memory may slip for a moment here and there, but I don't get big blackouts. Some people, you know, sleep-walk after fits and do all sorts of things, even murders, without knowing it. I daresay they'd like me to be as bad as that, so they could shut me up like the man in the iron mask and not have me hanging about embarrassing people.'

A sickening thought struck him. If he did go into automatism, he would never know. They would keep it hushed as the facts of life. 'You'd tell me, wouldn't you,' he said, 'if I ever did anything like that? *They* wouldn't. They're all against me, but you're on my side.'

'Oh, don't talk like a schoolgirl,' said Daniel impatiently. 'I'm going in. I won't listen to any more of your horrible, vindictive lies.'

'But it's true!' Geoffrey's voice was shrill. He clutched Daniel's bare ankle to stop him getting up.

'None of it is true.' Daniel hit his hand. 'And you're not to say these things to anyone.'

'Oh, I don't. They won't listen. That's why I like you, because you're the only one I can talk to.'

'Well, you can't any more' – Daniel wrenched his ankle free and got up – 'because I don't like you.'

'Oh, you *do*!' Geoffrey could not believe this. He threw sand at Daniel, thinking it was a joke. 'You must, because no one else does.'

By now he had talked himself into believing that this was true. It was quite a surprise, therefore, when on the next morning his sister brought him his breakfast in bed unasked, his mother came to kiss him very tenderly, his father gave him a book he had long wanted and even Aunt Florence asked him if he would like to go with her to Penzance for lunch and a film.

As the end of Daniel's time at Mara Rocks approached, Geoffrey grew disgruntled. He did not want Daniel to leave, and he resented it that Daniel wanted to go.

'Where to, anyway?' he grumbled. 'You've got nowhere to go to.'

'That's the beauty of it. There's nowhere I *need* go. I can go anywhere.'

'It must be wonderful to be free,' sighed Geoffrey, putting on a cage-bird act of pathos. Thinking he had captured Daniel's sympathy, he said: 'Stay here and keep me company.'

'No fear. I'd die here in winter.'

'It is a bit bleak,' Geoffrey admitted. 'I love it. The wind tears at the house and roars in the chimneys. Storms excite me. They make me want to stand on the rocks and wave my arms and scream like a gull. I have more fits in winter.'

'I'm not surprised.'

'But I wouldn't if you were here. Do you realize I'm two weeks overdue for one? You must be good for me. Stay a bit longer, Daniel.'

'Oh, for God's sake,' said Daniel, 'don't cling. You make me quite ill sometimes.'

Geoffrey was not offended. 'I suppose you could marry Eileen?' he suggested. 'You could live here free then.'

'Why don't you think about getting married yourself?' Daniel changed the subject. 'You're a big boy now. I saw you the other night with that girl from the village.'

'Oh, did you?' Geoffrey was unabashed, although what Daniel must have seen was not creditable. 'What did you think of her?'

'Too fat.'

'I like them fat. And squashy. We had a maid once called Ruby ... but they got rid of her. I shan't marry, you know. They wouldn't let me. I had a girl once. She was fun. Then she saw me have a fit one day. I know what I look like when I'm having one, I've read about it. No wonder she never came near me again. Poor Jane.'

'Who?' Daniel looked up.

'The girl I was telling you about,' said Geoffrey irritably. 'Half the time I believe you don't listen to me.'

It began to be an obsession with him that Daniel should not go. He prayed to his own particular God, a Being seated exactly above Geoffrey's head, occupied exclusively with his welfare, that Daniel might get ill or hurt in some way – anything to keep him here a prisoner. He could not bear people to escape him. He had not even wanted Woodie to go to the Isle of Wight. It was disturbing to think of anyone going to any place where Geoffrey did not exist and did not count.

However, the days ran out and nothing happened to Daniel. He was to leave two days after Woodie returned, to give Woodie time to recover from his inevitable train sickness. He would probably even be sick crossing the Solent in the paddle steamer.

Geoffrey always swore that it was seeing Woodie that gave him a fit. On Tuesday evening, as he watched Woodie get out of the car teeth first, he suddenly felt that he had seen it all before. It had all happened exactly like this: the green taxi, Woodie's narrow hat, a bird harping on a phrase of song, all together in this same combination of hidden meanings that were just beyond his grasp.

Here we go – o – 'Daniel!' he yelled, not aware of Woodie any more. 'Daniel!'

His mother woke him, coming in to draw the curtains. It was morning. 'What's the time?' he asked suspiciously, for she was not in the overall she wore in the early mornings.

'Nearly half past twelve.'

'Why did you let me oversleep? I've got things to do.' He could not remember what, but he had a feeling there was something. Or was that yesterday, and he had done it?

'Well, dear, you know you –' She had on her screwed-up 'fit' face, a bogus smile struggling with unease.

'No, I didn't. Don't tell me that. I expect I shall have one today, though, when Woodie comes back.'

'But he is back! He came yesterday. Never mind, dear. Don't worry.'

'I'm not worrying.' He rejected her balm. 'Of course I remember.' But he did not, so she must be right. He had had a fit. That was why he was so hungry.

'Get Daniel to make me some sandwiches,' he said. 'He's the only one who knows how I like them.'

'Oh dear. Now, Geoff, I must tell you – no, later perhaps. Eileen shall make the sandwiches for you. She does it very nicely.'

'Where's Daniel?' he asked Eileen, as soon as she came in with the tray.

'I don't know. He didn't tell us where he was going.'

'You mean he's gone? But it's not Thursday. Here – what day is it? How long have I been asleep? Why did he go too soon, without saying goodbye?' His feverish questions brought confusion to Eileen's freckled face.

'Didn't you know? Oh no, it was while you were asleep. It was quite a bad wound. No, I must begin where he hurt himself. Well, before that he was in the garden.' Eileen always told stories with the minimum of dramatic effect. 'There was an accident, you see, though I can't think how it could have happened. Nor could anyone, but Daniel said – I *am* telling you, Geoff. Don't shout at me like that. Yesterday evening, apparently, he took Reggie's German revolver down to the end of the garden to shoot rooks, he said. I can't think how he had the nerve to take it, but still. Anyway, he shot himself in the ankle. Wasn't that silly? I can't think how he did it. Yes, quite nasty. I had to tie it up, though I'm afraid I didn't do it very well, but Aunt Florence came in and did the bandage all over again. Mummy wanted to keep him in bed, but he wouldn't. He wouldn't stay here at all. I can't think why, unless he was afraid that Daddy would be angry about the gun. He left a note for you.'

The envelope was propped against the coffee-pot. As Geoffrey flattened the bedclothes to receive the tray from her, he noticed that there was some mud on the sheets. How on earth had he brought mud into his bed? Extraordinary thing.

117

DEAR GEOFF [the note said]

Next time you go sleep-walking take a water pistol. I got you back to bed O.K. without anyone knowing you'd ever been out of it, so don't tell them. Take care of yourself. My ankle hurts like hell, thanks.

DANIEL

CHAPTER SIX

Valerie

'It still hurts, you know,' Daniel said. 'Don't press on it like that.'
'Don't fuss.' Valerie compressed her lips as she always did when she was concentrating on doing something with her hands. 'It's practically healed. About time, too. You must be terribly unhealthy, Dan, to have gone so septic.'

'It wasn't me. It was that bullet. It had been in the gun seven years, fermenting germs from a dead German. Thank God that boy didn't know how to aim.'

'He sounds a menace.' Valerie smoothed the strapping round Daniel's ankle and sat back on her heels to look at him. 'Why do you go to these peculiar places?'

'Got to go somewhere. It was free living, and remote. I was in hiding at the time.'

'What for?'

'Stealing a car.'

Valerie laughed and got up, collecting the dressings into her first-aid box, which was as neat and well-equipped as her workbasket, her kitchen, and her wardrobe.

'I suppose that means it was something worse,' she said, 'something too bad to tell me. Never mind. You're respectable now.'

He wiggled his ankle, made a face, and complained that she had made the strapping too tight. 'Is it so respectable,' he asked, 'my living here with you?'

'Heavens.' Valerie realized that it was rather unflattering to Daniel that this had not occurred to her. 'No one thinks anything of women having P.G.s nowadays. Especially widows. They used to be merry and dangerous. Now they're just a nuisance, because there are so many of them.'

'And there's always Mr Piggott.'

'Oh yes,' she sighed, 'there's always Mr Piggott. Shall we ever get round to calling him Alec, do you suppose?'

'Steady,' he said. 'He's only been living with you for six months.'

Valerie March and her husband had not been rich while he was alive. After Philip was killed in the last month of the war Valerie found that not the least of her troubles was that she was very badly off. Unless she added to her pension, she could not go on living in the Chelsea flat or send her son to the school that Philip had wanted. She was thirty-five then, and young Philip was seven.

Having abandoned office work gratefully to get married ten years ago, she could not face the idea of starting again. It had been depressing enough when one was a girl with hopes instead of a widow with none. She had forgotten how to type, and her shorthand had always been amateurish. Her employer had thought it more important that his secretary was beautiful and companionable than able to do eighty words a minute, but she would never find anyone like dear Dobbie again. The world was different now. People moved faster and were less charitable. No one would ever give her a job and she could not cope if they did.

She was wholly feminine, utterly dependent. Marriage to Philip had been her refuge as well as her joy. She loved home like a cat. All her talents had gone into the big-windowed, airy flat which opened straight on to a quiet green garden. It had been her home for ten years and she could not leave it. If she must earn her living, she would stay there and let her living come to her. When she had recovered from the first lassitude of grief, when she could be with people normally again without suddenly having to rush from the room, she began to take paying guests.

Since then, the years had made her more independent. She had learned to discuss money without embarrassment and not to lower the rent to everyone who made her feel sorry for them. She had learned to be tough about damages and grumbles. She knew how to get rid of people she did not like and men who liked her too much. In spite of this last complication, she had found that men were easier to have in the flat than women, if only because they talked less. She had learned how to combine privacy with companionship and to jigsaw bath and shaving times. She did not have to learn how to make people comfortable. She had always been able to do that.

She had no difficulty in getting paying guests. Sometimes they were friends, or country friends' husbands who went home at week-ends. Her two spare rooms were hardly ever empty, because people who had been with her would always recommend her to anyone looking for a bed in London.

That was how Daniel had come: through a man in the advertising agency where he had a job doing strip cartoons. Mr Piggott had appeared out of the night six months ago, pale, like a little deep-sea fish and faintly common, murmuring that he had got into conversation on a 31 bus with her son, who had told him that his mother needed a lodger in her back room.

Mr Piggott always spoke in a tiny voice because he had some chronic affection of the throat. He had warned Valerie that it would become worse in autumn and winter, and as September paled into October it did. He could not call from room to room as one does in a flat. If Valerie were in the kitchen while he was in the drawing-room next door waiting for his supper he could not call out, as Daniel did occasionally: 'Need any help?' He had to get up and go padding out to her on his little turned-out fishtail feet, following her round the kitchen, getting in her way, until she sent him kindly back to the drawing-room.

She was used to his voice. If she listened carefully, she could hear nearly everything he said, which was seldom worth the effort. Daniel said that she was like a dog that can hear a whistle pitched on a note inaudible to humans. He nearly always had to say 'What?' to Mr Piggott.

In the mornings he did not even say that to him. Valerie knew that to have Mr Piggott at breakfast passing him things he did not want was about as much as he could stand, without conversation as well. So she, in a housecoat, but with her hair and face properly done, would talk to Mr Piggott while Daniel read the paper. Mr Piggott did not want to read the paper yet, for he had quite a long train ride out to Isleworth, where his business was. He read the evening paper in the train coming home, so when Daniel came home and wanted to read the paper Mr Piggott was ready to talk. They would have a drink. Mr Piggott had quite taken to cocktails since Daniel kept the flat supplied with gin, but he insisted on paying his share, and came home now and again with a bottle of British sherry.

When he had had a drink, Daniel would discuss bits of news with Mr Piggott and ask him if he had had a hard day at the office and say 'What?' to his answers. Daniel was quite nice to Mr Piggott. Valerie was very nice to him, but since Daniel had come, he seemed sometimes *de trop*, because she and Daniel got on together so well.

Daniel was often out in the evenings and sometimes away at week-ends, but Mr Piggott was always there, with his chlorotic, transparent skin and his whisper. She heard his key in the lock punctual to the minute at six-thirty, and, picturing him attached to the door by his key chain, like an umbilical cord, thought how terrible it would be if Mr Piggott was your husband and that was all a key in the lock meant to you when it ought to be the most exciting sound of the day.

If Mr Piggott were your husband you wouldn't go out to the hall with floury hands and have to brush the collar of his coat afterwards. You would let him come to you in the kitchen.

Mr Piggott liked to find Valerie in the kitchen, which was where he usually did find her, for she cooked, as she did everything else – housework or sewing or dressing herself or doing her face – with care and artistry that took a lot of time. She gathered, for he never made direct personal remarks, that he liked her as a Domesticated Little Woman, and never admired her so much as in an apron or overall. When she was dressed to go out, in one of the frivolous hats which were all she retained of a once too ornamental taste in dress – the rest of her was now slick and tailored – Mr Piggott was not at ease with her.

He was part-owner of a small firm that manufactured in a small way very small articles like shirt buttons and press studs and gilt safety-pins. His partner seemed to take only a small share of the work, for Mr Piggott was always bringing home letters and accounts that he had not had time to finish during the day. Valerie offered to help him, but he would not allow it, not because he thought, as she herself did, that she would not be much help, but because such things were not for her. She must be forever the Little Woman, shielded from the coarse world of commerce.

Daniel, on the other hand, resented her domesticity. She wondered how his wife had managed if he was always shouting at her to come on out of the kitchen and have a drink and be sociable. If Valerie forgot to take off her apron after she had put dinner on the table he would undo the knot behind her and tear it off.

He liked her in hats and high heels. He liked her with groomed hair and ear-rings. He liked her nails to be long and red and her fingers white and perfumed. Mr Piggott, no doubt, would have preferred them to smell of onions.

Unlike Mr Piggott, Daniel wanted her to be interested in his job, which she was, and to help him in the evenings, which she enjoyed. He used to make rough sketches at home for his work next day, and Valerie's help took the form of posing for the various roles required by the products whose merits he must dramatize in a way that even the semi-literate could understand.

He was working on a laxative at the moment. Valerie had been the Girl Who Came Top In The Exam because her inside was as slick as her mind, with pigtails, spectacles, and her moroccobound edition of Browning clasped ecstatically to her chest. She had been the wife of the Man Who Lost The Job because he was sluggish in the mornings, and the wife of the Man Who Got It because he was foully bright. She had been the men themselves, too, crawling out of bed with a hangdog look, or flinging off the sheets with a glad cry. Mr Piggott had been quieter than usual that evening, and would take no part in the fun, because he did not approve of Daniel going into Valerie's bedroom, even in the cause of art. He would not come in himself to see Valerie's masterly interpretation of a costive riser, but had gone to his room which looked up into the well at the back of the flats and had not even come out again to clean his teeth.

Daniel was now doing the Man No Girl Would Kiss. After supper he would not let Valerie wash up, but made her put a flower in her hair and portray the nauseated expression on the face of the girl at the dance when she smelled the breath of the man who did not take Evacu-pep.

Daniel sat on a stool looking like a pixie, viewing her with his head on one side. 'Won't do,' he said. 'Much too refined. You look like a district visitor. Think of the most disgusting thing you can – no, don't tell me. Your face is bad enough. That's fine. Hold it. Now lean over backwards, as if his clammy hand had you in the back of your waist.' Valerie overbalanced and fell on to the sofa.

'I can't do it without the hand,' she complained.

'Let's get Mr Piggott to be it. His is clammy enough. Where is he?'

Valerie went to fetch him. He had sneaked into the kitchen to do the washing-up for her. He had one of her best towels round his waist and was using the last of her soapflakes. She dragged him away. He let her lead him into the drawing-room, but he did not want to pose.

'Think,' said Daniel. 'You'll be seen in every newspaper in the country. That's fame.'

'I – no, I couldn't do it correctly.'

'Oh, come on,' said Valerie. She took the towel from his waist, planted him opposite Daniel and stood facing him. 'Now the clammy hand – there !' She picked up his cold, limp hand and put it in the small of her back.

'Here,' said Daniel. '*She*'s supposed to look disgusted, not you. You're supposed to look desirous,' for Mr Piggott was leaning back with an agonized expression, sweating lightly. They could not get him to lean forward. It was as if Valerie had the plague.

'Never mind,' Daniel said. 'I'll just do you, Val. That's fine.' She put on a face of unutterable loathing and Mr Piggott looked hurt.

Daniel sketched rapidly before he could break away. When Valerie relaxed, Mr Piggott took away his hand and stepped back at once, breathing quick and shallow.

'Now,' said Daniel, 'we'll do the Man The Girls Queued Up For. You stand there, Mr Piggott, with an air of lustful triumph, and Val – fluff out your hair a bit – you're swooning towards him as if you were smelling violets, or a steak.' She swooned. This was too much for Mr Piggott. He broke away with a low cry, and they heard him lock the door of his room, as if he feared for his honour.

'Poor little man,' Daniel said. 'We shouldn't have made him do it. It wasn't fair, when he's so crazy about you.'

Valerie was startled. This had never occurred to her. Because Mr Piggott was unlovable, it had not seemed possible that he could love.

'That's a typical woman's reasoning,' Daniel said. 'You're so busy analysing your own emotions that you never think about other people's. You should think of these things before you take lodgers. For all you know I might be in love with you.'

'You want me to ask you if you are,' she said, 'so that you can say No.'

'That's it,' he said. He had a disconcerting way of admitting or pretending things against himself..

'It's late,' she said. 'I'm going to bed.' She wanted to lie and remember things about Philip. She could do this now, sweetly, without anguish. It was a great comfort.

'Half a minute.' He was finishing his drawing of her smelling a steak. 'I want you to be the Happy Bride.' But she would not wait. She was weary of his pictures, and of the futility of being kept from one's bed for something that would be looked at once and then go round the fish and chips.

One Sunday in November, after a week of rain, it was suddenly a bright day. When Valerie got up to make the tea, she found Daniel in the kitchen in pyjamas and bare feet, trying to make tea with water that was not boiling.

'Are you ill?' she asked. 'Why are you up so early?'

'Look at the weather.' He took her to the window and stood with his arm along her shoulders, looking out at the gardens where the sun glittered on the wet uncut lawns like scattered glass.

Although his arm meant nothing to her, she was aware of it, if only because of noticing that it did mean nothing. It seemed that one was never cured of the habit of speculating about every man long after one had ceased to want any of them ever again. She wondered if men were the same, if he was at this moment idly speculating what her shoulders under the dressing-gown meant to his arm.

'I'm going to borrow Willie's car,' he said, 'and take you out to the country somewhere. Get a move on with breakfast, and then throw some kind of a picnic together while I go and get the car.' He went away and sang in the bathroom. She did not mind that, although Philip used to sing in his bathroom, for it was quite different. Daniel sang in tune and either gaily or not at all. Philip used to dirge off-key, mournful bass themes which sounded like a tuba being played by a novice.

It was typical of Daniel to take it for granted that she was free today. She was delighted to go to the country with him, but as she went about her neat breakfast preparations misgivings began to spoil her pleasure. She usually walked in the park on Sundays with Mr Piggott. When Daniel came back dressed, she said unwillingly, her heart sinking at the cussed kindness which made her say it: 'Dan, could we possibly take Mr Piggott? It seems unkind to leave him here alone, and he'd enjoy it so.'

'Oh, for heaven's sake,' Daniel said, 'what are you running – a lodging house or a charity home?'

'Please.'

'No. We either go without him or not at all.'

Having already struggled and lost to her conscience, Valerie had to stick to her point. 'He wouldn't be in the way. He could sit at the back. I'd take a bit of food for him –' She sounded as if it were a dog she was trying to insinuate into the car.

They had a small argument about Mr Piggott. The toast caught fire and the milk boiled over, and Mr Piggott came in in the middle of it. He always looked surprisingly miniature in the mornings. One had forgotten overnight how small he was. From his room at the bottom of the well he had not seen what the day was like, so he now exclaimed softly when he saw the sun shining on the china in the plate rack and said in the confidential whisper which sounded as if he were giving racing tips that it was a jolly day for a stroll in the park.

It was no surprise to him that Daniel would not answer, but his pale brows went up and his eyes looked blank when Valerie, glancing at Daniel and prepared to stop if he dared to look triumphant, explained over-elaborately to Mr Piggott why she had to leave him alone for the day.

'That's quite all right,' said Mr Piggott. 'I shall do very nicely. A pleasure really. I hope it keeps fine for you.' But his eyes were sad. Valerie wished that Daniel had not said that Mr Piggott was in love with her. She did not believe it, but it made her anxious.

When Daniel came back for her with the car, she got in beside him feeling a little less guilty now that she had left Mr Piggott a tempting tray of cold food and a rice pudding in the oven, which he loved.

'Where are we going?' she asked, bringing her hand in through the window as they turned the corner out of sight of the doorway of the flats where Mr Piggott had stood waving them God-speed like a dwarf retainer.

'Where do you want to go? I don't care. West – south –? Want to go to the sea?'

'Dan,' she said, 'let's go and see your cottage.'

'Oh, you don't want to go there.'

'I do. I've always wanted to since you told me about it.'

'There's nothing to see.'

'I want to see it. Please. I did give in about Mr Piggott.'

'Oh, all right.' He turned the car northward and they made their way to the Great North Road and Cambridgeshire.

The first thing that Valerie noticed about the cottage was that it did not look empty, although there had been no one in it for months. The windows were shut and grubby with rain. The chimney was the only one in the village without its pennon of smoke. The garden was a tangle of coarse grass and dead leaves and vegetation blown and smashed by autumn gales, and a broken toolhouse door banged with a doleful creak, but the house did not have that obstructive, discouraging look of buildings that are going to take a long time to come round to being lived in again. You could pick up life here at any moment.

Inside it was ghostly with dustsheets and upturned chairs, and the tiles on the floor shone with damp, but it still looked as if a few minutes of people about would make everything all right.

While Daniel collected wood from the shed and made a fire, Valerie ran about in delighted curiosity, exploring everywhere.

'There's a forest of cobwebs under the beams upstairs, a leaking tank in the linen cupboard, and a terrible mess in the kitchen where the mice have nested in a packet of cornflakes,' she reported briskly. 'I'd like to put a kettle on and do some cleaning up.'

'What's the point?' he asked. 'No one's going to live here.'

'Oh, Dan, it's a *shame*. I thought so before, but now that I've seen it I don't know how you can bear to let this place stay empty. If you don't want to live in it yourself – which you ought – you should really do something about letting. It's such a waste, and bad for a house to be empty, too. Look at this!' She touched the brass kettle which hung from a spit in the fireplace. 'This mildew will corrode it, and everything's getting so damp.'

'Oh, for God's sake!' he exclaimed, with extreme irritation. 'Stop running about being housewifely.'

'Well, I'm sorry,' she said, dashed. 'It just seemed such a pity. And when you think of the housing shortage –' As soon as she began to say this it sounded as silly and smug to her as it evidently did to Daniel.

One would have thought that he would have a lot of things to do, coming back to his own house after all this time, but he was sitting at the desk, staring out of the window at nothing in particular. Valerie felt bad. Of course, he was thinking about Jane. It did not matter now that he had spoiled her pleasure in coming to the house. It was her fault for expecting to get pleasure out of what could be nothing but sadness for him. She should not have made him come here. She tried to picture him and his wife here together. She did not know what Jane had looked like. He had never told her, but she could imagine how happy two people could be here. To live in this house would be good enough; to be in love in it would be almost too much.

'Look at that darn tree,' he said, as if he had not been thinking about Jane at all, 'trailing all those broken branches.' He went to get a ladder and saw.

The day had spoiled, and the white, clear-running clouds had spread and massed together into a sludge of grey. Valerie, who was sitting on the doorstep with her feet on the path, saw a spot darken on one cobble, then on another, then all were freckled and in a moment the whole path was glistening wet except the place under the thatch where her feet were.

She called to Daniel. He did not come at first and she again had a picture of him here with his wife, and Jane calling him in to meals to which he would not come.

When he came in, treading wet shoes on the floor which she had surreptitiously swept while he was outside, he seemed happier. The fire was burning well and they sat by it and ate the food Valerie had brought and drank some whiskey which Daniel found in a cupboard.

'I didn't leave any here,' he said. 'Those old girls must have been toping.'

'Perhaps it was for the one who was ill. Which one was it who died?'

'I don't know,' he said. 'I never asked, because I liked them both so much. What's the good of upsetting yourself about someone who's nothing to do with you.'

'It must be nice,' she said, 'to have your emotions so well-drilled.'

'It's the only hope,' he said.

They sat and ate amicably. They liked each other. Daniel was the first man whose company Valerie had really enjoyed since Philip, although they were not alike. Philip had been kinder and more predictable.

'Aren't you glad we didn't bring Mr Piggott?' he asked.

She thought of Mr Piggott eating his rice pudding with the eager little dabs he made when he liked anything particularly. But no, he would be washing up by now, for he was sure to have lunch punctually at one-fifteen, whether he were alone or not. 'Yes, I'm glad,' she answered.

'He might have wanted the rest of that chocolate,' Daniel said, taking it.

Later, when they were sitting idly and talking unwillingly about going home, Valerie thought that the friendliness of the house was working on Daniel. He liked it here. She could see that.

'Dan,' she said, taking a chance, 'why don't we come and live here in the spring?'

'Lord, no,' he said. 'We couldn't. There's too much to do to make it liveable again.'

'I'd do it. I could fix it.'

'No,' he said, and suddenly the shell of content that had enclosed them was broken and he was outside, away from her. 'Besides, I don't know where I'll be. I might be abroad by then.'

'Oh,' she said blankly, 'are you going to leave your job? Won't you be staying on at the flat?'

'I don't know. How do I know where I'll be? Don't try and pin me down.'

'Well,' she said huffily, for her mind had been racing ahead to all kinds of plans – letting the flat, buying a car on credit, perhaps, country clothes, friends down at weekends, Pip here in the holidays with his bicycle – 'Well, I do like to know, that's all. Someone might want your room.'

Soon after that they went home. She turned at the gate to look back, and wished that she had money and could buy the cottage. She wouldn't have Daniel in it. She was annoyed with him and sat as far away as possible in the front of the car. People had no right to behave as if you were trying to trap them when you only put out a vague feeler towards the future. Daniel had no right to make a show of being so fugitive in a world where people had to share each other's lives or die of loneliness. Who had let him get like this? She felt resentful enough to blame his wife.

Coming out of London this morning, she had been looking forward to seeing the cottage, pleased with the whole expedition and laughing and talking with Daniel. Although she had been along this road many times before, she had not been in the mood for nostalgia. Now that Daniel was driving in silence, much too fast on the wet roads considering it was not his car, she looked out of the window with pain at the landmarks of fifteen years ago.

Philip had been in his last year at Cambridge when she first knew him. She had met him at a dance to which they had both gone with different parties. On the lawn he had met her, breaking the buckle of her sandal on her way back to the marquee from the ladies' room. This was his college and he had taken her back to his room to mend the shoe clumsily with wire. After that, they had not gone back to their own parties, and had both been unpopular, particularly Philip, who had left a hot-cheeked girl in green broderie Anglais superfluous among the yawning duennas round the walls of the marquee.

It had not mattered, because from that time Philip and Valerie were seen together everywhere in Cambridge, and he was struck off lists as a dead loss. Valerie came to Cambridge nearly every week-end. Philip, who had a little open car, often drove her home again, after a Sunday on the river punting through the warm afternoon until they could find somewhere to tie the boat up under a tree, or a winter Sunday with a lot of people having tea in his room and Valerie making the toast, and everybody going away after tea except her and Philip.

Nights when they had driven back to London with the roof down and her hair in a tangle that took half an hour to comb out. Cold nights when he drove with one hand and the other arm round her. Wet nights when the rain came through all the holes in the roof and the celluloid windows would not stay up.

Daniel swished her through Stevenage, and here, just beyond the town, was the place where they had stopped to put the roof up at last after Philip had driven on for miles saying that you didn't get wet as long as you kept on going. She was very wet by that time and not speaking to him any more. Here was that house covered with painted wooden figures, where Philip had stopped one night and tried to wrench off one of the figures for her, but the cunning owner had nailed them on too firmly.

How many times she had driven down this long straight road between the poplars! Philip had said it was like a French road, and when they drove through France on their honeymoon she saw that he was right. Here was that shack of an all-night transport café with the terrible name of the Dew Drop Inn. It looked exactly the same and probably had behind the counter the same black-jowled man who never found the hour too small to make puns as excruciating as the name of his café. They used to stop here coming home from dances. She craned towards it as Daniel flipped her by, and on the rutted cinder lorry park in the middle of which the little café sat like an oasis in a desert, the memory of Philip and his snub-nosed car was very strong.

She sat back and sighed. 'It's funny, isn't it,' she said, 'how you can be sensible for months – years even – and then suddenly something puts you right back into the first pain?'

'Usually when you're tight,' he said.

'Roads,' she said. 'Roads you've been on with someone are one of the things that bring them back.' He was pulling out to pass an obstinate lorry, hooting at it, and did not hear her.

She would have liked now to talk about Philip and tell Daniel about driving back after dances in May Week. But what was there to say that would not sound silly? The feeble jokes of the man in the café, sausages, coffee made out of a bottle, the stiffness of one's face, made up so many hours ago, how drab a white evening dress looked in the light of dawn, its hem trodden and grass-stained. Philip's beard pricking through his chin, hurting when he kissed her good-bye, both of them too tired to want to kiss at all, seeing the milkman – he came earlier in those days – swaying up through the ticking house, clothes on the floor, bed, meeting Philip next day looking as fresh as if she had slept for nine hours. She wouldn't nowadays, but one could then.

Daniel and she both felt tired when they got home, and she wished that Mr Piggott did not have to be there and wanting to hear all about their day. But he was there and in high fettle, for he had cooked supper for them. He had been preparing it for hours, but it was still not finished, so she and Daniel had to wait in the drawing-room while he skipped in and out from the kitchen, forbidding Valerie to go in there, assuring them that in one minute everything would be ready.

When at last he came in and whispered that they must come to the table now, Daniel went away to wash. 'But it will spoil!' protested Mr Piggott in what was as near as he could get to a cry. Cradling it in a cloth like a mother taking her baby to its cot, he put the dish back in the oven until Daniel returned.

After all that, it was only spaghetti with some kind of tomato mess on top. Planning and cooking this had quite made his day. He knew a shop in Soho that was open on Sundays and he had been all the way there on a 22 bus to get the spaghetti, and the man had let him have some mushrooms and a tin of some special tomato purée. He told them this as he served it out.

'Oh, not too much, please!' said Valerie; 'for a start, anyway,' she amended as she saw his face fall.

'Where did you say you got this?' Daniel asked, tasting it.

'Soho,' said Mr Piggott proudly. 'The home of La Spaghetti. What's the matter?' he asked as Daniel laid down his fork. 'Don't you like it?'

'Oh yes, it's fine, fine,' he said, cocking an eye at Valerie. 'I suppose these *are* mushrooms? I mean, they wouldn't be likely to sell toadstools –?'

Valerie made a face at him. 'It's lovely, Mr Piggott! Simply delicious. I don't know when I've enjoyed anything more.' It did taste rather peculiar, but she conveyed to Daniel that he must eat and he picked up his fork again and played about with the spaghetti. Valerie managed to hide some of hers under a piece of bread; but when he saw that she had stopped eating, Mr Piggott insisted that she must have some more.

'Come along do,' he said. 'I'm going to. Mr Brett, you ready?' Daniel pretended not to hear.

Valerie took a little and toyed with it, trying to hide some more under the bread. Daniel had given up the struggle and was drinking water in an alarmed way. Mr Piggott, in honour bound to see the dish emptied, ate on, nodding and smiling encouragingly across the table, valiantly stuffing himself until his eyes popped.

In the night, Daniel met Valerie in the passage and complained that he felt queasy. She felt queasy, too, but there was no time to pay attention to her stomach or Daniel's, for Mr Piggott was very ill indeed.

Mr Piggott was ill for quite a long time. At frequent intervals he said: 'No, no, please don't bother about me. I hate to give so much trouble,' which was really more trouble than if he had been demanding and captious, since it moved Valerie to give him extra attention to show him that he was no nuisance.

Apart from a sister in Swansea who sent him a book of Bright Thoughts for Dark Days, he did not seem to have any relations or friends who cared that he was ill. The responsibility fell on Valerie, and in nursing him she grew almost attached to him, as a foster mother to a weakly orphan. He was a heartbreakingly good patient. He was so long-suffering, so tractable, so ready even when he was most ill to assure her that he was doing very well, that she was ashamed of being sometimes reluctant to go into his room. In this cold weather, the electric fire had to burn all day, but he had a Victorian dread of fresh air and suffered so acutely if she opened the window that the room became as stuffy as a boothole.

Although he was so undemanding, Mr Piggott's illness claimed a lot of Valerie's time. She went in to him as often as she could, and knew that when she was out, he just lay waiting for her to come back. Reading hurt his eyes, and since he did not like jazz or light music or variety comedians, the wireless was little use. He loved Valerie to read to him, and because he never asked her, she felt that she had to do it as often and as long as she could stand the atmosphere and his favourite second-rate thrillers whose horrors made him exclaim and chuckle softly.

It took an age to make his bed and get him fixed up in the mornings, and an age to settle him again at night. He would not let her even wash his face; and when she brought the basin and left him, he was hours in there splashing gently and making mysterious rubbing and scrubbing sounds. He liked a good wash, he said. It freshened a person up. If Valerie opened the door too soon, he would twitter like Nausicaa surprised bathing with her nymphs. When at last he allowed her in again, the smell of soapy water and toothpaste and damp flannels made the atmosphere more than ever like a bedroom in a Sickert painting, where the slop pail is not emptied for days and the bed slept in so late that it is not worth making.

Being at the bottom of the well, the room was always dark. Mr Piggott was painfully conscious of the price of electricity; and since the doctor had insisted on the fire, and since he would have died rather than disobey the doctor – or perhaps thought he would die if he did – he would hardly ever turn on the light. So in airless obscurity, his thin, greenish hair wetted and combed flatly to his head, Mr Piggott lay neat and straight as a child's corpse, not nearly reaching the end of the bed, looking more than ever like a little fish that lives far under water and does not know that there is day beyond the surface.

At Valerie's insistence, Daniel would put his head round the door in the mornings to say: 'Everything all right? Fine, fine,' and put it round again in the evenings to say: 'Had a good day? So glad.'

'I hear you're better,' he would say, whatever he had heard, for he did not want Mr Piggott to go on being ill. He resented that Valerie had to spend so much time in there and could never go out with him to dinner or the cinema, because of leaving Mr Piggott. When she had time to pose for him, it was with half an eye on the clock for the time of Mr Piggott's medicine and half an ear for the infrequent tinkle of the little brass bell which he rang half-heartedly as if he almost hoped it would not be heard.

Daniel did not like her in the white overalls she had bought to nurse Mr Piggott. He did not like to smell Dettol about her, nor to see her making arrowroot pudding and cutting the crusts off thin bread and butter. When she said to him: 'You are terribly selfish. Poor Mr Piggott needs me. He has no one. You don't need me, or anyone, but you think only of yourself,' he simply answered: 'Yes.'

When Mr Piggott's food poisoning was on the way out, it took a turn into gastric flu and plunged him back into being quite seriously ill again. When Philip came home for the Christmas holidays, full of plans of what he and his mother were going to do, he found her still tied to the sickroom.

When Pip was disappointed about anything, everyone suffered. He had always been uncontrolled about parties missed, or the wrong present from an aunt, or quarantines, or a rainy day when he had planned an outing. When he found that Valerie could not spend all day with him travelling the bus routes from Ponders End to Plumstead Garage he stamped at her and gestured with his hands like a foreigner and said in a caustic, elderly voice: 'I consider this has utterly spoiled my holidays.'

'Well, darling, Mr Piggott is your responsibility, too. You brought him home,' Valerie said, reasoning with him as if he were the adult he often seemed to be.

'I never would have,' he said tragically, 'if I'd known he was going to ruin my life. Why did you tell me you weren't going to be a proper mother to me these holidays? I'd have brought Edmunds Two home with me.'

'You couldn't have,' said Valerie, knowing she should not argue with him when he was in this mood, but unwilling to let him have the inevitable last word too soon. 'There's nowhere for him to sleep.'

'Damn, damn, bloody, damn,' Philip reeled off, hoping to impress Daniel. 'I wish we didn't have to have lodgers.'

'If we didn't, there'd be no school for you, and no Edmunds Two.'

'Neither would be any loss,' said Philip coldly, and Valerie wished that Daniel would not laugh at him.

She lived for Philip's holidays. She, too, had planned so much that now they could not do, and his disappointment made her own more difficult to reconcile. It seemed wrong to put a stranger before one's own child, but Mr Piggott was ill and Pip was not; and having decided what she ought to do, she could not stop herself from doing it. She had always been like that. As a child, she had been afflicted with a morbid conscience that made her stay behind on walks to talk to unpopular governesses, miss the best cakes and the biggest strawberries and always pick the worst side when she was captain, because she could not bear the expression of the duffer children trying to look as if they did not care.

Daniel said morosely that she was a good woman.

'And they're the end,' added Philip. 'They wear bonnets and sing in the street.'

Daniel said that she was lost, sold to her conscience like Faust to the devil. Philip agreed with him, adding, with Daniel's approval, that charity began at home. They ranged themselves against her, and she longed to be on their side, glad that they had taken to each other, if only through the common bond of selfishness.

Daniel started a saga of advertisements for cod-liver oil, and Philip, who had a high sense of drama, posed delightedly as the Child Who Couldn't, and the Child Who Could. 'I'll be famous,' he said. 'This will make my name.'

Daniel helped himself generously to time off from the office and did with Philip all the things his mother should have been doing. They went on buses and trams and trains. They went round and round the inner circle on a penny-halfpenny ticket and explored the central line to darkest Snaresbrook. They went to the cinema and the circus and queued for an hour to see a broadcast variety show to which poor Mr Piggott was made to listen to see if he could hear them laughing.

One night, when Philip had been telling her of What me and Daniel did and What me and Daniel think and What me and Daniel are going to do tomorrow, Valerie could not help saying, as she kissed him in bed in the dark: 'Love me, Pip?'

'Oh *yes*, Mum.' His cheek was cool against hers and she sensed that his mind was away. 'I love Dan, too,' he said. 'He's not like a lodger. Mum, it is nice to have a man about the house.' Valerie kissed him again and went away without speaking, glad that the light was out. She had never let Pip see her cry about Philip. She did not want him to think of his father as sad.

On Christmas day Mr Piggott was better and allowed to sit shakily up to lunch in a dressing-gown and eat a little breast of turkey and sip, since Valerie said he might, a little wine. Half-way through the meal he was looking so wan, though bravely smiling, and agreeing with remarks he was almost past hearing, that Valerie took him back to bed.

'You're trying to run before you can walk,' Philip said with his mouth full of pudding, as the pitiful figure tottered from the room with its slippers flapping and the dressing-gown its sister had sent for Christmas hanging like a tent from its drooping shoulders. Shortly afterwards, Philip was found to be drunk on cider and had to be put to bed himself with tears and a headache.

Daniel had been going out that night, but he stayed at home, since Valerie was alone. She wore the stockings and the scent that he had given her and they had champagne and cold turkey and afterwards talked by the fire in the effortless intimacy that had circled them round that day they had the picnic at the cottage.

Philip, bored with his bed, came wandering in to them in his pyjamas and stood by the door, approving the scene.

'That's nice,' he said, sensing the atmosphere. 'You look like two married people. Why don't you get married?'

Valerie looked at Daniel. He was looking into the fire, and said nothing. She laughed awkwardly. 'Oh no, darling,' she said. 'I've been married. So's Dan. People don't get married twice.'

'They do,' he said. 'Edmunds Two's father did, and Jefferson's mother has been married three times, *and* had her picture in the paper for it.'

'Is that why you suggested it – so I could be in the papers?'

Valerie asked, wishing Daniel would say something to help her out.

'Well, that would be super, of course, but I'm afraid they wouldn't put you in, Mum. You're too ordinary. I just thought it would be a good thing. You like each other and I like you both. We might let Mr Piggott get up to be best man.'

'Come on,' said Daniel, going to him. 'I'll put you back to bed.'

'With chocolate biscuits?'

'With chocolate biscuits.' He picked him up and took him away. Philip was too old to be carried. He usually hated it, but when he was in pyjamas and had been asleep he seemed several years softer and younger. Valerie went to her room before Daniel came back; and when she went in to kiss Philip and try to say something that would stop him harping on marriage, he was asleep with a chocolate biscuit melting between his hair and the pillow.

On Boxing Day he and Daniel came home from the fun fair at Olympia, penniless and exhausted. Daniel had not wanted to go. He had complained at lunch that he was tired; but when Pip wanted you to do something, it was less tiring to do it than to argue.

Valerie came out of Mr Piggott's room as they came into the flat.

'Have a good time?' she asked.

'Super. Mum, we spent three pounds, and Dan was nearly sick on the moonrocket.'

'I'm so glad,' Valerie said abstractedly, for she was thinking about Mr Piggott, wondering whether she ought to send for the doctor. 'I'm worried about him,' she said. 'I do wish I hadn't let him get up yesterday. He's not nearly so well. Do you think doctors mind being rung up on Boxing Day? I don't like to, but really, the little man –'

'Oh blast the little man,' Daniel said. 'Bloody little hypochondriac. If he felt as ill as I do he would have something to complain about. I feel like death.' He leaned against a bit of furniture and put his hand to his forehead in what Valerie thought a rather theatrical gesture, for her benefit.

'You're the most unfeeling man I ever knew,' she said angrily. 'Here's this poor little man really ill and never a murmur, and you moan and groan just because you were silly enough to go on a roundabout after eating and drinking too much yesterday.'

'Mum!' cried Philip scandalized. 'It wasn't a roundabout. It was the moonrocket. I told you.'

'Whatever it was,' she said, 'your friend Dan is nothing but a mean-natured egotistical hog, and now perhaps you see why I'm always on at you about being selfish. You'll grow up like him.'

'Well, I'd like that,' said Philip cheerfully. 'Go on. Say some more.' He liked to see grown-ups having a quarrel.

Valerie stalked away to the telephone. Daniel gave her a filthy look, pushed himself away from the furniture and went out, dragging his feet. While she was dialling, she heard him go to the bathroom and rattle about in the medicine cupboard.

'The aspirin's not in there!' she called. 'Oh – I beg your pardon. Hullo? Is that Doctor Mather's house? Could I possibly ... ?'

When she went to tell Mr Piggott that the doctor was coming, she met Daniel coming out of the bathroom with a face of doom. 'Get the doctor?' he asked. 'Good. He can see me, too.'

'Oh now, Dan, just because –'

He cut her short. 'I'm very ill,' he announced sepulchrally. 'I have a temperature of a hundred and two point one.'

She cavilled, not wanting to believe it. 'It can't be. The thermometer's measured at two-point intervals.'

'It's *exactly* between the two marks,' he said in a crushing tone that was spoiled by a stammer, and ended in a slight muzziness which Valerie, knowing him so well and knowing, in her maternal heart, the difference between illness and shamming, had to accept at last.

Daniel was the worst patient Valerie had ever nursed, and she had nursed her father through an illness which nearly killed her before it killed him. Daniel had Mr Piggott's flu, and although he had it less severely he made a hundred times more fuss. He took his temperature ten times a day and kept flinging off the bed-clothes. He would either demand attention and keep calling to her wherever she was in the flat, or refuse to let her do anything for him and growl at her if she tried to tidy his room or straighten his bed. Between him and Mr Piggott, Valerie was nearly demented. She became so tired that she began to think it would serve them both right if she got flu herself.

Poor Pip. This was no holiday for him. She tried to send him to his cousins, but he would not go. He wanted to stay and look after Daniel. The doctor had said that he must keep away, but since he went into Daniel's room, anyway, Valerie thought she might as well take advantage of it and let him be useful. They would be in there together by the hour, playing chess like a couple of old men: Pip on a stool drawn up to the bed, fondling his right ear, just as Philip used to; Daniel with his brown face sharper-angled now at the cheeks and jaw, his hair rumpled, his pillows in chaotic discomfort, for he was not a neat invalid like Mr Piggott.

Philip took his meals and posed for him when he wanted to draw, and when Daniel was allowed to have a bath, insisted on supervising, ordering him about like a male nurse.

'The boy's been good to me, anyway,' Daniel said, rolling his eyes at Valerie when she told him one day that he would have to eat plaice or nothing.

'You know why?'

'Because he likes me. No, take that away, Val darling. It smells of railways. Give it to Mr Piggott.'

'Because he likes you?' she snorted. She was tired, and sick of everybody's nonsense. 'Don't flatter yourself. It's because he's hoping he'll get flu and not have to go back to school.'

'Valerie,' said Daniel, breaking off a branch of the grapes she had brought him and holding it above his mouth like an Andalusian dancer, 'you are an embittered woman.'

'Dan,' she said, smitten, 'don't say that. It's what I'm always afraid of. Widows do get bitter. When they're widows too young.'

'Oh darling.' He closed his mouth and dropped the grapes on the floor. 'Don't talk like that. You'll marry again. You'll have other children, too. Look what you've produced. You've had one success with Pip. You'll have others.'

'I'll never marry again,' she said, 'any more than you will.'

'What he said on Christmas night – my God, children do get down to the bones of things sometimes – I know you didn't think much of it at the time, but I've been thinking about it a lot since I've been out of circulation. It makes you think, you know, being ill. It makes you think of being old and feeble and not able to get along on your own any more.'

'I see,' she said, still holding the plate of cooling steamed plaice. 'You want me to marry you to be a comfort in your old age.'

'Don't mock me. I say things all wrong, I know. Haven't had much practice. Even Jane had to propose to me. But you know what I mean – you and I – it could be worse. We get on fine, we laugh at the same things, enjoy the same things. We wouldn't get in each other's way. You know what I'm like; you wouldn't expect me to be too connubial. You've always said you'd like to live abroad. We could do that.'

'Italy?'

'If you like. We could scrape up some money there somehow. I might even get on with my book.'

'I doubt it.' She paused, and they studied each other's faces for a moment. 'I don't believe you really mean any of this, Dan,' she said, skirting decision. 'It's only because you've been ill and had premonitions of senility, and because you like my son.'

'Don't you want him to have a father?' Daniel asked. 'God knows he needs one. He's terribly spoiled.'

'He's not!'

'You said yourself you thought he was.'

'That's different.'

'He'd be pleased, anyway, if we got married, even if no one else was. Your mother would be furious.' He laughed, enjoying that thought.

'Yes, she would.' Her mother would distrust Daniel because he did not hunt, or even ride. For a long time she had had a square, prosperous fruit farmer lined up for Valerie, who dreaded going to visit her mother, because the fruit farmer would call and they would be left alone in rooms together.

'Dan, I don't know,' she said. 'It might be right. It does seem the answer to a lot of things, but – I don't know. Doesn't it seem awful to be discussing marriage dispassionately like this? Like a couple of French mothers arranging a *mariage de convenance*.'

For that was what it would be if she married Daniel, and with her single experience she could not imagine what a marriage without love would be like. It was difficult enough sometimes with it. Without, what should make two people stick together?

'Dan,' she said. 'You see, I . . .' She wanted to say: 'I don't love you'; but if he felt the same, and had discounted that, it would be silly to bring it up. She did not think he was at all in love with her, but you never knew. Look at Mr Piggott. She had lived with him for six months without knowing. 'I'll think about it,' she said. 'Thanks for the offer.' They smiled at each other like very old friends with a lot of unspoken things understood.

Pip bounced in and said: 'Hullo, you two. How's the romance getting along?' and she left them.

That afternoon she rode on a bus to Oxford Street to buy Philip a new blazer. She had needed to get away from the flat, away from the concentrated atmosphere of sickness and inaction and her own indecision. She had to be alone before she could think straight. Being an only child, she had never understood how anyone thought at all about anything in one of those big family houses where no one ever shuts a door, and each borrows the other's clothes, and there is always a wireless or a gramophone or a child practising some instrument, and always an argument at meals.

It was difficult to think, because she was so tired, but she had got to think wisely. Easy when you were a girl to make your decisions. Either you were in love or you were not. But when you had been married and did not expect to be in love again your decision was complicated by reason. She must do the right thing, because this was probably her last chance. She would never like anyone as much as Daniel.

You could not pray for guidance on top of a 73 bus, with a fat woman trying to oust you off the seat with a black mackintosh shopping bag. If it had been summer she would have gone into the park and let thoughts come to her, which was her experience of the answer to prayer. As it was winter and very cold, she went into Lyons Corner House, which was warm and bright and full of unknown, disinterested people. You could even sit at the same table with them and be alone. It was not done to talk in Lyons. If you only asked for the salt, it might be taken as a liberty. You stretched out a hand and took it for yourself. That was not rude.

Valerie found a place at a table for four and asked for tea. It was only just after three, but already tea was in order. Lunch began before twelve; tea followed hot on its heels, and by half-past five people would be eating roast joint, vegetables, and suet roll. Valerie knew. She had not lived in London on a small income for ten years without knowing and cherishing Lyons as the one single institution whose loss would probably mean more to the city than anything else. Let the Houses of Parliament be bombed, St Paul's gutted by fire, even Buckingham Palace razed to the ground and the lawns and lakes no more than a seed bed for fire-weed, if you could get a cup of tea and a toasted snack at Lyons the end of the world had not come after all.

It was raining outside, and the light was already beginning to go out of the day, but in here the lights were ablaze, mackin-toshes steamed, girls peeled scarves from their heads and shook out their hair, and the band was playing 'Voices of Spring'. At Valerie's table were a young, speechless couple and a worn-out, potato-faced woman who looked as if she had always got up too soon after having her babies. She had cocoa and rolls and butter. The young couple, in a hideous embarrassment which prevented their enjoyment of the food, since they could not talk about it, had tea, baked beans on toast, and trifle with a golf ball of ice-cream. Valerie had tea and biscuits.

The others at the table took no notice of her. She was just a woman in a brown coat and a beret put on at rather a smart angle, having tea and digestive biscuits. She sat and enjoyed the warmth and heard the music with the back of her brain while the front part tried to sort out whether she was disloyal to Philip, whether it was wrong to marry someone you did not love, and why, in fact, she was toying with the idea of marriage at all. Sud-denly looking over her cup between one sip and the next, the answer came to her like one of those revelations you get under gas at the dentist, when you think you have discovered the secrets of the universe, and, coming round, with the galloping in your ears slowing like a run-down machine and the voice of the dentist booming, insistent, you struggle to tell him, but he, the fool, only says: 'Spit here, please.'

This time, however, she did not think she understood; she knew, and it did not escape her, as the gas dreams do with return-ing consciousness. Often before in Lyons she had marvelled at the shy, ill-matched couples and wondered idly how, but not why, they came to choose each other and cling. Now she saw clearly what was between the ugly young man with the cactus forehead and nicotiny forefinger, and the plain girl with hair like a loofah, who had had all her teeth drawn before she was thirty and replaced with long new ones that gave her trouble in eating. Inarticulate, unattractive, they were heading for a life where the girl would become like the beaten woman with the cocoa and rolls and the young man would grow slovenly and a little pompous perhaps with the facile philosophy of the workshop, go collarless and stubbled on a Sunday and be drawn home after work not so much by the thought of his wife and children as by a good hot meal.

They were going to be married. The girl had a small stone on her left hand, and they had too little to say to be only mildly courting. Product of crowded families who only spoke their minds when quarrelling, they wanted each other because they had never before come first with anyone. They mattered to each other, if not by emotion, then by the circumstances of betrothal and marriage. They were not in love. There was no spark between them at all. Valerie, who had been in love, could tell that. When the boy, reaching for the pepper, touched the girl's hand, neither of them noticed it. They needed each other more for comfort than passion. They had found, as they grew forlornly up, that human beings are not strong enough to carry their lives alone, and that neither families nor friends nor even doting mothers can give the secret, saving support that comes only from the mysterious relationship of marriage.

The woman with the cocoa and rolls knew that, she said: 'My old man may give me trouble, but I wouldn't change him,' that was what she meant.

The trifle and ice were finished and the plates scraped. 'Well, what's it to be,' the young man asked the girl. 'Dottie Lamour or Bette Davis?'

'I don't mind, Ron,' she said. 'Let's see which is the shortest queue.'

'Miss!' He snapped his fingers unsuccessfully. He flushed as the waitress turned her back. The girl looked away. She was used to their being embarrassed by waitresses. It did not matter. When they were married they would go home together and be themselves and no one to see. No waitresses to belittle. No women in smart brown berets to stare and criticize. Valerie, realizing how she had been staring, pulled out of her thoughts and also tried to call the waitress.

'It always seems as if they deliberately don't look.' She smiled at the couple opposite. 'Like programme girls.'

'That's right,' the young man mumbled, not looking at her. The girl turned with the air of being a little deaf, making finicky, chewing movements with her mouth. When they got outside, she would ask: 'What she say?'

'I dunno. Something about the Nippies. I don't know,' and they would go off together, secure, two people who had each other, independent of Valerie, not needing her or anyone else. In the cinema they would cling, not so much from a sex urge as from their fundamental need to cling.

All the time while she was buying Philip's blazer, queueing for the bus, fighting on to it, and hanging on the strap, Valerie was warming with tides of relief. The hard-won independence that she had thought she would have to keep all her life – she could let it go. She was not breaking faith with Philip, because this would not be the same. You could marry and be happy without being in love. She needed someone of her own; so did Daniel. It was as simple as that. She smiled in the faces of the people who hung and swayed and read folded bits of the evening paper and tried not to be pushed farther along the bus.

Going in at the front door, she thought that she must go and see Mr Piggott and be nice to him. Oh, the relief it would be not to have paying guests; the relief of not being responsible for earning your living!

She went in to Daniel first. He was lying moodily with his knees drawn up. 'You've been a bloody long time,' he said. 'I've had no tea.'

'I've been getting Pip's blazer,' she said. 'He had to have another. The old one was simply bursting at the seams and –'

'All right, all right,' he said, turning his face to the wall. 'Spare me the domestic details. Get us some tea, there's a good girl.'

Valerie went to the kitchen. Now was not the moment, but it

would keep. The young man with the prickly forehead and the girl with the false teeth had probably waited years before they came to their understanding. She could wait, too.

When Daniel was better and Mr Piggott was better, and Philip had gone back to school – taking his temperature unsuccessfully for a week beforehand – Daniel took Valerie out to celebrate.

'I haven't worn an evening dress for ages,' she had said one day when she had been looking through her clothes. 'Come to think of it, I haven't been out in the evening for ages.'

'You shall go tonight,' said Daniel, grabbed the telephone and bullied the Savoy into keeping him a table.

At the Savoy there were girls who reminded Valerie of herself many years ago. Harmless, amiable girls, conscientiously vivacious to dull men who were paying. Girls who thought this was all of life until they were one day shocked into love and found that this was a part of life you did not need to have. There was a woman friend of Valerie's who said about Daniel in a meaning way, for everyone was always trying to remarry her : 'My dear, who is that man?'

Daniel heard, and they laughed quite a lot about that, keeping the joke going, thinking themselves funnier than they were, for they had a lot to drink. Afterwards they went on to a night club and had quite a lot more to drink and Daniel kept telling Valerie she was beautiful. Although he said it in a rather remote, technical way as if he were painting her, she was pleased. There was no room on the floor to do more than dance in a shifting dream. Valerie, leaning against Daniel, half asleep on her feet in an uncaring haze, imagined that if they were married this was how she would feel about him. When one is rather drunk one cannot imagine what it will feel like to be sober. When one is quite sober, one can remember the emotions of drink; well enough at least to drink oneself back into them if necessary.

Then they went home together. Of course, she remembered in the taxi, this was why she was going to marry him, so as to be able to go home with your head on somebody's chest, instead of propped upright on a corner of the taxi, with yawns flooding your eyes and stiffening your jaw, warding off middle-aged men, or making bright conversation to people you hoped you need never see again.

'I think,' Daniel said, and she could feel it in his chest as he said it, 'you'd better marry me, Val.'

'All right,' she agreed. They said no more until they were home. Daniel was asleep. Valerie was not even thinking. She was not going to have to think for herself any more.

As he put his key in the lock, Daniel said: 'If Mr Piggott is waiting up with cocoa, I'll slay him.' But Mr Piggott had gone to bed hours ago, leaving a note on the hall table. 'Cocoa in a saucepan in kitchen. Mrs Pegg phoned. No message. Will phone you at the office.' Mrs Pegg was a persistent woman who called Daniel Danny Boy, because she said that she had Irish blood.

'That's one person you can cut out of your life from now on,' Valerie said. She stood in the drawing-room by the embers of the fire that Mr Piggott had optimistically made up to be burning for their return, and waited for Daniel to come to her.

When he kissed her, she stood stock still and the world went cold and dead. She was suddenly in despair for Philip.

'Dan!' She pushed him away and looked at him in horror. 'What's happened?'

'I don't know.' They were sober. 'It's all right, darling.' He kissed her again, but her lips and body were frozen. He dropped his arms, and she began to cry, carelessly, like a child, without putting up her hands, not thinking how she looked.

The next day, Daniel said that he was going to find somewhere else to live. 'If I stay here,' he said, 'I'll only start thinking we ought to get married next time I get ill or tight.'

'Yes,' Valerie said. 'I suppose you'd better go.'

'One day, perhaps when we're – what was that Noel Coward line? – "When we're old and tired and the colour has gone out of everything a bit," I might come back.'

'Yes, Dan. Come back one day.'

When he had gone, Valerie began to look for another paying guest. She could not be in the flat alone with Mr Piggott. He had said to her, the day that Daniel had left: 'I say, don't think it cheek, but I do wish you'd call me Alec.'

CHAPTER SEVEN

George

'Ah well,' said George, making no move to get up from the café table, 'this won't buy the baby new clothes.'

'Not if she likes mink, it won't,' said Uncle, who was always one for a joke at any hour of the night. He never seemed to sleep, didn't Uncle. Couldn't afford to with the trade he had, for the Dew Drop Inn was just a nice distance from London for the first cup of tea on the way north, or the last coming south, to keep you going till you had clocked in with the lorry and gone home to breakfast.

'What time you due in then, George?' he asked, catching on to his underlip with his long black front teeth as he reached up to fill the urn from a gallon jug.

'Eightish.'

'You've got a hope in that old crate,' said Fred, sopping a bit of hard pastry in his tea. 'Better get going, mate.'

'Yes, I did,' agreed George. He sat a moment longer to prove he had a will of his own, then got up and went to the counter to pay, yawning and scratching his chest as if he had just got out of bed, which was where he felt he would like to be.

'Better not sleep on the job tonight, son. Might wake up dead,' Uncle said, raking in the coppers. 'See where it says about the Tattoo Slayer?' He swivelled the evening paper across the counter, stabbing a column with his cigarette finger, which was like a stump of charred stick.

George read: *Austin Clay Maverick, who was questioned by the police in connexion with the headless, limbless torso tattooed with the words 'Happy Easter', which was left in a basket outside the back door of the Home Secretary's house, has since disappeared. He is believed to have been seen in a café in the Hatfield district. Maverick is thirty-five, thin, medium height, with black hair, brown skin and very white teeth. 'Like fangs,' said Mrs Nora*

Stringfellow, the proprietress of the café, who served a man answering his description with tea and Swiss roll.

'Coming out this way, you see,' Uncle said. 'I got me bullet-proof waistcoat on.' He slapped his chest, then pretended to double up in a fit of coughing, which was one of his favourite jokes.

'Fangs, eh?' George murmured, finishing the column. The things they had in the papers nowadays! It was like reading about another world, where things happened to people all the time. Nothing ever happened to George in his world.

'Ta-ta, Fred. Good night, Nob. 'Night, Bill.' He called out to people he knew as he left the shack. When you had been doing the Great North Road as long as George, there was always someone you knew at all the stops.

'Ruddy awful night,' answered Bill Nix, who was picking his teeth by the door. 'Inverness, for crying out loud. Mean driving half through Sunday. Good Friday, they call this. Muckin' Bad Friday to me.' He screwed up the side of his nose in a tremendous sniff.

George had started up his lorry and was a good quarter of a mile away from the Dew Drop before he realized that his face was still set in a disapproving expression to match his thoughts. He had not liked Bill making that crack about Good Friday. It wasn't right. That was one of the things that got him about Edie, that she laughed at him about going to church. She wouldn't go herself or make the kids go to Sunday-school, and with George away so much the little blighters hadn't got a chance. One day he'd chuck this lark and start in being a good father to his kids.

As he slowed down for the lights at Bignell's Corner, a man stepped into the road and stood jerking his thumb in the head-lights. The firm forbade their drivers to give lifts, but the lights were red, so George had to stop. The chap came to the near side of the cab and had the neck to open the door and start climbing in.

'Hey!' George began, and then he thought, Oh, what the hell. It must be pretty lousy hanging about on the road, seeing car after car go by. 'O.K.,' he said. 'Hop in quick. The lights are turning.'

'Thanks a lot,' said the chap, who was already in. He sat down with a thankful sigh, putting his case on the floor.

'Thumbing it north?' George asked, as he got into top gear again and settled down to his cruising thirty-five, which he could keep exactly without looking at the clock.

'Got to,' said the other. 'Missed the last train, and I must be there first thing tomorrow. I got a lift to that corner, but the blighter turned off. How far do you go? Anywhere near Northport?'

'Middlesbrough,' George said. 'You could get a train from there.' He did not mind taking him all the way. It kept you awake to have a bit of company, though the chap didn't seem very chatty. After a few trial remarks, George dropped it and drove in silence, until soon after one, he pulled in to the muddy park of Paddy's place, just outside Grantham.

'On me,' he said, as they sat down with tea and cakes, for chaps didn't hitch-hike for pleasure. He never believed those stories about missing trains.

The chap began to protest, but then agreed. Nice smile he had. Quite a nice young fellow all round, but George couldn't think of anything to say to him, so he picked up a morning paper and read some more about the Home Secretary's Easter present.

Miss Ivy Adcock, domestic servant, who opened the basket thinking it was the laundry, is now in hospital suffering from shock. She is twenty-two, and when on holiday last year won the title of Miss Budleigh Salterton.

'Better be shoving,' George said. While he was buying cigarettes at the counter he looked round to see that the chap was reading the bit about Miss Ivy Adcock and laughing. George suddenly noticed that his teeth were very white.

'What's biting you, George?' Paddy asked. 'That old ulcer again?' All the Great North Road knew about George's duodenal.

'No thanks to them cakes of yours if it isn't,' George retorted, pleased at being able to pull himself together quickly. For a moment he had almost told Paddy, but a look at his shiny, cocky face stopped him. Paddy would not believe him. No one would expect someone like George to have found what every policeman in England was looking for. If he was wrong, what a fool he'd look; and if he was right, why should he let that crumby little Irishman into the glory of ringing Whitehall 1212?

'Come on, fella.' He touched his passenger on the shoulder as he went out.

When George's lorry was in low gear, you couldn't hear yourself speak. When they were out on the road in top, the chap said: 'What do you think of the murder? Rather fun. Brightens up the paper, a thing like that.'

There. They always harked back to it. They loved to see themselves in the papers. As the lights of an oncoming car brightened the cab of the lorry, George gave him a sideways look, but there he sat, looking as innocent as you please. He couldn't have done a thing like that and sat there looking like this. George was glad now that he hadn't said anything to Paddy. After all, it stood to reason, not everybody wanting a lift on the Great North Road was a murderer on the run.

The chap began to whistle softly. 'Mighty Like a Rose', it was. George's spine crept, because he remembered a film where Emlyn Williams had whistled that tune in a sinister way when he was going to kill someone. He glanced sideways again. The chap had his lips parted, whistling through his teeth, and in the faint glow from the dashboard they were very white. Not really like fangs, but perhaps this Mrs Stringfellow had been a bit the hysterical type, like Edie. Black hair, brown skin – almost foreign-looking, something like those Wop prisoners. Travelled abroad, no doubt. Sailor perhaps; that would be where he'd learned his tattooing.

'Sweetest little fellah ...' the chap sang softly. Ah, but of course, the radio in Paddy's place had been playing that. That was why he was singing it. He was O.K.

From Newark, on through Doncaster and Knottingley and Tadcaster, George veered between thinking the chap was It and thinking he wasn't. When he thought he was, he felt a thrill of excitement, not fear. Odd that. The chap did not seem frightening, but when you *thought* what he'd *done* ... jointing that corpse as neat as a butcher parcelling out the rations. George was glad to find himself so brave. Each time he decided that the chap was not he felt almost more disappointed than relieved.

Seeing a church clock in Doncaster, his passenger fidgeted and said: 'Doesn't this bucket go any faster? What time do you get to Middlesbrough?'

Ah, in a hurry. You would be, cock, with the CID on your trail and a tattooed torso on your conscience. He was quite the gent, though. He seemed too well-spoken, too well-dressed for a murderer. But then, what about Buck Ruxton, Neville George Clevely Heath, whom George had seen in Madame Tussaud's, that Haigh and the gallstones? Weren't they all well-dressed and nicely-spoken?

But how could a man have done that, not two days ago, and not carry something of it in his face.

'Look out,' the chap said, wincing. 'That was a near one. Why do you look at me instead of the road? Afraid I'm going to bash you over the head?' His laugh sounded natural, but George was not deceived. Not he, not old George Bolton, who was smarter than people gave him credit for. Everyone from Edie down – her brother, the boss, the chaps at the depot, even his kids thought they could put things over on old George, but this time he was going to put one over on them and bring off something that would make them sing a different tune from now on, and put Edie's brother and his two-hundred-pound win on the Pools properly in the shade.

He would draw this chap out now, cunning, get him to give himself away without knowing that George had caught on. Useful later for evidence.

'Smoke?' he suggested.

'What?' The other jumped. 'Sorry, I was asleep.'

Oh, were you, my lad? Foxing, more like. People don't sleep when they're on the run. 'I said, what about a smoke?'

'Sure. Have one of mine.' He put his hand in his pocket, but George got his packet out first. No one was going to catch him with doped cigarettes, though Dick Barton himself had fallen for one only last week.

When they had lit up with the chap's silver lighter, that looked stolen all right, George blew out a cloud of smoke. He couldn't do it through his nostrils, because the doctor had dared him to inhale, but he put on a voice as casual as if he had.

'Going up after a job?'

'Sort of. I've got to go to a holiday camp to do some sketches of happy campers for publicity. My firm handles their advertising.'

Well, it came out glib enough, but it sounded fishy to George. Whoever heard of going nearly three hundred miles to draw pictures of people when you could just as well get snaps?

Going over the bridge at Wetherby, the chap yawned and said: 'Any chance of a cup of tea soon? I feel like death.'

It gave George quite a turn to hear him say that. Harping on the subject. They always did. George was not keen to stop anywhere, for fear that someone else might spot Austin Clay Maverick and rob him of his prize. They had to get juice, however, and when he stopped by the pumps at Meggy's All-night Pull-in, the chap had climbed out of the lorry and was away into the café before George could say 'Give us eight' to Bob, looming sleepily up by his window.

When he went inside, he found that the chap had bought him tea and bangers and mash. Decent of him. George was hungry and he weighed in, but suddenly, between one chew and the next, his jaw stopped working and the next mouthful was arrested on his fork half-way to his mouth.

Bought with dead man's money. As he stared at his plate in horror, the sausages seemed to be dismembered fingers; the mashed potato was brains spilling out of a head; the gravy was rich, sluggish-oozing blood.

He clattered down his knife and fork, pushed the plate away and took out his cigarettes.

'What's up?' the chap asked, eating happily. 'Can't you take it?'

'Sorry,' said George in a jerky voice. 'I don't fancy it just now. It's my ulcer. Chronic.'

'Oh, bad luck. All drivers get them in the end, don't they?'

George did not like to hear him say that. His duodenal was something that made him individual. The chap had said that with an air of knowing a thing or two about medicine. He remembered that the morning papers had said: *The body had apparently been dismembered by someone with an expert knowledge of anatomy.* Medical knowledge. There you were.

'Come on.' He got up. 'Let's get going.' The sooner he turned him in the better. Driving on, he planned what he was going to do. He had got to get to Middlesbrough. That was more important than anything, murderers included, because it meant his job, and with a wife like Edie and three kids bursting out of their clothes like ripe chestnuts you couldn't take chances. He would tell Maverick – he thought of him now as that – that he was driving him to the station, and that was one hell of a joke, because it would be a station, but not one with rails and a ticket office. Tickle Uncle, that would. He would tell it him tomorrow on the way home.

Tomorrow everyone in England would know George's name. From café to café all along the Great North Road the word would pass : 'Old George Bolton. Who'd have thought it? He was here, you know. Here with *him* ! Talk about nerve ... Never so much as wink an eyelid he didn't, though he knew he was riding with a killer. Plucky as they come ... Here he is, boys ! Give him a cheer. Good Old George – what'll it be? This is on the house.'

He saw it all. Back in London the boss would grunt – he wouldn't raise a smile; that would crack his face – 'Good work, Bolton. Proud of you. Like to show our appreciation.' With that and the police reward he might get enough to retire. He and Edie could go to Letchworth garden village. George had driven through it once and never forgotten the clean toy houses with neat gardens, which looked as though the town council had banned dirt and weeds when they banned alcohol.

And Edie – what would she say? She would read about it in the paper before he got home. The whole street would have read it. They might even be decked out in welcome like they were when Mrs Slater's Joe came home after getting his medal at Buckingham Palace. The kids wouldn't be at school Saturday. They might be watching in the street for him. And Edie, she might – there was just a chance she might – run out, too, and jump at him with her arms flung wide and her mouth soft for a kiss, like she used to do once, long ago before they had the kids.

George's thoughts travelled on, faster than the trundling lorry. Maverick was asleep. Good thing. George would try and keep him sleeping until he drew up outside Middlesbrough police station with a squeal of brakes fit to wake the dead, grabbed Maverick in a bear hug while he was still fuddled, and yelled like mad for help. If he woke before and turned suspicious, George would simply drive straight up to the first policeman, shout: 'Get him – he's the tattoo slayer!' and leave the rest to the copper. Any copper would do. As a law-abiding citizen, George had as trusting a faith in them all as in the Almighty.

His mind elsewhere, he drove automatically along the road he knew so well. The tarmac rolled towards and under him like a black ribbon. He steered unthinkingly by the cat's-eye centre markings which were fading now as the night cleared away, taking with it the brightness of his headlamps. He dreamed on into the future. He was at the trial now, giving evidence in his new brown suit. Edie was there, proud of him in a flowered hat instead of the turban scarf she always wore. The barrister shouted some mad mumble that rang in his ears without words, and George knew he was falling asleep. He was broad awake in the split of a moment, and wrenched the lorry back to the left of the road, but soon the dreaded heaviness crept back. He blinked and squinted, shifted his position, gripped the wheel tight and sat stiffly upright, counted all the towns he knew beginning with B, went over the form for the runners of the Two Thousand Guineas, banged the side of his head with his fist. All those things one used to try desperately, driving in convoy during the war, until, like magic, they stopped the column just in time and you were made to get out, cursing, and run up and down in the cold night.

'What's up?' Maverick was awake. Cunning brute. Probably been awake all the time with his eyes shut. 'Why are you knocking yourself about?'

'I had a itch.' Wouldn't do to say you were sleepy, sitting next to a murderer.

'Some itch,' he said, 'that needs all that hammering. Want me to do it for you?'

He would, too, as soon as look at you. All right, cock. Have your little joke. In two hours' time you'll make no more.

It was getting lighter every minute now, and for a moment George had a pang and a sadness to think that, because of him, this man would not see the early-morning sky any more, except through bars. George had seen many dawns, but he never failed to enjoy the moment when all at once it wasn't the ending of night but the beginning of day. It made him feel like a poet, though he could never make words of it. Once he had tried to describe it for Edie. 'You should see it, E,' he had said, and she had snapped back: 'Think I've got so little to do all day I can stay up all night to see the sun come up? There's some as can, no doubt. Thank you very much. Not me.'

To the right the sky was getting that queer colour before it went pink. George jerked his head. 'If you're a painter,' he said, 'how'd you set about getting them colours down now?'

'Well,' said the other, 'I'd have a bash at mixing gr – g –'

Got you now! George could have cried it aloud in triumph. I knew you were no more a painter than my foot. All that fishy talk about advertisements, and now you stammer and flounder about the first mention of a colour.

'I knew then,' he would say in the statement to the police, and the reporters' pencils would go scribble, scribble. 'If you're an artist,' I said to myself, 'I'm a murderer.' Ha, ha, they'd go, with the willing laughter they always give to someone famous.

'Green,' Maverick suddenly said, finishing his sentence. 'That's the dominant colour. Sorry. I always stammer when I'm tired. Chronic. Like your ulcer.'

I'll teach you to make jokes about my ulcer, thought George, making his lips grim. He felt so powerful that he risked pulling in to Mac's at Thirsk for a last cup of tea. Heaven knows when he'd get the next, with all the business there'd be at the police station. Maverick must take him for a mug to go with him into the café so calmly, so sure of being unsuspected. George rolled in his walk. It was too easy. He was as sure of him now as if he had him handcuffed.

He looked at those hands breaking up a roll and thought that they soon would be. Those hands had – ugh! You couldn't bring yourself to think of it. Doing to human flesh what they were doing to the roll. You could always tell with those long fingers, square nails, and knobbly knuckles. That came to George on the spur of the moment, but it seemed so true that he thought he must have read it somewhere. 'I knew at once,' he would tell the reporters, 'when I saw his hands. Killer's hands, I said to myself, I said.'

The radio stopped talking about Shannon, Fastnet, Irish Sea and gave six pips. Seven-o'clock news. Time to get going if they were to make Middlesbrough by eight.

'... Austin Clay Maverick, who disappeared yesterday after being questioned by the police, was found last night at a cinema in Welwyn Garden City and arrested on a charge of murder. Miss Muriel Popham, who was on duty at the cash desk, recognized him when he bought a ticket and telephoned the police.'

'Smart girl,' said Mav – No. George's mind tumbled away from the name as if it was falling downstairs.

'I dunno, lad,' Mac said. ' 'Tis easy. You or I could have done it – or even old George there. You can always spot a murderer.'

CHAPTER EIGHT

Dickie

DICKIE was only properly alive from Easter to October. The rest of the year he was dormant, waiting like a hibernating animal for the opening of the holiday camp to bring him into the sunlight of his best self.

He had been one of the hosts at the Gaydays Holiday Camp for three years. Blue Boys, they were called, because they wore white slacks and bright-blue sweaters, and their job was to go around organizing everybody into having a good time. Dickie, who followed the stars in the Sunday papers, had applied for the job on a propitious day. He thought that must be why he had got it, for he had no particular talents. He was not handsome like Larry, nor a great joker like Barney, a tennis champion like Pete, an acrobat like Johnny, an accordian wizard like Kenny. But he tried very hard at being an all-rounder with a bit of something for everybody. He never relaxed all season or took any extra off-duty, and with his smile that was so broad it seemed to be hooked round his ears he kept to the spirit of the camp as conscientiously as even Captain Gallagher, that stickler for 'Gaydays Atmosphere', could wish. So while other more dilettante Blue Boys came and went, Dickie was back on the job year after year, and campers who had been there before were glad, when they arrived, to be able to shout: 'Hey there, Dickie!' and show off a little to friends who were new to the camp.

When the camp closed in September, and most of the staff said Thank God, Dickie was not happy. He put on ordinary, towny clothes again and went back to his room in Earls Court, hoping, but not expecting, to find it cleaned of the traces of its summer lodger. He lived as long as he could on his summer's earnings, and then, with his money gone and his tan faded, took a Christmas job at the post office, or went as an extra assistant for the shopping rush. After that, if he was lucky, there might be a few days of crowd work in films to keep him going until he could earn his six pounds a week demonstrating something at the Ideal Home Exhibition. With the first buds of spring, his smile began to creep to his ears again, for it was time to get his white slacks cleaned and his jerseys washed and to buy a new pair of shorts and some snappy swimming trunks. When blossom was on the almond trees, he was heading happily for Whitby to be Dickie again to all comers, a successful somebody, a feature of the place, instead of a nonentity struggling to keep afloat among the rest of the unskilled driftwood of London.

In the winter there were only a few people who knew that he existed. In the summer, among eight hundred people he was one of the twelve most popular. Besides the Blue Boys, there were six Green Girls, who wore white skirts and green sweaters with built-in brassières, were beautiful and gay, kind to old ladies and little children and healthily tolerant of anyone who wanted to feel a bit of a dog.

The Girls and Boys had glamour. It went with the job. Dickie, who knew that he had no glamour in winter, put it on with his uniform and was a new man. Although, as Captain Gallagher stressed in monthly pep-talks, the campers must be to them the most important people, the Blue Boys were invested with a golden aura that made them seem important to the campers. They had been deliberately and subtly built up, not so far as to be out of reach, but so that people should feel gratified to discover that these supermen were so breezily friendly that each camper seemed to be the one thing on earth that mattered to a Blue Boy.

On Easter Saturday morning all was well with Dickie's world. After the long limbo of the winter, he was alive again. The camp was full, with no hooligans, or carping snoopers who stood about in groups and hats making no attempt to look anything but Government. All the coloured woodwork was freshly painted, blossom was on the cherry trees between the rows of cabins, Dickie's clothes felt clean and light, and his summer was before him. The sun shone and the sea sparkled, although hardly anyone went in it, with the swimming pool so much handier.

Dickie had been along to the pool to feel the temperature of the water. Some small boys were fooling about on the edge, and Dickie scuffled with them, pretending to push them in and letting them try to push him, bracing himself, delighted with his strength against their insect struggles.

Above their shrieks, Barney called: 'Hi, Dickie! You've got to take a car to the station to meet a bloke – publicity or something.'

'O.K.' Barney had probably been asked to do it himself. People were always shouldering things off on to Dickie, but he did not mind. The small boys clamoured to come, too, and one climbed up his back and clung like a starfish, for children were not in the camp a day before they discovered that they could do what they liked with the Blue Boys.

Dickie could not take them in a staff car because of the insurance, so he gave them sixpence each for ice-cream and went off to the garage.

When the train came in, Dickie stood on the platform prominently, displaying the 'GAYDAYS', which was written in an arc across his chest, like the name of a fisherman's boat. The Green Girls did not have it on their sweaters in case it led to suggestive remarks, for Gaydays camp was, as the slogan tacked up in Captain Gallagher's office put it, 'Clean, healthy, and moral as a family circle'.

A thin, youngish man with untidy dark hair and loose legs dropped out of the train and stood uncertainly, looking at Dickie with some suspicion. Dickie advanced, gave him a hearty handshake and took over his bag, swinging it easily as they walked to the car. He liked the look of him, but then Dickie liked everybody on sight and tolerated even those who palled on further acquaintance.

This Mr Brett had come to do some sketches for publicity. Dickie did not like the tone of voice in which he referred to 'Happy campers', but the man was an artist; that was why he looked a little crumpled.

'Sorry I look a bit scruffy,' Mr Brett said. 'Got involved in a party last night and missed the last train, so I had to jump a lorry to Middlesbrough of all God-awful places. Any hope of a bath at your concentration camp?'

'Oh, sure. Boiling water all day and all night,' said Dickie, as proudly as if he stoked the boilers himself.

After they had checked in and collected the cabin key, they

walked past one of the milk-bar cafés, and Mr Brett peered through the big glass window, which was steamed over from the crowd inside.

'There are people in there drinking something *hot*,' he said. 'It couldn't be coffee?'

'Coffee, tea, chocolate, anything you like. People have snacks all day long here, in spite of the whopping meals. Stimulates the juices, I suppose, to want more. That lot only had breakfast an hour ago.'

'I didn't have any breakfast,' said Mr Brett wistfully, like a child outside a sweetshop.

Inside the air was thick with steam and gabble and the smell of wet clothes, for it had rained that morning and campers always made straight for the tea urns when they got wet or cold. Several people sitting at tables or waiting in the queue at the counter hailed Dickie.

'Hey, hey!' he called back, giving them his catch cry. Each Blue Boy had one of his own, which campers soon learned, and threw back to them in full-throated recognition at every opportunity. Barney always said: 'Watcher'; Larry's was: 'Hullo, folks'; and Kenny, who crooned, which gave him a stake in the States, said: 'Hiya!'

'Hey, hey!' As he passed among the crowd, Dickie slapped men on the back, chucked girls under the chin, winked, laughed knowingly at a couple sitting very close, did Thumbs Up, and the Victory sign – all the little tricks he had learned to do to keep the party gay.

When they were sitting with their coffee, Mr Brett asked, not disparagingly, but with the fascinated disbelief of someone studying pond life: 'Do you have to go on like that all the time?'

'Like what?'

'All that Hey, hey, and –' He winked and jerked his head and went click-click out of the side of his mouth.

'More or less. Keeps things going, you know.' A girl at the next table thought Mr Brett was clicking at her, and pretended to put her nose in the air, but Dickie could see that she was looking sideways down it to see if there was any future. Even when he was talking to someone, he was aware all the time of what the crowd was doing. You had to learn never to be monopolized by one person, since you belonged to everyone. While he talked with Mr Brett of the things he might sketch, people passing by kept greeting him, ruffling his hair, teasing him.

'They like you,' said Mr Brett, still with that air of viewing the wonders of nature.

'Oh well,' Dickie grinned. 'They like to see someone else fooling about. Saves them having to do it themselves.' He thought Mr Brett was a bit superior, but he would soon come round. They always did, even the aldermen's wives, who had arrived in a body and stayed in a body for three solid days until they began to filter about to see what their husbands were up to.

'Watcher!' The door banged open and Barney came in through the café, jokes flying off him in all directions like raindrops from a shaking dog. Everyone laughed, even those who could not hear, for Barney was comic. They knew that as they knew the rising of the sun. Whatever he was saying must be a scream. He stopped by Dickie's table, but did not sit down, for the Boys were not supposed to congregate too much on duty.

Dickie introduced Mr Brett. 'He's up for the week-end to draw some pretty pictures for publicity.'

'Right,' said Barney, 'he can start with me.' He stuck a hand on his chest and struck the pose of a Victorian statesman, for, although Mr Brett was not a camper, Barney could never stop gagging. It came as naturally to him as showing his best profile did to Larry.

Barney was a huge, bear-headed man with a ruddy skin, a chest expansion that could break string, and a laugh, it was said, they could hear on the Dogger Bank on a clear day. He was the most popular of all the Boys, for in spite of his ribaldry he had a healthy, family quality. He could get away with anything, even slightly *risqué* stories, on which he was able to raise a dividend laugh by slapping himself with a noise like a pistol shot for having been so unbridled. Like Dickie, he was a regular Blue Boy, returning year after year. What he did in the winter no one knew. If you asked him, he would say that he was kept by a woman, or went to jail, or played the back legs of the horse in pantomime at Llanfairfechan. Never the same answer twice.

Larry, who was in his second year, had been working for a model agency out of season. Dickie had seen his face in haircream advertisements and illustrations to magazine articles about Love. He did not have to be especially comic or athletic. He just had to be around with his smile and his eyelashes, in and out of the pool all day long when it was warm enough, for he looked his best in swimming trunks. Pete was the one for those who took their games seriously. Everyone wanted to be on his side at hockey, and each week a new tennis racket was presented to the camper who took most games off him in a single. John was popularly known as Spring-heeled Jack. A whirl of colour with his red hair and bright blue jersey, he did acrobatics at the concerts, led flocks of bicyclists round the countryside, and organized romps in the gymnasium when it was wet. Kenny, who was long and Latin, carried his accordion almost permanently strapped round him, like a part of his anatomy, and could be found striking up Old Favourites in any part of the camp. When the bars were full, he would wander through with his teeth agleam, playing 'Black Eyes' and 'Sous les Toits'. It lent a Continental air.

Dickie was the youngest of the Boys, although he was older than he looked. He was not very tall, chunky, bounceable as sorbo, with snub features and fluffy blond hair which he wore ungreased, by order of the management, since he was the ingenuous boyish type. Girls were always falling in love with the Blue Boys on and off during the season. It was always the older ones who fell for Dickie, the plainer, shyer, last-hope ones, and sometimes after they went home they knitted him socks and pullovers. Although he had to go about pretending to be madly susceptible, kissing any girl who won a prize or had a birthday or came in late to lunch, and begging to be held down when he saw a choicely-filled swimming suit, Dickie was not really interested in the seductive campers. He hadn't time, with so many others less seductive claiming him.

He had a real girl-friend once – not a camper, for you were not allowed to have even mild liaisons with them. This was a girl he met at the Ideal Home Exhibition, where she was demonstrating cooking oil. Frying chips all day long, poor kid, with all the biggest queues to cope with, since it was free food. When

Dickie took her out to supper, she could never bear to have anything fried, and turned her head away if he had anything cooked in fat. She was always a little sharp with him, and he persuaded her to come to the camp in the summer, so that she could see him in his glory. She came, and that was the end of it. She did not like him kissing other girls and not being free to spend all the time with her. On the fifth day she talked him into a first-class row in the passage between the bath houses, said that she liked him better when he was selling Nocurl Lino, and left the camp two days before her time was up, although she had paid in advance. Afterwards, Dickie persuaded the accounts department to refund her the money. Barney said he was a craven worm.

The cabins at Gaydays were set in blocks of six, radiating out from the central buildings where the dining-hall and theatre and lounges were. As Dickie led Mr Brett along the concrete paths to B.39, a piercing wind harried them at every gap between the blocks.

'Interesting study for future historians,' Mr Brett said, clenching his teeth. 'Why atomic age man always built his communal pleasure resorts on the bleakest parts of the coast.'

Dickie did not mind a bit of wind. He was used to it, and he was fit. His one real interest during the winter was keeping himself in trim for next summer. He walked at least five miles every day in any weather, circling Battersea Park at great speed, played golf every week-end in Richmond Park, haunted the YMCA gymnasium, and kept his smoking down.

No one could deny, however, that there was seldom a windless day at Gaydays, but Dickie was not going to have anyone calling it bleak. 'Healthiest climate in the world,' he said, quoting the advertisements with conviction. As the next gust came between the cabins, he threw out his chest and breathed deeply. 'Invigorating.'

'Yeah. Like a cold bath.' Mr Brett swore and huddled his coat round him. These office workers. Dickie was sorry for them. Mr Brett had been given a double cabin, with one bunk above the other. He stood in the doorway looking in, like a dog inspecting a new kennel. 'Who sleeps on the top deck?' he asked, with a resigned air of being surprised at nothing now.

'Who would you like?' asked Dickie. 'We aim to please.' He laughed, and a monstrous woman who had been listening from the next cabin laughed, too. She and her husband, in overcoats and hats, were sitting under a string of washing in the porch. Two babies played round them, one wearing nothing but a vest and the other nothing but knickers, and another child staggered about in corduroy leggings, several jerseys and a woollen tam-o'-shanter rising off the top of its head like an ill-fitting kettle lid.

'Hey, hey, Dickie,' the fat woman said, and the children echoed: 'Dickie! Dickie!'

'Going to be our neighbour, dear?' she asked Mr Brett. 'You'll have to get us to show you the ropes. Been here five days, we have, and feel we've been here all our lives, don't we, Tom?' Her husband grunted peacefully. He was enjoying his holiday.

'Only a couple of days, I'm afraid,' Mr Brett said, and Dickie was relieved to find that he was not going to be stuffy with the other campers. He stepped back from his cabin and stood looking at the family with his head on one side, smiling faintly. 'I've got to make a few sketches,' he said: 'and, I say, would you mind if I start on you, just as you are now?'

'Well!' The woman tweaked at the skirt that had ridden up over her thighs when she sat down. 'What do you say, Tom?' Her husband grunted.

'I'll just get my things out.' Mr Brett went into his cabin, and Dickie followed him.

'But look here, Brett,' he said. 'I was going to show you all round the camp – the places you'll want to draw. The pool, the kiddie's playground, the ballroom, the Olde Taverne bar –'

'I'm supposed to do pictures of happy campers,' Brett said. 'This lot'll do for a start.'

'Yes, but I mean –' began Dickie. He knew about publicity. He had not worked in films for nothing. The family next door was hardly the type, but he would not say that. He was already afraid that Brett might be going to laugh at people, not with them. 'I thought you were going to have a bath,' he said.

'Well, I will,' said Brett impatiently, tipping his case upside down on to the lower bunk to get at his sketch block. 'But I want to draw this first while I've got the urge. I don't often get it these days. You go and organize somebody else, there's a good boy. I'll find my way around. I might even find the Olde Whats-it bar. Meet you there for a drink before lunch.'

'Thanks,' Dickie said, 'but I don't. Got to keep fit, you know.' He kept off drink during the season because he knew himself too well, and knew that he would never stop at the two gins and a couple of pints which was the Blue Boys' ration on duty.

Mr Brett took the chair out of his cabin and settled on the other side of the path. Dickie automatically squatted down to the eldest child and asked it what its name was. It goggled, chewing at something which was choking up its mouth.

'What's he eating?' he asked the mother, who was sitting for Mr Brett like a petrified mammoth, only the great black bow on her hat quivering.

'Tassel off his tam,' she answered out of the side of her mouth. 'He will have it, sew it on as I will. Michael's got his tassel again, Tom. Take it away from him.' Her husband grunted peacefully, tipping his hat forward in a holiday attitude, although there was no sun.

'Come on, old chap.' Dickie held out his hand and put on his Uncle Dickie voice. The child gave a woolly yell and retreated, knocking over the baby in the vest, who screamed.

'Oh, go away,' Mr Brett told Dickie. 'You're spoiling the group.'

Before meals, the Blue Boys went through the bars, rounding campers up towards the dining-room, for the waitresses could not cope with mass feeding if people came in late. Dickie found Mr Brett in the Maxime Bar, which was done up in something that looked like red velvet, with can-can dancers painted round the walls.

'Getting on all right?' he asked.

'Fine,' Brett said. 'I've been snooping round. Oh God, this is an incredible place.'

'You're dead right,' said Dickie, choosing to take this in a proud Gaydays spirit. 'Come on, soaks!' He raised his voice. 'Grub up! Come on, let's see some action there. Time gentlemen, please!'

Brett sat with him at one of the staff tables near the door. Every time a girl came in late Dickie had to get up and kiss her, while people called encouragement and rattled knives against glasses, and the girls shrieked, scuffled, and ran. He had to do it with middle-aged women, too, for part of their holiday fun was that they were as carefree as girls again, with no thought for where the meal was coming from or who was going to wash it up.

'Why don't you sit still and get on with your soup?' Brett shouted at him when he sat down after the fifth embrace. You had to shout, with two thousand people eating in here.

'What's this?' said Barney. 'Sedition? Mustn't discourage a keen young chap from his duty. Men have been shot for less than that. O.K., Dickie boy, you can relax now. All the skirts are in. Oh God, my turn for it tonight, and my *dear*, what it does to my *digestion*!' He put one hand behind his head and the other on his waist, affecting the traditional stage pansy voice. People at nearby tables, not hearing the joke, but seeing that he was fooling, told each other what a scream Barney was, and an old lady, who had to laugh every time she thought of how he had teased her at the concert on her first night, nearly choked herself on a piece of suet crust.

Camp announcements were read out at the end of meals, when the fury of knives and forks had abated and tea drinking had set in. It was Dickie's turn at the microphone today. Leaving his pudding, for rhubarb was the only thing about the camp he didn't like, he went to the middle of the room, grasped the stand of the microphone and said into it at the right strength for coming out a yell: 'Hey, hey, campers!'

'Hey, hey, Dickie!' they yelled back at him and his heart glowed. He felt that the whole vast room was with him.

The list of announcements had a few suggestions for jokes pencilled in the margin, for no notice, except the times of Divine Service, was ever read out straight and seriously. Adding a few of his own, Dickie followed up most of the suggestions, for Captain Gallagher liked you to use his jokes. He was listening now from the corner of the room, for, whoever you were at Gaydays, you took your soup, joint, and sweet with the mob. 'The dreams of

Democracy,' said another notice in the Captain's office, 'have here become flesh and blood.'

When Dickie made a pun, or put a whistle in the middle of a word, or made one of the deliberate Spoonerisms suggested in the margin, cries of 'Good old Dickie!' rose at him from all sides like the surge of waves to the shore. At the end he got them all singing the chorus of the camp song, 'Gaydays are playdays for you and for me,' dragging it a little, because they were full of food.

When he went back to his table, Mr Brett, who was frowning as if the noise hurt his head, asked: 'Do you have to do that at every meal?'

'Mm-hm,' said Dickie cheerfully. 'Someone does.'

'Breakfast, too?'

'Mm-hm.'

Brett groaned. 'What time does the bar shut in the afternoon?' he asked.

'Not till three,' Barney said. 'We've got a club licence.'

'Thank God,' said Brett, looking at his watch. 'Please may I get down?'

Although the day-by-day organization of Gaydays Camp was tightly planned and enforced, the Blue Boys were cunning enough to rearrange things among themselves behind Captain Gallagher's back. If Pete, for instance, wanted to sneak a day off to see his girl-friend, the others would cover up for him, taking over his jobs and saying he had 'Just gone down to the other end of the camp' or was 'Here a minute ago', if the Captain was looking for him. If damp weather made Barney's leg disinclined to lead the Boomps-a-Daisy or the Hokey-Cokey round the ballroom, he would swap it for the spelling bee with John, who in turn would swap with Pete, who had a cold, for a netball game on the wind-swept sports field.

Dickie never wanted to unload any of his jobs, but was always happy to take on someone else's. There was not a job in the camp he did not enjoy, except seeing people off at the end of their holiday, and on to him were unloaded all the things that no one else wanted to do. It was always Dickie who had to take the indefatigables for cross-country hikes in the rain, Dickie who conducted the various denominations to their temples of worship in Northport, Dickie who had to organize the Old Folks' whist drive. He did not mind. He liked the older campers, because they were fond of him.

'You ought to be married, dear,' they told him. 'When are you going to find yourself a nice girl?'

He hedged, joking that there was safety in numbers. He had not been interested in any particular girl since the chip-fryer had gone out of his life. He was adept enough at the flirtatious quips and banter which the Blue Boys were required to bandy with the girls at the camp, but he did not want any of them for his own if they expected you to treat them like that all the time. The strain would be too great. Besides, marriage would mean chucking the camp, and that he would never do until it chucked him. How long could one go on being a Blue Boy? Old Charley was only forty when they unfrocked him, but he looked more, and was getting rheumatic, which did not do. A Blue Boy had to bounce. Nora was forty-five, but she did not have a bounce. She was the babies' guardian angel and the kiddies' Auntie Nora. Perhaps when Dickie lost his bounce he could make a niche for himself as Uncle Dickie. His fondness for children was the only thing that might persuade him to marry, if ever he could find a girl who was beautiful without being smart and quick at repartee. It was always Dickie who dressed up as a clown at the children's parties, Dickie who was an unseasonable Father Christmas when there was a present-giving.

It was also always Dickie who had to be pushed into the swimming pool with all his clothes on. This little ceremony took place every Saturday whatever the weather, and those who had seen it before enjoyed it just as much for being flavoured with anticipation instead of surprise. It was the most popular joke in the whole of the camp repertoire, working on the infallible principle of the banana skin or custard pie.

It started after lunch on Saturday with a mass parade round the camp, led by the band. Ronnie Cucciara's band deserved their respectable, restful position in a Torquay hotel during the winter, for they led a chequered career at Gaydays. In the morning, wearing lounge suits, they played light music in the lounge, or, if fine, put on uniforms like commissionaires and played marches in the bandstand. In the afternoon, wearing Tzigane costumes in which they looked as silly as they felt, they played for the tea dance in the ballroom, or, if warm enough, in the outdoor Viennese café, which meant lugging their instruments right across the camp. This was all right for *some*, grumbled the double bass, but he didn't see why he couldn't have several instruments at strategic points, like the pianist. After supper, the band were in the orchestra pit of the theatre in evening dress, and then at last in the ballroom, coming into their own as Ronnie Cucciara's All-star Melody Band, 'bringing it to you hot and strong and sweet to urge your dancing feet', with Ronnie's wife Mara, in a too-youthful chiffon dress, to sing the numbers.

For the Saturday parade through the camp the band were dressed as the Seven Dwarfs, with Mara in a kind of nightgown as Snow White. All the Blue Boys turned out for this. Kenny with his accordion and a string of children trailing him, so that it was a safe bet that at least fifty per cent of the campers would tell each other he looked like the Pied Piper. Johnny doing cart-wheels and flip-flaps, finishing with a handstand on the edge of the pool, bending his legs back and back until everyone thought he *must* fall in, for they knew someone had to; but no, it was not him, and he just flipped himself upright on to dry land again at the last split second of balance.

Larry walking arm in arm with as many girls as could hang on to him. Pete chivvying the stragglers along in the rear. Finally, when everyone was round the pool and the Seven Dwarfs struck up 'I Do Like To Be Beside The Seaside', Barney chasing Dickie up the ladder to the high diving-board, where they struggled together on the edge until Barney said: 'You've had it,' and pushed him off to turn a double somersault twenty feet to the water, while the crowd went mad with joy. One day, Dickie would manage to pull Barney in with him. Then they would go madder still.

The water was icy cold today. As Dickie turned in the air with one fleeting upside-down glimpse of pink gaping faces, he could feel the coldness rushing up to meet him, then – Bang! he was in, and thought his heart had stopped. But when he broke surface again, flinging back his hair, he was grinning and waving and shouting 'Hey, hey!' to the crowd, the centre of attraction in his big moment of the week.

When he swam to the side, showing off his crawl, and climbed out, everyone gathered round him, touching him in surprise to see how wet he was. There were always one or two dear ladies who thought it was cruel and a shame, and he must go straight in for a change and a hot cup of tea.

In hot weather he usually let his clothes dry on him, enjoying the vitality of generating enough heat to evaporate cold and wet. Today, however, he made for his cabin, sneezing.

'Hey, hey!' said a voice calmly, and he turned to see Brett with his sketch-book, grinning. 'Got a swell one of you doing your act,' he said, 'though I doubt if anyone will believe it; and if they do, they'll think this place must be a madhouse.'

'Which it is,' said Dickie happily. 'Let's see.'

'No, get *away*!' cried Brett as if he were a dog. 'Don't drip on it. You're *wet*. I'll show you later – if you're still alive.'

'Never killed me yet.' Dickie felt warm now, and very well. He walked jauntily, knowing that people were looking at him, pointing him out.

'Do you have to do this every week – in this climate?' Brett asked. 'There must be easier ways of earning a living.'

'I don't mind, honestly,' said Dickie. 'Really I quite like it.'

'Who are you kidding?' They parted at the end of the line of staff cabins, and Dickie went whistling away to change and fling his wet clothes at Dillie, who was good to him, and would dry them in one of her private corners where hot pipes ran.

At the concert after supper Brett was in the audience with his sketchbook. Dickie, on the stage in the opening tableau of Blue Boys and Green Girls, hoped that he would be recognizable in some of the pictures. It would be fun in the doldrums of winter to get the publicity book and cheer himself up with his summer self. He would take it to the Ideal Home Exhibition and show it to the boys and girls of whatever stand he was on. He was going to try for the lime-juice stand next year. They had a bar behind the scenes, where they kept gin, to show trade buyers how good the lime juice tasted.

Brett was looking full at him. He must be drawing him. Dickie gave him a big wink. In spite of his still unconverted attitude, Dickie could not help liking him. He felt that he knew him quite well, even just meeting him on and off during this one day. He would win him round yet, if only for the sake of the camp, for what was the good of an advertising man who did not like the product he was boosting?

Les Cowan, the entertainments manager who compèred the show, was tall, thin, and bald, with trenches of surprise across his never-ending forehead. He had two stock tricks. One was to outline himself with his hands in a kind of Mae West figure that wasn't there. The other was to sweep a hand over his shining dome and shake back the illusion of glorious locks. He frequently alluded to himself as a gorgeous beast. He was not very funny, but he was a north-country man, which helped. In winter he toured in pantomime, as a broker's man or an ugly sister, or Tweedledum (or dee), pitting gents against ladies to sing the words of a song on a screen let down from the flies, and making the children shout, 'Hello, Les!' every time he came on to the stage. If they did not shout loudly enough, he went off and came on again with his hat turned back to front. It never failed.

He did that tonight, and the campers, sorry to have disappointed him, greeted his second appearance as the Nazis used to greet Hitler.

The concert was an informal, haphazard show, with laughs as easy to get as water from a tap and the willing unselective applause of a BBC studio audience. The campers were encouraged to perform. The trouble was to stop them. Tonight Mr Reg Barber of Darlington had been trying for five minutes to turn a ping-pong ball into a hard-boiled egg. Every time he whisked away his handkerchief and said 'Oh, darn it!' with a fallen face, the audience clapped hopefully, not sure if that was meant to be the trick.

Reg Barber tried again. He seemed prepared to go on trying all night. Dickie in the wings saw that Brett was asleep with his sketchbook fallen from his knees. The clapping threatened to become ironical. There were cries of 'Wot, no eggs?' and a bunch of youths at the back began to stamp, when the loudspeaker suddenly crackled into the announcement: 'Will Mr Barber of cabin A.43 please go there at once as his children are crying !'

Genuine applause now, for Mr Barber was a sympathetic character again, having children.

'But look here –' he protested, but Les Cowan was saying: 'Come on, Pa,' and hustling him off, handkerchief, ping-pong ball, egg and all, and out through a side door like a popular murderer being sneaked out of the Old Bailey.

'Only way to get him off,' said Les returning, mopping his forehead.

'No wonder he didn't want to go. He hasn't got any kids,' said Nora, who always miraculously knew the life history of all the campers. 'His wife had an operation when she was only twenty-five.'

'Ee,' said Les. 'Poor soul.'

On the stage, the inevitable solemn, wrongly taught child was dancing, hopping backwards as if she had a stone in her shoe, with a basket clutched before her like a bowl held out for free soup. After her, the inevitable man with a troublesome Adam's apple swallowed half of 'Who is Sylvia?' and let the rest out in uncertain baritone bubbles. Loud applause from the third row showed where his family was sitting. Mr Brett woke with a start and seemed surprised to find himself where he was.

Two girls in identical cotton dresses crooned a duet, bothered by their hands. For a while it was questionable whether they were singing the same song, but Kenny at the piano sorted them out, and they finished more or less at the same time, if not in the same key.

A small boy with adenoids recited, his eyes on his mother, who was performing a kind of mime in the front row, so that his prompted gestures did not always synchronize. A pretty girl in shorts did a tap dance, and a young man took his girl on a very slow boat to China indeed. No one minded how bad the concert was. They were here to enjoy themselves and sing any choruses that might be going. Les kept the thing together with patter, the girl in shorts won the prize and was kissed by all the Blue Boys, and everyone was happy.

Dickie found Mr Brett in the bar. 'Better have a drink,' he said, 'after all you've been through.'

'I'm O.K.,' said Dickie. 'I enjoyed it. Wasn't so bad tonight, I thought. The campers liked it, anyway.'

'Mass hypnotism,' said Brett hollowly into the bottom of his glass.

'Bilge,' said Dickie. 'They like it. We wouldn't do it if they didn't. That's the whole principle of the camp. They love it.'

'That's what you keep saying, but really it's you who like making them like what you think they ought to like.' If that meant what Dickie thought it did, he did not want to hear it.

'I must go,' he said. 'Got to do my stuff in the ballroom.'

'Dancing with all the wallflowers, I hope?'

'Of course,' said Dickie. 'That's one of the things we're here for.'

'You're a marvel.' Brett laughed. 'A bit smug at times, but I like you. I wish I had half your enthusiasm.'

Dickie grinned at him. 'Come and dance then. Do you a power of good.' He wanted everyone to be happy.

'When the bar closes I might,' said Brett.

Ronnie Cucciara's band was giving of its best, and the vast painted ballroom, which was the pride of the camp, was a kaleidoscope of coloured lights whirling over the heads of the shifting, shuffling dancers. You saw good dancing at Gaydays, better than Dickie ever saw in London. There were solemn couples, making an art of it with complex steps; lively young ones, laughing at each other; romantic ones, jammed very close, with moony faces; jitterbuggers who had to be curbed by the Blue Boys, for Captain Gallagher black-balled jive.

Dickie was a good dancer himself – all the Boys had to be – but most of the girls he plucked from the walls were not. He pushed them gently round, making jokes for them, blaming the congestion when they missed his steps, and saying: 'Whoops! My fault, lady,' when they fell over his feet. There were comic community dances, and Dickie, doing 'Knees up, Mother Brown' with an energetic matron, whose dress was going under the arms, saw Brett's face as he came in at the door and viewed the hilarity.

'What I can't get over,' he said afterwards, 'is that everyone is *sober*.'

'Well, of course –' began Dickie, but having been called smug once he did not like to expand on the Gaydays spirit. Brett had better meet the Old Man tomorrow and get the benefit of some of his slogans. Dickie was going to introduce him to some girls, but when Ronnie and the boys picked it up sweet and hot again, with Mara in apple-green organdie sobbing into the mike, he saw that Brett had found one for himself. The best-looking girl in the camp, of course, Shirley Ann, who had won the beauty contest last year and been given the job of a Green Girl as part of her prize. She should not be dancing with Brett. She was supposed to be doing for shy men what Dickie was doing for shy girls. When the Paul Jones started, Brett would not let her break away from him to join the ring in the middle of the room, but kept her dancing in a corner while everyone else changed partners.

Shirley Ann came up to Dickie later at the soda fountain and asked him who Brett was. 'He's all right,' she said. 'He's going to get a car tomorrow and take me for a drive.'

'The hell he's not,' said Barney raising his head from a glass of ginger beer with foam on his moustache. 'You're on the job tomorrow. What d'you think this place is anyway – a holiday camp?'

'Oh, darling Barney,' said Shirley Ann in her soft pouting voice, 'you are a hard man.' She stood on tiptoe and kissed the foam off his moustache. Bystanders whistled and cheered, some youths made the sucking noises they were wont to do at the cinema, Barney raised clenched hands above his head in a prize-fighter's victory gesture, and everyone was happy.

At midnight the camp song was followed by 'God Save the King', which Ronnie pitched too high, so that it sounded a little thin after the rousing, roared rhythm of 'Gaydays are Playdays'. The crowd dispersed, and Dickie called hundreds of good nights and responded to hundreds of jokes about not being late in the morning for his Easter egg.

A few children who had escaped bed were collected asleep from corners where they had finally succumbed. Dickie was carrying one away pick-a-back when Brett caught up with him on the brightly lit path where campers were loitering along to their cabins with the lazy, easy air of people going home after a good party.

'When you've parked that,' he said, 'come along to my cell and tell me what you think of the sketches.' He lifted the tangled hair that flopped over Dickie's shoulder.

'Nice-looking child,' he said. 'Girl-friend of yours?'

'She loves me,' Dickie said. 'She woke up to ask me to marry her, only she went to sleep in the middle.'

'What is she – about eight? And you're what – thirty? Queer to think that in ten years' time at a pinch you could.'

It was queer. Ten years would change this little girl so much, but Dickie, with luck, would not be so different at forty. He might even still be here, although he would be on the wane, not in his zenith, as he was now. 'God,' he said, 'I don't want to be forty. Getting older is horrible.'

'Oh, I don't know,' Brett said. 'It helps, I think. You expect less, so you seem to get more.'

When Dickie had left the child and made his way to B.39, he found that Brett had got a bottle of whiskey and was pouring some into two celluloid tooth mugs. 'Oh, come on, smug,' he said, when Dickie began to refuse. 'I pinched one of these mugs for you from an old gentleman's cabin. He'll have to put his teeth in his handkerchief. Don't let him make that sacrifice for nothing.'

Dickie giggled and someone in the next cabin thumped on the thin partition. Brett stuck his tongue out at the wall.

The sketches were good, though slapdash. They were lively and true, but Brett had drawn peculiar, derogatory things. Gaping faces turned to the sky with Dickie rolled up in a ball half-way between the diving-board and the water. The vastness of the woman in the next-door cabin half obliterating her husband beside her. A hungry camper shovelling in food. A chinless youth vacant-eyed over a straw in a bottle of Coca Cola. A child crying at the Punch-and-Judy show. The back view of a skinny, bowlegged man with a plump, knock-kneed girl, both in shorts.

'That one looks like a dirty postcard, doesn't it?' Brett said with some pride.

'It does a bit. I say,' Dickie said uncomfortably, 'these are awfully good and all that, but surely your firm can't use them for advertising?'

'That's their worry. They told me to draw what I saw. This is it.'

The whiskey tasted good, even out of celluloid. Brett filled up the mugs again and Dickie looked in vain round the untidy cabin for somewhere to sit.

'Get up on the top bunk,' Brett said, and Dickie climbed up and stretched out on the blanket, cuddling his whiskey to his chest.

'I'm tired,' he said in surprise.

'I don't wonder.' Brett was sitting on the edge of the lower bunk, leaning forward with his arms on his knees. 'I'd be dead. Never mind. Sunday tomorrow. You can have a lie in.'

'Not me. I have to drive the Papists to church.'

'For crying out loud,' said Brett, peering up at him. 'What kind of a job is this? Don't you ever stop?'

'Not till the winter,' Dickie said. 'Don't want to either. I like it. I told you. I like all of it.' The whiskey was beginning to glow through him, making him feel expansive. Lying up here where Brett could not see him, he felt that he could tell him things. 'It's the winter I don't like,' he said. 'That's the worst part of this job.'

'Why?' The lower bunk creaked as Brett lay down among the litter of his clothes and sketches. 'What do you do then?'

'Nothing much. Nothing I can do, except this. Didn't learn a thing at school, and nothing since. I thought I was going on the stage, so it wouldn't matter. I could dance and sing a bit, and I got a few chorus jobs on tour. Then it was the war, you know. My first real break, the chance to get into a London show, came at the same time as my call-up papers. So there I was. Lots of people the same – chaps who've never learned a thing except that they don't ever want to be a soldier again. You meet us around the studios getting our guinea a day – thirty bob if you've got a suit of tails. We sell you things rather inefficiently at Christmas – can't wrap parcels, you know. There are thousands of us at exhibitions demonstrating things we care sweet damn all about. Last year I sold patent sink traps. Year before I was on Nocurl Lino. That was more fun.'

'Doesn't sound it.' Brett reached up a hand. 'Here, give us your mug. This bottle's got a long way to go yet.'

Dickie had been right about himself. Once he started on whiskey there seemed to be no reason why he should ever stop. He was not worrying, though. He felt delightful. He would go to sleep up here in his clothes maybe.

'What happens,' Brett asked, 'when you sell a sink trap to some-one who's seen you here?'

'Oh, they never recognize you. Different clothes, and hair grease, and you have to put on a treacly kind of voice you'd be slung into the pool for using here. There was a woman once – a bit awkward. I'd sold her a roll of lino, and she turned up here next summer and said in front of a whole crowd of people: "Didn't I see you selling at the Ideal Home?" I had to pass it off as a joke. I said something like: "Any home's ideal when I'm around." You know.'

'Yes, I know,' sighed Brett settling back on the bunk again.

'People laugh when I make jokes here,' Dickie said sadly. 'No-body laughs in the winter. I wish this place was open all the year round. It's a patchwork life – I say, this whiskey's good – that's what it is, a patchwork life. Sometimes I wonder whether I'd be better off with a steady office job, like you.'

'Steady!' From below, Brett thumped the springs which sup-ported Dickie. 'Don't make me laugh. I've never stuck much more than a year at any job yet, except the Army, and that was only because they shut me up in a prison camp. I couldn't desert.'

'But this advertising agency –'

'I'm chucking it after this job. Time I had a change of scene. If you stay in one place too long it begins to own you, instead of you it. Life traps you. You've got to watch it.'

Dickie's trouble had always been that he could never stay as long as he wanted in one place. He felt sorry for Brett. It must be awful to be so restless. 'What'll you do then?' he asked, com-fortable in the thought that he was only at the beginning of his summer.

'Not sure. I don't think I'll go back to London. I'll send the sketches down and they can use them or do the other thing. I'll go abroad, I think. You can't do what you like in this country any more. I might go back to Italy; I was more or less brought up there. I could scrape up a living. There's the fare though. I haven't saved a bean. I'll get a job for a bit up here, teaching or something.'

'Can you teach?'

'No, but they don't find that out for quite a while, and the kids certainly aren't going to let on. They're delighted to find someone who knows less than they do.'

'Takes some nerve, though,' said Dickie. 'I'd never even get the job, let alone keep it. I couldn't bluff like that.'

'What else do you think you do here all day long?'

'This isn't bluff.'

'Oh no? The whole place is one vast, successful spoof.'

'It's not, I tell you. It's real!'

'Real my foot.' The springs of the lower bunk creaked as Brett shifted irritably. 'You talk about your winter life as if that was unreal and this was reality, when really it's the other way round.'

'What do you mean? Look at all these people.' He flung out an arm, although Brett could not see him. 'They're real enough.'

'In ordinary life, yes. Not here. Why do you think they come? Because it's everything their lives are not. Food and drink and cleanness and good temper all laid on without them having to lift a finger. And they can *be* everything they're not, too. Why did those terrible girls sing and that man make a fool of himself with the ping-pong ball? No, I wasn't asleep all the time. This is their escape dream, and you're part of it, my chick. Their real life goes on for the other fifty-one weeks of the year. You're living in a dream world and calling it reality. God, if this is what life is really like give me death. Whiskey?'

'No thanks. Haven't finished this yet,' said Dickie abstractedly. He was worried. 'What's wrong with it here?' he argued. 'People like it. They're happy here.' He raised himself on his elbow and looked over the edge to emphasize what he knew to be true.

'Well naturally.' Brett was over by the basin, trickling a little water into his mug. 'Anyone can be happy in heaven. Cheers.' He raised his mug, then sank on the bed again. 'Happy, happy camper,' he murmured drowsily.

'It's not your idea of heaven, obviously,' Dickie said huffily.

'Never mind. Everyone's heaven is different. That's what the place is – the favourite idea in each person's mind. A kid I knew once said to me – nice boy; I was nearly his stepfather – he said: "I think heaven is a big kind of stableyard with everyone in loose boxes all round, doing just what they like." You ought to get out of your box, Dickie. You're anticipating. There's plenty of time for heaven when you're dead.'

'Who knows? There's the other place,' said Dickie, seeing it as something like a coloured documentary film of a steel foundry.

'Not for you,' Brett said. 'Hell's only an idea in the mind, too. You make it yourself. There's none in yours.'

'Oh, rot,' said Dickie, embarrassed. 'I'm no ruddy saint.'

'I never said you were. The saints had plenty of hell in their minds. They wouldn't have been saints otherwise, because it would all have been too easy.'

Dickie was not feeling so happy now. He took another gulp of whiskey, but his swallow rejected it, like peppery soup. It was bitter in his mouth and he could taste the celluloid mug now that the first sting of the spirit had worn off. 'What do you want me to do?' he asked flatly.

'Lord,' said Brett. 'I don't want you to *do* anything. I'm only talking, not giving advice. I never do that. Everyone's got to run their lives as they want. No good ever came of meddling. People ought to leave each other alone. You want to watch out who you marry, Dickie. They don't grow on every bush – wives who'll leave you alone.'

'Oh, I shan't marry. I could never cope with living up to what girls expect of you.'

'There you are! That's what I meant. They're always trying to change you, to trap you within the limits of their minds, just as this Belsen has trapped you and narrowed your horizons. God, it's worse than working in films.'

'Oh *no*!' cried Dickie, horrified at the comparison. 'Because everyone in films is half out of his mind with worry or jealousy. Everyone here is happy and friendly. It's the Gaydays atmosphere.'

'Don't be wet.'

'But it is!' Dickie sat up and swung his legs over the edge of the bunk.

'I daresay, but one doesn't say such things.'

'You do here.' Dickie put his mug on the shelf. He wished he had not had the whiskey. He had a taste in the mouth and he felt bleak and cold. 'I think I'll go to bed.' He dropped to the floor, stumbled, and turned to look at Brett stretched contentedly on the bed with his mug on his chest and a pipe in his mouth.

'Good night, dream boy,' Brett said.

'You're not allowed to smoke in the cabins,' said Dickie and thumped the notice on the wall. The woman next door banged again and shouted something. Brett laughed, and Dickie went out.

The cold starry air made him feel better. The wind had dropped, the main lights were out, and only here and there a cabin window laid a panel of yellow across the concrete path. The camp was sleeping and quiet, black and white under the moon. Dickie loved to walk round like this when no one else was about. It made him feel like a night nurse, glad with the responsibility of being the only one awake. He warmed with tenderness towards the people behind the cabin walls, tired out after a day that he had helped to make happy. A woman in an overcoat and metal curlers stole from under a porch and made for the doors marked Girls and Boys, and Dickie drew back into the shadow between two cabins until she had passed. Farther on, the watchman going round in gym shoes walked with him for a block, talking of the night, but after that he walked alone.

He went right round the camp that was dearer to him than home, trying to reassure himself with the familiar things: all the places of pleasure, purposeless in the night, waiting for life to flow back into them and the pleasure to go on.

The tennis courts with each net neatly furled – Pete was strict with the groundsmen about these things. The playing field, full on the edge of the sea; the putting course, smooth as baize, the concrete of the roller-skating rink white as ice. The slides and ladders in the children's playground threw skeleton shadows on the pale grass, and in the swimming pool the moon lay on the water like a mirrored face. He sat down on the cold parapet and trailed his fingers in the water. It was warmer now than when he had bowled down to it between the gaping faces, as he would do next week and the week after and the week after that, right through the days of warm water until the autumn chill again.

Unreal? All this an escape dream? If so, what was there real for him?

'... is half past seven and it's Easter Sunday. Good morning, campers, and a very happy Easter to you! The sun is shining, so don't delay, get up and enjoy this lovely fine day!' Dimly through sleep came Ada's voice, breaking the day through the loudspeakers.

Fully awake, Dickie was immediately conscious that something was wrong. Why didn't he feel the happiness that always flowed into him as Ada's voice brought him the promise of another day? Then he remembered. Not real.

He paused while he was shaving to stare at himself in the glass and wonder if it was the face of a fool. He thought of the day before him and wondered whether the things to which he had looked forward yesterday were worthwhile today. If Brett was right and the whole job was not worthwhile after all, what was there to be proud of in having got it and kept it for three years? It was all a second-rater like himself was fit for.

Usually, while the Catholics were in church, he waited outside in the station wagon. Today he sneaked in behind them and slid into a back pew, not following the service, but standing and kneeling and sitting when everyone else did; not knowing how to pray, but putting two shillings in the plate and hoping that miraculously the little bell would tinkle away his troubled thoughts.

He went out before the end in case one of the Catholics should see him there and track him down to convert him, although he had nothing to be converted from, for he had no religion beyond knowing that God existed. His mother had taught him: 'Your religion is in the life you lead,' and 'I would rather say my prayers in an open field,' which saved her the trouble of going to church or saying prayers at all, since there were no fields at Hammersmith except Brook Green, and you would probably be arrested if you knelt down there.

Breakfast had started when they returned, and when he went into the roar and clatter of the dining-room and saw the women in their bright dresses and the men with their shirts open-necked, the collar thrown over the jacket, sure enough, he was happy again. Dickie wished he had put five shillings into the plate instead of two.

The people who greeted him as he passed among the tables were real enough. They were eating bacon and eggs and they were happy. Everything was all right, as it had always been. He wished that it was his turn to announce, so that he could hear the affectionate roar of 'Hey, hey, Dickie!' and be completely reassured.

Kenny, in the middle of the room, waited for the cry of 'Hiya, Kenny!' to subside, and then with the slight American accent that he affected over the microphone read out the list of birthdays and wedding anniversaries and made the people stand up, chewing, to be cheered red in the face and have their hands shaken by everyone within reach. Most popular of all was the announcement: 'And now, campers, I want you to meet a very lovely little lady and a handsome young man, who are, yes, a little bird told me they are – wait for it – on their HONEYMOON!'

It seemed that the ceiling and floor must fly apart at the shriek of delighted voices and the stamping of feet. 'Stand up, Mr and Mrs Davies – Peggy and Stan to you, folks. Stand up and let's give you a big hullo!'

They had to obey, looking anywhere but at each other, a shining boy with crimpy hair and a girl with the wrong colour lipstick, biting most of it off in her embarrassment. Kenny went along to kiss her, putting up his hands in pretence that the young man was going to attack him. Whistles and catcalls came from all over the room, and the children cheered as if they knew what it was all about. It was quite indecent really, yet somehow perfectly proper.

Dickie was enjoying it, until Brett, who was sitting at the next table, tipped back his chair to talk over his shoulder. 'You see. Just what I said. Not true. That kind of thing can't really happen at breakfast. It's all just a dream. Pinch yourself and everything will be all right.'

'Oh shut up,' said Dickie. 'They love it. Can't you see?'

'You make them love doing what's unnatural. It's genius, but is it right? It reminds me too much of youth rallies in the dictator states. Hitler would have been quite capable of holding a Jugend Versammlung at breakfast-time.'

Dickie went about his morning's duties uncertainly, with his grin assumed like a false moustache and dropped again when no one was looking, trying not to see everything he did through Brett's eyes. He despised himself for being influenced by him, yet he could not help it. The man had shaken him. He wasn't right, of course, but he had seen more of the world than Dickie. Could he be right, and was Dickie only daydreaming here, wasting his time on a thing that, in the phrase the camp had used last year, long after London had finished with it, couldn't matter less?

He had signed his yearly contract. He must stay now for the full season, but if he could not shake off these misgivings how on earth could he get through the summer? And if he decided that it was not worth coming back next year, *what* could he do? It was unthinkable. He had nothing in the winter. If his summers were to be taken from him, too, there would be no purpose in his life at all. He could not remember whether anyone had ever thrown himself under a train at Earls Court. If one could make one's mark on the world no other way, it would be something to make station history with the last act of one's life.

Going into the Olde Taverne before lunch, he found Brett with a pink gin in his hand, although beer was the drink there, typically talking to the barman instead of fraternizing with the tankard-holders. That was the trouble. If only he would take more part in the life of the camp, find out how people felt instead of just how they looked, he might think differently.

Dickie suddenly had an idea. He ran a hand through his fluffy hair and grinned his first spontaneous grin that day. 'Hang on a minute,' he called to Brett. 'I'll be right back.'

When he ran back from Captain Gallagher's office, the bounce was in his feet again. 'Brett, old man,' he said, 'I want you to do something for me.'

'Sure. Buy you a drink? One of these? It's mostly water.'

'No thanks. I wouldn't mind a ginger ale, but that's not what I meant. Look, Brett. You're an artist. I thought it would be fun if you judged the beauty competition this afternoon.'

'You thought wrong, chicken. Nothing would induce me.'

'You must. I've told the Old Man you would. He's got it down on the list for announcing at lunch. He's tickled to death.'

'Then he's as silly as you are. I'm leaving by the two-ten. Going to York to do a bit of sight-seeing.'

'Who's silly now?' cried Dickie with glee. 'That's the weekday train. The Sunday one's not till four.'

Brett groaned. 'Why did I never learn how to use a timetable? O.K. I'll do it. Lord, you're getting me as organized as the rest. Don't tell me I'm getting the Gaydays spirit. I'd shoot myself. I'd better have another of these, Fred.' He gave his glass to the barman. 'Cheerio,' he said gloomily when it came back. 'Happy camping.'

The beauty contest was held in the theatre. It was as much a show for the campers as a serious competition. The important thing was to get as many girls as possible up on to the stage, no matter what they looked like, just so long as they were girls.

The Blue Boys ranged among the audience, pouncing on anyone presentable. Some were keen and had come all ready in swim suits under their dresses, like people who leave their music in the hall. Others were not so keen and had to be dragged, pushed, or even carried on to the stage to make up the numbers. When there were still not enough girls giggling and eyeing each other at the side of the stage, the Blue Boys ranged again, hunting down any woman under forty who had the right number of arms and legs and features in more or less the right place.

Les Cowan stood at the microphone, keeping the patter going, enticing the girls with the prospect of a free week in London for the finals between all the winners at the end of the season. 'There's a smasher!' he would cry, pointing to a shrinking girl in the audience, and the Boys would descend on her like hounds on a carted stag. Dickie, eager to do his best on any occasion, made it a point of honour with himself to produce more girls than anyone else. He desperately wanted the show to be a success today, with Brett sitting in judgement not only over the girls but, it seemed to Dickie, over the whole camp and even over Dickie himself.

When the other Boys had given up, Dickie was still arguing with a lint-haired girl with pale startled eyes and a queer hunched figure, who sat gripping her chair, shaking her head, while the people all round urged her to go with Dickie.

'Now we've got the girls,' said Les, 'all we need is the judge. So, campers, let me introduce you to the gentleman who has sportingly agreed to agitate – beg pardon – arbitrate between this lot of lovelies. Smashers, though, aren't they, eh?' he appealed to the audience, who responded.

'Ladies and gentlemen, that celebrated artist, Mr' – he glanced at the paper –'Mr Daniel Brett, who has been up here making sketches of you lucky campers, so don't be surprised if you find yourselves in the Academy.' Laughter, during which Brett, looking rather hunted, walked on to the stage with his hands in his pockets and sat down at the table trying to look as if he was not there.

'Half a mo'!' Dickie was still struggling with the lint-haired girl.

'Go on, Lil,' her mother said. 'They're all waiting for you.'

'Yes, go on, Lily,' said her father. 'They can't eat you.'

'Go *on*, Lil,' said her much prettier schoolgirl sister, who was too young to enter the contest, but knew she could have won it. 'You are a drip.'

The Blue Boys were on the stage lining up the girls and pinning numbers onto them, which involved a certain amount of scuffle and giggle, and Barney having to slap his own hand frequently and chide it as if it were a dog.

'Come on, Dickie!' Les shouted. 'Last orders, please. Bring 'em back alive!' Dickie picked up the girl and carried her, kicking and muttering and thumping him in the chest, up the steps to the stage, where he deposited her right side up and retired panting but triumphant. The girl stood there scowling with her toes turned in, Barney pinned a number on her green blouse, chucked her under her lowered chin, and sent her off parading round the stage after the others.

Most of them, especially the tall girls, and the ones who regretted having worn swim suits now that they found themselves exposed to public view, walked badly, with bent knees and caved-in chests. Dickie's Lily stooped worse than any of them, and he saw with a pang that she had a very slight hunchback. Never mind. The audience applauded every girl and she would get her powder compact for having been in the competition, and probably live in the memory of her brief glory for weeks to come, and let Brett call that a daydream if he liked. It was, and a good one.

In turn, the girls came singly before Brett, who frowned, blinked, bit his pencil, and scratched his head with it, getting no help from the audience, who applauded each girl impartially and hooted at every swim suit, as if they could not see hundreds any day round the swimming pool. The Boys and Girls watched from the side of the stage, Shirley Ann a little blasé, as one who had been through this and triumphed. Barney was trying to lay bets, unsuccessfully, for there was a dark girl who would obviously win on face and a blonde who would obviously be second on figure. The others were nice girls, but no oil paintings, and were only made to revolve in front of Brett to spin the thing out until it was time for the Easter-egg hunt.

When it was Lily's turn, she came forward like Mimi going to the guillotine in the third act of *The Only Way*. Having flashed one terrified look at Brett, she dropped her angora eyes and stood looking down at her feet, her light hair sticking out from her head, hands held straight down the sides of her tight brown skirt. She wore no stockings, and from where he stood Dickie could see her legs trembling with nervousness. Brett had a faraway look, as if he had already decided on the winner. Still, he might have given the girl a break. Dickie felt responsible for her, and wished he had not made her come on to the stage with that back.

He smiled at her when she came to the side, but she would not look at him. She would not look at anyone, and stood apart while the other girls jostled together, waiting for the marks to be counted, talking to each other over-affably and pretending they did not care.

Kenny played 'She's My Lovely' on the accordion. The girls were lined along the back of the stage, still pretending not to care; Barney prepared to lead forward the dark, juicy-lipped girl; Les stood sideways to the microphone and whispered tensely into it: 'And the winning number is –'

'F-fourteen,' said Brett, stammering a little. For a moment no one could see who it was, then Les, with the furrow in his brow as deep as the Grand Canyon, said: 'Fifteen, is it?' Because fourteen was Lily's number.

'Fourteen,' said Brett belligerently, got up and left the stage.

There was nothing for it. The audience, though startled, broke into applause, and Les had to lead Lily forward, her pale eyes staring in unbelief, her jaw slightly dropped at the shock of it. The other girls were furious, and drifted off the stage, muttering. Les said all the usual things about lovely little ladies, and hoped, creakingly, that she would win the finals, while Lily stood stumpily beside him with her queer colouring, and her hands still hanging straight by her skirt.

Dickie tracked Brett to his cabin, where he found him cleaning his teeth as if he had just been through a distasteful experience.

'Why did you do it?' Dickie asked. 'Why did you choose her? You've made a farce of the whole thing.'

Brett rinsed his mouth, spat and wiped his toothbrush on a towel. 'I was sorry for her,' he said.

'You!' Dickie held on to the sides of the door, blocking the light. 'I thought you were a mizzo-whatnot.'

'I am, in the mass,' Brett said. 'Not individually. Get out of the light. I want to pack.'

'But look here,' said Dickie, 'if you're going to choose just any girl you're sorry for what's the point of the competition?'

'Don't ask me. I asked myself that hours ago, and got no answer. It's your fault anyway. You shouldn't have dragged the wretched girl on to the stage.'

'Are you trying to teach me my job?' asked Dickie, who was cross and confused. The competition had gone wrong, and nothing ever went wrong at Gaydays. His own plans had gone wrong. Brett had turned them upside down.

'Not your job,' Brett said. 'Just the most elementary psychology.'

'It's yours that's wrong. How do you think that girl is going to like being made to look a fool at the finals?'

'Well, it's your fault,' Brett repeated. 'You shouldn't have asked me to judge.'

'I wish to God I hadn't. I believe you did this on purpose to be awkward, to spoil the competition and upset the atmosphere of the camp.'

'Yes,' grinned Brett, and before Dickie could decide whether he meant this seriously one of the camp messengers came running by, saw Dickie and skidded to a stop with a squeak of his rubber soles. 'Dickie! Quick!' he panted, as if the Furies were after him. 'The Old Man wants you. He wants you now. Quick!' he repeated, although Dickie barely hesitated a moment, for when Captain Gallagher summoned you, you had to go at the double, as if you were a Dartmouth cadet.

Dickie entered the office jauntily, trying to look innocent, but his grin faded when he saw the Captain's face. It had that liverish, putty colour which boded ill. He was not sitting safely behind his desk, but standing up by one of the big charts on the wall, tapping a ruler into the palm of his left hand, like a schoolmistress waiting before the blackboard to cane the boy who had flipped the blotting-paper pellet.

'Well, Dickie,' he said in a clipped, consciously Service voice, 'you've done it this time.'

'*Me*, sir?' Dickie feigned surprise. 'I haven't done anything.'

'Oh, I see. It wasn't you, I suppose, who urged me to let That Man judge the beauty contest. Oh no! Couldn't have been you.' His sarcasm was stodgy as an ill-cooked pudding. It lay on the air like indigestion, and the Captain left it there and tried something else. 'Yes, Dickie,' he said sorrowfully, 'I was there, watching from the gallery. You must have known he couldn't be trusted. That was light of you, Dickie. You can't *be* flippant about your job, you know. It matters.'

Dickie could not frame words. He stood vaguely to attention and stared at a notice by the electric light switch, which said: 'A Penny Saved Is A Penny Gained. Switch me OFF.'

The Captain flung down the ruler and sat at the desk, drawing a sheet of paper towards him and making earnest pencil marks on it as if he were planning an exercise for the Home Fleet. 'What you've got to *do*,' he said, emphasizing his words with jabs of his pencil, 'is to think up some excuse to get the girl out of the finals.'

'Oh, I can't, sir –' But Captain Gallagher pointed his pencil over his shoulder to a notice which said: 'Can is a shorter word than Can't. Use it.'

'It would be more cruel to let her go on with it,' he said. 'And what would the London judges think? We have a reputation to keep up. Everything at Gaydays, including the campers, is the *best*. See what you can do, will you, there's a good chap?' This last was said with a deceptive geniality which meant, Dickie knew, Or else.

He went away down the concrete paths, unable to react properly to campers who hailed him, or small boys who tweaked his jersey as they ran by. He was bent on finding Brett, for he knew he could not tackle Lily. Brett must do it. He had made everything wrong for Dickie; now he must put it all right.

'Looking for your friend?' asked the fat woman in the next cabin as Dickie rattled at the locked door of B.39. 'He's gone, dear, didn't you know? Packed his traps, said good-bye to us, given the kids a bar of chocolate, kind as you like, and gone.'

'Hey, hey, Dickie!' A pigtailed girl came along with her mouth full of sweets. 'Why aren't you on the Easter-egg hunt? It's super fun. I've found six.' Dickie smiled at her and walked on, barely noticing that she was clinging to his arm, trying to match her steps to his.

So it was over. He couldn't say anything to Lily; he knew that. So he would have to go. 'The job matters,' the Captain had said, and oh God, didn't he know now just how much, faced with the idea of losing it! The seeds of doubt that Brett had sown were blown away long before they could germinate. Brett was a fool, trying to pose as a cynic because he did not know what Dickie knew. This place was important. It was necessary to his life. But too late. The very thing that had proved to him where his treasure lay was taking it away from him.

'Not that way, Dickie. Come *on*!' The little girl tugged at the sleeve of his blue jersey, and looking down, he saw it no longer as a part of himself, but just as a garment, the kind of things that other people wore, and were bright to see.

'Come on?' he said vaguely. 'Where to?' But there was no going anywhere, for round the corner, like an overblown cabbage in a dark-green overcoat with flapping pockets, came Lily's mother, and blocked their path.

'Aha!' she cried. 'I've been looking for you. What's all this I hear?' Whatever she had heard, Dickie did not want to discuss it. He would rather not know that she existed.

'Well, you see ...' He stood drawing his foot along a crack in the concrete while the pigtailed girl pulled steadily at his left arm, trying to get him moving again. 'Well, you see ...'

'Oh yes, I see all right,' boomed Lily's mother, as if she were part of the camp's loudspeaker system. 'All too clearly do I see. Two-piece bathing-costume indeed! If you think Dad and I are going to let Lily parade herself in London in a brazier and pants, well, you've got another think coming.'

'You mean you'll not let her go for the final?' Dickie lifted his head. The grin glowing all over his face, he could feel the muscles lifting of their own accord, and the small girl nearly fell over as he yielded suddenly to her pull.

'Come on!' he shouted and raced her down the path, feet hardly touching the ground, pigtails flying out like whips. He did not know where he was going. He just wanted to race round the camp as if he had been away and was coming home. He did not care where they went, but the small girl did. As she pulled him into the café, someone greeted him: 'Hullo, smiler!' Others called to him: 'Hey, hey, Dickie! Come and sit here, Dickie! What's new, Dickie? Look, there's Dickie.'

'Hey, hey!' he called, as the child dragged him towards the ice-cream bar, and he couldn't have stopped grinning if he had wanted to. Everything was going to be all right. Everyone was happy, and it was only the beginning of his summer.

CHAPTER NINE

Pamela

WHEN Pamela was at the High School, each term had a personality of its own: a flavour, a smell, a colour in the mind's eye; but now, at Rosemount, the whole school year was like wet sand.

At the High School the winter term was brown with the smell of October bonfires in a corner of the hockey field, and the fog in your throat as you pounded up and down on the left wing. It was dark when you went home to tea, most people wore two pairs of knickers and you were allowed to wear a jersey instead of the uniform blouse under your tunic. The spring term was the green buds in botany classes, which you put in jars by the windows to see whose came out first. Your lacrosse stick smelled of linseed oil, nobody came or left and the term was over almost as soon as it began. Summer was the white of umpires' coats and bowling screens and the grey-green smell of mowings behind the scorer's table, and chlorine and rubber bathing caps and the hollow echoes of Miss Ringer's voice, challenging you to try the high board. Blue poplin dresses and chewing grass in outdoor history lessons and finding with dismay that the endless halcyon days had suddenly accelerated into a fever of exams.

But at Rosemount, which was called on the prospectus 'a Co-educational Progressive Community', the terms were all the same, because there was no hockey, no cricket, no lacrosse, no change of uniform to mark the season, for you wore what you liked when you liked, exams were called intelligence tests and held spasmodically according to Peter's whim, and if you wanted to take Matric or School Certificate you had to get extra coaching in the holidays. The terms all smelled of boiling rice and Alice's carnation scent, and differed only in that the summer term was the worst because it was the longest.

It stretched before Pamela like eternity. Going north in the train, she thought it typical of the upside-downness of life that the higher up England you went the lower fell your heart.

It was a terribly long journey, so your heart had a long way to fall. Long and dull, and the book that Estelle had given her had become unreadable even before Hitchin. Pamela had known it would, but had not liked to say so, for it was all about modern ballet, and Estelle was very keen for her to know about that. It was boring in a train by yourself. Looking out of the window was fun for a while, but what was the point of seeing a man fall off a bicycle, or a street decorated with flags if there was no one in the carriage to whom you could turn back and tell about it?

Next door eight girls were going up together to another boarding school. Whenever the train stopped, you could hear their talk and laughter through the partition, and the man in Pamela's carriage, who looked like a monkey himself, said to his wife: 'Like a cage of monkeys.'

At stations the girls all crammed their heads out of the window to shriek at the one who had dashed out to try and buy chocolate or cakes or magazines. When Pamela went down the corridor at lunch-time she saw that they all had sandwiches and oranges and bottles of lemonade. She would have liked to picnic with them like that, but she was a rich man's daughter now and must go along and eat grilled halibut and rhubarb tart among the elderly people in the dining car.

The girls next door reminded her of the High School. They all wore dark-green tunics and blazers with a crest and hard round hats with bands that matched their green-and-white-striped ties. Pamela wore a grey flannel coat and skirt copied from one of Estelle's and a grey beret with a real gold clip that Eric had given her last birthday, when she had wished desperately for riding lessons. In her suitcases were some new cotton dresses that Pamela thought much loo long, but Estelle said that fourteen was not too young to start being fashionable. Look at the Americans, she said. Pamela was tired of looking at the Americans. Estelle turned her eyes Westward all the time, but Pamela couldn't see what was wrong with England.

It was quite nice being able to wear slacks or shorts or anything you liked at Rosemount, but all the same, there was something about a uniform. It gave you a safe feeling to put on the same things in the same order every day, and to mark Sunday with your own clothes. There was nothing to mark Sunday from the rest of the week at Rosemount, except chicken for lunch, and the few cranks who went defiantly to church. Pamela would have liked to go, for the sake of clinging to old custom, but she did not dare, because they thought her queer enough as it was. Peter made jokes about clergymen, and didn't approve of morning prayers or grace before meals, like there had always been at the High School.

At York, the eight girls spilled out on to the platform, dropping books and cricket bats, and were set upon by other girls in the same uniform who had been farther down the train. They made such a chattering crowd on the platform that passengers and porters had to steer round them, until a red-faced open-air-looking woman came up in a hard green felt hat and a blazer and started to bully them into collecting their luggage.

'Oh, Miss *Feeny*,' they clamoured. 'Oh please, Miss Feeny!' and Pamela wished that it were her Miss Feeny, too. At Rosemount no one bullied you into doing anything. If you had luggage, you must look after it yourself or lose it. That was Independence. There were no Miss Feenys, for everyone, even the Head, was called by their Christian name. That was Equality. No teachers really, for they were called Helpers, which was Encouragement; and if they cursed you, you were entitled to curse them back. That was Liberty of the Subject.

Pamela had to change at York, to take the branch line to her country station. There was no one she knew on the second train, for you were allowed to trickle up to Rosemount when you liked within the first two or three days of term. She was not disappointed, for she did not like any of the others very much, except Linda, who had got TB from not changing her wet clothes and would not be coming back this term or probably ever again.

Pamela took a taxi from the station to the school, which was a spectacular red house with gables and towers and unreasonable windows, on a windy hill above a huddled stone village. She paid the driver without feeling grand, for she was quite used to taxis by now. She left her trunk for Jock to bring in when he had finished with the cows and went along to Peter's room. Although he was the Head, you were allowed to go in there whenever you liked, without knocking. It made Pamela laugh when she remembered the trembling line in clean blouses waiting outside the headmistress's study at the High School. She had only been in that study three times in her life. Once when she came, in tears of fright; once when she was rude to the French mistress, in tears of shame; and once when she left, in tears of real distress. Everyone was always in and out of Peter's room, for it had french windows and was a short cut to the garden.

When Pamela went in, he was on the floor, cutting out curtains.

'Hullo,' she said. 'I'm back.'

'Who's that?' He looked up. He was a lean grey man with a face like a wolf and huge spectacles shaped like an eye-bath, with half-inch-thick horn-rims. 'Oh, hullo, Pam. Had a good Easter? Christ is risen, and all that?' That was the kind of joke he made. After a while you just paid no attention.

'Yes, all right, thank you. I've got that book you wanted. Estelle – my mother – got it from America for you.'

'Oh great, great. Thanks most tremendously.' When he smiled, his teeth were long and narrow and even and looked false, although they were not, or the school would have known it. They knew all the intimate personal details of the staff.

'Come and look at this,' he said, crawling about among the bright cretonne. 'Don't you think it's rather exquisite? Angles, you see, to counteract the bulges of that extraordinarily ugly bow window. How anyone in their senses could have perpetrated a monstrosity like that – but typical of the whole house, don't you see. Polypi and pustules breaking out all over it like a Rowlands print.'

Pamela sighed and shifted her weight to the other foot. This was one of his favourite themes – the faults of the old house and the iniquities of the family who had lived in it for hundreds of years. She thought the old red house was lovely, and the legends of the Torrin family, which she had found in a book under the stairs, fascinated her, but she did not say so. Rosemount had taught her one thing, anyway. She had dropped so many bricks in her first term that she had learned now to hold her tongue among alien minds. She never said what she thought.

When Peter held up the bizarre cretonne, draping it against himself as if he were a fashion model, Pamela said: 'Yes, it's wonderful. How bright of you to have found it. Oh look – there's Babette!' She hopped over the bunches of material and jumped down the three steps into the garden, glad of an excuse to get away, for she never liked being alone in a room with Peter. It made her feel somehow like seeing snakes in the reptile house at the zoo; wanting to draw back, your spine shuddery a bit, although you knew they could do you no harm.

'Three more bloody months,' Babette greeted her gloomily, kicking at a drooping peony, although she did not particularly dislike Rosemount. She did not like any school. She had been expelled from three and refused by two before she was taken in here. She would not be expelled from Rosemount. No one ever was. You could never do anything bad enough.

They walked together to Lady Torrin's summer-house, a little filigree retreat among the rhododendrons, in which she used to receive her soldier lover, while the old earl they had made her marry lay crippled in his bed, calling for her. Pamela knew. She had read it in the book, but she would not tell the others, least of all Babette, because they would turn it all into sex. You could not be romantic at Rosemount, for there was an explanation for everything. Sometimes at breakfast Peter made all his 'friends', as he called the children, tell him their dreams of the night before. Then they would all have a long discussion about what the dreams meant, sitting on and on at the table, forgetting about classes, until it was almost lunchtime, and old Pearl, who tolerated anything that Peter did because he had once saved her from the consequences of infanticide by a petition to the Home Office, simply swept a few crumbs on to the floor and laid the places round them.

The others all loved to discuss their dreams, but when it was Pamela's turn she always said: 'I didn't have any.'

'You wouldn't,' they scoffed. 'Your subconscious is atrophied.' But she would not tell them about the flying horse that came to her window and took her away to where Bucephalus and the Tetrarch and Brown Jack grazed on pastures wet with stars; and about the time she heard moaning in a ditch and it was the Queen knocked down by a lorry, and Pamela saved her life and lived ever after at Buckingham Palace, 'like one of the family'.

'I didn't dream,' she would say. Her dreams were the treasure that gave life its only value. She wasn't going to have them pulled to pieces and scattered on the table like sham jewels for everyone to despise.

They sat in the summer-house and ate chocolate. Babette said her father was on the black market in sweets. Whether or not this was true, she had an unlimited supply, which she kept in a locked drawer, for things of value were not safe at Rosemount.

'D'you know what?' Babette asked, while Pamela was sitting trying to feel like Lady Torrin waiting for her captain to come shouldering through the rain-wet rhododendrons.

'No, what?' She hoped it was a secret. Secrets were exiting, but you were not supposed to have any at Rosemount. The contents of everyone's mind must be as free to the community as a convent wardrobe. That was Sharing.

'Old Gabriel's sick,' Babette said. 'We've got a new stooge. Male, I'm glad to say.'

'What's he like?'

'Wet, I expect. They always are, especially the floating ones.'

'He couldn't be worse than what we've got already,' said Pamela. 'Perhaps he'll be nice.'

'Oh, don't be so naïve,' said Babette, getting up to leave her. 'How could he be? He *teaches*!'

If only he would! If only someone would come here from whom she could learn, someone she could admire. A mistress for preference. At the High School she had had crushes on elder girls and mistresses like everyone else. Here, the Helpers were not remote enough to be hero-worshipped. You could not have a crush on someone who called you a stinking little twerp, or took your hair grips without asking, or wandered about the corridor cleaning his teeth, with his braces hanging down. You might have a 'Thing' about someone. Most of the elder boys and girls had it about each other, and Selina had one about Peter, but that was different. Pamela knew. Estelle had told her the facts of life long before she wanted to hear them. She took her to all the most unsuitable plays and films and explained the mystifying parts in forthright detail, although Pam would much rather have gone to see a Western, or *Where the Rainbow Ends.*

Her foster-mother and father – Estelle and Eric as she had to call them – were very kind. Pamela was conscious that it was generous of them to have adopted her, for there was nothing special about her. She was not even pretty, with her straight black hair and solid face, so she tried her best to please them and to do what they wanted. She had never known her real parents, who had been killed in a skidding car soon after she was born. She knew only that they had not been married. Estelle, with her passion for honest statement, had thought it her duty to tell Pamela this, and, having made quite an important thing of it, then tried to explain that it didn't matter at all.

Pamela had been brought up by an aunt, who had died when she was at the High School, and the aunt's rich, childless friends had taken over Pamela, body and soul and even name. They might have had a name like anyone else, but no, they had to be called Ruelle. Pamela Ruelle. She hated the sound of it. Before the year was up, just when she might have been captain of Under Thirteen cricket, and was in the middle of a crush on Miss Parkins, they had to remove her to Rosemount. After that, they talked of sending her to a college on the Isle of Skye, where you learned how to coordinate your body with the elements. It meant health for the rest of your life.

Eric and Estelle were homoeopaths, so Pamela had to be, too. They did not hold with things like magnesia and syrup of figs and Friar's balsam, on which she had been reared, but gave her drops of colourless liquid or tiny white pills which did not even give you the illusion of doing good. Pamela suspected that although the pills came out of differently labelled bottles they were all the same. Once when she was in a homoeopathic hospital with a broken ankle the night nurse had told her that they had special pills made only of sugar and milk which they gave to people who made a fuss, and they slept, thinking they had been given a power-ful drug. Pamela had to stuff her face in the pillow when she heard the dying-duck woman in the next bed say to the nurse: 'You must drug me again tonight – heavily,' and then sleep like a log on her harmless sugar pills; which proved, Estelle said in her 'explaining' voice, when Pamela told her the story on visitors' day, 'that illness comes from yourself and can only be cured by yourself.'

'What about my broken ankle? Being kicked by that milk pony was nothing to do with me.'

'It might have been a subconscious wish to hurt yourself that made you go near the pony at all,' Estelle said. 'That's what Freud believed. When his children got hurt he used to say : "Why did you do that?" '

'How infuriating,' Pamela said, snuggling her chin under the sheet and glad that, although she had odd ideas, Estelle was better looking than any of the other visitors.

'I don't think so,' Estelle said, drawing on her gloves as the bell rang. 'Most interesting.'

At Rosemount you could take homoeopathic medicines, or none if you liked. There was no matron to hand out pills and cough syrup, and if you cut yourself you went to the cupboard in Peter's bathroom and found some strapping among his talcs and toilet waters. Bobby Manning, who was a diabetic, had to do all the syringe business himself, unless he felt generous and let someone else have a go at stabbing him in the arm or leg. You could put yourself on any peculiar diet you fancied, and no one but the vegetarians ate their cabbage.

You could do anything you liked at Rosemount, it seemed, except learn anything useful. Pamela wanted so much to learn, so that she could have a job and be independent in the world. Eric and Estelle were very kind, and her home with them was so beautiful that she hardly dared to go in without taking off her shoes. She could manage with them for now, but she must be able to get away and change her name and earn her own living as soon as she was grown up.

At Rosemount, the Helpers and the twenty-odd children had their meals together at a long table down the middle of what had once been the dining hall of the Torrins. There were no places. You just grabbed a seat anywhere as you came in. That was the way it was. No privileges were necessary because there were no restrictions, and the staff must not be put before the children, because that would retard progress. Pamela was willing to be progressive if she must, if that was what Eric and Estelle wanted, but she would have preferred meals to be like at the High School, with the staff talking soberly and eating genteelly at the top table on their own. She did not like having to eat with the Helpers, for Kathryn always had a drop on the end of her nose, even in summer; Humphrey's Adam's apple looked as if it were perpetually trying to swallow a lump of gristle, even when it was mince, and Alice's scent overpowered everything, even curry. Alice and Humphrey were married. At least, Pamela thought they must be, whatever the others said, for only married people went in the bathroom together.

There was nothing about the new Helper to put you off your food. Pamela thought he looked quite nice, but he would probably turn out to be just as bad as the others in the end.

'Looks a pretty good wet,' said Mervyn, who was next to her. 'Daniel, his ghastly name is. Well, he's come to the lion's den all right. Haw, Haw.' He laughed the coarse, exaggerated guffaw which the boys had picked up from the lads of the village and used at all times.

The first thing Pamela noticed about the new Helper was his look of horror when he saw the *hors-d'œuvre*. It was one of Mrs Harvey's Vitamin C days, and she had arranged on the dish every available kind of raw vegetable, shredded coarsely, with a few tired old prunes in the middle.

You were allowed to criticize the food at Rosemount. Peter did it himself. 'What's this?' he demanded, picking out one of the prunes with his long fingers, which always looked cold. 'The by-product of a gasworks?'

Brian, who was top boy this term, which didn't mean much except having a room to himself and being allowed to ride Humphrey's motor-cycle, flicked a bit of bread at him. 'That's a pretty corny joke, Peter,' he said.

'Well, make a better one. You're all so ruddy dull. The new member of our little community will think us a sadly-lacking lot and wish himself back in the gay metropolis.' Peter often talked like this, in a kind of quoting voice, to show that the clichés were deliberate.

'D'you come from London?' Babette asked Daniel. 'Why on

earth d'you want to come all the way up to this God-forsaken hole?'

'Oh well, you know.' The new Helper eased his tie and stammered a little. 'If you want to teach, you've got to go where the job is.'

'You haven't come here to *teach*? I say, what a scream.' Babette appealed to everyone to giggle at him. 'You can't teach here, because we never listen.'

'We'll see about that,' said Daniel a little grimly, jerking back his head as plates of cauliflower cheese began to pass down the table under his nose.

Peter stopped serving it out to shoot him a look through the thick-lensed glasses that hid the expression of his eyes. The new man must not get bossy with his friends; that was not the idea. 'You'll be surprised, I daresay, by our freedom from rules here. The children make their own. A self-governing community, you might say.' He gave his wolfish grin, lifting his lip from his long teeth without moving the rest of his face.

'What are the rules then?' asked Daniel.

'None,' said Babette. 'Haw, haw, funny joke.'

'Pass the potatoes, dear,' said Alice. 'Humphrey wants some.'

'Why the heck doesn't he ask for them himself then?' retorted Babette, not passing the dish. 'I knew he was dumb but not about food.'

'Mind your own business, and pass the potatoes, if there's any left after they've been down your end.'

While they were wrangling, Peter was telling the new Helper: 'We have made a lifelong study of the fundamental motives of original child-nature, don't you see. On that we base our system, which I beg leave to say is the finest in this God-awful country. No is a word that has fallen into desuetude here. If you don't forbid them to do wrong, they will do no wrong, because they don't know what it is. Look at Adam and Eve. Everything in the garden would have been lovely if they hadn't been *told* not to eat the apple. Not that I believe in the Old Testament, mind. I am merely illustrating my thesis for your enlightenment. Now cads, who wants some more of this muck?' He swashed the ladle around in the cauliflower dish.

The studio at Rosemount was a converted barn a little way away from the house. It was used for dances and had a radio-gramophone, which was played all the time during art lessons. It was blaring away, and Mervyn and Wanda were doing a Samba among the easels when Daniel came in for his first class. 'Shut off that ruddy noise!' he shouted. He was learning fast how to talk to his pupils.

'Let's make it a dancing lesson instead,' Wanda pleaded, jigging up to him and raising her left hand to his shoulder.

He brushed her off. 'You've come here to draw, and draw you damn well will. Now get on those chairs, everybody, and pick the easels up and let's see what we're going to do.'

Gabriel always let them draw what they wanted. He insisted on it, in fact. They must paint to express themselves. 'It doesn't matter if it doesn't look like anything,' he said. 'Draw the inside of your brain.'

So they splashed on blocks of mad colour and explosions of zigzag lines, and women with two heads, and men like playing cards with eyes in the wrong place. You could paint on the walls if you wanted to, or draw caricatures of the Helpers. That was Observation.

Pamela always wanted to draw neat little pictures of cape gooseberries, or kingcups in a green glazed vase, with the reflection of the window highlighted in squares on the bulge. But when she drew flowers that looked like flowers, Gabriel ran his hand through what there was of his hair and said: 'What do you think this is – a botany class?'

'I've been told I can let you draw what I like,' Daniel said.

'What *we* like,' they corrected him, lolling. John Birch was sharpening pencils with a Japanese dagger with which he was making great play this term, even eating his meals with it and using it on onions in the cookery class.

'We'll start with the human form not so divine,' Daniel said. 'One of you sit out here. You – girl with the red hair – come on.' He put Eileen on a chair in the middle of the room and arranged her arms and legs, which she rearranged as soon as his back was turned.

'Now you others get on and draw her. Draw, I said,' as Mervyn began to flourish a brush. 'No colour until I see how you can use your pencils.'

While they began, with sighings and groans, he went to look out of the window where the grassland dropped downhill to the village among oak trees stunted by wind and pulled at odd angles by the slope. Pamela liked the view, but Gabriel would never let them paint it. He said it was bucolic, and made them look out of the other window and paint the slagheaps instead.

Perhaps Daniel would let her paint the rolling green view. He seemed to like it, and dragged himself away reluctantly to walk round the room and quell the scufflings that were breaking out as people got bored with drawing Eileen.

'Good God,' he said, as he looked at the drawings. 'What is all this – spirit drawing? None of them are anything like.' He picked up Mamie's drawing, tried it upside down, turned it round again and said: 'Ghastly.'

'Well, it's how I see her,' said Mamie, who fancied her art, and was going to design materials for her mother's shop.

'If that's how she looks, God help her,' said Daniel, and Eileen stuck her tongue out at him.

'We're always allowed to draw how we like,' said Mamie smugly. 'You mustn't repress us.'

'It's just a waste of my time,' he said, flinching at what he picked up from Mervyn's easel. 'You could scribble that nonsense in the playroom.'

'Ah, but we haven't got a playroom, and it isn't nonsense. It's the expression of our inner selves, Daniel.'

'If that's the expression of yours,' he said, tossing the paper back to Mervyn, 'I don't want to know it – and don't call me Daniel. I've never been a schoolmaster before, but my impression is that I should be called Mr Brett, or even Sir.'

'Oh no, not here, Daniel,' they chorused.

When Daniel came to Pamela's sketch, which had a head, two arms, two legs, buttons down the dress, and was just possibly recognizable as Eileen, he said: 'Ah now, this is better. Here's something sane at last.'

'Oh, her,' Mamie said scornfully. 'She doesn't count. She's

203

not been here very long. She hasn't progressed as far as us.'

'Anyway,' said Babette, 'she's wet.'

'I'm not!' Pamela picked up a ruler and fell on her. She had progressed far enough anyway to fight in class. Most of the others joined in, and Daniel wandered over to the gramophone and began to look through the records.

'Oh, look,' he said, 'if you're going to scrap, you might as well go and do it somewhere else. What time is this class supposed to end?'

'We go when we like,' they said.

'Well, you can go when I like today. Scram.'

When the others went out, Pamela was left behind snivelling in a corner. Someone had hacked her on her weak ankle and it still hurt too much to walk, so Daniel said: 'Sit down and finish your drawing. It's not bad, you know. Those others – ye gods! How old *are* those dead-end kids?'

'About fourteen or fifteen, this class. Babette's sixteen, but she's backward.'

'Hardly the word I'd have used.'

'They say I'm retarded,' Pamela told him, limping over to her easel, 'because I still like playing games. But I can't see the point of being grown up too soon, can you? After all, you've got to be it all the rest of your life.'

'Too true.'

Pamela was surprised to find she could say such things to him. The other Helpers would have told her to get wise to herself, or given her a little lecture on infantilism.

Daniel played the gramophone and wandered round looking at the pictures on the walls, while Pamela put shading into her drawing of Eileen. She was quite pleased with it. At the High School, when her cape gooseberries were successful, she used to take them home for Aunt Winnie to hang in her bedroom, but Estelle would not want Eileen on the candy-striped walls of her bedroom, which had just one picture that Pamela thought must be the wrong way up.

Presently Daniel said: 'Don't you want to go?'

'Not particularly. It's not Sociology till after lunch, and there's nothing to do. We're supposed to fill in our own time between classes. I wish we had them all the time. I get so bored. When we do have classes or lectures, you can't hear, even if it was worth hearing, because the others make such a row, or get the Helper sidetracked into some discussion about sex or something.'

'Not in my classes they won't,' Daniel said. 'I'm going to bring a new régime to this reformatory.'

'Oh do, Daniel. I'm sorry, would you like me to call you Mr Brett?'

Feeling much happier, she went away to strum on the piano in Peter's Room, until he told her for God's sake if she didn't know anything else but the Jolly Farmer to go and drown herself. She banged down the piano lid and went into the garden, where some of the younger ones were having secrets under the weeping birch and would not let her in. She didn't mind. She felt happy. She believed she was going to have a crush on the new Helper.

She was, and it made all the difference to her. Life now had some purpose. Having crushes on people kept you very busy, for you had to scoot about all day trying to see them as often as possible. Her life revolved round Daniel's. In the morning she dressed quickly and hung about outside his room until she heard him drop his shoes on the floor – one, two – which meant he was going to put them on. When he came out, she would be casually sauntering by and they would walk to breakfast together. If he had been late getting up, Pamela was in a fever, in case there might not be two seats left next to each other. If she could sit by Daniel and pass him things, it was a propitious day and she knew that she would see him often, and he would talk to her and perhaps ask her to run an errand, having learned already that it was a waste of breath to ask any of the others.

She dogged his movements all day, not following him about, but always managing to turn up at strategic places; and when he walked down to the village through the park Pamela would sit on the terrace wall and watch him appear and disappear among the trees. It was worth waiting about for a glimpse of him coming back, although she would get down from the wall before he could see her, for she was terrified of annoying him. If he was cross with her, she was suicidal. If he was nice, she burst out of her skin with happiness. She did not know how to contain herself, and people asked her why she was going about with that silly grin on, and had she been to Peter's drink cupboard?

Every word that Daniel said to her was printed on her brain, to be gone over and over in bed at night. Sudden sights of him made her breath catch and her heart hammer, and his day off was as flat and forlorn as the third act of the Chekhov play they were rehearsing. It was a real, slap-up crush all right. Just as good as the one she had had on Miss Parkins.

The summer term footled itself away, and Peter bought a set of ribbons and bells and instituted morris dancing on the lawn. He tried to make Daniel teach it, and quarrelled with him when he refused. Selina, who was in Peter's room mending his socks, heard it all and reported to the others some of the things Daniel had said about the school.

'You could be sued for saying things like that,' Brian said. 'I admire the man's mastery of language though, if he really put all those words you said into one sentence.'

'He's shockingly reactionary,' Mamie said. 'I can't think why he came here.'

'That's what Peter said,' Selina told her, 'and Daniel said he was a snooper from the education authorities and had come here to bust this place wide open.'

'Haw, haw,' went the boys, but Eileen, who lacked thyroid and always took things literally, said: 'I say though, suppose he were? He'd spoil everything.'

'Of course he's not,' Pamela said. 'I think it's mean of you to suspect him.' They looked at her slyly, and Bobby whistled 'Love Is The Sweetest Thing'.

'We all know what you think, O foolish virgin,' Brian said. 'Thank God you're growing up at last.' She did not know what he meant. Getting up, she parted the curtains of the weeping birch and left them, for it was time to go and offer to help Mrs Harvey with the vegetables, so that she could be in the kitchen when Daniel came in for his coffee.

In July there were fewer and fewer lectures, because everyone had to help with the haymaking. Even Peter, who had recently discovered Outdoors, toiled in the heat in a yellow shirt and orange linen trousers, his peeling nose reddening like a slowly boiling lobster, his spectacles perpetually misting up with sweat. John Birch was working on an invention to fit them with little windscreen wipers, although Peter, who was a man of brief enthusiasms, would have given up working in the sun long before it was finished.

Pamela, whose new cotton dresses were still in her trunk, wore an old shrunken gingham, and got Selina to cut her hair very short with Kathryn's cutting-out shears. She worked as near as she could to Daniel, standing with him on top of the stack, raking the next row to his, or riding on top of the cart when he was leading away, so that she could watch him from above. He wore khaki shorts and a white shirt and his skin was browner than anyone else's and his hair blue-black in the sun. She thought he looked very romantic.

When the rain came they retired to the house again and got on each other's nerves. It soaked down for three days and no one would go to the studio because it meant a dash through the wet. Peter revised the curriculum to keep them quiet with more lectures, because he was trying to finish his novel, which was called *I and Not I*, and took place entirely in the mind of a schizophrenic postman.

Kathryn gave some talks on ballet, which she called bal-lée, and Humphrey intoned in his usual half-hearted way about modern music, illustrated by a gramophone which he always forgot to wind until it ran down with a groan. Alice, who had once done two years' medical training, gave some snappy little talks on the reproductive system, which Pamela could not understand, and Daniel organized a Brains Trust, which would have been quite fun if only people would stick to the point and keep off insults. Daniel was question master, which meant sitting at the middle of the table smoking and saying: 'Shut up, boy,' or: 'One at a time, girl.'

'Why don't you call us by our names?' someone asked. 'You're damn rude.'

'Can't be bothered to learn 'em,' he said. 'I shan't be here much longer, thank the Lord. Now shut up and let's get on with the next question. "Why does a woman –" er – no, I think we'll skip that one. Which of you scum sent that in? O.K. I know the writing. I'll deal with you later. Here's a better one: "If you were a Russian and came to England –"'

Pamela was sitting in a daze of shock. She had never thought about Daniel not being here any more. It had been bad enough before; it would be impossible without him. He was the sun and moon and the only thing that made the days go round at all.

'Pam.' He was speaking to her. 'Pam, wake up and answer this question. What's the matter with you?'

'You upset her,' Mervyn said calmly from across the table where he had been watching her, 'with your talk of going. Can't you see? How blind men are. . . .' He hummed an airy tune and studied his finger-nails. Daniel appeared not to have heard him.

When the lunch bell rang he went out, and the others clattered their chairs back or on to the floor. Someone blocked Pamela's way before she could get to the door.

She was surrounded by sniggers. 'Pam's got a Thing about Da-niel!' they chanted. 'Ain't love grand?'

'I'm not surprised,' Babette said. 'He's got something. I might take an interest myself if I wasn't elsewhere involved.' She put her arm through Brian's.

'Good old Pam,' Mervyn said. 'Sex rearing its ugly head at last. You look out, kid. He's the kind who likes 'em young.'

'Has he kissed you yet? Oh bliss, girls!' cried Wanda and pretended to fall into a swoon.

Pamela did not go to lunch. When she got away from the others, she ran through the rain to Lady Torrin's summer-house and wept. It was all spoiled. No one understood. Her glad, exalted crush was turned to Rosemount smut. Babette and her Brian – as if it was anything like that!

Or was it? Was it true what Mervyn had said, and her feeling for Daniel no more than the manifestations of adolescence about which she had heard so much? She hated herself. Her body was growing a shape and she didn't want that. She wanted to stay a skimpy child always, never to have to grow up and get married. Everything was spoiled, and the romance of the summer-house was spoiled, too. Pamela had vaguely imagined that what Lady Torrin felt as she waited for her captain was the same innocent delight that Pamela felt when she waited to catch Daniel coming round the corner of the house to the studio. But if love was only what those others made of it, then Lady Torrin's romance was only the sniggering she sometimes heard behind the cubicle curtains in the dormitory. There was only one pure affection, and that was hers for Daniel. She knew what it was, but no one else did, and they had wrecked, defiled, and stamped on it.

She went out of the summer-house. Pushing through the polished rhododendron leaves, she nearly died of fright, as a voice said in her ear: 'Whither dost thou wander, my pretty?' It was Peter, lurking like the wolf in Red Riding Hood.

'Oh – oh, hullo,' Pam said shakily and ducked under a branch to go on, but he caught her arm and held it behind her so that she had to turn round to untwist it.

'I was just going to the wigwam for five minutes' peace,' he said. 'Come, you shall share it with me.' He drew her towards the summer-house, but Pam hung back.

'No – if you don't mind,' she said. 'I want to go back to the house.'

'But I do mind. I want to recite poetry, and it's no fun doing it to oneself.' As she still pulled away, he put his hand on her other bare arm, not holding it, but stroking the skin, and now he was not holding the other any more but stroking that, too, while Pamela stood petrified as a rabbit before his intent look.

'Why,' he said in a funny purring voice she had not heard him use before. 'My little schoolgirl's getting quite grown up. Your flesh has the soft exciting promise of a woman's. Come here, my dear. . . .' He bent his head and she smelled his breath and the first cold touch of his glasses galvanized her into a wild shriek as she pushed him into the bushes and fled, with his chuckle following her through the clattering wet leaves.

Her instinct was to destroy. She wanted to beat his brains out against a wall, as she had seen Brian kill a rabbit. Without thinking, she ran through the french windows into his room, swept all the papers off his desk, pulled out the drawers and scattered what was in them, like a naughty child revenging itself in its mother's bedroom. She found the manuscript of his book and stood stock still, with the package in her arms, calmed to deliberation.

Just what she wanted. *I and Not I*, his precious novel that was to shake the world. Gleefully Pamela threw it into the grate and set light to one corner, striking match after match to make the thick pages burn. When it was only a charred mess with little shreds flying off it round the room she dusted off her hands and pranced out, feeling as if she had taken a dose.

Pamela Ruelle was in trouble. It was epoch-making. Just like a real school. There was no proper punishment, however; that was against the system. She was just completely set aside. She had been odd man out before; now she was a pariah.

No one spoke to her, except Daniel, who said that he personally thought it was a good thing she had burned the book, for Peter would never have the guts to write it again, and there would be that much less paper wasted, and the world be spared that much tripe.

After a tortured lunch, when people had talked round and across her and just looked through her when she asked for bread, Daniel found her crying in the summer-house. He sat beside her and patted her shoulder awkwardly.

'I hate this place,' she sobbed. 'I don't *want* to belong to it, but, oh, Daniel, isn't it awful when everyone's against you !'

'I'm not,' he said. 'I've got a fellow feeling. I was a misfit, too, at school. I was slung out of Eton, you know.'

Interest checked a sob. She looked up. 'Lucky you,' she said through the only handkerchief that Kathryn had not pinched. 'You couldn't be slung out of here.'

'You could for what I did, I bet.'

'What did you do?'

'Something like you, only mine was real arson. I set fire to a housemaster's car.'

'Daniel, you didn't !'

'I did. I dropped a match in the petrol tank. It burned like all-get-out.'

'Why did you?'

'Because I hated him – and life in general. I was half crazy that term for want of someone to talk to. I wasn't any good at anything and, being me, couldn't bear being a nonentity. The masters, I believe, had been told to go easy on me because I was bereaved, so I didn't even have the distinction of being cursed. I was passed over, forgotten at the back of the class, stuck in the deep field in the third cricket game which no one bothered to umpire, lost at the end of a stone corridor in one of the little cold cells which opened off it like the snuggeries in a family vault. I *had* to call attention to myself. I thought they'd send me to prison, but they didn't. Just sacked me. First time a Brett's ever been sacked from Eton, don't you know. Still, it got me to Italy. That saved my life, though the family thought it was my downfall.'

'Why?'

'Oh – I went properly wrong after that, and ended up as you see me now. But anyway, I enjoyed seeing that car burn to scrap metal in Founder's Yard more than anything else at Eton. I'd like to burn another some time.'

'Let me help,' said Pamela eagerly. 'Let's burn Humphrey's motor-bike. They might sack us both.'

'I'm going anyway,' he said, 'as soon as I've got my money. Back to Italy. I'm going to get me a room above a café and live on aubergines and figs and Orvieto Secco and not ever do a stroke of work.'

'Let me come, too. I like figs. It's the only part of the food I like here.'

'What would you live on? I couldn't support you.' He stretched out his legs and leaned against the wall with his hands behind his head. 'You haven't got any money, have you?'

'Estelle has. She's got a diamond bracelet worth two thousand pounds. I could steal that.'

'I say,' he said, 'you are getting progressive. Quite the Rosemount spirit.'

'Don't say that,' Pamela said fiercely, 'even in fun. If I thought I was getting like them here I'd die.'

'Poor old soul.' He smiled at her. 'You do hate it, don't you?'

'I loathe it,' she said solemnly, 'with my heart and soul, I swear.' She licked her finger and drew it across her throat from ear to ear. 'That's what we used to do at the High School. I wish I was back there. Daniel,' she said suddenly, and the simplicity of the idea stunned her, 'let's run away!'

'Oh, we can't,' he said lazily.

'Why not? They always do in school books, why not in real life?'

'Where to, though?' he asked, leaning forward.

'Well, you'd be all right. You're grown up. I could go home. To Estelle and Eric I mean. They couldn't send me back if once I'd run away. Peter wouldn't have me.'

'He would. He'd call it an extravasation of the freedom syndrome and love you all the better for it.'

'I'd tell them what he did. Then they couldn't send me back.'

'What did he do?'

'Here, it was.' She told him about it.

'God!' he said. 'You poor kid! Of course you can't stay here. Why didn't you tell me before? I'd have damaged more than his book for him.'

'Oh, I couldn't. It made me feel awful. I didn't think I'd ever tell anyone. I'd hate to tell Estelle, because she'd analyse it, but you could tell them for me. You would, wouldn't you? Make them send me back to the High School?'

'Oh don't, Pam,' he said. 'Don't get me involved. You've got me wrong. I don't go round being a benefactor.'

'You could start now,' she said happily. She believed that he would do it. It was going to be the biggest adventure of her life, and when it was over she would write a book about it. She bounced on the plank seat, thumping his knee with her fists. 'Oh, come on, Danny! Let's make plans. It's going to be terrific.'

'Danny ...' he said. 'I haven't been called that for years.' He looked at her with his eyes half shut, as if he were trying to blur her into someone else. 'When I was married,' he said, 'my wife wanted us to have a son, because she thought that was what I wanted. But really I wanted a daughter. You can't talk to boys, because they're as tied up as you are. And they get to despise you. Girls will put up with you when you're senile because you bring out their maternal instincts. But whoever heard of a son feeling paternal about his father?'

Pamela wished that he would hurry and not talk about irrelevant things. There was so much to do, for they must go today, now, while the idea was still hot in their brains.

He opened his eyes again, yawned and stretched himself, looking at his watch. 'Oh well,' he said, 'if we're going, we'd better step on it. There's a train in an hour.'

They were both so tired when they got to London that they could not decide what to do. Pamela wanted Daniel to take her with him to a hotel. She was too tired to face Estelle and Eric tonight.

'They'll know,' she said. 'Peter will have rung up and told them. He may even have followed us.' She had had this prickling in her spine ever since they stole out of the coalhouse door at Rosemount. She looked over her shoulder and up into the black vaults of the station roof, shivering, dizzy with fatigue, seeing things that were not there.

'Don't be an ass,' Daniel said. 'How could he?'

'In a plane or something. He'll pounce.' She could feel his cold fingers on her arm.

'Rot,' said Daniel. 'Home for you, and bed. It isn't a hotel anyway, where I'm going, just a lousy kind of boarding house. I couldn't take you there.'

She was afraid he wanted to be rid of her. Often on the journey down he had said: 'I need a drink.' It must be wonderful to be a grown-up and be able to have a drink and suddenly feel much better about life.

'Not home, Danny,' she begged, standing looking up at him, while people pushed and jostled round them. 'There'll be so much talk.' Oh how Estelle loved to talk about things! 'Not tonight. Tomorrow.'

'Tonight,' he said, picking up her bag. 'Let's get a taxi.'

'No, a bus. It's slower.' She trotted by him as in a dream. She had a horrible feeling, like being drawn powerless towards some suffocating terror in a nightmare, that when she got home Peter would be there, grinning like a werewolf on the brocade sofa.

Half-way across the main road outside the station they had to wait on an island for a gap in the buses and cars. Under the flat green light their faces looked as though they were dead. Still with that prickling in her spine, Pamela looked back and saw, stepping towards her off the pavement they had left, a man in a mackintosh, with grinning teeth.

'Danny!' she cried. 'He's after us!' She reeled forward into noise. A scream, a great grinning radiator on top of her, Daniel in her ear, 'You bloody little –' and she was knocked forward, stumbling to the pavement among the screams, and turned to see Danny's suitcase scattered open on the road and the crowd beginning to gather.

CHAPTER TEN

The Nurses

SISTER Ferguson liked to see her fractured femurs all together on one side of the ward, with their Balkan beams exactly parallel and the foot of their beds raised at the same slope. She would really have liked them all to have identical fractures, so that their legs could be slung at the same angle and the tin cans with the extension weights in them all hanging at the same level.

She would be glad when this new patient had had his operation and was settled down for at least a month with his beam and pulleys. He was at the top of the ward now, by the desk, where she could keep an eye on him, but as soon as possible she would move him half-way down and line him up with the other femurs.

Sister Harvey had her Balkan-beam women scattered about all over the ward, which was not only insulting to Mr Pennyfeather and inconvenient for the nurses, but spoiled the look of the ward as much as bed wheels akimbo and counterpanes awry. But Sister Harvey thought more of her wireless and her artistic flower arrangements than of tidy lockers and undeviating beds, and there were nurses on her ward with hairstyles that – well, that was the way things were in the profession nowadays.

The ward clock was out of order. Sister had rung down to the electrician three times about it, but he did not seem to think it as important as she did. A voice called from a bed behind her: 'Half-past ten by my watch, Sister. Time you went for your coffee.'

'Thank you, Sonny.' Sonny Burgess had been in her ward for two years with his spine in a plaster cast. They were part of each other's lives. On her way out of the ward she stopped by the new patient's bed. He was asleep, and he still looked very shocked, as far as you could see for the dirt and grazes on his face.

'Nurse Saunders!' she called. 'I'm going to coffee. Keep an eye on this femur man, and if he wakes you can start cleaning him up. I can't think what the night nurse was about to leave him like this. She had plenty of time.'

She would have to speak to her about it this evening, and the night nurse would be furious and do no mending, or mark all the new pillowcases in hideous letters an inch high, as she had done last time Sister had scolded her. She always said she had no time, but Sister believed she spent half the night reading, and didn't wake people up for their fomentations. In her day, night duty had *been* duty, with three night sisters prowling round to keep you on your toes, but you couldn't say a thing to these girls nowadays. All this extra money and heated bedrooms and dances every Saturday had gone to their heads. It might recruit more nurses, but what kind? 'When I did my training at the Northants General,' she was fond of saying, 'we were there for work, not for sport.'

The nurses at St Patrick's quoted that, she knew. 'When I did my training at the Northants General –' she could hear them giggling, when they thought she was not near. They thought her an antiquated martinet. Ferocious Fanny Fossilson, they called her, but it could not be helped. Whatever the younger ones like Sister Harvey thought, she believed it was impossible to run a ward properly without rigid discipline. A man had died once, twenty years ago, because she had not done what she was told. She had never forgotten that.

In the sisters' room they were reading the papers and talking excitedly. 'You're in the news, Fergie,' they greeted her. 'At least your new femur is. Look, he's got quite a write-up.'

'I suppose that will mean those reporters trying to get into my ward at all hours,' she complained, but she could not help being quite thrilled at what she read in the paper. 'Fractured humerus!' she scoffed. 'They always get it wrong. I daresay the whole thing is a tissue of lies.'

'Oh no. The policeman told Nurse Jones about it in Casualty. He's quite a hero.'

'Well, he'd better not try any heroics in my wards,' Sister Ferguson said, pouring herself some coffee.

'I don't suppose he's as brave as all that, Fergie dear. He only argues the toss with lorries, not with you.' They laughed. They always laughed at everything Sister Morris said. When she was in training she had won the gold medal three years running and was the youngest staff nurse ever to be made a sister, but she was going to throw it all away to marry Dr Methuen next month. Already she had cast off all sense of responsibility, and Sister Ferguson was sorry for whoever got Out-Patients after her, for the linen cupboard down there was a shambles.

She started to tell them about her osteotomy case, which had taken a really interesting turn; but with their thirst for sensation, they only wanted to hear about Mr Brett, who after all was only just another fractured neck of femur with slight concussion, and everything going according to plan.

'I see old Penny has got the reduction down for his list this afternoon,' Theatre Sister said. 'You coming with him?'

'I suppose I shall have to,' Sister Ferguson said, although she always deliberately fixed her staff nurse's day off for Mr Pennyfeather's bone days, so that she could go to Theatre. Mr Pennyfeather was one of the few people who had been at St Patrick's as long as she had.

'The old Thomas' splint and Balkan beam, I suppose?' said Sister Harvey. 'Penny hasn't altered his technique since the first war.'

'And what's wrong with that? His femurs knit. That's more than Sir Isaac's elbows do, with all his new-fangled gadgets. The old ways are often best. I hope I may live to see steam kettles come into fashion again.' She took some pins out of the front of her dress and plunged them here and there in her cap, which would not settle this morning, because she had washed her hair last night. She did this regularly once a week, although it did not show, since she wore her cap covering practically all her hair, which was what she had been brought up to believe a cap was for.

'I suppose,' said Sister Morris, 'if your hero goes septic he won't get penicillin?'

'Ah, now you're laughing at me,' said Sister Ferguson, and went back to her ward.

She made the nurses go round tidying all the beds again before Matron's round, although Matron, who was fifteen years younger than Sister Ferguson, always said that she didn't want her hospital to be all mitred corners and no fun. She was one of the new sort. Matrons had been matrons in Sister Ferguson's day, without all this talk of democracy and taking the nurses to the theatre. Oh well, her own kind was dying out. She would retire soon and leave the field to nurses without stockings and taps that stayed polished without daily rubbing. Where would she retire to? She never thought of that, for her life beyond the hospital was a blank. She could not imagine existence without it.

When Matron came into the ward, willowy in her high-necked navy dress, one of the probationers, who was scrubbing out a locker, scrambled to her feet and scuttled away in search of her cuffs, but Matron told her to go on with her work and not bother. Sister bit her lip. It might be her hospital, but it was not her ward, and she had no right to come in undermining the discipline that Sister took so much trouble to establish.

Mr Brett was awake, and Matron asked him what he would like her to do about his family.

'Family?' he said thickly, for one side of his mouth was bruised and swollen. 'I haven't got any.'

'I've had enquiries from people who've seen it in the papers,' Matron said. 'A Mrs Brett, who said she was your aunt –'

'Keep 'em all out,' he said. 'I don't want anyone. There was a girl called Pam though. Can't remember her other name.' He put his hand up to his head and seemed surprised to find the hand in bandages.

Sister thought it sounded like some girl he had picked up somewhere, but Matron said: 'Oh yes, the child whose life you saved.'

When Sister came back to him after Matron had gone Mr Brett said: 'What was she talking about? I saved Pam's life?'

'Yes,' she said. 'You're quite a national hero. I'll bring you the papers when you're well enough to read.'

Nurse Saunders was in trouble with Hodgen's splint, so Sister, who believed in helping with the practical work in her ward, rolled up her sleeves and cleaned up Mr Brett and prepared his leg for the theatre herself, as it was Mr Pennyfeather's case. She never took any off duty on her staff nurse's day off, although Nurse Saunders in her impulsive way was quite good; better than Staff Nurse Fitt in many ways.

'Why don't you go out and get some sun, Sister?' Nurse Saunders sometimes said. 'I'll be all right on my own.'

'But you're not State-registered.'

'That makes no odds. The men aren't going to die because I'm wearing the wrong colour belt.'

'It's not ethical, Nurse, to leave you in charge.'

'But all the other sisters do it –'

'Nurse. I am not all the other sisters.'

Mr Brett seemed a pleasant young man. He swore a little, but she was used to that. She thought he was going to be quite an amenable patient, although when she came to give him his injection he made a fuss and jerked his arm so that the needle jabbed him and he said: 'There, I told you it would hurt.'

She was tired when she came back from Theatre. Mr Pennyfeather was very slow and it was no joke to stand on the alert for an hour when you were fifty-five. She went into her office to change her shoes and Winnie the ward maid brought her a cup of tea and told her that she'd missed a bit of fun.

'There was two reporters come up while you was in the theatre, wanting to talk to our 'ero. So I tell them 'e's gone and show them the empty bed. Laugh! they thought he'd kicked the bucket and dashed away like lunatics so as to get their story in first.'

'Winnie, you didn't tell them that? It'll be in the paper.'

'What's it matter? Brighten it up a bit. I didn't tell them, anyway. I just said, "He's gone," I said. They can't sue me for purgatory.'

Winnie, like the other ward maids, did and said more or less what she liked, for she knew she was as gold. She looked like nothing on earth, wore her stockings spiralled round her legs and her cap hanging by one pin from hair that Sister itched to get at with the Sassafrass bottle, but she did her own work adequately and anyone else's with enthusiasm.

Sister had sent the nurses to tea, but she stayed in her room for a few minutes while she drank hers. Sonny would keep an eye on the ward. When she went in, he had raised himself on his elbow as far as his plaster would allow and was shouting at Mr Brett, who was hazily reaching for the glass of water on the next man's locker.

'Doesn't know the first thing about operations,' Sonny complained to Sister. 'I should have told him before about not drinking. Bad as having kids it is, trying to run this ward. Here you – young Michael ! Stop playing with them ropes. You'll have them off the pulleys.'

Sonny had been in the ward so long that he knew more about it than anyone except Sister. He instructed new patients, organized convalescents to sweep the floor and lay the fires while Winnie amused herself with someone else's job. He watched the visitors of patients on diets to see they did not slip forbidden food into their lockers, and kept an eye on crafty old men who tried to get out of bed. The nurses told him about their love troubles, and anyone new to the ward always came to Sonny if she wanted to know what to do or where to find things.

When he was back to his normal senses Mr Brett turned out to be not so amenable after all. Sister had got her twenty men almost as well trained as her nurses, and always made it clear to new patients from the first that she would stand no nonsense. Most of them were a little afraid of her, if only because their well-being was in her hands, but Mr Brett gave her a lot of trouble.

He made a fuss about everything. He complained of the pain, and of Mr Pennyfeather, and of whoever had built the hospital on a hill where buses changed gears. He complained of his bed, the heat, the cold, the food, and every time Sister passed his bed called out plaintively that he was hungry. He refused to let the night nurse wash him at six in the morning, was rude about the hospital pyjamas, and smoked at all the times when it was not allowed. When the house surgeon came to put up his leg into the extension tackle, he cursed Mr Dearmer, who cursed him back, and made such a commotion that the porter, who was fixing the beam, said it was as good as a pig-killing.

Afterwards, every time a nurse went by he called her to adjust the pulleys or the padding, swearing that he was dying of agony. Sister wanted to tell him about the bravery of men she had nursed during the war, but she had once said that to a man in Casualty who was making a fuss about a splinter under his nail, and he had calmly pulled up his trousers and shown her two quite new aluminium legs.

She told Mr Brett that if he wanted to behave like a private patient he had better go up to the fourth floor.

'Can't afford it, my dear woman.' She could not get him to call her Sister. 'I'll have this on the Government.'

'Well then, you must behave yourself. I can't keep you here if you're going to upset the whole ward like this.' For he was a subversive influence. The other men took courage from his insubordination, complained about things they had accepted cheerfully before, and were impossible to get back into bed at night when they had been up for tea. Mr Brett led a strike against rice pudding and plums. He got an irresponsible up-patient to give him the ends of his ropes and let his leg down himself, and soon all the femurs were doing this when they were uncomfortable. Sister had to ask Mr Pennyfeather to speak to them, which was extremely mortifying.

The newspaper men, quite disappointed to find he was still alive, had been back to see him once or twice, but they had dropped him now for more topical things. It showed how much people were influenced by the papers, however, for strangers kept writing or sending him parcels and one girl wrote a letter every day asking him to marry her. He always read it aloud after breakfast to the men, who made remarks about it that Sister did not like.

Sometimes people came up to the ward wanting to see him. He had forbidden her, on pain of setting fire to his bed, to let any strangers in to him, so when a wealthy-looking couple came inquiring for him, she took them into her office to find out who they were.

The lady was tall and elegant and looked rather like the Duchess of Windsor. She did most of the talking. Her husband, who looked well-fed and easy going, stood jingling his money and looking nervously at a collection of splints and cradles in a corner of the office, and backed up everything his wife said.

Their name was Ruelle. 'Oh, you must be the parents of the child who was involved in the accident with him,' Sister said. She was not going to speak of him saving the child's life. She was cross with him today about the carrots at lunch and was not going to soften into consideration of him as a hero.

'*Foster* parents,' Mrs Ruelle corrected her. 'We make no bones about her adoption. The other is so foolishly escapist, don't you think?'

'Quite,' said Mr Ruelle.

'But of course she's just like our own child to us,' Mrs Ruelle went on, 'so naturally we want to offer her rescuer our gratitude, even though it was his fault in the first place. Oh, not the accident,' she explained, as Sister looked surprised, 'I mean their being in London at all, though no doubt something similar would have happened wherever they had been. The intrinsic causation of these things is always more psychological than functional.'

'Clearly,' said Mr Ruelle, although Sister could not agree with him.

She went into the ward to ask Mr Brett if he would see them. 'All right, all right,' she said. 'There's no need to be violent about it. Just say No and have done.' She hated to tell untruths, but she had to tell the Ruelles that he was not well enough for visitors, hoping that they would not look through the glass doors on the way out and see him sitting up, as far as his splint allowed, drawing a picture on the plaster cast on Mr Foley's arm.

'He's asking about Pamela though,' she said. 'He'd like to see her some time.'

'I'm afraid that's impossible,' said Mrs Ruelle in her high, enunciating voice. 'We've sent her away to a farm in Cornwall. She was in a terrible state, and not only because of the accident; all our careful guidance of her development abrogated. The whole thing was most unsatisfactory, you know. I won't impose on your time with the details, Sister, but she must not see him again. It would be the worst thing for a child of her irregular nature.'

'He'll be disappointed,' Sister said. 'He talks about her quite a lot. He told me once that he'd been in a madhouse and she was the only sane thing in it, though I'm sure I don't know what he meant.'

'You see, Henry?' Mrs Ruelle turned to her husband, generating a slight disturbance of perfume on the air. 'Just what we thought. A *mésalliance*.'

'Of the first degree,' he said.

Mrs Ruelle asked Sister if she would convey to Mr Brett what they had come to say themselves: that they wished to make him a present of a hundred pounds for his service to their foster daughter.

'Guineas, dear,' amended her husband.

'All right, Henry. My husband is very profligate.' She smiled at Sister. 'Pamela said that Mr Brett seemed to be very poor, so we thought this would be the best thing to do.' When they had gone, Sister went back to the ward, not liking her errand. Mr Brett was a gentleman and you did not buy gentleman off with a hundred pounds – guineas – just because you did not approve of their influence on your daughter. Although Mr Brett was always on about something for nothing out of the Government, he did not look or behave like someone who was very poor. What tale had he been pitching the child? It sounded uncomfortably to Sister as if he might be a scrounger, knowing that she came of wealthy parents.

'You should be in bed by now, Mr Foley,' she said and sent him away with the drawing on his cast half finished. Sister would not look at it, for from what she could see at a glance it was going to be some kind of pin-up girl.

'You're lucky,' she told Mr Brett. 'I've got some good news for you.'

'The only good news you can bring me,' he said, 'is when you come and tell me I can get up and go.' That was the way he spoke to her. She was getting used to it.

When she told him about the money, to her surprise, he said: 'Oh gosh, I don't want it,' and then she was sorry she had thought of him as a scrounger. The Ruelles had hurt his pride.

'I didn't think you'd accept it,' she said, liking him better, but he spoiled it by saying: 'Well, it's no use now, as I can't go to Italy. Not for ages, anyway. When d'you think I'll get out of here?'

'Not for some time yet, I'm afraid. Mr Pennyfeather's still un-decided about putting in that peg.'

'That butcher,' said Mr Brett disgustedly. 'If you don't have a compound fracture, he has to make it one. He's not happy unless he can see torn and tortured wounds.'

'I won't have you saying such things, Mr Brett, in my ward.'

'I won't be his guinea-pig,' Mr Brett groused on in the grumbling monotone he fell into when he was fed up. 'I'll get up and crawl out of here – you wait. You can't keep me here against my will. I've got a life to live like everyone else, but not here, strung up by this blasted thing.' He kicked his sound leg towards the beam. The jerk hurt his bad one and he yelled once and then was quiet, turning his head to one side with his eyes closed, looking pale.

Sister Ferguson stood looking down at him for a moment and then went off duty and back to her room at the hostel, where she had her many photographs and her own bedspread and cushions and doilies, to make it quite like home. It was her home really, for her other one was in Liverpool, and she only went there once a year and then felt out of place, because her sister didn't want to talk about hospital all the time, and she could talk of very little else.

She took off her cap and smoothed down her slate-coloured hair and thought about Mr Brett having a life of his own outside here, and was unable to imagine what it was like. She could never think of her patients as having any existence outside the hospital, for her only contact with their lives was here. When they went home to pick up lives she knew nothing about, she did not like it, not only because she grudged them their independence, but because she had usually grown a little fond of them.

Willy-nilly, although she disguised it, she had a feeling for everyone who was entrusted to her, even Mr Brett. She wanted them all to like her, but if they teased her, affectionately as they sometimes did, something tightened up inside her and she could not respond. She suspected that they had more fun on her day off.

Sister Ferguson's day off was Staff Nurse Fitt's favourite day of the week. Not that Sister bothered her much when she was there, for Nurse Fitt had her own ways and was not one to be dictated to by anybody, even Ferocious Fanny, who was the bossiest sister in the hospital. If Sister told her to do something she did not want to, she would either pretend to be deaf in both ears, instead of only the mastoid one, or say: 'Of course, I don't know about

you, Sister, but I always think the modern method is the best.'
That made the old girl hopping mad, because half the modern
methods she had not even heard of, and was too pig-headed to
learn.

On Sister's day off Nurse Fitt sailed into the ward with more
bombast than usual, and started right away ordering the juniors
about, chivvying the men and catechizing the night nurse. She
sat straight down at the desk and didn't take off her cuffs, because
she was in charge today and she was blowed if she was going to
make beds. If the nurses were pushed, Winnie could help them.

When Mr Pennyfeather pottered in to do his round, with his
white hair in a fluff, although she privately thought him a dodder-
ing old back number, she put on a full show for him. She led
the parade from bed to bed, with herself in a clean apron carrying nothing, Nurse Saunders trying to hide her dirty apron,
carrying the case history folders, Nurse Barnes with the X-rays,
and Nurse Potter, scuttling away just in time to fetch her cuffs,
bringing up the rear with the sphygmomanometer and patella
hammer.

Nurse Fitt tried to do the same thing for Matron's round, but
Matron would not have it. 'Let the nurses get on with their
work, Nurse,' she said. 'What are you about? You need not
trouble to come round with me either. You've plenty to do. Your
dressing-trolley looks as if it could do with a good clean.'

Nurse Fitt retired and jerked the dressing-trolley out to the
annexe in a dudgeon, which she vented on Nurse Potter for
leaving a bottle of Lysol about. Nurse Fitt always suspected the
men of suicidal intentions. Drinking Lysol would be just the
kind of thing they would do to be awkward, and then Matron
would have an even bigger down on her than the one she had
already. Nurse Fitt declared she would give in her notice tomorrow if the hospital were not so short of staff.

Mr Brett's leg was not uniting properly. He took this as a personal insult. 'It would have to be me. Look at those others –
George, Knocker, Old Jonesey –' he waved a hand down the line.
'Lying there smug as you like with their bones joining away like
mad. But me – oh no, mine couldn't, just because I'm in a hurry
to get out.'

Nurse Fitt was rubbing his back. She had very strong hands and made him wince occasionally. 'What for?' she asked, not because she really wanted to know. After six years' nursing, she had come to the conclusion that the patients were more interesting as cases than as people.

'Nothing particular. I just want to get *out*. This place is worse than being in prison camp. At least that was all male.' Holding himself clear of the bed by the handle fixed to his beam, he looked back over his shoulder to see how she liked that.

Nurse Fitt pretended not to hear. She had one for him, anyway. Rubbing spirit in at a speed which nearly set his flesh on fire from friction, she said: 'Mr Pennyfeather is not at all pleased with your X-rays. He's definitely decided on artificial fixation.'

'Oh no!' Mr Brett let his body sag and she smacked him to make him lift it up again while she applied the powder. 'He can't do it yet,' he said. 'I don't know that I want it done. I'll have to think about it.' Then, in a few moments: 'Fitt,' he said suspiciously, 'what are you doing to my foot?'

'Taking off the splint. He's going to put a peg in this evening. Theatre can just fit you in.'

Sister would be hopping mad. She did not like to miss Penny's cases. Mr Brett was hopping mad, too, as far as he could be with that leg. Socked and gowned and capped and snowed under with blankets, he was still grumbling while they waited in the anaesthetic room for the case before his to finish.

'Pegs!' He had been on like this ever since she told him. 'Just experimenting on me. It's a scandal. This is the only time I've ever wanted to have a large outraged family, so they could write to *The Times* and get questions asked in the House.'

'It happens,' said Nurse Fitt smoothly, seeing herself in a glass-fronted cupboard and pulling forward a curl from under her white theatre turban, 'to be necessary — always presuming you want to walk properly again.'

She did not like Mr Brett. From the first morning that she had come on duty and found him full of morphia, but muzzily anti-everything, he had shown no respect at all. He did not seem to appreciate his luck in getting a good staff nurse. Some of the other S.R.N.s — even some of the sisters — were not fit to hold a syringe, let alone wear the key of the dangerous-drug cupboard. How they had passed their exams was a mystery to her. Some of them were quite common. Nurse Fitt was very careful about grammar and pronunciation and never called the patients Dear.

The men were not familiar with her, as they were with some of the nurses. Disgracefully so, she thought, although people like Saunders did not seem to mind not getting the respect due to them. With her Roman nose, imperious bust, and massive swoops of bronze hair, Nurse Fitt, queening it round the ward, was a figure to command respect. But not from Mr Brett. He mocked her. When she came round with what was called the Cocktail Tray, handing out her special concoction of cascara and paraffin, he said: 'Go away. I don't want to have a Fitt,' an elementary form of humour from which she had suffered all her school and nursing career and was not disposed to enjoy now.

They had to wait a long time in the anaesthetic room. 'I wish they'd hurry. I've got a date at half past eight,' Nurse Fitt said meaningly, for everyone knew about her boy-friend, who owned a chain of milk bars and provided ice-cream for the hospital parties. They did not know that he was middle-aged and rather coarse-looking and not really her boy-friend. He just liked to have someone to take to shows, but she had hinted so long at a romantic affair that she almost believed in it herself.

'I could get married and leave here any day I want,' she would say when afronted, but Stewart had never asked her, and she would not accept him if he did. She had a cushy enough job here. Why should she give it up to be some man's slave – an aproned nobody, instead of a staff nurse who wore a special cap and belt and made the juniors scuttle like ants before a treading foot?

From behind the sliding doors of the theatre came clinks and murmurs and a roaring, snoring noise. 'This is hell,' Mr Brett said. 'Why did they send for me if they weren't ready? If this is nationalization, they can have it.'

'The case before you is taking longer than they expected. You're not the only patient in the hospital, you know.'

'That's all too obvious –' he began, when at last the sliding doors parted and Dr Mooney, the anaesthetist, breezed nervously in, rubbing his hands.

'Hullo there, my boy! Ah yes, Nurse. Mr Pennyfeather's case. Let's see now. What's he for?' he fumbled about with a list.

'Insertion of peg in right femur,' said Nurse Fitt, standoffishly. She had never cared for Dr Mooney since he had had the cheek to try and kiss her in a cupboard during Sardines at the Christmas party last year.

'What's the peg made of, anyway?' asked Mr Brett, swivelling his eyes to where Dr Mooney was filling a syringe with Pentothol.

'Bone,' she said. 'Everybody uses wire nowadays, but Mr Pennyfeather has his reasons, I suppose.'

'What kind of bone?'

'A boiled beef bone usually.'

'No!' He struggled to sit up. 'How horrible – I won't –' But Dr Mooney had plunged the syringe into his arm and he was out like a light between one word and the next.

Mr Brett was low for several days after his operation, but as he picked up he began to annoy Nurse Fitt again. Coming back from lunch one day, she saw him making Nurse Potter pull the ropes of his extension about, and bustled down the ward.

'Nurse Potter!' she cried. 'You know you're not allowed to interfere with the Balkan beams.'

'I thought I was supposed to do what the patients want,' said Nurse Potter, who was very young, very small, and very cheeky.

'It's a pity you don't remember that more often. There's old Daddy Ledward been wanting his toenails cut for days. You can go and do that now.'

'Oh, must I? I can't bear it. It makes me retch.'

'Then you'll never make a nurse.'

'Don't want to if it means getting like you,' retorted Nurse Potter.

After this interchange, Nurse Fitt was out of humour when she turned to Mr Brett. 'Now what's all the fuss about?' she asked. 'Anyone would think you'd got every bone in your body broken instead of just an impacted extra-capsular fracture of the base of the femoral neck.' She liked the long names of things.

'I don't care what you call it, it still hurts; more so now it's got the remains of the week-end joint in it.'

'It wouldn't if you didn't fidget about so.'

'This damn machine's strung up too tight.'

'Nonsense. I fixed it myself this morning.'

She was going away, but Sonny called across the ward : 'It is too tight, you know. That rope is caught up at the top, look.'

He was right, of course. He always was. Sonny was a terrible know-all, and Nurse Fitt, who liked to have a monopoly of being right, thought he had got impossibly spoiled from being so long in the ward. She did not approve of the licence that Sister allowed him. However, he was useful for things like cutting swabs and rolling bandages. She gave him some to do now.

As Mr Brett's condition improved, his manners deteriorated. Although he did not make so much fuss now, he was growing very saucy and even encouraged his visitors to give sauce to Nurse Fitt. If Sister were off duty, she was very conscious of her position on visitors' days, sitting at the desk ostentatiously writing in ledgers, or looking through X-rays, as if she could understand them, raising her head to answer relatives' anxious questions with grave reticence. She felt that the visitors all looked at her and thought to themselves : 'That's the staff nurse,' and envied and admired her. There was a lady, however, who came quite often to see Mr Brett – chic, Nurse Fitt supposed you'd call her, though she herself preferred more colour and trimming. She thought perhaps that this was Mr Brett's girl-friend, for they seemed to have a lot to say to each other and giggled in a juvenile way, and Mr Brett would always try and keep her there over-time after the bell had rung. It would be just like him to be carrying on with a married woman, which she proved herself to be one day when she brought her small son into the ward, strictly against rules.

Nurse Fitt caught him wandering round the ward, eating the men's sweets, listening in to their earphones, and reading everybody's charts.

Nurse Fitt went to Mr Brett's bed, looking across it at the boy's mother who sat quite at her ease and so perfectly groomed that it made you involuntarily put up a hand to your hair and glance down at your apron. Mr Brett looked from one woman to the other, as if he found it amusing.

'I'm afraid I must ask you to take that child out of the ward,' Nurse Fitt said. 'They are not allowed in under twelve.'

'But he is twelve,' said Mr Brett's friend. 'He's small for his age. I'm really very worried about him.' Nurse Fitt did not believe this, especially as she saw Mr Brett's visitor give him a wink which she did not even trouble to hide properly.

'Even so,' said Nurse Fitt, 'they are only allowed in to see their fathers.'

'Well, how do you know –' began Mr Brett, and his friend said: 'Dan – really!' and put her hand up to stifle a giggle.

'Short of having a blood specimen taken for a paternity test,' he said pompously, 'I don't see that you're justified in turning the poor kid out.'

'Well really, Mr Brett!' Nurse Fitt was very shocked, and walked away, feeling in her spine that they were giggling about it together. She thought them disgraceful and retired to the desk, where she dealt haughtily with old Daddy Ledward's daughter, who wanted to know why Dad was breathing so funny, although she could not have understood if Nurse Fitt had told her.

Nurse Fitt got her own back, however. Next week, when Mr Brett's friend had the colossal nerve to bring the child again, she intercepted them in the corridor outside the ward and told them that Mr Brett was not well enough to have visitors today. 'Just a slight reaction to sulphonamides,' she said, 'nothing serious,' for she did not want her ringing up Sister and making trouble.

'What's he having M & B for?' the small boy asked, as if he knew something about it. Children were fiends. Nurse Fitt had always thought so. They invariably asked the one awkward question.

'You wouldn't understand, dear,' she said, faking a smile for him and putting a hand on his hair, from which he jerked away as if she were contagious.

'Oh, come on, Pip,' his mother said. 'Don't make a pest of yourself. We're obviously not wanted here. Poor old Dan.' She looked towards the ward doors and then took the child away.

Nurse Fitt went back into the ward, stepping on the balls of her feet with triumph. Mr Brett called out to her: 'Fitt! Here a moment. Fitt!' She pretended not to hear. She would not answer to that in front of the visitors. He would have to call her Nurse if he wanted her.

When he did, she went to him, in her own time, and he asked her if Mrs March had rung up. 'I can't understand it,' he said. 'She said she was coming at two, and she's never late. She's not that sort of woman.'

Nurse Fitt implied by her manner that she was not interested in what sort of woman Mrs March was. 'I'm afraid you're not to have any visitors today,' she said. 'It's too tiring.'

'What on earth – who's damfool idea is that?'

'Sister said so. She thinks you need more rest.' She could make it right with Sister afterwards, if he complained. She would pretend to her that she had said that, and old Fergie, who was getting forgetful in her old age, and selfconscious about it, would not dare to contradict.

Mr Brett flopped back on his pillow and sulked. Nurse Fitt sat at the desk and kept an eye on the door to intercept any more of Mr Brett's visitors. A few more people came, but certainly no one for him. There was only George's mother and Daddy Ledward's crooked-looking brother, a few more of Sonny's interminable family, and an enormously fat old Jewish woman in a flowered hat, who waddled down the ward weighted down on both sides with loaded bags. She was obviously bound for Joe Levi at the end, who had a locker full of stuff already.

But when Nurse Fitt went round with the ward Christmas box, she saw to her astonishment that the fat old woman was sitting by Mr Brett's bed, leaning on it with a doting expression and feeding him with little sugary cakes out of a paper bag, as if he were something at the zoo.

Daniel laughed. 'Beaten you this time, Fitt,' he said. ' "I'm afraid you're not to have any visitors today",' he mimicked. 'But this one got by you, didn't you, Mumma?'

'So thin, I was,' said the fat woman and chuckled, overflowing the chair. 'It is necessary that I come, to keep my poor Daniel alive at all.' She took bars of chocolate and cakes out of her bag and began to put them into Mr Brett's locker.

'The patients are not allowed to have food brought in from

outside,' said Nurse Fitt feebly, making a last attempt at mastery, but Mr Brett said: 'Now that's a lie, Fitt, and you know it.'

'Never mind, my dear,' said the fat woman. 'Here is something for you.' She put sixpence into the slot of the Christmas box, and Nurse Fitt went away and rang the bell for the end of visiting hours five minutes too soon.

When Jacky Saunders was going round tidying up after the visitors had gone, she asked Daniel what he was grinning at.

'I've just scored off old Fitt,' he said.

'Oh, good. Damn – I shouldn't say that. Where is your loyalty, Nurse?' She looked over her shoulder as if she expected to have been heard. She never got away with anything. She was in trouble all the time – had been ever since she started nursing, and before that in the typing pool at the Bank of England. Other people got away with far worse things, but she was always found out. It was her fate whenever possible to run headlong into trouble like a runaway horse into barbed wire.

When she had tidied Daniel's locker, he reached over and untidied it again, looking for chocolate to give her. He asked her to adjust the padding under his splint, and she said: 'I can't for a sec. I've got masses to do. I'll come back. Oh no, look, I'll do it now. Come on.'

The other nurses seemed to get through their work fairly calmly, but Jacky lived in a perpetual state of being always behind, undecided what to do next when there were so impossibly many things to do, knowing she had no hope of getting finished. Scrambling through somehow and getting off duty only half an hour late, she would remember, when she got across the road to the hostel, that she had forgotten someone's medicine or left a glass syringe boiling in the sterilizer, and rush back to the ward again before Night Sister caught her.

'Don't you ever get tired of us?' the men would call out. 'What's it this time?' Whenever there was a crash in the kitchen or annexe, someone would sing out: 'What you bust, Nurse Saunders?' and when Sister discovered some abomination, she would stand at the top of the ward and rap out: 'Nurse Saunders!' before she investigated further.

Jacky believed that the men were fond of her. They said that she was the finest nurse in the hospital, but she knew that was not true, so it must be just their instinctive championing of the underdog. Daniel said she was a rotten nurse. He and she got on very well. He annoyed the others, but he was all right with her. They talked the same language and it was fun having him in the ward.

She had been asleep in her off-duty today, and woke to find she had only five minutes to put on her uniform and dash across the road to the hospital.

'And you look it,' Daniel said. 'It's a pity you're such a mess, Jacky. You could be quite pretty with those grey eyes and that long, soft mouth.'

'Oh, shut up, Daniel,' she said.

'*Nurse Saunders!*' Sister had come up behind her. People were always surprising Jacky from the rear. She lacked that instinct that makes you turn and see them just in time.

Sister drew her aside, for she never criticized a nurse before a patient. 'Nurse, you are *not* to call the patients by their Christian names. Nor the nurses either,' she said. 'I've heard you ever so often, calling out to each other like schoolgirls.'

At that moment Daniel chose to shout: 'Hi, Betty! Any chance of another cup?' to Nurse Barnes going round with the tea-trolley.

'There, you see,' said Sister. 'That's what happens. You can't expect respect from anyone else if you don't give it to each other.'

'But who wants respect, Sister? I mean – I'm sorry – I mean it seems so silly when we call each other by our Christian names off duty.'

'It's a question of etiquette. If you can't understand that, I'm afraid you'll never make a nurse, Nurse. You must root out this slapdash streak in yourself, and you'd better start by cleaning that blood transfusion set. You forgot it before you went off this morning. Now Nurse Fitt is going off duty, and I am going to the plaster room with that Hip. Can I trust you on your own?'

'Oh, Sister, of *course*.'

Sister Ferguson treated her like a child. Matron, too, was always giving her homey talks and telling her she must mature, which was so absurd, when she was one of the oldest nurses in the hospital. Most of them had started their training at eighteen or twenty, but it was not until she was thirty-three that Jacky's desire to nurse had overcome everything else – family, job, prospects, and her half-hearted attachment to Paul.

Perhaps it was because she had come later to hospital life that it had not chastened her. The others came to it when they were still suggestible and accepted the system, but Jacky had to sift it for herself and reject what she could not stomach, and be called a rebel about once a month, although she was really more passionately heart and soul for the hospital than anyone. But in her own way. The others had come with their characters still malleable, and by a too early contact with the unadorned issues of life and death had grown up too quickly, like flowers in a forcing-house. But Jacky could not change now. She was too old, although when she saw people like Fitt, joyless at twenty-five, she felt very young indeed.

When the staff nurse had gone and Sister was safely in the plaster room for at least an hour, the men all got out of bed again, Winnie put the kettle on for tea and came in to play cards, and one of the walking patients went into the kitchen to fry chips for supper. The two probationers sang different tunes at the same time as they made beds and whisked through their evening duties, careful, however, to leave one job until the end, for if you finished before time Sister might find you something to do that would keep you late on the ward.

Jacky spun hectically round, taking temperatures, giving medicines, starting one thing before she had finished another, leaving Mr Foster to soak his septic finger while she tried to pacify a doctor about a missing X-ray, and chasing all over the hospital for it, so that poor Mr Foster's finger was like a washerwoman's when she remembered him.

Daniel and Sonny Burgess, who had long been conducting a game of chess on two boards by calling the moves across the ward, wanted her to move their beds together so that they could play properly.

'Oh no, look, I can't,' she said. 'You know Sister hates the beds to be moved, and, anyway, I haven't got time – oh well, come on then. If I must. Here, someone give me a hand.'

They could not move Daniel, so they pushed Sonny across and fitted his bed in askew among the Balkan beams, sticking out into the middle of the ward.

'Let's pray Matron doesn't choose to do a snap round,' Jacky said. 'What I risk for you – oh, not you, Daniel. I wouldn't do it for you. Only for Sonny.'

Everyone in the hospital liked Sonny because he was an institution, but Jacky truly loved him for his own staunch self which had never sagged under his load of bad luck. He aroused all her campaigning instincts. She was always wanting to make causes of things – van horses, lunatics, old people who didn't want to go to the infirmary, the bath water in the nurses' hostel. It was terrible about Sonny. Someone ought to do something about it. If she had been in court when they dismissed his claim she would have told them where they got off. The unspecified thems and theys of the world were all Jacky's enemies. She could not read a newspaper without getting incensed.

Sonny had been twenty-two when his life went wrong, a house painter, engaged to a quiet girl called Nelly, whom he was going to marry if they could ever find somewhere to live. Painting the outside of a third-story window two years ago the cradle rope broke and pitched him to the pavement, and since then he had been in and out of plasters and splints and jackets, manipulated, operated, drugged, and X-rayed, but all the orthopaedic surgeons in London could not say whether he would ever walk again. His claim against his firm had failed, because they said it was his duty to check the ropes each day. When his appeal failed, his mother, who was pugnacious, wanted to go on with it, but Sonny, who had taken to books since his accident and had just finished *Bleak House*, said he didn't want the case hanging round his neck for the rest of his life. When Nelly's parents went away to Scotland she stayed behind and lived with his teeming family so as to be near him. Patient as a dog, she waited for him to come out of the hospital and marry her, although if he ever did they would have no home and no money for the hope of one.

Sonny had a perfectly round head with sandy hair which had to be cut very short because it preferred to stand straight up in bristles instead of lying down. After his accident, when it had not been cut for weeks, he had looked like a porcupine. He had vivid blue eyes with stubby fair lashes that looked as if they had been singed, and with his smooth face and gap-toothed smile, his neck and arms grown thin with disuse, he seemed more like a small boy than a man of nearly twenty-five. Strange chaplains and good women visiting the hospital were apt to call him Sonny, which was how he got his nickname.

Galloping up and down the ward, for if she obeyed the maxim that a nurse never ran she knew she would never get anywhere, Jacky was touched to see him and Daniel, propped sideways with pillows, contemplating the chess-board contentedly there. Every time she went by she asked Daniel to put out his pipe and told them that they must finish the game so that she could get the beds straight before Sister came back. They waved her away and she became involved with something in the specimen room, until the bump and sigh of the swing doors brought her flying into the ward to see Sister coming back too early with a strange and impressive doctor, and the most unholy row blew up and it was all Jackie's fault.

Probationers Barnes and Potter thought that Sister had got Nurse Saunders put on night duty because of spoiling the pattern of her Balkan beams. What a sell for old Fergie that she had got her back as night nurse on her own ward! She played war with her in the mornings over the report, for Sister thought that everything was always the night nurse's fault, and doubly so when it was poor old Jacky, because everything was always her fault anyway, night or day.

The day nurse they had got in her place was a God-bothering drip who was heading for heaven, but if Barnes and Potter had anything to do with it would go through hell on the way. They had liked Jacky. She had let you alone and was good fun and not uppish. Fitt was a sow, but they paid no attention to her. Sister was just Sister, inevitable as clouds over the sun, but Nurse Fewling was the end, a pain in the neck that would get you down if you didn't cut her right out of your life like a carbuncle.

You had to watch out that she did not corner you in the annexe and try and convert you, and Winnie was more use on the ward, for when something was really up and a man trying to beat you to the pearly gates, Fewling would be crying for his soul instead of running with hot-water bottles and trying to get the bubble out of the saline drip.

So they ignored her, and the creature, who was terrified of Nurse Fitt and almost fainted when she heard Sister's skirts coming, had to go to Sonny for all her information. She *would* have to be there for the wedding. It was going to be the biggest thing ever, but Fewling would probably sing hymns or forbid the banns or something mad. She was queer, said Barnes and Potter, who applied this adjective to everyone who was unlike themselves.

The wedding was not for three weeks, but already Sister had started sending Barnes and Potter up step-ladders to wash down the walls, or on the floor with a knife to scrape bed wheels. Anyone would think it was going to be a surgical operation instead of the happiest day in Sonny's life.

Ever since what he called his little tumble he had been trying unsuccessfully to persuade Nelly not to ruin her life for him. He had finally decided that if she was going to wait, as she said morbidly, to the grave, she might as well be Mrs Burgess while she was doing it. He had prevailed on the hospital chaplain to let him be married in the ward, and Nelly was going to be there in white satin and a silver headdress, with two children in organdie, and be joined in holy matrimony to Sonny in his plaster trough. Potter had started his nails on an intensive course already, and in her off-duty Barnes was making a white and gold satin banner, which was to hang over his bed saying Good Luck. The newspapers had got hold of the story through Fitt's milk-bar man, and there were going to be pictures taken, and a great crowd of guests, and altogether the wedding was going to put St Patrick's, which had always played second fiddle to the bigger London hospitals, right on the map.

Then Sister launched a bombshell by saying that one of the probationers must have her day off on the day of the wedding. They could decide between themselves, she said, and they had a terrible quarrel about it in the linen cupboard and didn't speak to each other for a whole day, except through the patients: 'Please tell Nurse Potter to pull the draw sheet tight her side.' 'Ask Nurse Barnes whether she's *eaten* that last bit of soap or what.'

Although they were bosom friends and shared not only a bed-room but each other's aprons and stockings, they fought often. They were either as thick as thieves, so that no one could get a word in edgeways through their giggling gabble, or waging war in every way they knew.

They had entered the hospital on the same day, but because one must be senior on the ward Barnes was put over Potter, since she had actually entered the portals first, having come by a slightly earlier train. This Nurse Potter could not forgive. As first and second probationer, they had their own jobs allotted, and if Barnes was up to the neck in dirty linen and the bell long gone for supper, would Potter give her a hand? Like hell, she would, for Barnes would not dream of helping her clean the bedpans except on her day off, and then she did not do them properly, so that Sister raised Cain and it was Potter's fault, for the bedpans were her responsibility, her sacred trust.

They had their ways of getting back at each other, a never-ending game, because each dirty trick must be countered by another. When Barnes, who was bulky, and slow in her move-ments, but thorough, had spent an hour cleaning tooth-mugs, Potter would stain the insides of half of them by using glycothy-moline too strong. So when they were making the bed of a heavy, helpless patient, Barnes would get him rolled over to Potter's side, and then while she was standing on tiptoe, red in the face, burst-ing her heart to hold him, Barnes would remember that she had left the sterilizer boiling dry and leave her – 'But don't let him go, or we'll never get him over again.'

At dinner-time Potter would stay in the kitchen, soaping round Sister by offering to put the spinach through a sieve, so that Barnes would have to feed Daddy Ledward, who would not swallow, but just held it in his mouth, moving his gums feebly, until you nearly went mad. On fish days Barnes hurried out with the first platefuls and took them round the top of the ward, where the men felt too ill to complain, so that Potter had to suffer the grumbles of the far end, where they always said the fish was stale. When Sister had gone to lunch, they both made a rush from wherever they were to finish up the pudding before Winnie got it.

When Sister allowed Barnes to take out some of Mr Brett's stitches, there was no holding her. They were the first stitches she had ever removed, so she looked on him thereafter as her private property. Until Potter was allowed to take him downstairs and help put the plaster on for his walking splint, so yah.

They came together somewhat over Mr Brett, who, now that he had got over making a nuisance of himself, was becoming quite ward-minded, and was always good for a laugh. He had got a sketch block and would draw anybody's picture, as good as the lightning caricaturist at the Olympia fun fair. There was not a plaster cast in the ward which was not adorned with some of Mr Brett's art work, and Winnie took twice as long to sweep the floor that side because she had to stop halfway and pose for a few touches to her portrait that Mr Brett was doing for her young man. Barnes and Potter were always hanging round his bed giggling and making him draw things for them, and Sister said she didn't know what young girls were coming to, but then she had never known that within living memory.

He had better visitors than most of the other patients. There was a dear old girl called Mrs Weissmann who always brought him bags full of cakes and sweets. One day, Barnes stopped, goggling by the bed while she was unloading them.

'I hope it doesn't matter that I bring these, Nurse dear?' she said. 'But I am sure this poor boy goes hungry here.'

'Too true,' said Barnes. 'So do we.' Mrs Weissmann was horrified, so Barnes, calling Potter to corroborate, drew a heart-breaking picture of the food in the nurses' dining-room. Ever after that Mrs Weissmann never came without bringing cakes and pies and a loaf of her own braided cholla bread for the starving nurses.

There was also a visitor called Ossie, who made a joke every time you came near the bed, and seemed to be telling Mr Brett funny stories all the time, judging from the laughter.

'He's a scream,' Barnes and Potter said afterwards. 'You have got killing friends, Brettsie. What was he telling you that was so funny?'

'Nothing special. Telling me about his girl, among other things. She's gone off with a man from some dog kennels.'

'Was that funny?' asked Potter.

'He's doing his best to think it is.'

'Gosh,' said Barnes, 'how *queer*.'

'What are you doing gossiping there, Nurses?' Sister called. 'Get on with your work.'

'We are,' they said. 'We're making a bed.'

'It doesn't look like it. Anyway, Mr Brett is to get up for bed-making now. You're not to baby him any more. Come along now, Mr Brett. You're not going to stay in my ward for the rest of your life. You've got to start using that leg.' She came clapping her hands at him and he groaned and turned up his eyes at her. 'You made enough fuss about getting out of here at first,' she scolded him, 'but now you've got too spoiled and lazy to make the effort.'

'Yes,' he said.

Barnes and Potter giggled. 'He's afraid you'll send him home before the wedding, Sister.'

'He'll walk for the wedding,' she said, 'or not see it at all. I'll need to have half these beds out with the crowd there's going to be, and Daddy Ledward will have to go in the side room, poor old soul. It's a terrible upset. I can't think what the Reverend was about to allow it to happen on my ward.'

But the probationers, who knew all the gossip of the hospital, on every stratum, knew that Sister Ferguson was really as excited as anybody and had bored everyone to death in the sisters' sitting-room by talking about nothing else.

On the morning of the wedding she was in a flat spin and had been over to the hostel to change her apron at least three times, although nothing would happen until after lunch. Nurse Fitt had washed her hair the night before and wore it in rolls under her cap, ready to comb out later. Nurse Fewling was not there, for Barnes and Potter had resolved their argument by foisting the day off on to her. They were both as excited as if they were going to be married themselves, and kept goading Sonny for lying there so calmly, although he could do nothing else. 'You are queer,' they said, 'you're not a bit romantic.'

One of the men said something which made Potter collapse on

to the end of a bed and stuff her giggling face into the blanket, but Barnes did not understand, so Potter took her out to the annexe to explain it.

When they were not teasing the bridegroom, the men spent all morning shaving each other, and there was a constant stream to the door of the ward of wives bringing brown-paper parcels of clean pyjamas. People kept coming along from other wards to ask if they could come and bring their up-patients, but it was to be the fracture ward's day, and no outsider was invited except Matron and Sonny's gallery of doctors and surgeons. There would not be room, because of the size of his family. They began to arrive even before lunch was over, and Sister kept them lined up in the corridor in their wedding clothes, until the last plate of treacle batter had been served, although no one wanted treacle batter with the sight of the wedding feast arriving on trolleys.

Then the sheer weight of Sonny's mother burst open the doors and the guests streamed in, aunts, uncles, cousins, fat and thin, shy and jolly; pimply youths and vague old men who were steered about and told: 'Not there, Grandpa!' Children who stared at the patients, and Sonny's twin sisters, who stared at them, too, but in a different way. Sonny's father, with a strawberry nose and a buttonhole as big as a cauliflower, and Sonny's mother looking like a bulldog in an aggressive black hat and a young tree of carnations hanging upside down on the shoulder of an edge-to-edge coat that was made to be a wrap-over.

The Press arrived in mackintoshes, although it was a fine day, and took up strategic crouching positions. The chaplain arrived calmly, as if this was like any other wedding. Barnes and Potter held hands and their breath, Sonny began to giggle, and then, with the doors held back by two porters in white coats and theatre caps, came Nelly, overpowered by her headdress and looking as if she wished she were the least instead of the most important person.

It was all over too quickly. Old Fergie dropped a tear; Barnes and Potter didn't miss that, and then everyone was breaking into noise and kisses and the flash bulbs were going like a film première. The nurses had to come forward and be photographed with the married pair, who should have looked somehow different, but didn't. Jacky was there, with circles under her eyes. She had stayed out of bed for the wedding, 'just to get her picture in the paper', said Nurse Fitt, shoving her own head well in front of the cameras, and oh, joy! that one never appeared in print. Potter and Barnes were in the paper, however, and although Barnes was all teeth and Potter had her apron hitched up, their mothers sent for copies and had them framed to stand on their mantelpieces, where they may be seen to this day.

That night the ward was very difficult to settle. The wedding had gone to their heads, and they were laughing and calling out ludicrous jokes about Sonny's wedding night long after Jacky had turned out all the lights except the desk lamp and the shaded light over Daddy Ledward's bed. The noise did not disturb the old man, for he was miles away from them already, fighting out the last battle between body and spirit.

Jacky went out to the kitchen to set the breakfast-trolley, for she was always one mad rush in the morning. While she was stacking the plates, Winnie arrived in a long brown coat, a green dog hairslide, and orange lipstick overrunning the edges of her mouth like the colour in a badly printed comic paper. Jacky was not surprised to see her, for Winnie often came back after the day staff had gone, with fish and chips or sausage rolls for the men to eat in bed. Tonight, however, she had brought nothing, for she reckoned that everyone had had enough to eat today. She had certainly cut enough sandwiches to bring up a callous on her finger.

She had come for a cup of tea. 'Got a bit of time to fill in, because I can't meet my boy till half past ten. He's on the late run now, on the seventy-sevens.'

'Useful for you when you want a free ride.'

'Not bad. It was better when he was a dustman. All kinds of things he used to bring me. You couldn't believe what people throw away. How's your fellow, Nurse, by the same token? We don't hear so much of him these days.'

'Nor do I,' said Jacky. 'I think he's given me the chuck, because I can't be bothered about nail varnish any more. He didn't like me going on night duty, anyway.'

'Ah no, that you can understand in a man, when he's on days,' said Winnie, who led a full sex life in spite of her appearance.

Jacky had not seen Paul since they met for a drink one evening before she went on duty. She had been tired and vague from having got up too early. It was six a.m. for her, and that was what she felt like, not yet come to life, remote from the crowd in the bar to whom it was six p.m. Paul was irritatingly lively. He had finished his work, while hers was still before her.

'It seems terrible,' she said, 'to be drinking gin and French before breakfast.'

'It's a terrible life you lead altogether,' Paul said. 'You should just be starting out for an evening with me now, not going back to that mausoleum to put on those black stockings.' She had told him about those and he could never forget it. The black stockings came into every argument they had about the hospital. 'What am I supposed to do with the rest of my evening?' he asked. 'You put that place before me. It's damned unfair.'

'Nonsense, Paul. You've got plenty of friends. You don't need me, and there are lots of people in the mausoleum who do. That's why I like it.'

'I don't want you to like it,' he said sulkily. 'It's ruining you. Drop it and marry me, Jacky. You'll have much more fun.'

When he could have had her he had never asked her. She would have married him once. Now she knew that she would never give up nursing for him. Or anybody. This loving need that drove her could never be satisfied anywhere else.

'You must have done something awful in your past life,' Paul said, 'so you have to half kill yourself in that place to expiate it, or something.' He always said 'Or something' when he had made a serious remark, to leaven it. 'Still, I'll say one thing for you being a nurse. It saved you wanting to be a nun. Or something.'

The ward settled to sleep at last. Only Daniel was awake. Jacky could hear him fidgeting and muttering as she sat at the desk filling in charts, the corner of her eye irked by the vast pile of mending that Sister had left out for her. She was clumsy and slow at sewing and Sister always complained that the pile looked no smaller in the morning, so Jacky had taken to hiding bits of it in odd cupboards, banking on being off night duty before Sister discovered them.

Daniel lit a cigarette and she went to him. 'Look out. Night Sister hasn't been round yet.'

'What the hell. I can't sleep. Got any dope?' He lay with his hand behind his head, looking at her with wakeful eyes that were black in the dimness of the ward.

'Nothing for you. You're supposed to be convalescent. You're going home soon, aren't you?' She realized that she would miss him. Odd how your life was made up of little bits of other people. You were close for a time, but it was touch and then away, like flies on a ceiling. In hospital you got to know people so intimately, and then never saw them again. For a few weeks you were the most important person in their world, but soon afterwards they would have difficulty in remembering your name.

She would miss Daniel, but there would be others, and after them others, so many people to whom you mattered, who mattered desperately to you.

'You can have Mr Price's Veganin, if you like,' she said. 'He's sleeping like the dead.'

When she had brought it, he said : 'Don't go,' and caught her apron. 'Stay and talk to me.'

'I can't. I've got a million things to do. That old man –'

'How is he?'

'Not too good, but there's nothing one can do. He's so old.' She looked down the ward to where Daddy Ledward was propped high on his pillows, his chest moving at long intervals, the light sharp on the pale ridge of his nose. She looked across the ward to where the bridegroom slept in his coffin of plaster with his arms flung out and his fists clenched like a child.

'Look at him,' she said. 'And that poor girl going back to that rabbit warren in Camden Town and taking off that dress in a room she shares with three other people.'

'Seems so pointless getting married.'

'Don't you know why he did it?'

'Bit of sensationalism, I suppose.'

'No. Remember that American surgeon that came up that day Sister was so wild with me about moving the beds? He's going to try something a bit drastic, and there's a chance Sonny won't come through it.'

'Oh God!' said Daniel. 'Poor kids. I wish there was something one could do to help. But I haven't got any money. What could I do? I haven't got the habit of being any use to anyone. It's easy for you, because you do it all the time. Comes naturally, like breathing.'

'That's a nice thing to say.' Jacky was touched. 'You have got much nicer, you know, since you've been here.'

'Oh me. I'm lovely.'

'What about saving that child, anyway. That wasn't so useless.'

'First disinterested thing I've ever done for anyone in my life, and look what it got me.' He kicked his leg under the bedclothes. 'Oh Lord,' he said, as the swing door sighed, 'here comes Lady Macbeth.'

'I suggest, Nurse,' said Night Sister, picking up Daddy Ledward's little claw to try to find a pulse, 'that instead of hanging round young men who are quite well you pay a little attention to old men who are very ill.'

'But, Sister, I – ! What can I do for him, anyway?'

'Nothing,' said Night Sister unreasonably.

'Jacky,' Daniel called softly, as she passed his bed early next morning. 'I want to tell you something.'

'Tell me later,' she said. 'I can't stop now. Daddy Ledward is dying.'

He died just before the day staff came on, but none of them would help her to lay him out. 'My nurses have their own work to do,' said Nurse Fitt. 'Anything that happens before eight o'clock is your affair.'

When she got to her room, late and very tired and past caring that Sister had discovered the concealed mending and was going to speak to Matron about deceitfulness, Jacky remembered that she had never been back to hear what Daniel wanted to tell her.

CHAPTER ELEVEN

Nellie

NELLIE had made such plans. For a month now, ever since Sonny had told her, she had been giving her mind to it all the time, and she saw it all, exactly as it was going to be. She had even cooked meals in her imagination and argued with herself whether to have potatoes baked or fried.

When Sonny had first told her, squeezing her hand so hard that she could almost have cried out if it had not been for all the other people in the ward, Nellie could not believe it for a long time. Things like that just did not happen to people like them.

Mr Brett had asked them to come and live with him in his cottage when Sonny was out of hospital. Mr Brett had asked them. . . . She made Sonny say it over and over. She was always slow to take things in. Often she did not see Sonny's jokes until he explained them, but he did not mind. Once she got hold of a thing she never lost it. He was proud of that in her.

Once she had got hold of the idea that they were really going to live with Mr Brett the thought was never out of her mind. She saw it all. He had never had a home, poor Mr Brett, since his wife died, but Nellie was going to make it just like home for him again. Not pushing herself. She and Sonny would never get in his way, but Nellie would cook and work all day long and Sonny would do odd jobs and there they would be, the three of them, as happy as birds.

'I'll pay him back,' Sonny said. 'You'll see. As soon as I can get about a bit I'll get my job back, or a better one. I'll earn good money, and I'll not forget. I'll pay him back.'

But Nellie knew that she could pay him back long before that, right from today when she was going to start making things nice for him. He must have the say-so about everything, of course, since it was his house; but in the cottage, Nellie had decided, no one was going to dictate to anyone else, because people could not be happy except in their own way. She had had enough, first with her own parents, and these last two years with Sonny's people, of everyone prying on everyone else and taking you up if you didn't go exactly their way. At Camden Town, where there had been such a noise all the time, and everyone trying to live everyone else's lives for them, Nellie had kept herself to herself, and she knew that Sonny's family thought her a dull nothing. Even Sonny did not know that she was really a person on her own, because she had made herself a part of him. That was what she wanted.

He knew so much more than she did. He had had more schooling, and had read books there in the hospital that were nothing like the magazines that Nellie liked to read. Sonny was clever. He had ideas about every subject you could name, but sometimes Nellie felt that there were ways in which she knew more than he. She was not always worrying away at the thoughts of what life was all about. The ideas she had of it were so few that they were all the clearer for being on their own, not crowded up by other notions coming in all the time.

At the cottage, if Sonny and Mr Brett got talking cleverly, as she had heard them going at it there in the hospital, Nellie might get ideas of things to say, but she would keep them to herself. When you tried to voice your thoughts, they always came out differently from what you meant, and people took you up wrong.

She had not yet been down to see the cottage, because she wanted to see it first with Sonny. She did not quite know what to expect. The word cottage in her mind conjured up the only cottage she had ever known, her aunt's tumbledown brick box near Dorking, with a slipping tiled roof, hens on a rubbish heap, and tin sheds stuck all over the place.

When the station taxi stopped at the white gate and Nellie got out and looked over, she could not believe that they had come to the right house. It was like a fairy tale, the sort of house you might see from the road, cycling, or from a train. You were not envious, because it was the kind of house other people lived in, not you. But this – this ! If Sonny had built it for her with his own hands it could not have been more perfectly right.

Mr Brett had said that it looked like a cross between a calendar and a tea cosy, so Nellie was prepared for it to have a thatched roof and lattice windows. But she was not prepared for it to look one with the earth, as if it had stood there from the beginning of time, to have walls the indescribable colour of sunlight, geraniums all along the window sills and a cobbled path that led straight to the front door between borders of crowding blue primulas. Behind them were daffodils, a rose arbour, and then a lawn on each side with a bent old fruit tree, and beyond that more daffodils, all along the thick hedge that folded in the garden like a sanctuary.

She was going to live here. She couldn't take it in, couldn't see herself coming down that path as casually as coming home. But – well! She lifted her chin from the gate and brisked herself up. Couldn't stand there goggling all day. Whatever would Mr Brett think?

She turned back to the car, where Sonny was craning from the window. 'Sonny, Sonny – oh, it's lovely! It's ever so – oh, come and see!'

'How can I till you get me out?' he grumbled practically.

With the help of the driver, she got out the collapsible chair, helped Sonny into it and wheeled him down the path. He was as staggered as she was. Sonny usually had plenty to say for himself, but all he could do now was give little whistles and murmur: 'I say, Nell, I *say*,' as she took him slowly, trying not to bump him on the cobbles.

Outside the front door, between the rosemary bushes, they looked at each other. What should they do – knock or call for him or what? It seemed silly to knock, when you were going into your own home, like.

'Go on in,' Sonny said. Nellie tried the latch and the door opened.

It was a long, low room with rugs on a tiled floor and beams not only across the ceiling but up the walls as well. There were spring flowers everywhere, oak furniture, chintz, a great open hearth like a cave, with logs burning. Nellie could not take in every detail, but it was like one of those English films that critics in the Sunday papers said it was too olde-worlde to be true.

'Sonny, it's – it's –' But he was fuming outside, and rocking the chair dangerously in his impatience. She tipped the wheels to go over the step, and deposited him in the middle of the sitting-room with a proud 'There!' as if the cottage were all her own work.

'Gee, Nell, do we *live* here?' He looked round quickly, then raised his voice as Nellie could never have done in a beautiful house like this, or any house for that matter. She could not shout. Her voice did not run to it.

'Daniel!' Sonny yelled. 'Where are you? Daniel? Hi, we've come!'

While he was shouting, Nellie noticed a bit of paper on the table by the door. *Back soon*, it said. *Make selves at home. Have tea.*

'*Should* we?' Nellie showed Sonny the note.

'Well, that's what he says, isn't it? If he says "Have tea", he means "Have tea", and it's the one thing I want.'

'Me, too; but, Sonny, it's his house, not ours.'

'You're running it now, though.'

'Yes, but not to presume,' Nellie said. 'Don't ever forget, dear, he was here with his wife.' As she looked at the chairs by the fire, she saw it, with a saddened heart. 'I mustn't ever do anything to make him feel I was setting myself up to take her place.'

'Hey,' said Sonny. 'You're not his wife, you're mine. Come here.' He wheeled himself towards her round the furniture. Deft, he was already in that chair. Sonny could always master anything mechanical.

'All the same,' said Nellie, as she straightened herself up from his boyish hug, 'it's his house, and we mustn't ever do anything to make him feel sorry he asked us to share it. Why did he, anyway? Why *us*?'

'Because he's so damned nice,' said Sonny. 'He can be murder, mind, if something gets his goat. You should have seen him on the ward. Poor old Fitt. I thought she'd take a stroke that time he called her a —'

'You told me once,' said Nellie. 'There's no call to repeat it.'

She helped him out of his wheelchair into the armchair by the fire, and left him chuckling while she went to find the kitchen.

At Camden Town the damp basement kitchen had also been the living-room, and Sonny's family had a taste for fried food. It had been a dark and greasy inferno, always full of the smells of cooking and people, always a string of babies' nappies steaming under the low ceiling. The windows were not cleaned from one fog to the next; the walls were spattered with grease, the worn-out carpet repatterned with spilt food and the stove coagulated with years of gravy boiling over. The whole place had got beyond cleaning long ago, and no one was going to embark on it now, even if it had ever been empty of people for long enough even to sweep the floor.

Before that, the kitchen at Nellie's home where she had lived with her parents had been no more than a tin-roofed shack, stuck slightly askew on to the back of the house by the railway line. Every time a train went by, the little oil cooker teetered on its rickety table, and Nellie's mother, who had few subjects of conversation, remarked yet once more that they would all be burned alive one day.

There were coals in there and piles of boots and shoes, dead ferns, and two broken rabbit hutches that Nellie's father had been going to mend for years. In summer flies were on everything and food and milk went off almost as soon as you bought it. In winter it was almost more than you could do to make yourself wash your face under the cold tap when you crept down in the dark morning to make the tea.

But the little kitchen at the cottage was like nothing Nellie had ever seen, except in magazines. White-walled with a red-tiled floor, and the stove, sink, draining board and work-table fitted round the walls with cupboards underneath. Pans, pots lids, jugs, eggbeaters, painted canisters, were on hooks and shelves in a satisfying pattern of ornamental usefulness. Red-and-white-check curtains were frilled over the little square window, beyond which was an apple tree with the evening sun coming through to hit you as you stood at the sink. Who would mind doing nothing but wash up all day in a place like this?

It looked spotlessly clean. Mr Brett must have got someone from the village to look after him. Nellie hoped she wouldn't come back. That would be dreadful. She stood quite a time in the doorway before she dared go in.

When she did, she told herself, for she liked to savour such moments: This is the first time. To think I shall be in and out of here all day and every day! She turned on the stove, put the kettle on, and unpacked some of the things she had brought – milk, tea, bread, butter, jam – for she was going to be very careful about using Mr Brett's stores.

She opened a white-enamelled door. It was a refrigerator! Instantly she saw herself making ice-cream for Sonny, and dashed in to tell him. He was reading one of Mr Brett's books.

'Oh, Sonny, ought you –' A piercing scream came from the kitchen, and he dropped the book and stared at her aghast.

'Silly,' she said, proudly domestic. 'Have you never heard a whistling kettle?' She picked up his book and went back to make the tea.

She hardly liked to use Mr Brett's china, but if they were really living in the house it must be all right. Two coffee-cups and saucers were upside down on the draining-board. In the plate-rack there were two plates of each size, and when Nellie opened the silver drawer she saw two napkins rolled through rings. Mr Brett must have a friend with him, and Nellie shrank from the thought that they might be staying here. It would have to happen eventually, of course. There would be visitors. Sonny would know how to talk to them and Nellie would just have to keep silent, but she didn't want it to happen now at the beginning, when everything was strange.

When they were having their tea, however, on a table before the fire, it didn't feel strange at all. She and Sonny might have been there all their lives. The fire crackled like a Christmas story. Outside, the wind was getting up, but in here they were at home.

'Isn't this cosy?' Nellie kept having to say, and Sonny said it was a bit of all right and made her cut more bread.

'I do hope it's all right,' Nellie said. 'Do you think Mr Brett would rather we'd have waited for him?' She looked in the tea-pot. 'This will be dreadfully stewed. I wonder when he'll be back? Shall I just go and pop the kettle on again so I can make some fresh as soon as Mr Brett comes in? What do you think?'

'Don't fuss, girl,' Sonny said. 'And you'll have to call him Daniel.'

'I know,' she said, 'but not yet. That will come.' She was glad, although she knew she ought not to be, that they were alone just for this beginning. However nice Mr Brett was, she was going to be shy of him. She could not say this to Sonny, because he was his friend. She could not tell him what, in the happiness of this tea-time, she couldn't help feeling: that she wished it could always be like this. Just the two of them alone here.

But what was she about, having a thought like that? If it wasn't for Mr Brett they wouldn't be here at all, would not have a home at all, might not even be together, for there would not have been room for the two of them at Camden Town. This was the most wonderful, impossible thing that could ever happen to them, and it just showed how the devil got into your thoughts uninvited if you could even for a moment wish for anything more than the heaven that had been given you.

Had the same thought come into Sonny's head? No, because he was a nicer person than she. The devil was not able to put thoughts into the heads of people like Sonny.

'Either drink that tea or put the cup down,' he said. 'What have you gone so broody about? Come and sit by us over here.' She sat on the arm of his chair and stroked his stubbly hair.

'Few weeks,' he said, 'when these legs firm up, I'll be able to have you on my knee. I asked the doc.'

'Sonny, you didn't! Whatever must he have thought?'

'Said he wouldn't mind having you on his knee himself.'

'He never did!' You never knew whether Sonny were having you on or not. He said these things with a dead solemn face. Never dull, you couldn't be, with Sonny. He had so many jokes. She was so proud of what the matron had said to her about him always having a smile for everyone, even in his worst time of pain. How Nellie loved him! Like a wife and like a mother and like a dependent child, all in one.

From where she sat she could see now that there was a woman's coat hanging among the macintoshes and jackets behind the door. It must have belonged to poor Mrs Brett. That made Nellie feel awkward. She was going to point it out to Sonny, when there were footsteps on the cobbles outside and Sonny's face lit up as he cried: 'Here he is!'

They came in together, Mr Brett and a dark, graceful woman

with a smooth, oval face. Nellie jumped off the chair, tweaked at her dress and put up a hand to her hair.

'Don't get up, don't get up,' Mr Brett said. 'You look wonderful like that. Just how I planned it.'

'I hope you didn't mind us having tea –' Nellie began, but Mr Brett did not hear, because he and Sonny were greeting each other like long-lost brothers, and started kidding together, something about the hospital.

'Of course not.' Mr Brett's friend smiled at Nellie. 'I'll just go and make some for us before we go.'

'Before you –? Oh no, let me!' Nellie darted forward to take the tray.

'Sorry we weren't there to greet you,' Mr Brett said. 'I was just saying goodbye all round the village, and we got involved in the story of Mrs Langdon's varicose veins. You'll like her. She's promised to look after you with milk and eggs and all that.'

'Daniel, what on earth are you talking about?' Sonny said. 'Saying good-bye? You're not going away?'

'Didn't you get my letter? Damn, I was afraid I'd got the address wrong.'

'But you can't,' Sonny said. 'We can't stay here without you. It's your home.'

'You keep it warm for me,' Mr Brett dropped back on the sofa and put his feet on a stool, mud and all. 'You know me. I can't stay in one place long.'

'It's not right,' Sonny protested, leaning forward sharply, and grimacing at the jerk to his back. 'You must settle down some time. Everyone must. What's the matter with you that makes you so jittery?'

'Oh shut up,' Mr Brett said. 'I'm not. I'm calm as a ruddy mill pond. Don't nag at me. You picked that up in hospital. Nellie, don't let him. You don't mind my not staying here?'

'Well, you know how we feel about being here at all,' she said, looking down at the tea-tray which she held before her. She could never find words for her wonder and gratitude. 'Mr Brett's right, dear,' she told Sonny, who blinked, because she hardly ever disagreed with him. 'We have to let each other alone. Everyone must live how they must.' Mr Brett was delighted at this. She had said the right thing. She was not as shy of him as she had expected. He was different from what he had seemed at the hospital. It would have been nice if he had stayed on there with them. But – she and Sonny were going to live here together on their own! Inside her, this thought of joy was forming, growing, but she could not consider it now. Later she would go over and over it, think all round about it, and savour the dream come true of all the days that were before her.

She heard a clatter from the kitchen. 'I'll just go and see if I can help – er ...' She did not know who Mr Brett's friend was, although Sonny called her Valerie and seemed to know her from visitors' days at the hospital. Nellie did not mind even if they had been staying here together. Her morals were strict, but somehow someone like Mr Brett seemed to be outside the rules that you were taught in chapel.

Halfway to the door she had a cold, upsetting thought, and turned round with the tray. 'Mr Brett,' she said bravely. 'I'm afraid – Is it because you don't like the idea of living here with us that you're going away? Because if you –'

'Hey, Nell!' Sonny said, but Mr Brett laughed.

'Got it in one, Nellie. How did you guess?'

She went quickly into the kitchen, where Valerie was making toast, and asked her quite boldly: 'Does Mr Brett pretend things he doesn't mean, to have you on?'

'Gracious, yes. If you accuse him of something, he'll always take the wind out of your sails by agreeing, whether it's true or not.'

'Why is he going away then?' Nellie set down the tray and began to put cups and plates into the sink, marvelling at the boiling water that came from the tap.

'Because he wants to go to Italy,' Valerie said. 'Oh – and other reasons.'

'It seems like he must be unhappy,' Nellie said, looking out of the window, not turning round, because she was shy of discussing Mr Brett like this. 'Always to be so restless, never able to stay long in one place.'

'He was.' Valerie brought a cloth to dry the things that Nellie was washing. 'This time, though, he's going away because he's happy.'

'I'm glad of that,' Nellie said. 'I'd feel awful else, when he's done so much for me and Sonny.'

'That's why he's happy, you idiot,' said Valerie, and then the whistling kettle suddenly began to shriek, so that Nellie could not be sure whether she heard her say: 'And me too.'